2000

Karl Drinkwater

ISBN 978-1-326-27483-2

Visit my website at karldrinkwater.blogspot.com

Cover design by Karl Drinkwater.

Contents

Strangeways, here we come

A HISTORY OF MANCHESTER MUSIC

- **…bum:** Strang…
- **Year:** 1987
- **Label:** Rough Trade Records

The Smiths' fourth and final album: a farewell maybe, but Morrissey and Marr a… created something that acts as an introduction to Manchester via the unpredictab… changing rhythms of real life, real people, rather than polished bubble pop…

… …adness of Last Night I Drea… …ne Loved Me, …ano fronts the sound of a crowd from the miners' strike. These are everyman songs to hum afterwards at the bus stop, in your council flat, walking to work or queuing for chips. We identify with the perspective. "Eighteen months' hard labour" sings Morrissey – about Strangeways, or just the grinding boredom of doing a job you hate? I'm not too sure.

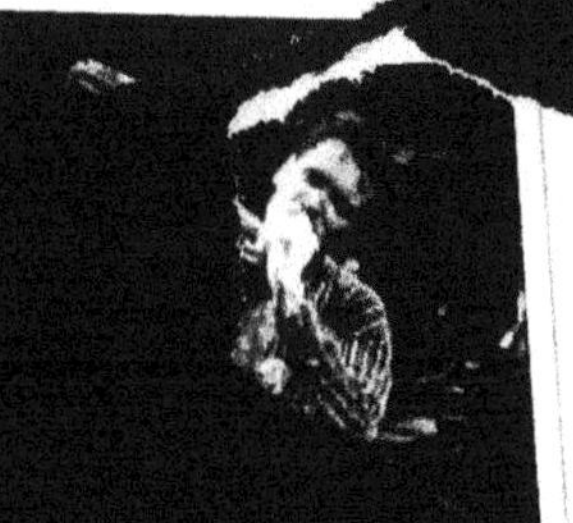

e… undercuts the … the blow of the most downbeat ones. The a… of references to love, that force of power and happiness: but that gets undercut by the idea that love is something we only get in dreams, because the reality is a series of false alarms and yearning for "the right one". There's …ys a loser left behind, saying goodbye to love.

…e or harmony, Morrissey tells us as Dea… Disco Dancer's yearning buildup evolves into awesome quasi-military drumwork blowouts. We all blow out one last time. There's always Death At One's Elbow. The kicker is that this song is like an upbeat Elvis on a train, enabling us to smile in the face of death. We can be strong, the music tells us. We're in it together. After all, the album's name is a nod to crammed Victorian prisons: people need to get along.

It ends with slow fade-out h… …ding, The Smith…

Mark Hopton shuffled along the road, a striking bunch of black and yellow flowers dangling from one hand. Hair brushed and centre parted but still hung in his eyes, hid them from strangers.

He walked in the shade when there was any. Out of the way. With his black clothes, slow pace and shaggy dark hair he could almost disappear into the shadows, a young city ghost who walked like an old one. Today, anyway. Today was a day for thinking about loss.

Life wasn't fair. Why did all the good ones go first?

It was Sunday 21st May, year 2000. Some 18 years ago there was a hopeful beginning, now dead. Never grew up to be an adult. Mancunian potential killed in its prime.

Samantha Rees thrust money into the taxi driver's hand and hurried away. Stopped, smoothed down her black skirt. Was it too short?

Too late if it was.

The white-washed Presbyterian chapel was built on a hill and the graveyard sloped down to dry stone walls. A bank of dying daffodils bent their heads towards her in the breeze. When she was a little girl her uncle had tricked her, making her believe they were really called *Taffodils*. She shook her head and climbed the steep stone steps, worn from two centuries of comings and goings.

People in black milled around outside under incongruous sunshine. She spied smokers having a quick ciggie behind the holly trees. She'd have joined them if she wasn't so late. Just a one-off to settle her emotions.

The mourners admitted her, welcomed her. Hugs and questions but she pushed her way through as quickly as she could without seeming rude. It smelt like a flower shop. Overpowering sweetness of the white lilies. Snippets of conversation heard in passing.

"Such a nice day for it..."

"Aye, booked the weather in advance, knowing her."

"Joined her husband, that'll be a reunion..."

"Always said they didn't want to outlive each other."

"Shouldn't be in here really, I'm a pub man..."

Inside was dark polished wood set off against pale walls. Pews and a small gallery were filling with those too tired to stand around. She spotted her mam and they hugged. Seconds without words, but which said everything, before Sam moved to arm's length. "Sorry I'm late. I dropped my bags off at your house first, and the trains were –" but Mam silenced her with a waved hand.

"I knew you'd be here, *bach*. We waited. She'd have wanted that."

Despite all the murmurs the atmosphere was hushed, heavy, like a gap in sound before an approaching storm. Noises seemed further away than normal, vitality cut off from conversation, words disconnected from their source, just as Sam's mother was now disconnected from *her* source. Organisation rippled through the crowd as people moved to seats. Some mourners had to spill over into the small gallery.

Mamgu was in the coffin at the front. It hurt to look at the box, to picture Mamgu's face without a living smile on it; so when the minister stepped into the pulpit and began speaking Sam was glad to focus on him instead. The service was in Welsh. Before long there was sniffing and nose blowing as the eulogy continued.

They stood to sing. Calon Lân began, beautiful music and strong voices. Sam tried to sing along but felt her throat tighten so she mumbled, "*Calon lân yn llawn daioni, Tecach yw na'r lili dlos.*" *A pure heart full of goodness, Is fairer than the pretty lily.*

She had to look up as her eyes brimmed, lights hung in threes, the images spilt over and she realised she hadn't brought a hankie but was definitely going to need it.

Mark Hopton knelt on the hard pavement of Whitworth Street West and laid the flowers reverently at the steps of the former Haçienda. They spread like a swarm of dying wasps. "I miss The Smiths," he muttered. "The Happy Mondays made me happy. Joy Division offered joy. New Order gave my life order." He continued his Madchester Mantra in a tone of prayer undiminished by the fume-farting traffic behind.

The Haçienda had opened on 21st May 1982. Rather than the date when it closed in 1997 he had chosen the opening date for his annual pilgrimage (he'd walked all the way from the concrete gardens of Piccadilly; it took more than 20 minutes). This way he could mourn, but with a touch of hope: by celebrating its birth it would be an optimistic ritual. It *could* re-open, he told people. Just look at the wall, the graffiti saying "rewind and repackage" – the people wanted it. They'd *always* wanted it. An idea moved to the brick; the brick housed a club; the club transmitted a lifestyle. The music that grew from this seed could live again too, Haçienda womb, Factory Records progeny, Tony Wilson magic, the best of Manchester. Music, bands and people were always connected to a place. Everything had to grow somewhere, it just needed the right environment, time, and a bag of that funny-smelling soil from garden centres.

It could re-open. It had been before so it could be again. It was just … in a coma. Yes. He knew it was serious. But you woke from comas didn't you? It happened in films. It wasn't yet the death of a disco.

Dancer not romancer; drinking in The Haçienda on a Monday, leaning on one of the many black and yellow hazard-striped pillars. Music blaring out dancing beats and rolling guitars. Stage crowded with happy dancers in floppy hats. Darkness at the edges. The darkness of anonymity.

It had been a surprisingly small place compared to its size in his memory.

"Unhappy birthday. Please live again."

Maybe this would be the year. People said the year 2000 was special, a year of change. Chuff all so far though, and the year was nearly half over. The doors in front of him were still locked. He stood, knees sore from the unforgiving Manchester hardness.

Then again, you can't just see things as they look. You've got to see them as they *could* be. The secrets behind the signs. Over to his right was G-Mex, a huge converted railway station. Nearby winding steel steps led up to the platform of the Metrolink station where a tram trundled to a stop. Mark continued to rotate. City Road Inn on the corner, people sat outside drinking and inhaling exhaust fumes. Unfilled train arches opposite. Cars queued up at the lights. That was it – trains, trams, cars, all leading here to *this* spot. The nexus, the ley line, the place where all the veins meet (as Richard Ashcroft once sang). *The Haçienda.* Mark was right; his true faith was justified.

"Oy, you! Clear off you fucking weirdo!"

Someone hard-faced yelling at him from a window above, with a gesture that was absolutely uncalled for. So much for peace and harmony. Maybe in the next world. Until then it was time to move on in case they started throwing things.

The congregation stood round the graveside. The breeze rustled leaves, made the trees sigh. Horribly bright green fake grass surrounded the hole, a depressing focus for all those shuffling awkwardly.

A little boy whispered a question into his mother's ear. "I don't think Jesus is buried in this graveyard, sweetheart," she answered.

A ripple as necks turned. Mamgu was being carried up the precariously steep hillside on four strong shoulders. Breaths held when Uncle Joe slipped, but he kept his balance, kept the coffin proud, waved a hand to say "No problem!" and they continued up. Slowly the wooden box was lowered down into that damp-smelling darkness until it thudded into place, punctuating a life's full stop.

Dust to dust.

When the time came to take a handful of clumped earth from the mound and throw it onto the prison of a coffin Sam had to borrow more tissues from her mam. That was her *gran* in the box. Mamgu would never talk to Sam again. Never cheer her up and tell her everything was okay. Never need help getting a jar open. So many nevers meant this was final. There was no Mamgu any more.

While he waited for the bus Mark thought about Lana.

He'd seen her at a gig, stood nearby until they got talking, and they hit it off talking about bands. So they met up again a week later and ended up in bed.

On the fourth date she told him, "You know we're not going out, right?" She was stood by the bar in Rock World, looking stunning with her hair brushed back and extravagant eye make-up, every punk colour spiralling in.

"No. I thought we *were* going out."

"I'm not ready for that. For now we can see other people." She was glancing around the room as if bored and already seeking another partner.

"I won't share you."

She looked back at him. "That's a deal breaker."

He sulked. She left with someone else and ignored his calls.

He was angry for a while. Almost wished she'd fall into a coma. But then he realised that was petty and he had to grow up. It was as much his fault. Lesson to learn: don't fall for someone so quickly. Establish the groundwork first, make sure you both want to hum the same song. Otherwise you just end up singing alone, busking in a lonely subway that stinks of urine and violence.

So much noise now they'd moved from the house of the divine to somewhere secular. Chatter and clatter, laughter, hubbub that hid the remaining occasional snifflers. The furniture had been moved to the edges of the living room to create a space for the mourners. Priorities: a long table laden with four-packs, cider, and spirits, stacked up, mixed up, then drunk up. Oh, and a bit of space for food.

This had been her gran's home, a narrow terraced house in Neath. Its name was proudly carved into an oak plaque over the door, *Tŷ Pili-Pala* – Butterfly House. Her granddad had liked insects and when he died gran renamed the house. She'd then lived alone but was never alone really, with so many family and friends in the town. She never lost her mind or wit, Mamgu.

"Auntie Samantha, it was sad, wasn't it?" Sam's cousin's daughter, Angharad; nine years old, proper Welsh pretty, tugging at socks she seemed to feel were never pulled up enough. Her dark grey dress looked like it was part of her school uniform.

Sam bent down to kiss the top of her head. "It was. I cried," she whispered.

"Me too!" Angharad's eyes widened. "I couldn't stop crying! It was the kind of crying where snot is coming out of ya nose 'cos your eyes can't cope with it all." The girl hugged Sam's waist, brief and fierce. "Don't tell anyone I was snot crying," she added shyly.

"I won't. We'll keep each other's secrets."

More hugs, welcomes, condolences as Sam mingled and drank, letting the booze float her into acceptance. Drink was always good for that. Shaved off splintery edges in her life.

It was a shock when her mam came in from the kitchen carrying a tray of sausage rolls. Just for a second it was like seeing a ghost: her gran when she was younger, here through a time warp. The way she walked, the sharpness in her eyes, the shape of a face. Her mam was even wearing Mamgu's old apron. Sam swore under her breath as something burned inside her. Just a cruel trick, a memory overlaid on the world, similarities merging, subconscious desire. Maybe not all sad, though. It showed that Mamgu lived on in her daughter. Maybe a little bit in Sam, too. She downed the rest of her drink as her mam got rid of the food and approached her, tea towel in hand. Sam noted her red and puffy eyes.

"You're taller than me now. You ever noticed it?" her mam asked.

"No. How are you doing?"

"As you'd expect."

"You look tired."

"I'm glad you're here too, you know." A brief smile, then lost. "It's hard doing this without your dad. I miss his clumsy big arms."

"Me too. He always smelt of carbolic soap."

"Cigarettes, knowing him. But even when I was mad at him, like during the anniversary when he told people you normally only got 30 years for murder, or when he rolled in at all hours singing 'Hob Y Deri Dando', I…" She petered out.

Sam smiled as she pictured the scene, made worse by her mam's teetotal nature; Dad may have towered over her mam but he was never the boss. "Go on."

"Well, he was serious when it was needed. It's hard but it's life. Families get smaller." She had been twisting the tea towel absently but now adopted a sly look. "I thought you might have brought your boyfriend, the new one?"

"I don't think he's ready for you all yet."

"Does he respect you? Treat you well?"

"Oh, he does."

"Not like those others in the past."

Sam ground her teeth before replying. "No."

"Still, would be better if he was Welsh."

"It's nice being back in Mamgu's house."

"Is this one serious? Steady?"

"I'm trying not to look ahead just yet. It's good seeing so many people here again."

"So you don't love him?"

"I don't know. Do you want a drink?"
"Don't give it away so easily, Samantha."
"Bloody Hell, Mam!"
"Don't blaspheme in my mam's house, not now!"
A few people looked round at the angry words.
"Sorry." Sam lowered her voice so only Mam could hear. "But I don't get it. You want me to have a boyfriend but not sleep with him? Make your mind up. *This* is why I left Wales! Nose jabbing in all the time, advice about who I should or shouldn't see!"
"I don't know why you say such mean and untrue things, Samantha. You left to get educated."
"Just swapped one type of lecture for another," she said under her breath.
"Anyway, that wasn't what I'm saying, you always twist things, too clever for your own good. I still love you though."
"I know."
Brightening. "You know about Mam's will?"
"No."
"She left this house to me."
"What will you do?"
"Keep it. For now." Something implied. "You never know –"
"Ha ha, little Sammy!" Uncle Joe lifted her off the ground with his hug while she struggled.
"I'm not little, put me down you pillock!"
He let her go, sheepish grin.
"And don't call me Sammy, I hate it." She'd wanted to say something stronger, but not with her mam there. Her mam seemed to take the half-glance as a hint and left to organise more food.
Uncle Joe took Sam's arm, moved her towards the drink table so they could both get another.
"How long you here for then?" he asked, swigging from a can.
"A few days. Staying with Mam."
"Looked like arguing?"
"Just nagging."
"What about?"
"Boyfriends."
"Well, are you courting?"

"That's an old-fashioned word."

"Seemed more polite than asking if you're fucking some Englishman's balls off."

"You really only do extremes, don't you?"

"I say what I think."

"I don't want to talk about my boyfriend."

"Shy in front of your old uncle? When'd this happen? No secrets, me. This woman I met last week, right, tits like Snowdon –" he started to gesture with one of his hands when Sam told him to stop and remember where he was.

"Work then, that going okay?" he asked, defeated.

"It's great. I think about quitting at least once a week."

"Ha ha. You should then. Come and work for me in Swansea." Joe owned a few mobile phone shops, which seemed to be doing well judging by the suits he wore.

"You shouldn't joke about that."

"I'm not! And I'm a good boss. Friendly and helpful. Even to fuckwits. You know, there was this English guy, right, he was with his family. Came in the Swansea shop last week. 'Hey man, can you tell me where Traeth Beach is? I came here last year and it was really nice.' Can you believe that? For fuck's sake. Don't they realise how bilingual signs work?"

She laughed at the exasperation on his face.

"Hey, fancy popping out with us?" he asked. "I was going to skin up."

"Not here."

"Why? Fits in. You know: soil, plants, herb."

"Not today."

One of his friends appeared from behind, smiled at her, then eagerly told Uncle Joe, "Hey mun, come and get some pasties, they're putting pasties out, proper ones!"

That was it. She couldn't compete with proper pasties.

Across the room a male voice sang a few words – "Bread of heaven, bread of heaven." The refrain was picked up by others, and as their voices grew others were silenced, conversations faded and became admiring gazes as the men plus a few of the women began to join in. Some sang in English and some in Welsh but it came together, all flowed into one whole which moved up and down scales leading to a chorus that always said "funerals" to Sam. Her family had songs for everything when they were drunk. Thousands of them, stored in minds to be taken out and shared. The voices rose, filling the room. Sam stood still, hairs on the back of her neck prickling, chin raised and eyes watering, proud and hurting.

Mark sat on the top deck of the bus, feeling the precarious tilt as it cornered too fast. He absently picked at a hole in the seat while looking out at the grey buildings, sunlight-washed bones embedded in the ground. The writing was on the wall for this place. Literally. The pink spray-painted words past the traffic lights said "Sorry about your wall".

Without the Madchester music that ruled the world, what was left?

A city of arches and canals, graffiti and art, litter, chimneys, tower blocks and walking cocks, posh and poverty, the mindless and museums, Moss Side and Sale, black and white, buses and trams, blood and brick and Sunday morning sick. Carrier bags and kicked-in teeth, short skirts in winter, tall tales with bitter, a brew and a lager, shaved heads and shopping on red brick and grit, endless suburb houses, long roads and alleys, gorillas and galleries, Salford scallies, prohibition signs and double yellow lines, shops shuttered on Sundays: no ram raids, no green ways. Hulme not short of bullets for the M60 as even the roads run past cloned housing estates. The bus passed Maine Road and Old Trafford, commercialised games of faded glory, the rain and the thunder, rushing and pushing, scaffolding and cranes. A mix of all things human because it was built by MAN. This was life's backdrop, his be all and end all. Separated from the beats that made life worth living, the reality was clear: Mancunians were just knuckle-dragging animals trapped in time, caged in the year 2000, a zoo with an extra character, sniffing each other's arses because there were no forests left to swing in. He'd be here forever. That's what tradition means.

A buzz in his pocket. Mark fumbled his phone out. A text off Denny.

`dad wants 2 c u`

Mark stared at the letters until they burned. Looked outside, squinting at the sun. Gazed around the bus for someone to cheer him with a smile. There was only a guy with a shaggy mop top who looked vaguely familiar. When the guy winked Mark glared at the message some more.

The place traps you.

Eventually he shook his head and triple-tapped a reply.

`ok will see im tmw if i can or on bank hol week after`

The latter would be better: he'd have a week to psych himself up for the visit. Failing that, a week to get drunk and not think about it.

Kinky Afro

➢ **Album:** Pills 'N' Thrills And Bc
➢ **Year:** 1990
➢ **Label:** Factory Records

Kinky Afro acts like a manifesto of intent to

hey, t… …py Mondays … …, brother.

The song is a conversation between a bad dad and his estranged son. Reconciliation is impossible: the dad won't hear what the son says. Once, twice, say it again: he never will. Words are a barrier that can't be passed as they stand across a gulf of difference. Tony Wilson described it as "the greatest poem about parenthood since Yeats". Shaun Ryder, Bard of Salford.

Kinky Afro was one …

music forever. Baggy … you can indulge?

The album's name is all sex, drugs and rock and roll, but with a hint of recognition of the comedown after the indulgence is over. A mix of the high life and the low life. That fine line between satisfaction and going too far, overindulgence that leaves you tetchy, flaking at the seams, having to put on a front to scare off the vultures that prey on the dying. Life and death in there (hey, it's Grandbag's Funeral they tell us, skin up on both sides of the line).

And so this band of excess, discovered by Tony Wilson during one of The Haçienda's battle of the bands nights, became one of the most influential UK bands of the early 1990s. At that time Paul McCartney said they reminded him of the Beatles. It's no surprise that The Happy …day… …lped pave the way for the

The dark-haired boy's floppy fringe shaded his eyes, hid their defensive, withdrawn look. He wore a tracksuit with dried mud at the bottom, and sat next to his dad inside the gloomy pub that smelt of old beer and old men. Occasionally he would sip lemonade. The green straw was a special treat.

His dad drank Pints. Sometimes a lot of them. Like today. Even if the boy didn't count them he could usually tell when it had been a lot because his dad got words wrong, or stayed quiet for a long time staring at his glass, or forgot to get them any food.

"We'll get a chip barm in a bit, on the way home," his dad said with a smile that crinkled his unshaved face. "A treat, eh? Nice chip butty?"

"Yeah. I love chips, Dad."

There was music on the jukebox. It was a tune that seemed to be all slow sad drums and a sad man singing in a deep sad voice. The boy had heard it before in this pub. He liked it. The man was singing about silence. It sounded peaceful.

"Oy, Jacko, you be wantin' another?" shouted the barman. He always called the boy's dad "Jacko". It wasn't his right name though.

"No, we'll be gettin' off after this. Got business to take care of."

"That business being a certain big-tit slag?" The people who spoke to his dad in the pub always used Bad Words, ignored the boy's presence.

"Nah, had a barney. Stuff her!" His dad laughed, though the laugh wasn't a laugh of fun. He turned to the boy. "That's your Auntie Mary he's talking about. We won't be seeing her again."

"I liked Auntie Mary."

"Yeah, well, she was too grabby. You'll get a new Auntie soon enough. Always do, don't you, Mark? It's one of those things about life. Here's a tip for nowt – always keep a bit back, son, whatever it takes to keep the bastards guessing. Applies to everything. Remember it."

"I will, Dad."

"Hey, Jacko. Guess who's walking past?" said a man with a beard and fat arms who sat by the window looking out on to the main road –

– and he woke on the bus with a shudder and a tight feeling in his gut. The same feeling he always got on a visit. He shouldn't have dozed off. The sun was hot on his face.

"Are you okay?" asked the bloke sat next to him.

"Yeah. Just kippin'."

The man nodded and took a swig from a litre bottle that was wrapped in a plastic bag. He had ugly scars running up his cheeks:

Mark recognised him then. A drunk who travelled on some of the same buses. The bloke stunk a bit, but Mark always felt sorry for him. The old guy was round but compact, like a grey-haired human cannonball squeezed into a black leather jacket. The seats weren't big enough for the two of them, and scarface was only half on.

The plastic bottle was offered to Mark. He couldn't imagine anything more trampy than to swig from it, yet he almost did, just to show that he didn't think the guy was a leper.

"Can't, thanks. I'm going to prison," Mark said.

"You seem happy about it,"

"That's because I'm only visiting."

"Strangeways?"

"Yeah."

"Well, bless you lad."

Mark got off the bus. Only a five minute walk from here. Plenty of time to get his head together. He took a deep breath of hot air. Then sneezed. Snitting pollen. He removed a can of pop from his bag and gulped down the warm fizzing sweetness.

It had taken years to track down that sad song from the pub. Then he was in a video rental shop one day and heard it playing as background music. He'd rushed over to the counter staff to ask about it. "Atmosphere. Joy Division. Fucking class," the teenager behind the desk had said. Mark had written it down on a scrap of paper.

It was Mark's first single. He'd played it again and again until he hadn't just learnt the lyrics: the music became part of him. He always did that with the good stuff, until he could almost believe the musicians were his friends and were always somehow nearby.

The can was finished and he threw it over a wall, heard it clank down a pile of rubble, bouncing bum over boob like most things in his life. Rene had been irritated earlier, when he'd asked for leave at short notice. Then he'd told her he was going to see his dad in prison and she went quiet and signed the form. It was a passport to special treatment. The only passport he had.

The streets around here were a ghost town. All tight roads, shuttered doors, yards topped with barbed wire. The only outlets were for van hire. On the rare occasion when a car went past you suspected they were prison spies: undercover patrollers in unmarked cars.

Whenever he was in this area he felt watched, judged. As a result he looked ahead, walked stiffly, and probably seemed even more suspicious.

He soon reached the intimidatingly huge walls. The prison was a red brick castle, massive doors like a drawbridge, but designed to keep people in, not out. And overlooking the whole prison and surrounding area was the balconied red watchtower. "Stuff Big Ben, we've got a big fucking bell-end," his dad had once said. It was supported by the higher-tech security cameras on poles. Eyes and fences everywhere. He bent his head forward, uncomfortable.

He knew where to go, what to do. Through reception, handed in his visiting order, let them check his ID. A quick frisk. Mobile phone taken off him and put into a locker, gifts checked, then he was escorted to the visiting hall. His life had always been dragged into these places.

Two other prisoners were sat with their visitors. Prison officers stood nearby, joking with each other. The hall was surprisingly cool. Even the summer heat wasn't allowed in without a pass. Mark sauntered over to the drinks machine and bought two teas. Dunk, whirr, sloosh, gurgle. Cheerless brown liquid squirted into white plastic. He took the teas to the grubby table he'd been told to use, careful not to spill the one he put down on his dad's side. He sat and waited with his hands on his lap, still apart from the nervously tapping toe.

Sound always echoed in these places. Footsteps and the clang of gates warned him that people were approaching long before his dad was shown into the hall. Dad. Tall and wiry yet solid-looking, like the handle of a hammer, striding with the cocky walk of a much younger man. Mark noted that the officers adjusted their positions to keep a better eye on Jack Hopton. They knew their troublemakers and the lines on Jack's craggy face weren't from smiling.

"A brew, great. You get the cigs?"

Mark pushed three packets over. The cellophane was gone because of the guards' checks. "60. Like you asked."

"Good lad." Jack slipped them into a pocket on his overalls.

"Glad to be out of solitary?" Mark kept his voice neutral, but when he'd found out he couldn't visit his dad last time because he was in the

SSU – Special Segregation Unit – he'd sighed with relief. It was like a present from the prison service.

"Makes no difference to me, son. It's all the same boring nick." He sniffed.

"What was it for this time?"

Jack cracked his first crooked smile. "I bit part of someone's ear off in the textile workshop. Don't look worried, the bastard had been acting the cock, got me razzed. He'd been warned. So I laid into him. You've got to or they walk all over you. Here's a tip for nowt – biting an ear off takes all the fight out of them. Just like that." Jack smacked a fist into his palm with a hard thwack, earning a glance from the officers. "Just don't swallow any blood unless you know they haven't got Aids. If you're sure they haven't and you really want to piss them off, it's even better to swallow the ear. They can't sew it back on then."

"That's disgusting."

"I didn't swallow it. You get too many extra days added. They sewed the bit back on, but I've heard the joke when he walks past and the blokes all say, "Ere, 'ere, look who it is?"" A deep gurgle came from Jack's throat. "Thing is, the bastard of a wing manager had it in for me, he was in there with C&R right away."

"C&R?"

"Control and Restraint. Two of 'em got me down, the dogs. I was hoping for more, bragging rights, see. Then they put me in segregation for fourteen days. Threatened me with a body belt. I reckon they wanted to punish me for fucking up their Safer Prisons Award or something. In the end they slapped on thirty days, but that's just adding drops to a puddle. My first parole will be fucked though, unless I go on a load of the education and training schemes to get my record back in the black. Actually. I'm thinking of reading up on the law, learn more about it. I spoke to this other con who was studying legal shit. You find out so much then. The whole law, it's as crooked as I am."

"That'd be good. Learnin' stuff."

"Got a new guy in my cell. Shifty Shane. He's really into all them courses. Bricklaying, plastering and the rest." Another phlegmy sound from his chest as he leaned back. "Ah, he's a good laugh. Dry sense of humour. When he was being sentenced for dealing he thought the judge was looking at him in a way he didn't like, so he got nowty and said, 'Yer can luke yer septic twat.' Classic. Got contempt of court but didn't give a shit. Best cell mate I've had. Anyway, what about you? How's life on the outside world?"

"The usual stuff. Work. Listening to music."

"Fucking *music*! What about *women*? You putting it out there?"

"A bit."

"A bit?" His dad sized him up. "You're lying to me. I can always tell. Nice try, but you can't shit a shitter. Lie to others, yeah, never give the game away, it's only used as evidence against ya: but don't lie to me. So let's try it again. You putting it out there?"

"Not at the moment."

"Are you gay or something?" Jack scowled at Mark.

"No! I've just not met anyone."

"Fuck, you're wasting the opportunity of being outside! Don't let the Hoptons down. You should be enjoying all sorts of lasses. Just don't get tied up with one. You don't want to lose your freedom when you're not even inside. That's why I'm glad your mum died."

"You said she left."

"Left: died to me. She was always a dirty, mithering witch."

Mark squeezed the thin plastic cup, looked down as he felt tea spill over the top. "I don't like you talking about Mum like that."

"Yeah, yeah, okay. I'm just thinking of you. Just some advice for nowt – whatever you do, don't leave your cock-snot up a bitch's chuff. Only ties you down."

Mark looked out of the barred window. The sunlight seemed dirty. "Do you regret us, then?"

"Denny sticks up for hisself."

"And what about me?"

His dad slurped the hot drink. Stared at Mark's face, making him uncomfortable. "You're doing your best," he eventually said. "Visit your dad when he asks, bring him things. So there you go. I'm lucky enough." Jack grinned, showing nicotine-stained teeth, one of which was chipped.

Mark sat up straighter on hearing this thing that was near to praise.

"Yeah, you're very good at bringing me stuff." Jack fidgeted with the now-empty plastic cup. "Your main skill, that. I know you don't throw your weight around. Not like our Denny, limping fuck that he is. Remember that time your brother decked a Chinky with a plank? Hit him so hard the wood broke, and you just stood blubbering about it, yer mardy arse. I shoulda forced you into boxing or something, shape you up." He see-sawed his forefinger under his nostrils like a jittering moustache. "Don't make it obvious, just look over my shoulder and tell me if the cunts are in listening distance."

"They're not."

"Good. You know what I'm saying, son?"

Mark shook his head.

"Shit-for-brains! I want you to bring me something next time. Something special."

"What, something I'm not *supposed* to bring in?"

"Now you're thinking."

"I'm not –"

A palm was held up. "Just hear me out. It's not for me. I'm not a user. But there's so many of 'em in here, no hope, just time. Spend so long in a cell that by lockdown they need the escape, will do owt for a head-change. All you see is white-washed walls, white faces – apart from coloureds and pakis, obviously – it's enough to make anyone desperate for something to bring a bit of colour to this place. And if you have the key then it's *power*, Mark. Power over other lives inside; outside too sometimes, when there's debts. Set yourself up."

"Drugs?"

"Don't paint it on the fuckin' wall!" he hissed. Lowered his voice. "This is where I need you. It ain't so easy to get away with catapulting it over the wall in a dead pigeon nowadays, and chances are another con would swipe it first anyway. Works best if someone brings it in."

"You're getting me mixed up with Denny."

"No I'm not! Denny can't do it. He's got unpaid fines and probation orders he's barely sticking to. Probably breached a few conditional discharges too. Too risky for him; if he gets caught he definitely goes inside. It would only be a first offence for you. And anyway, they watch him like a hawk. Not you, though. You're a good boy."

"You must think I'm stupid. I'm not risking prison!" Mark whispered harshly. "How could you ask me to do that?"

"I already said, you wouldn't *get* caught, you soft sod. It's dead straightforward: nowt tricky, nowt rough. Denny will organise it. All you'll have to do is bring me what they give you. Just this once."

"Things are never that simple."

"They are."

Mark put his heels on the floor, ready to scoot his chair back. "No."

Dad's eyes fixed on him, unblinking. "Don't say that yet. Just think about it."

"I don't need to."

"This isn't something for the future. This is already being worked out. I've made promises. Don't let me down, unless you want to see me in trouble. It'd be worse than I'd get off the screws. So shut your gob and listen. Don't answer. Just *think* about it. If you care anything for family then when Denny gets in touch you'll do the right thing. We don't do charity but we should do anything for family. I would."

"I don't believe you."

His dad's fist pounded on the table, rattling loose bolts like jarred teeth in a slapped skull. "I don't believe you either, you ungrateful shit! Don't make me fucking tell you twice!"

Mark had scooted back, almost fallen from his chair; he saw two officers rushing over; his dad turned to them with palms held up. "No problem, just telling my boy not to disrespect his old man," he said, smiling at them to show he was calm. How his dad could ever think that smile reassured anyone, Mark never understood.

"I think the visit is best over for the day. We don't want you getting excited, Jack, do we now?" The officer's tones were as cold as Mark's dad's.

Mark stood too. "I'm going. See you, Dad. Take care of yourself."

"Aye, I'll do that. Stay in touch with your brother."

As Mark left he heard his dad telling the officer, too loudly, "A good lad, really. Both me sons are."

Despite the sweltering heat outside Mark was glad to be on the other side of the big walls. Cars were pulled up there, bleached blonde women combing their hair in front seats, shifty-looking lads smoking with the back door open, legs out of the car blocking the pavement. Mark to walk around them. They stared at him all the while.

Once out of sight he leaned back against a chainlink fence, legs weak; it rattled in protest. He squinted up at the sky and the blinding sun. Family had so much weight, so much gravity. It wasn't easy to escape.

ever fallen in love (with someone you shouldn't've)

...rus in the verse "You make me feel I'm dir...
punk song to swap the last words for "You ...
Buzzcocks. This is a personal situation, a lonely problem. As the guitar shreds at the end,
and the drum whacks into the last chorus, Pete Shelley is still repeating the complaint.
Nothing's gonna fix it. Sometimes love's too broken for you to do anything but grit your
teeth or walk away.

Not humourless...
...the B-sid...

...visualisation. Innov... an ability to upset the establishm... ...nued the pop punk tradition.

And so a song released in the year that Joy Division made their first TV appearance has been chosen to represent this band whose punk attitude had a huge effect on the indie and Manchester music scenes.

"Body language is key. Sell yourself and you unlock the door to selling your product."

The trainer moved to the next slide. A list of body Dos and Don'ts which he highlighted with the sniper's dot of a laser pointer. He stood with legs planted slightly apart, shoulders back. So manly. So slick. So fucking fake. His hair was so thick and mahogany brown that Sam called wig.

She yawned. Wouldn't it be beautiful to just stand up and walk out? Wave as she left. Out the door, through reception, into the sun. Look at the sky, find a tree, eat an ice cream, paddle in a fountain. Then onto the first train back to Piccadilly.

But the workshop was expensive. Rene would blow a gasket if Sam didn't stay for the whole thing. No escape, physical or mental.

"Look people in the eye. This is something many people pick up on, but be aware that you especially need to do it if you are lying to someone. That's when we would naturally want to look away. What do we do?"

"Over-ride your instincts!" some of the people in the room chanted with varying degrees of enthusiasm. Sam stayed silent, watching how others reacted to being told that it was perfectly acceptable to lie.

Many were making notes.

The trainer chose a volunteer and did some role-playing to back up his points, involving variations of evasive eye movements against direct looking. He managed to make his lies about failed orders and shoddy products more convincing.

Bravo.

Sam looked down at the blank sheet of her pad. Then she scribbled her only notes:

- Unethical.
- This environment is undoing my goodness.
- I don't want to sell myself.
- I <u>really</u> want an ice cream.

The day had even begun badly. She couldn't find the place, had to ring the organiser. Told him she was by the train station and asked for directions.

"Okay, do you see a big hill?" he'd asked.

She'd glanced around. It seemed flat. A small slope, maybe. Nothing she would think of as a big hill. "Errr, no."

A sigh from the other end.

"I'm from Wales..." she'd tried to explain.

Work. Grind to the end so playtime can begin. Evil and good, dividing up the clock of our time: that's life, see.

"Wish the weekends lasted more than two days," muttered Benjamin Lawrence as he hefted a box from the cart into the back of a white van. "So many ladies to love, so few hours." His black skin glistened with sweat. The warehouse by the side of the main building was spacious and cool but for now they were outside, loading the latest orders for the afternoon delivery.

"At least you'll be back inside soon. I've got to drive this bloody thing," moaned Dave Chambers, stacking piles of boxes inside the van. Its suspension creaked as he walked back and forth.

"Yeah, but I have to work with him, sniffing all the time," said Ben.

"It's not my fault. Hayfever," Mark told him.

"I don't care. Get some tissues or something. It's disgusting," Ben replied.

They were quite a contrast. Ben was stylish and good-looking, whereas Dave resembled a boxer with his shaved head, flattened nose, and big biceps. Mark and Ben sometimes referred to him as "Bulldog"; Mark suspected Dave secretly liked that.

Mark had opened one of the boxes to take a peek. From the looks of the book covers they were all school and FE college orders. He took one of the books. Flicked to the back of the title page. Date of publication. Place of publication. He liked that. An indelible stamp which showed where things were from. The setting that made them.

"Oy, lazy arse, keep the boxes coming," snapped Dave from above. "It's not like you can read anyway."

Mark hoisted the box up, not deigning to answer, and became aware of a figure watching them from the dark rectangle beneath the warehouse's rolled-up corrugated steel door. He expected it to be their boss, Rene, checking up on them, but before he could subtly warn the others she stepped forward. The slim legs, short skirt and trainers blew that expectation away: it was Emily Garfield. Just like the blue hairclips holding in her sandy hair, she looked cool and controlled, not ruffled and sweaty like Mark.

"Hey boys, working hard?" she asked.

Ben smiled and sat on a crate, adjusting his collar. "Yep. Always."

"Always? Didn't I overhear you two this morning, and it sounded like you were talking about erections?"

Dave stopped loading his box and grinned. "The walls have ears."

"Pretty ones, too," Ben added.

Dave sat at the edge of the van, making it creak. "You're sort-of right. We were discussing the difference between a *cob on* and a *lobon.*"

"I wouldn't get those mixed up," Emily replied smoothly.

"You're a no-nonsense girl, Emily, and I respect you for it," said Dave.

"No nonsense then." She held out a sheet of paper. "Additional order from Rene, do you want this?"

"No."

She ignored him, folded the sheet and put it into his shirt pocket. "Tough. Send Ben and…" she glanced at Mark, confused. "They'll get it."

Mark looked down at the worn orange road markings that delineated the loading area, let his hair fall forward, hoping she'd leave.

"How come you're giving out work today?" asked Dave.

"Sam's on a training course."

"Wish I was," Ben said. "Free dinner, smart women, have a snooze at the back."

"She's there under protest. Hates anything to do with management. I think Roger wanted to go. He's gutted he had to stay here."

"How is old Gel Head?" asked Dave.

"The usual. I asked him if he wanted a coffee earlier, and he said 'Nopey dokey'. I asked him if that meant no. Then he said 'Yuh-huh' and nodded." She shook her head. "I looked into his eyes and said 'The thing is, Roger, when you speak it *sounds* like English, but I can't understand a word you're saying'. I don't know what his problem is, but I'll bet it's hard to pronounce."

"It isn't really," said Dave "It's pronounced 'fucktard'."

Emily and Ben laughed. Mark pretended to read a label.

"Lovely to talk to you all, as usual," said Emily, looking from one to the other. "There is nothing like having some adult conversation."

"Why, thank you," said Ben, standing. "We –"

But Emily interrupted him. "And that was *nothing like* having a mature conversation. You're all idiots." She entered the building with a wave and a smile.

Ben wolf-whistled after her. "One-nil to Emily."

"Nowt like a bit of banter." Dave jutted his chin at Mark. "What about you though? Did you even speak to her?"

"Can't remember."

"I don't think you did."

"If you're shy around the ladies, I can give you advice," said Ben.

"The only advice he needs is to open his mouth and say something."

"And maybe get some new clothes."

"And try looking up for once."

"Leave off," muttered Mark. "I know how to talk to women."

"Don't get your face all red. You white boys give everything away," Ben added.

Mark's palms were sweaty. He stood stiffly. If he leaned on the van he knew it would look stupid, not casual like when they did it. Always so sure of themselves. And so sure of Mark. What he'd do, what he'd say. As if he had no punk in him. "We could go out tonight. See who's shy then," he blurted.

"Ooh, sounds like a challenge! What do you think, Dave? Three Musketeers? Tuesday night in the city?"

"I was going to stay in with Suzannah … but why not? Okay, you're on."

"And Mark can show us his smooth moves outside of work when he's not acting so … *professional* in front of women."

Oh sugar fudge. Why'd he suggest something so stupid?

Finally back in Chorlton. Flat land of bedsits and burgled flats. Sam was exhausted. She'd lugged bags from Neath straight to the training course then home. Her arms were six inches longer.

She looked at the wind-up clock again. A smiling frog pranced in the middle of the clock face, his arms pointing to the time, but they hardly seemed to have moved since her last glance. When she'd left Neath the tears and the smiles had dried up. Now it seemed like time had dried up too.

She finished the box of Cadbury's Animals and stuffed the carton into the overflowing litterbin in the corner of her room. It crinkled above the Nurofen packaging and mini vodka bottle. It wasn't much of an evening meal.

The shower shut off in the room above her with a clunk. Leigh's skin must be like a prune by now. She'd probably spend another half hour in there doing whatever she did after her shower.

"Pube trimming and eyebrow plucking," Sam muttered to the frog teddy sat atop the LPs she couldn't listen to any more since her old record player broke. He didn't reply.

Sam had the room by the front door. She shared the ground floor with the living room, kitchen, and toilet. Better companions than Leigh and Robin, who had the rooms upstairs. The kitchen never went quiet when she walked in. The living room didn't go out with the toilet without inviting her. It was better when she was alone here; there was more of an illusion of it being her home.

If she squinted, the clock hands had maybe inched round a bit more. Russell would be finished at the bar in an hour or so. She could escape from this white-walled prison.

She heard the bathroom door open and close, so grabbed a towel. The floor above was always alien territory but she wanted to freshen up before meeting him. Kill dirt, kill time, in one fell swoop.

"Playtime!" laughed Ben, as they grabbed jackets from the free-standing lockers.

"This'd better be worth it," grumbled Dave. "Suzannah's pissed off with me."

They stopped off at a newsagents because Ben wanted cigarettes. Mark bought a bar of chocolate. "It's bad to drink on an empty stomach," he explained, tucking in as they sauntered down the road. They were turning a corner when Dave asked, "What the fuck are you doing?"

Mark looked at him, confused. "Just eating?"

"No. That." Dave pointed to some crumpled paper on the floor. It was the wrapper Mark had dropped. "Pick it up."

"Why?" asked Mark. He felt his body tense.

Dave sighed. "Didn't anyone socialise you? Jesus, I guess not." Dave leaned forward and Mark flinched, but Dave just said, "What you cringin' for? Nobody's gonna hit yer," then picked up the scrap of plastic and dropped it in a bin. "Use your brain. Don't leave the world worse than when you came into it."

"Sorry," Mark said from a dry mouth.

"Erm, come on guys, night out. Cheery, yeah?" Ben said, looking from one to the other. "I've got a treat for you both."

A few streets' worth of sullen walking and they stood before the "treat".

"No way I'm going in there. It's for nerdy sci-fi geeks. Let's go Copperface Jack's instead." Mark thrust his hands into the pockets of his black jeans and stood in a posture of stubborn defiance.

"Christ," growled Dave. "It's only a bar. Don't be so boring, you lanky wanker."

"Yeah," added Ben. "Try it. There might be some Klingon pussy if we're lucky."

The bar was called F.A.B., and you had to go through a futuristic-looking steel door to get in. Traffic was roaring past along Portland Street. Mark sighed. "Okay. But you can buy first drink." As he followed them in he muttered, "And I'm not drinking anything called 'Laser Blast'."

It was dark inside, no windows, and it took Mark's eyes a few seconds to adjust after the sunny street. Fluorescent and UV light strips gave the place a twilight feel, illuminating futuristic decor and framed pictures from sci-fi or cult films. Then Mark almost grinned when he saw they had a full-sized dalek behind a barrier in a mock-rock grotto. He used to love Dr. Who as a kid. One of his earliest, blurriest memories was of Dad taking him and Denny to an exhibition in Blackpool; the only day out he could recall. The dalek's eyestalk pointed at Mark's face; it was comforting.

"And there's a monster in a cage round the corner," said Ben, who must have followed Mark's gaze and read his expression. "Something else from Star Trek I think. A cyber-bot or whatever."

While Ben ordered the drinks Mark had a proper look round. The place was a grown-up's toyroom, prized possessions highlighted with fairy lights. Reds the glow of engine ports, greens of alien birth chambers, blues of distant ice caverns. Painted girders and pillars combined 60s kitsch with steampunk engineering. A time machine escape to a kid's dreamworld.

He felt something tickling his neck. Reached up to scratch and then – *hairylegsscratchylegs* – let out a shriek, leaped back as the biggest motherflipper of a spider he'd ever imagined touched his head, it was about a foot long and was hanging from a web on the dark ceiling, and –

Dave and Ben were laughing, doubled over ... the pretty girl at the bar was grinning as she put a pint on the counter.

The spider whirred back up to the ceiling again.

On a motorised wire.

He realised his hand was covering his heart, feeling the racing thuds.

"Ha ha you comedians, very funny. I nearly dumped and you two find that amusing?" he snapped, but it just made them laugh all the more. Dave tried to say something but couldn't speak yet and gave up.

"Sorry ... your face!" Ben managed, wiping his eyes.

Mark looked at the spider. It seemed to lower and raise automatically from amongst the dangling spaceship models. It had a woman's face stuck to it.

"Did you two know about this?"

"I didn't, never been in here before," said Dave, holding up his palms.

"I'd completely forgotten about the Thatcher Spider. Honest!" apologised Ben. "It's just your luck to be in the wrong place at the wrong time."

"Look, just take a drink and stop being soft," Dave ordered. "And be thankful your sphincter didn't collapse."

They sat at a table in the corner, Ben and Dave still smirking at Mark's sulky face.

"Glad work's over," said Ben, fiddling with his new phone. "Rene had me running round like a blue-arsed fly."

"Wasn't all bad though, was it? Emily was looking pretty hot today. And I saw you joking with her after Rene had left. What was all that about, huh? You sly dog!" Dave poked Ben with a stubby forefinger repeatedly, making him squirm.

"Yeah, well, she wanted to know how to get free tickets to see bands at the Apollo. And to bask in my sexy personality for a while."

"You told me she needed more envelopes?" said Mark.

"Grass."

Dave asked, "Have they got boyfriends?"

"What do you think? Girls like that always have boyfriends. Sam's is a barman, big bloke. Cool motherfucker. Dresses well." A quick glance towards Mark. Only a split-second, but Mark knew what it meant. Ugly Manchester-monkey Mark.

"How'd you know all this?" Dave asked.

Ben lit up a cigarette. "It's my business to know."

"I thought you were giving up smoking?" Mark asked.

"Yeah, I can any time. Just not tonight."

"That's what addicts always say," Mark told them, leaning forward. "I know a guy who's addicted to brake fluid. He says he can stop anytime."

Dave rolled his eyes. "Punishment for that is your turn to buy a round."

A number of drinks later.

"Where next, chaps?" asked Dave.

"Home," suggested Mark.

"Forget that. I thought we were going to see red hot Mark action? Lessons in the ladies? If I'm busted with Suzannah then I want something to laugh about tomorrow."

"Rock World then," said Mark, but the other two jeered at him.

"No, it's a Monday, so 5th Ave. Got to be," said Ben.

"That's where you got off with the woman from the offices over the road, isn't it?" Dave asked.

"Yep!"

"You were all over her that night."

"Too right!"

"But you don't even *like* her."

Ben gave Dave a condescending look. "She was dressed as Lara Croft. That over-rides *everything*."

"Right. 5th Avenue it is."

"I object," Mark said.

"Tough," replied Ben, putting an arm round Mark's neck and pulling him in. "Two-to-one, old buddy. The battlefield is chosen, so you'd better go to the toilets and arm up. Tonight we're going to learn from the master – by which I mean *you* – so it's pump-action spunk guns at the ready."

Dave and Mark both groaned, but for different reasons.

She was waiting outside Russell's flat when he got home. He was doing well for himself: she knew Didsbury was one of Manchester's posh areas because of all the big trees.

"Ta-da!" She smiled at him.

"Oh. Hi." Hug. "Didn't realise you were back from Wales."

"I told you it was only a weekend."

"Yeah. Yeah. Right." Door unlocked, they went in. His flat was quite swish. Super-low sofa, minimalist chrome dining area, and space galore. She'd rather spend time here than in her own chipped-furniture hell cell.

"How was work?"

"Usual pissheads." He had a short-sleeved shirt on. It was tight enough to show his muscles, and the tattoos up his forearms were on full display. Celtic swirls and a red phoenix on his left, fading panther on the right. "Wanna drink?" he asked, going to the fridge.

"No. Had one already today."

"And?"

"I don't want to get pissed."

"Whatever." He poured himself some wine. She noticed the bottle was already open. "How was Wales?"

"I'm not in the mood to talk about it right now."

"Probably got jumped by a hairy-legged Welshman, eh?"

"I'm not like that."

"No. But I know what you *are* like." He downed his drink then kissed her, gripping her arse tightly in hands designed only for fists or clutching. She ran her fingers over his short hair, wondering if he'd look sexier if he grew it, until his hand went up her top and she stopped wondering about anything much.

Mark followed the others down the under-lit steps into 5th Avenue. He was soon holding a bottle of Hooch and leaning against a pillar. It wasn't a huge crowd and few were dancing.

"What about those girls?" Ben asked, pointing with the neck of his bottle. "Go and do some smooth moves on them."

"Not yet. Wait until it's busier." Mark tipped the bottle back, found it was empty.

"You've not even looked at them!"

"I saw."

Ben shook his head. "Putting it away a bit, aren't you?"

"It's all part of my plan. I'll go get us more."

Mark crossed the dancefloor without taking his eyes from the bar. He was aware of observers on the balcony above, leaning over the steel rails. Bars and eyes, even here.

"Hooch, Wicked blue, and a four X." Dave refused to drink "fizzy townie alcopop baby bottle shite".

The woman behind the bar had been laughing with a customer and seemed irritated at Mark's interruption. He noticed another group of girls coming into the club, all made up and ready to razzle. They were gorgeous. A glance back at Ben and Dave. They were gesticulating towards the girls. Mark turned his back on them all.

Three bottles in front of him. He chewed on his lip as he counted out the money.

Ben and Dave, egging him on. How'd he get into this?

"Can I have a double whisky too?"

With all the flashing lights and the bobbing bodies it was hard to tell if the room was spinning, or he was. They danced, a manly triangle on the royal-blue resin dancefloor. Ben's efforts to get any women to join them had failed, and Mark's one attempt – smiling at two girls dancing nearby – had scared them to the other side of the dancefloor. So he had another drink and was content to swagger. At least it was indie night, and the baggy music was a comfortably loose fit to his ears.

Ben danced with a bottle in his hand. His moves involved pelvic thrusts every so often. Mark dodged out of the way whenever it looked like a thrust was pointing at him. Bulldog's dancing resembled a boxer with the twitch. Yeah, they were hot stuff.

A whistle kicked in with an irresistible laid-back beat: Mark knew the song even before Shaun Ryder accused him of twisting melons. He leaned over to Dave, "Track 8! Step On!" Mark yelled. "The Happy's best album, 1990!"

Dave turned away, as if he hadn't heard Mark's words.

Mark started his bow-backed swagger, shoulders jerking to the indie jingle-jangle sound. He leaned over to Ben this time.

"This is better than the Kongos original because of the *attitude*."

Ben just shooed him away. No matter. Mark rolled his mouth and slurred the words, stepped and muttered while hands hung down on rubber arms, wobbling from those stampin' dancin' feet, head nodding, traffic noise like angry car horns whizzing past Stretford Arndale, sound of the streets. He was a music star, a highlife whistling man of happiness, legs open to the chunka thunka loose beat and wailing guitars. Be a man, step up or get stepped on, it's a world of conflict, no peace here except in escape: drugs, sex, raves, booze, rock 'n' roll, the ever-present icons of the album. Like Bez himself, the constant that keeps it together, part of the band's identity, a dancing logo, a walking riff, a stomp of identity. For now, at least, it was part of him. Figgy pudding, this was the good stuff.

When the song ended the floor was full of sweaty faces grinning at each other. Ben finished his bottle then stuck his tongue out, stained blue by the drinks. A promising new beat began and Mark hunched his shoulders for another dance then frowned, stopped.

He'd been tricked.

"What's up?" Dave shouted in his ear. "You okay?"

"This music. 'There's No Other Way'."

"What's up with it?"

"It's them southern Blur bumholes, trying to rip off the Manchester sound."

"Shit, you bear one hell of a grudge, Mark. That was a fucking decade ago?"

"No. April 1991. Same year Oasis formed. I'm not dancing to this baggy rip-off."

He stormed off the dancefloor. The unfinished bottle he'd left on a shelf was gone. Bloody over-zealous glass collectors. He checked his pocket. Wallet still there.

Busier in here now, correspondingly hotter. He licked his lips, throat feeling dry.

Had to queue at the bar. He tried the trick of holding a fiver out in his hand but other people still got served first. He always spent more time looking round than speaking to bar staff.

The balconies above were nearly full. Then in between the heavy lights and strobes which hung up there he recognised a face framed by distinctively curly dark hair. The girl wore a low-cut silver top and leaned over the railing on her forearms.

"Canagetcher?"

Buy posh stuff.

"Two bottles of Bacardi Breezer."

"What flavours?"

"Don't care. Different ones."

He was up the stairs, edging sideways through the hot bodies to the woman. The way she leaned over the railing pushed her arse out, skirt tight around it. She had a cigarette in her fingers: there were ashtrays round the upper balcony, making it the haunt of smokers as well as leching talent-spotters.

"Hi," he said.

She didn't notice him.

"HI," he repeated, louder, bending his neck to enter her field of vision.

"Oh, hi." Confusion.

"You live in the same flats as me, don't you? Off Barton Road?"

"Oh yeah. I thought I knew you."

"Yeah, I knew it was you. Silly, I've never spoken to you before."

"I'm not silly."

"No, I mean me!" They had to shout to be heard over the music, alternately leaning forward like polite seed-pecking birds. He thrust the two bottles out, clear glass showing the disco colours of the sugary liquids. "I got you a drink. Just to say hi, since you're a neighbour and stuff."

She smiled, took the red bottle, leaving him with lemon. "Thanks."

"I knew you'd pick that one."

"Yeah, right. I didn't realise I lived on the same floor as a smooth operator."

"That's me. Mark, by the way."

"Mandy." They shook hands and her fingers were small in his. "Though what do names matter, eh?" Her eyes were surrounded by blue eyeshadow, seemed large in her petite face, itself framed by a curly mane. The sort of girl he couldn't normally talk to without a skinful. Yet here he was.

"Yeah! Right! Who cares? Johnny Marr's real name was John Maher, he changed it when he was at school so he wouldn't be confused with the Buzzcocks' drummer. Names don't make you what you are!" She was nodding, smiling. Wow, she was on his level!

"Sorry, couldn't hear you, what did you say?" she asked, tilting her head towards him. Oh. She'd been nodding to the music.

They continued to shout into each other's ears as he asked questions and only understood half of the answers but laughed each time in case they'd included a joke. He was trying to act like Ben, and it seemed to be working. The music wasn't great so he didn't mind not dancing. Told her titbits about the bands and songs. She seemed interested.

"I was actually going soon," she said, finishing the drink. "Work."

"Don't want another?"

"No. Pissed already." She stared into his eyes when she spoke, a directness he wasn't used to.

"I was going too. I'm getting a taxi."

"Want to share it? Costs a bomb from here."

"Sounds good to me. My treat though, give you a lift back. It's nothing to me. The money."

"Okay, get me coat and meet you at the front."

He nodded. Waited until she walked off, then rushed down the other staircase as quickly as he could without causing a fight, twisting and pushing through the tide of sweating punters until he got to Dave and Ben.

"THERE!" he yelled, pointing at Mandy as she headed to the exit. "GIRL WITH SILVER TOP. TAKING HER BACK TO MINE!"

"What?" Ben.

"Bollocks!" Dave.

"Not *her*?" Ben.

"You *paying* her?" Dave.

Mark just grinned and waved to their shocked faces, made sure he caught up to her and said hi before she was out of their sight, let them know it *was* her, and she *was* leaving with him.

"Oh yeah, oh yeah, who's the man?" he grunted as he came, fingers holding on to her waist tightly from behind. Then he let her go. She collapsed gracelessly onto the black sheets and he left her there while he went to get cleaned up. He was so obsessed with looking tanned that he sometimes topped it up with fake stuff. Got her to rub it into his back. She hated that chemical coffee smell. Fake tan never fooled anyone. She once left streaks on purpose for a joke, but he checked in the mirror and made her do it again.

He came back with another glass of wine. She shook her head when he offered it.

"You were more fun when you drank a lot. When I first met you," he said, taking a gulp.

"That's a mean thing to say when we've just made love."

"Well I did all the work just then. Maybe that's what I mean about you being more fun in the past."

Rattled, she took a cigarette and lighter from her bag.

"Do you have to do that?" he whined.

"Sometimes." She lit up. He left her and returned with an ashtray. It had a photo of a naked woman in the middle.

"Classy."

"About as classy as a woman who smokes."

She inhaled more and frowned at him. He was examining his naked body in the mirror. Flexing muscles. He looked fucking ridiculous.

"I'm thinking of getting another tat. What should I get?"

"My name," she muttered. "You've got other girl's names on your back."

"Huh. Not doing that any more. Beginner's mistake."

She'd looked forward to this. Hoped it would fill her up. Despite the sex she was still empty.

"You mad or something?" he asked, turning to eye her up.

"Maybe."

He put his glass down. Sat next to her on the bed, his weight creating a dent, a slope that tilted her against his side. His arm snaked round her shoulder. He was solid and warm and she suddenly felt like crying.

"I'm sorry," he said. "Me going on … I didn't even ask about the funeral. I know you were fond of your mum."

"Gran."

"Yeah. Was it bad?"

She took another pull on the cig. "I miss her," she said, looking down at their bare feet.

He nodded.

"I feel guilty for not being there so much this last year."

"Guilty, yeah, I get it."

"I was thinking about –"

His phone buzzed. He pushed away from her, rolled on the bed, snatched it up. "Work," he told her, walking towards the bathroom. "Yeah, hi John, what's up man?" He was gone, laughing about something.

She couldn't bring herself to finish the cigarette. Ground it out on the ashtray's fanny.

"Call it thirteen," said the taxi driver.

Mandy was already getting out.

£13? He'd expected half of that. But then again, he didn't often splash out on a taxi. Mark looked in his wallet. *£13?* Did he even have that? He should have gone to Kickacars.

He tipped coins into his hand, poking through and adding up the shrapnel. The last of his cash. Tomorrow's shopping was a no no.

Should he have stuck with the bus?

A glance at Mandy as she waited.

No.

He shoved the coins into the driver's hand and slammed the car door.

They reached her flat first. It was nearer to the staircase than his.

"Thanks for getting the taxi."

"No problemo."

She stood close to him on the open concrete walkway, her short jacket unfastened at the front. The silver top rested on her curves. His ears were ringing.

"It was nice getting to finally talk to you tonight," she said.

"Yeah. When I saw you, I thought 'Hallelujah'."

"Why, you religious?"

"No. It's from a song by the Happy … never mind."

They both leaned forward together. In Mark's case it was a slight loss of balance, but *whatever.* She had thin lips but her mouth was open to him, almost frantic as the pointy tip of her tongue pushed against his; he stroked a hand through her hair until it got caught in some knotted curl and he had to apologise and extricate it. She pushed him up against the wall (great, would stop him wobbling) despite being a foot shorter than him. His hands were on her waist then moved up to hold her in his arms, kissing love, lip affection, her body doing things to him, then she cupped his crotch, stroked, he removed her hand despite the pleasurable hardening; she broke off from the kiss.

"Come in," she said, glancing towards the door of her flat whilst insinuating her body against his.

He slid out from her, shaking his head. "Like you, but … don't normally … on a first taxi ride. I'd prefer to get to know you first."

She blinked and moved her chin back, no smile. Then nodded. "Sure. I wasn't offering anything."

"No … oh?"

"I need to get some sleep." She unlocked her door, slipped inside. "Night."

"Yeah. Night," he said to the closed door.

He swayed to his own place at the end of the hall, tried to turn it into a swagger, got the keys in on the third attempt, told the flat it was twisting his melons, slipped off his trainers, thought about Mandy, smiled to himself, fell onto the sofa in the dark and crashed out.

cigarettes & alcohol

Could a title do more to glorify self-destruction? Maybe if it was backed up by a video where it is obligatory to have a bottle of booze in your hand or a cigarette hanging limply from wasted-looking faces; a video of people collapsing drunk, pissed snogs, smoky backgrounds, toilets as mixed-sex social spaces to show what things can descend into. Grainy black and white footage to imply a colourless life, fitting the lyrics – nothing worth making an effort for except drugs as escapism, go down the white line route. A seductive path to overindulgence reminiscent of the Happy Mondays. Even the single's sleeve reinforced the smiling nihilism: cigarettes (Liam dragging on a fag) and alcohol (Noel holding up ... le) cover the drugs ... Beds, beautiful women, guitars: h... of ... 's not subtle ... red home the ... view of ... nced pe...

BRITS, MTV, NME, and Q. Best Band In The World Today. They really do have awards coming out of their rear ends. Controversy too. The press loved the two oh-so-quotable foul-mouthed wild and hedonistic brothers, forever falling out. The Gallaghers couldn't ever settle their differences for long. Always another insult, another whack with a tambourine, another headline.

If we move on to a different type of bloodline it is easy to see that Oasis was influenced by the cream of

"Dooby dooby doo, gotta make it 'appen," Mark sang as he pulled the greying end of the cord to give power to the shower. The red neon light shone, saying "Ready to go, man!"

He was in his duds, dropped them round his ankles as he sang; kicked one leg so the underpants spun up through the air, a cotton Frisbee with legholes in, then as they reached his shoulders – snatch, scrunch, exuberant side lob into the cardboard box he used as a laundry basket. The sun shone through the window, buttery on his pale skin, and brought a message: the whole *world* was golden today.

He'd woken up early, so there was loads of time for a good scrub, posh breakfast (cornflakes with a cup of tea poured over the top), then maybe read a page of his favourite book before catching the bus. He'd run out of shower gel so had to use Fairy Liquid. He was soon squirting green fluid round and filling the cubicle with happy bubbles.

"Another day, another dollar," said the porter, looking up from a newspaper as Mark entered the work building. Above the reception was a blue sign which read "Packham Green, Manchester's premier book supplier to the academic market".

"Sure is, Taffy," Mark replied. "Another *lovely* day!"

"Bloody hell, you're like a dog with two tails."

Mark took the stairs two at a time, did a little jig at the top, threw things into his locker, and checked the clock. Yep: he was early, for once.

"Hopton," said Dave with a nod. He'd been kneeling on the hard rubber floor and fiddling with the levers on one of the office chairs. Mark's team always got cast-offs. They looked okay but usually one wheel was stuck, making the chair roll in circles, or an adjuster was jammed so you had to lean forward all scrunched up, or sit at the highest setting with your feet dangling like a child. One of the chairs was nicknamed Russian Roulette because it would drop a foot with no warning as some internal mechanism decided to liven up the day by splashing your cup of tea in your face.

"Chambers," replied Mark, grinning.

"You've got some explaining to do." He straightened up, wheeled the chair under a desk with a look of disgust, apparently giving up on it for now.

Ben appeared from the staff room, sunglasses pushed up on his head. "Yeah, what happened? She was *hawt.* You didn't even have time to get her drunk."

"You don't need to get someone drunk if you've got some Manc action."

"Manky action," Dave muttered.

"Are you seeing her again?" asked Ben.

"Er, sure. Tonight, I think. If I'm not too busy."

"Unbelievable," said Ben, shaking his head. "What was she like? Was she dirty? How many times –"

"I don't kiss and tell." Mark savoured the look on their faces. Surprise. Disbelief. Respect? He was having some of that.

Mark stretched and yawned, fists bunched and arms reaching back. He'd finished the last of the box packing. Always a boring job, in the isolated corner of the open-plan office, surrounded by bays of books and stationery. He liked looking at the covers but didn't normally read books. Covers had interesting pictures, colours, designs. Like presents all wrapped up. But words on pages were cold, transmitted after the event. He supposed books were no different from a tape or CD or LP though – the finished product, burned into plastic then cooled to leave the impression of the sounds and words, unchanging and final. That's why you couldn't beat a live performance. Heat, change, immediacy, closeness as the sound vibrations reach your ears fresh, feeling like contact with a dream.

The afternoon sun came through a skylight and slid across the wooden floor to his desk. He put a hand down, let the warm light play on it. There was no outside view from here, no nearby windows down onto the car park, little to see but cardboard and paper: this felt like the outside reaching in to befriend him.

Taffy brought the post up. Mark sorted it and put the envelopes and packages into a tray, humming to himself. Distribution was a brainless task but he could occupy himself with the game of kings, Manchester Music Associations. He felt like playing the interbreeding variant today, bands connected via members. He would avoid the obvious ones such as the formation of New Order or Electronic. Too easy.

He handed a few letters to one of the new keyboarders who was complaining to another about the confusing layout of the building. She thanked him with a smile. That was nice. He nodded with satisfaction.

The Seahorses. Formed by John Squire from The Stone Roses. 1996. 1 point.

The tall guy in finance took the post and stuck it on his desk without acknowledging Mark, just carried on working on some paperwork. Rude. But Mark wouldn't let it affect his mood today.

Around 1996… Ah! Monaco – side project by Peter Hook from New Order. 2 points.

Packham Green took up the top two floors of the building. Below them was some kind of archive connected to one of the universities. Most of the work took place on this top floor, with its warehouse-like corrugated and peaked roof, fluorescent lights hanging in strips, sets of free-standing shelves dividing the space up into discrete areas. At the floor's entrance was the staffroom and toilet, while at the far end were offices for senior staff like Rene. In one open-plan zone there were the teams who dealt with orders and finance, each sat around large desks. And off in a corner near the staffroom was the post and packing area, which also happened to be the base for Mark, Ben and Dave. There were two old PCs nearby. Most of their work didn't require using a computer so they only got to use them at breaktimes. Their small team was just "monkey workers, mooking our way round the Green jungle," as Dave would have it.

Could Mark count the fact that Noel Gallagher was a roadie for Inspiral Carpets before he joined Oasis? Maybe not. Noel wasn't actually in *that band. Thinking cap back on.*

He approached the orders team and separated out the items for their table. Samantha Rees was concentrating on the figures that filled her screen. She wore baggy black culottes and slip-on shoes. But she'd taken her feet out of them, was stroking one of them absent-mindedly with a toe. It slid back and forth smoothly. Her toenails were bright red.

"You want something?" asked Gel Head, bringing Mark's attention to the fact that he'd been staring at Samantha's feet.

"Oh, just doing the post."

"Well?"

"These for Gel–" and he just about stopped himself from saying "Gel Head" aloud. "For you." Roger's surname was Gelder. It was Dave who had come up with the nickname for Roger, who used loads of the wet-look stuff. It reminded Mark of chip-pan smearings.

Roger scanned an address then dropped that letter in the bin. "Junkatron," he muttered, before putting his payslip in a tray.

"And these for Samantha."

"Thanks," she said, smiling as she accepted the post. "And it's just Sam." That smile. Not just painted on. Warm light on a hand.

"No problem. I'll leave this payslip for Emily."

Mark moved on to the next team.

Sam.

He felt inspired. Rapidly he connected Happy Mondays to Black Grape to Paris Angels to The Stone Roses and Inspiral Carpets, hardly pausing as the burning links formed like a web, each node tracing fire to the next; he zoomed out mentally and saw that it was only a small section, a fraction of a whole, possibly a lifetime's work to map it all out.

He grinned. *Sam.*

"All done, all accounted for," said Emily as she got back from the warehouse, crumpling up the order sheet. Her blonde bob was cut to just above her shoulder, light and bouncy like Emily herself. "Ah, payslips. Great."

"Yours feels heavier than mine," said Roger, holding one in each hand.

"That joke was old in the stone age." Emily snatched hers back. "Sometimes it's hard to believe you're the same generation as us."

Sam returned to the spreadsheet, pulling figures off for her monthly report.

Em tutted at something on her own screen, muttered "Fuckwits". Roger leaned over, made a joke that caused Em to do one of her dirty laughs. Em started showing him things on her PC, with commentary.

"You two, please, this is important," interrupted Sam. "It's hard to think straight and avoid mistakes while people keep jabbering on."

"That's 'cos you want to know what everyone else is saying," said Em. "Nosy."

"No it's not!"

Back to the totals column.

Roger ran fingers through his hair, an unconscious habit. Sam decided not to let his phone touch her face next time she had to answer it.

"Just don't want to miss out," Em muttered.

"Shut up!"

Got to shut out distractions. Train her mind to deal with numbers, block out people.

Sam eventually became absorbed in the latest list of orders when a voice over her shoulder said, "Can you put the lid on that please?"

Rene Hacking, their boss, looking down at Sam. Rene was in her 40s, overweight, and from this angle appeared indomitable. Sam's confusion must have been obvious, because Rene nodded at the bottle of water on her desk. "Health and safety. It could be knocked over."

Sam looked blankly from Rene to the bottle, and back. She moved her hand to the bottle lid, then stopped. She could feel heat rising in her face. She forced her hand onto her lap instead. "Oh, come on. I'm not going to spill it. Health and safety also says we should sip water regularly, and it's easier without a lid on."

"Yeah, she'd get RSI from unscrewing it all the time," Em chipped in.

"Stay out of this, Emily," snapped Rene. "It is between Samantha and myself."

Emily frowned, but Rene's gaze stayed on Sam. It felt like the office's sound level had lowered a touch. Eavesdroppers. A wave of unreality washed over Sam. She could hardly believe this conversation was taking place. She glanced around at the other's faces for support, saw something in front of Roger, and pointed at it. "But he's got a cup of coffee! That's more likely to be spilt."

"You can't seal a coffee cup," Rene said, colour rising on her own cheeks. Their eyes locked uncomfortably. It wasn't worth it. Sam was reaching for the lid when Emily swiped it and put it into a pocket.

"There's no lid," said Emily. "So Sam can't put one on, and it's just like a glass of water now. Okay?"

Rene glared at her. "No, it's in your pocket."

"No it isn't," Emily replied calmly.

"You just put it there!"

"Didn't."

Rene's complexion was prone to flushes; right now it resembled a giant strawberry that had eaten a Madras. For a beat people seemed to hold their breaths. Then Rene stormed off without saying another word. Slammed her office door, making the blinds rattle.

Emily grinned. "Did I say something?" she asked innocently.

"Yes. Every time you open your filthy trap, you psycho," gasped Sam. "I can't believe you did that!"

"I won't have her picking on you."

"But she'll sack you."

"Nah. She's scared of me," said Emily with a smile, leaning back and swivelling in her chair. "Hell, most people are."

Sam put her face in her hands. "Great. In that case it's not you who'll take the flak, is it?"

"You said she bullies you. I'm just helping out."

"I don't want it making worse though." Now Sam would have to apologise to Rene, smooth it over. Again.

"I was going to step in too," added Roger.

"Yeah, right," Emily said.

"I was!"

"Wasn't."

"Give it up, Roger," Sam interrupted. "You know she always gets the last word in any argument."

"Not always," Roger replied.

Emily tapped the end of her pencil against his chin, making him recoil. "Always. Anything someone says to me after that is the beginning of a new argument." She turned back to Sam. "Hey, don't worry, it'll be fine. And after work I'll make it up to you. I promise."

Emily believed what she'd said. She really didn't seem to understand the nature of consequences.

Mark found a cup that wasn't too dirty to drink from a second (or possibly third) time. The cup bore the slogan "I Love Builder's Brew". The streaky brown stains weren't so noticeable once he poured in some lager for a pre-trip tipple.

Memories were a bit vague, but she had invited him out.

He was *fairly* certain.

A swig of golden brown wetness fizzed on his tongue.

The pitch of the tape rose as one spinning spool emptied, then stopped with a reassuring clunk. Mechanical rewind. If only life was so reliable. Mark pressed play and soon Shaun Ryder was drawling his lyrics about dirty mothers and crucified brothers. It was easy to imagine Bez the background dancing a bodily interpretation of "I don't give a fig".

Did she invite him out?

Yeah, yeah, course. So it would be rude not to go. It didn't matter that he couldn't really afford it and might be eating beans on toast (or just the toast) until pay day. He'd hammer his overdraft at the cash machine. Couldn't look stingy in front of a classy woman like Mandy.

He reached under his top and sprayed deodorant around, cooling and tickling his skin with scented hiss. Appropriately, the boppy tune now coming from the stereo was Bob's Yer Uncle: Shaun Ryder's husky-voiced drawl about sex, accompanied by cartoon moans. It reminded Mark of last night.

Mark and Mandy. It had a good ring to it. A bit like the Robin Williams TV programme he loved as a kid.

He just needed to be cool. Mark took a deep breath. There was no putting it off any longer: time to go and say Nanu Nanu.

Smooth strokes, glossy transformation, chemical smells. Emily and Sam both sported pink sponge separators between their toes, like pacifist feminine knuckledusters. Em was painting her nails neon punk pink, Sam was using a dark red which Em referred to as "blood clot". Radio music draped Emily's messy flat.

"Was the course good?" asked Emily as she painted, concentration pursing her lips. "I never even asked. Some friend."

"Wasn't good. Boring, immoral, overpriced. The veggie option was onion salad, and a weirdo sat next to me on the train back and kept staring at my legs."

"At least he had good taste."

Sam narrowed her eyes.

"Only kidding. I hate leches. Urgh." Emily went back to painting her nails. "Unwelcome ones, anyway. Serves you right though, for sending me to that supplier conference a few weeks ago. Cosmic karma. I've still not forgiven you. This one guy was staring, pretending he was trying to read the name on my ID badge. I asked him 'Are you looking for my name or my nipples?' He stopped then. I wouldn't have minded except that he was fugly."

"Swear shot."

"Fugly isn't swearing."

"It is."

"Fuck it, make me a double."

Sam poured vodka into the shot glasses. They clinked then downed them. A grimace that turned into a grin. Taste washed away by going back to the long glasses of cider.

"Happy now, Russell?" Sam muttered to herself.

Best to be with Em when you needed cheering up. Like having an alcohol-soaked flannel from the fridge slapped across your face a few times. Em's flat was in Eccles. It was a weird town. Dense population. Rich and poor rubbing shoulders. Most famous for its Eccles cakes (or "dead fly pies" as Angharad called them when Sam took a packet back to Neath).

"I don't want to talk about work any more," Sam said, returning to her nails. "I'm sick of it at the moment." Neat around the cuticles. "Bored." She leaned back, stretched. "And Rene's got it in for me. As today proved."

"Uh-huh."

"I mean, she rang me on the work mobile while I was on the course. Angry because of that order I'd been too busy to rush through before the funeral, just some out-of-print titles. It takes time to root around on second-hand sites, doesn't it?"

"Yep."

"The order had been in my tray, but before I could do it someone rang *her* up – idiots – to see when they'd arrive, and Rene couldn't find details of any order on the system so was embarrassed. And took it out on me."

"Shut up! You said no more work talk."

A sigh. "Yes."

"Good. I'll drink to that."

"Just that I feel like quitting every week."

Em thumped her glass onto the tabletop. "Then why the fuck don't you? Instead of bending my ear about it?"

"You don't just go with your feelings."

"*I* do."

"Fine. I'll quit."

"Don't you fucking dare!" Emily bared her teeth in threat then laughed.

The song on the radio changed. Staccato stabs and moaned affirmations, a riff that seemed to be everywhere at the moment.

"Britney Spears *again*," grumbled Sam, reaching for her cider.

"And?"

"Well. Blonde minx pretending to be a schoolkid. How can you compete with that?"

"You? Just be yourself and flutter those big fucking eyelashes. Can't believe they're natural." Em downed the rest of her cider then started bouncing up and down as she sang, "Oops! I did it again".

"Swear shots. You're doing it on purpose."

Emily laughed and hugged Sam with one arm whilst holding the nail varnish out with the other. "Just rack 'em up."

Sam's phone buzzed. She checked the screen. "My mam," she explained to Emily, who shrugged before putting the finishing touches to her toenails.

"*Shwmae*, Mam."

"Fine, fine. Where are you? I can hear music. Is it a pub?"

"I'm at my friend's."

"Boyfriend?"

"No. Emily."

"Say hello."

Sam did the honours: Emily's response was "Hiya to Way-*ells*!" in an exaggeratedly camp approximation of a Welsh accent. Sam walked over to the window.

"She's a funny girl," said Mam.

"I know."

"What are you doing now then?"

"Just painting our nails and having a drink." Sam looked down at the lights laid out below and running up into the sky. Em lived in one of the residential tower blocks which jutted up around Victorian terraces, like right-angled volcanic eruptions. 12th floor. Buildings as far as the eye could see, dominating the flat perspective. Sam missed fields. Hedges. Hills. Anything not chopped and blocked stone and brick. "I wanted to get out of my place for a bit."

"You know your mamgu's house is still empty." It was as if her mam could read her mind. Always knew the tender points.

"I know. You texted me that yesterday. And the day before. And you told me all my old friends are still around."

"I was just being helpful." She sounded hurt.

Sam waited a second before replying. Smiled, to make her voice softer. "I know. I don't wanna be rude, but can I ring you back later, Mam? Unless there's something you wanted to ask."

"Not really. I'd been watching the news, saw the thing about Manchester..."

"Why is it you always seem to find the horrible stories?"

"It's worrying. That poor girl."

"I know. But stuff goes on everywhere. Not just here."

"Still, cities..."

"I've got an attack alarm in my purse and I'm careful, so you can stop worrying, okay?"

"Okay. I was just seeing how you were. No need to ring back later, there's something on the telly, but tomorrow?"

"I'll try. *Hwyl*, Mam."

"*Hwyl, cariad.*"

Sam stared at her phone for a few seconds before putting it away. She sat, grabbed her cigs and lighter. It took a few flicks to get a flame, that comforting orange she could suck on to start the smoke dissipation ritual. Immediately things seemed better. Her own peace pipe.

"What's up, hun?" asked Emily.

"Nothing. Nothing bad, anyway. Just my mam. She's lonely, I think. Shit, I feel guilty for cutting her off now. Should I ring her back?"

"No, it'd seem weird."

Em poured out the shots they were owed. Sam itched to pick up her phone again but knew she'd have nothing to say. Next time. She'd do better *next time*.

"Is that all? Mums are always lonely. I wouldn't want to be a mum." When Sam didn't say anything Em gave her a questioning look.

"Who knows? Maybe I'll want a family. One day," Sam said, ignoring Em's scrunched up face. "Right time, right person. Anyway, there's one other bit. My gran, the one whose funeral I went to – she left her house to my mam. She wants *me* to live there. Be near them again."

"And?"

"It's tempting." Sam took a deep drag, making the tip glow like a sickly sun against the blackness of the window.

Em frowned. "You are de-calming me. Stop it."

"You asked."

"Down this and shut up."

They necked the shots, chased them with cider again.

"You'd miss me?" asked Sam.

Emily leaned over and surprised Sam with a warm hug that felt genuine rather than superficial. Emily broke it off with a smile. "Of course. Who wouldn't want to have you around?"

Sam leaned against Emily for a second, a nudge of thanks, then finished the cig and added the last touches of varnish to her toes.

"How come you're slumming with me instead of being with mister loverman tonight?" Em asked.

"He's busy."

"How's it going?"

"You're as bad as my mam."

"So? "

"It's okay. Hopefully will get better over time."

"Hardly a glowing report."

"Just the truth. All relationships have ups and downs. How can you have a day without a night?"

"Rubbish. As soon as there's downs, it's time to move on. It's a sign that maybe there are no more ups left. I know you, into all your 'fidelity' shit."

"What, you end a relationship the first time you're not enjoying it?"

"Yeah, usually. How long do you wait before giving up?"

"I don't know. Longer than this, though."

"When are you seeing him again?"

"Not till the weekend."

"Maybe you need to fuck him before that. Dress up, go wild. Do you dress up in sexy lingerie when you see him?"

"No. Just the usual."

Em shook her head. "Wrong answer. A basque? Or stockings and suspenders? Or a peep-hole?"

"I've not got any of them. Pointless if you're going to be naked after five minutes."

"Not pointless! It's part of foreplay. Teasing. Excitement buildup. At least *nice* underwear."

Sam stared at her.

"Oh, for fuck's sake. Right. I'm busy tomorrow but on Thursday we finish work early and go shopping. We've both got loads of leave. I'll hand the forms in, Rene won't say anything then."

"What for?"

"Duh! Get you something sexy he can rip off you. Put the stuff on under a dress, give him a peep, let him know what he's in for."

"We'll see."

"No we won't. You'll do it. I said so."

It wasn't worth arguing about. "You swore again."

"Did I?"

"Said fuck."

"Shit, I didn't even spot that one. Hey, look at my pretty toes!" Emily wriggled them, the pink tops made them resemble fat glowing matches but Sam kept that to herself. They downed their latest shots. Sam could hardly taste the vodka now. "Here's a question. It involves swear words so we're on a swear-shot amnesty. What do you call yours?"

"My what?"

Em pointed between Sam's legs. "Pussy? Vag?"

"I prefer fanny."

"That could be misconstrued. Anyway, isn't that a Welsh name, that aunt of yours?"

"No, that's Myfanwy."

"Oh yeah. Muff and fanny together."

"I'd rather you didn't bring my family into that."

"Sorry."

"What do you call yours then?"
"Kate Bush."
"But you're blonde!"
Em winked. "Anyway, what are we doing after this?"
"I'll get a taxi."
"I feel like partying."
"You always do. Can't face going out tonight though."
"Go halvies on an E with me then. It'll be a laugh."
"That's daft. I only take E if I'm dancing."
"We'll dance in here! Go on go on go on go on go on go –"
"What the hell… Okay, if you promise *never* to do comedy impressions again."
Emily grinned. "Cool! I'm bringing make-up out too. And my ABBA CD. This place will rock! It's good to see you happy, babes."
"It's you that cheers me up." Of course, a skinful of booze and half an E would help.

Mark spied Mandy and her group, up on a raised area to the right of the Lass O' Gowrie and taking up two tables that had been pushed together. The men all had suits on, the women in smart work clothes. The group was laughing at some joke, rowdy and white-toothed. They were all professionals. Had she said she worked for a law firm? Still, they looked like they were having a good time. Fun people. Friendly.
He brushed his fringe to the side, sniffed, straightened his top, and walked over.
"Hi!" he said with a big smile and wave. Blank stares. One guy looked him up and down. A woman sniggered.
"Oh. Hi," said Mandy. "Erm, this is a friend of mine. Neighbour," she explained to the others. "Are you –"
"Yes, I'll just get a beer and join you," Mark cut in. "Can I get anyone else a drink?"
Some heads were shaken. Others just stared.
He went to the bar, forcing himself to take more deep breaths.

The conversation kept pausing. Mandy had said the names of the other people but he couldn't remember any of them. He'd pulled a stool over and sat at the end of the table, because it was the only place free. He felt like an exhibit.

They talked about work, something to do with a change of manager, more names. He was desperate to contribute but couldn't. He felt hot. Pulled his sleeves up a bit but it didn't help.

Mandy was a couple of seats away from Mark. He glanced at her but she rarely looked his way. When she did the smile was weak. She was smoking a lot, tapping her cigarettes into the ashtray unfinished.

"Hey, Mandy, was work okay today?" he asked, leaning forward and trying not to speak too loudly. She didn't seem to hear him. He tried again a bit louder, leaned forward even more.

"Do you mind?" asked the woman to the left as his elbow knocked her glass.

"Sorry," said Mark.

"Yes, it was good, thanks," replied Mandy as she fidgeted with her drink. "And you, at the – what is it, bookshop?"

A few looked over.

"No, bookseller. Big warehouse place."

"Oh."

"I lead a team there," he added. "About ten people. Orders. Financial things. Letters. Stuff like that."

Someone whispered to her, she replied, didn't turn back to Mark.

Mark's nose was getting bunged up again. He breathed through his mouth so he wouldn't start sneezing. Hayfever seemed to be worse than usual.

They all spoke posher than Mark.

He didn't like the look of the woman on his left, whose drink he had knocked. There was a guy on his right, in a shirt and tie with his jacket over the back of his chair. "Are you in the same team as Mandy?" Mark asked, trying to get something started. Anything.

"No. She's in the floor above."

"Oh. Like your boss?"

The guy frowned, shook his head. "No. Not like that. She's just a legal assistant."

Had she invited him?

A bit of laughter at the other end of the table. Mark and those nearest to him looked over, hopeful, but it had petered out already.

So hard to recall her exact words in the taxi. Something about going to the Lass, about a crowded group, but the more the merrier?

He stared at his drink. A nearby TV was showing American football. One of the lads halfway down the table started talking about his interest in it, the skill involved. People seemed to be warming to the topic, but Mark knew nothing about it. A silly idea popped into his head.

The next time the lad mentioned football Mark said, as clearly and loudly as he could, "That's not football. That's handegg." He stifled his own laugh but it didn't seem that anyone else had to. They just looked at him.

"That's funny," said one girl, but not smiling.

Mark wanted to say "I'll get my coat" but didn't think they'd laugh at that either.

He stared up at the big shelves heaving with old barrels and jugs.

In the taxi. Mark had asked if she was tired, and Mandy had said, "Sleep'll be good, there's tomorrow night too." Maybe it *wasn't* an invitation, she hadn't been making a reference to seeing him again. He'd just put things together wrong. There was a sinking feeling in his gut.

He caught glances between them, raised eyebrows. He was an outsider.

Mark patted the pocket on his leather jacket, took his phone out. "Someone… Felt it vibrate… 'Scuse me," he explained, holding it to his ear. Repeated "Yes" a few times, pretended he was hearing words, then put his phone away. Stood. "Sorry, got to go, was nice meeting you all," he said, and swiftly exited the pub.

Mark hated kneeling over the toilet.

H-wuuuurunghaa!

After that mutated war cry of a teenage ninja turtle he wiped his mouth on his sleeve. His eyes were watering and the stench of sour vomit made him want to hurl again. His stomach was empty though. Another dry heave, then he reached up and flushed the chain.

He stood shakily and washed his face in cold water. In the mirror he saw something with clammy white skin beneath a shaggy helmet of dark and sweat-dampened hair. Dead eyes and a throat like a black hole, a shadow of the dead, black, night-time world outside. His brain was sore and he felt rough as sun-dried dogdoo.

He'd not gone straight home from the Lass. He'd felt like crying, knew the empty flat would set him off, so stopped off in Stretford and toasted oblivion. Bad move. Crammed by day, dead by night. Morrissey grew up in Stretford too. No wonder he was miserable.

When Mark had staggered up the stairs to his flat he'd almost bumped into a scruffy-haired guy in a baggy T-shirt, tattoos up his arms. He waved a "No problem, mate" hand at Mark, walked on with a laughable wide-legged swagger. While Mark fumbled keys from his pocket he realised it was the shaggy mop-top guy off the bus on pilgrimage day. Now he thought about it the guy often seemed to be hanging around here. Great, Mark looked like a prick to yet another neighbour. Keep this up and they'd probably sign a petition to get him out.

He started sneezing again.

Water. He needed to drink ice-cold water. Lots of it.

Mark filled a glass, chucked in a few ice-cubes, put the TV on and flicked through the channels. There was a dating show, but he turned it off once he realised every contestant was a wanker.

As he lifted the glass he noticed his hand was shaking. He put the glass down and held both hands out. The right one had a definite tremor.

He'd seen his dad's hand shake when he drank too much. Denny too. *Fig.*

Hopton DNA. Blood will out.

He clenched his fist, took deep breaths, then downed the water. Put the glass down gently. No. No!

1994. Buzzcocks supported Nirvana.

Mark wasn't like the rest of his family.

1994. Oasis debut album Definitely Maybe.

He just had to persuade his body it was true.

1994. Second Coming. Second album by The Stone Roses.

He sniffed again. He could be different. He could be better.

1994. Up to Our Hips. Third album by The Charlatans.

Mark put his face in his hands and cried.

this is how it feels

- **Album:**
- **Year:** 1990
- **Label:** Mute

This is a story of unhappy lives, misunderstandings and lack of communication, and a desire for escape that will not be realised. Who said the Inspiral Carpets, so much part of the late 1980s Madchester scene, were just psychedelic organs and hippy guita

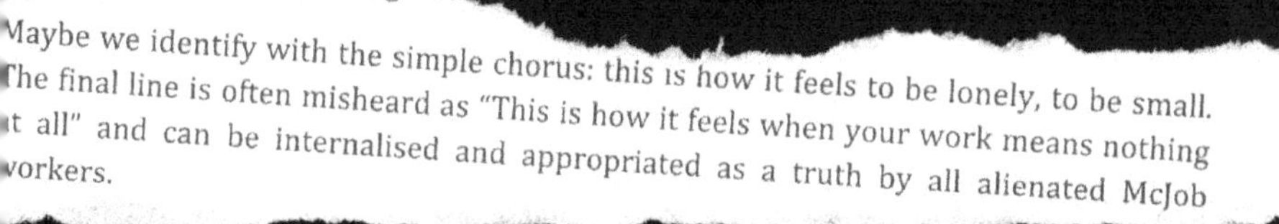
Maybe we identify with the simple chorus: this is how it feels to be lonely, to be small.
The final line is often misheard as "This is how it feels when your work means nothing
it all" and can be internalised and appropriated as a truth by all alienated McJob
workers.

"You ill, mate? You sound awful. Like gravel."

Mark and Ben stood weeing. There were three urinals, so they could leave an empty one between them as a universally understood masculinity delineator. Even if a third guy came in he'd go into a cubicle to wee rather than stand in the middle where he'd be suspected of wanting to glance at someone else's penis.

"The voice means I'm getting better," Mark rumbled. "I've had bad hayfever for days. It's like a cold. I get a red nose from all the sneezing and blowing, but know I'm getting better when the snot goes thick and green instead of runny and clear."

"Nice details there. Enough to put me off my guacamole sandwich. I've gotta tell ya, it's pretty disgusting at the moment. You're like those dogs that slavver everywhere, you pick up a stick they fetch and your hand's all covered in slimy goz."

"Thanks. Makes me feel good." Mark kept his gaze forward.

"Mad sound though. I should record you doing my answer message in that voice."

"That Emily, when I was doing this morning's post, she said deep voices are sexy," Mark boasted. "Like a white Barry White."

"It's wrong that you've got that voice and I haven't! Thing about Emily is," said Ben, doing up his fly, "if she said it's sexy, she doesn't fancy you. That's the way with offices. Arse about tit."

"I don't really care if *she* thinks I'm sexy."

"Just as well. You never could be, the way you look."

Mark yanked on the stiff taps, trying not to turn them on so hard he'd get splash stains on his crotch. Ben headed straight for the door.

"Hey, you didn't wash your hands!" Mark called.

"I just avoid pissing all over them in the first place." The door banged shut.

The dispenser was out of paper towels, forcing Mark to use toilet paper which dissolved all over his fingers like a sodden layer of dead skin.

Mark looked up as Dave returned from the ground-floor warehouse, clicking his fingers. It was like he had too much energy and it had to sneak out any way it could. Having worked at Packham Green longest Dave performed the liaison role with stock control. It was seen as a perk by the three of them because it got you out of the office. The opportunity for a skive was a bonus. Definitely better than Mark's current task, "library processing" – adding barcodes and security tags to books, putting paperbacks into plastic jackets. "A profitable premium service for Packham Green," Rene said. Monotonous work associated with paper cuts, bits of plastic sticking to your fingers, and glazed eyes, Mark said. Even worse when you had a banging head and dry mouth.

"You look rough," Dave told him. "Peepers like piss-holes in the snow."

Mark rubbed them. They felt gritty. "A few late nights."

"Too much wankin'. And what's he up to?" Dave jutted his chin towards Ben's back

Mark shrugged. There would be no peace, so he folded up the piece of paper he'd been drawing on, a mass of arrows and coloured blocks, and slipped it into his pocket.

Ben was at one of the two PCs in their area, supposedly accessing and printing the most recent jobsheets, but in reality chuckling to himself as he browsed photos on weird websites where strangers pretended to know each other. He was switching between one called Friends Reunited, and one called SixDegrees. It was all a bit peculiar and imaginary to Mark but he left him alone because Ben had earbuds in, presumably listening to the soulless dance music he favoured on his flashy MP3 player. Mark didn't need a music player: he knew his favourite songs so well he could conjure them up in his head note for note and word for word anytime he wanted. Today he was "playing" the rollicking northern rock of Embrace (who were from outside of Manchester but had enough northern soul to discount thirty miles or so) in lieu of conversation. Ben's music might be crap but Mark respected people's rights to immerse themselves in rhythm and melody undisturbed.

Dave had no such respect for the sanctity of music time.

"Hey, Lawrence!" Dave said, leaning over and speaking loudly into Ben's ear.

Ben flinched as if Russian Roulette had dropped him. "Don't deafen me! And I can do without your face so close to mine."

"You've gotta be careful: I could've been Rene stomping up on you."

"I'd have heard."

"Not with music on, dumbo."

"Uh? I'm not listening to music," Ben said, rotating his computer chair round in a leisurely way, legs open unnecessarily wide.

"Why you got earphones in then?"

"They're cutoffs," replied Ben.

Mark and Dave looked at each other, confused.

"What?" asked Mark.

Ben removed his earplugs and pulled the cable from under his jumper. No connector, no music player – six inches of thin wire just ended in thin air. He caught the frowns. "My Diamond Rio got nicked when I was mugged in the Arndale the other week. I can't afford another yet. Will probably get a Creative Jukebox instead, holds a fuckload of music. Anyway, these earplugs were broke so I just cut 'em off. Seems like I've got an MP3 player, so looks cool, but there's nothing for anyone to mug me for until I get another. Why you both gawping like that? It makes sense."

"You're a nutty fucker," said Dave. "You never cease to amaze us."

"And cutting earphones? Sacrilege," added Mark.

"There's just so much pressure nowadays, y'know, to look good and have the right clobber." Ben made a theatrical gesture at his branded clothes.

"But pretend music players? Now I've seen it all," said Dave.

"You say that, but you're wearing one of them daft tops that try to make it look like you've got a T-shirt underneath. That's just as silly. Why not just wear a T-shirt under it? Why *pretend* you have one? That's more gormless than anything, since a T-shirt is so fucking cheap. Do one, Dave."

"You can do two, yer twat," snapped Dave. "I'm just saying you're obsessed with appearances. You'll end up like Gel Head. Some of his sculptures look like they're modern art. Y'know: shit." Dave raised a foot, kicked the lever under Ben's chair so it dropped with a pressurised hiss. Ben laughed and readjusted his seat.

"It's called pride in your appearance. Some of us have it and some of you don't," he said smugly, then pointed towards the middle of the office without looking in that direction himself. "Look over at the chosen ones, boys." He was pointing at the ordering team's table. "The ones with more money and responsibilities than us. Do you think they'd be on that table if they didn't bother with appearances? You ever seen Sam with a hole in her tights? Emily looking like she fell out of a charity shop? Roger the Todger without a tie on? Then wonder why we're at the losers' end of the office with shit pay."

Mark looked over at Sam. She was frowning at her screen and clicking a mouse so furiously it almost made him laugh. She was wearing a navy blue skirt and short-sleeved top and *did* look smart. Then he looked down at his own clothes. The bottom of his trousers were a bit frayed, and he'd worn the white shirt for a couple of days because he couldn't be arsed walking to the launderette. Was it the fluorescent lights, or were the cuffs a bit yellow?

Shuggle. Now he couldn't think of anything else. Ben was right though. Sam's team weren't hefting boxes in and out of a warehouse.

"I doubt if you'd get in that team with a bowlhead either," finished off Ben, still swivelling back and forth in his chair.

It was the straw that broke the Manc's back. Mark dropped the book he'd been working on and headed off, pulling hair out of his eyes.

"Toilet again?" called Ben.

"Might be wanting a shady one," smirked Dave. "I reckon he got worked up looking at Emily's legs."

"I didn't look at anyone's legs!" he snapped. "I'm just regular."

"I find that hard to believe on your diet. I don't think you've ever had your 'five a day'."

"Five a day?" Ben looked puzzled. "I only go once. Is that normal?"

"Leave forms done, all sorted," said Emily as she returned. "Rene frowned like I'd let one off in her office, but she didn't say anything so we're fine." Em turned to Roger. "Hey, it's your turn to go out for sarnies," she said, throwing down a chewed pen.

"Right, right." He took up a pad of paper. "What do you both want?"

"I want chicken. White bread," said Em.

"Nothing else?"

"Well, butter. Make sure it's butter, not margarine."

"Okay."

"Make sure. Butter."

"I WILL!"

"There is a 't' in butter you know," said Sam.

"It's silent, like the 's' in island," Em replied.

"What about you, Sam?"

She had a funny feeling in her tummy and didn't fancy anything, but remembered what her Mamgu always said about eating properly. She'd only had a few hours' kip, the loss of appetite was probably just tiredness creeping up her body. Fill the hole then ride it out. It always passes. She asked for her usual.

"And a can of pop," added Em. "From the fridge."

"Rightie-ho."

"From the *fridge*. Remember."

Roger held up a middle finger then left.

"Isn't cheese and pickle boring?" asked Em.

"No. I like it."

"You can have a bite of mine if you want. It's only chicken. You can have that."

"Don't wind me up."

"I'm not."

"If it has a face I don't eat it."

Em leaned back in her chair, crossed her bare ankles. "I did go out with a veggie once. Actually, he was a vegan."

"Really?"

"Yeah. Made me brush my teeth before he'd let me put my tongue in his mouth."

"I bet it didn't last long."

She lowered her eyes. "Actually, I really liked him. He was super sweet. A good kisser, too."

"Is there anyone you haven't gone out with?"

"Roger?" Em suggested, chewing her pen again.

"Oh, I'd pay to see that."

"Wouldn't happen. He's so naff it goes full circle to funny again. Like humour, but different. There's some lines I wouldn't cross."

"First I've heard."

"Rightie-ho," said Em, impersonating Roger.

"Yes, you are."

It was Em's turn to flip up a middle finger, but they were both smiling. "Oh, now big ears has gone, you arranged a meet with lover boy?"

"By text. He's only deputy manager for a bar but it's like trying to schedule a meeting with a fucking MP. I'd see him more if I just went drinking in Kicks."

"Good job Operation Thunderthong starts tonight. All falling into place."

The end of the day at last. Mark examined a smudge on his shirt but realised it was an inkstain, and there was more under the elbow. It must have brushed one of the inkpads they used for rubber stamps. He threw the scissors, tape and pens into his plastic tray, put it on the nearby metal shelves ready for tomorrow.

His was the end locker with a dented door. Someone had used a marker to edit the label: instead of "Mark" it now spelled "Wanker". He yanked the locker open and rummaged through the pile of things in carrier bags at the bottom, found a T-shirt he'd bought in Afflecks Palace a couple of weeks ago. He kept forgetting to take it home. That meant it was clean.

A sticker inside the locker (where it was protected) read

LOVE, LOVE

WILL TEAR US APART

AGAIN

Mark touched it reverently. Gain power when you can.

No one around, he undid a few buttons and pulled the shirt over his head, threw it in the bin. Put the black T-shirt on instead. It was one of his favourite slogans: "And on the 6th day God created MANchester". He was just leaving when Ben and Dave saw him.

"Hey, look who's got changed! Must have a date," said Ben.

"But he's all in black! No offence mate," Dave said to Ben.

"None taken."

"But I mean, it's like he's turned into a fucking *goth*!"

"I'll stop wearing black when they invent a darker colour," snapped Mark. He looked down at his clothes. Suddenly felt like a fool.

"Ha ha, he does look a bit like that guy … erm, y'know the one … oh, the big hair one …" Ben began, turning to Dave who looked puzzled too, couldn't help him out. "Well, anyway, a big goth guy from that band. Look, his face is all white, and the mop-head, I hope we're not going pub tonight if he's going to look like *that*. I've –"

"Fig off, the two of youse!" shouted Mark. "I'm sick of it!" He ignored the surprised faces, jumped down the stairs half a flight at a time using the handrail as a brake on each landing, and stormed out of the building narrowly missing a dog turd where the dog walkers always stopped. That would have just been the brown icing on the cake.

The *bar stewards*. He wasn't going to catch the bus home. This called for more drastic measures.

His heart was like a slow breakbeat, seemingly controlled but just on the edge of a rock out.

He didn't want to go through with this.

He rubbed his chin. Wrong move – there was scruffy stubble there.

The shop was a *proper* men's clothes shop.

Why did this feel worse than going to the fudding dentist?

The bell jangled above the door as he entered, old-fashioned, not musical enough to calm him.

"I normally just wear these..." Mark pointed to his brown striped footwear.

The assistant in the smart suit smiled but it was a humourless cracking of the face. He shook his head.

"Athletic-inspired shoes are wonderful for the pub, sir – but not for work. Follow me, we'll see if we have anything more suitable."

Was he taking the mick? He *seemed* serious.

The end of the narrow shop had a shoe section. Racks of polished leather on display. Shoe boxes neatly fitted onto shelves behind. A smell of polish and aftershave combined to make Mark feel queasy. The grey-haired assistant was in his fifties.

"How about these? Slip-on loafers with squared toes and a one inch heel. It's a classic look, ideal for the office. They evince a sophisticated style, appropriate for any wardrobe."

"They look a bit long."

"That is fashionable. And elegant. What kind of work do you do?"

"Erm, office work. I have an office. Manage a big team of law people."

The assistant gave him a piercing stare that made Mark look down. "Is that so, sir? In that case you won't want to penny-pinch. If you wish to look right, then you will need to trust me."

Mark sighed. "Okay, can I try some in a ten?"

He was glad to get out and breathe the city centre air again. As well as the shoes he had two slim-fit dress shirts "in subtle pastel hues". Also a pair of "single pleat long leg office trousers" as an alternative to his black jeans.

He wished they'd given him a "single colour smooth sheen" carrier bag, not one with a poncy logo on. He scrunched it up as much as he could, was wrapping the top of the bag around his wrist a few times when from the background chatter he perceived lively voices that sounded familiar; noticed it was Samantha Rees and Emily Watson, talking fast and gesturing. *They* didn't have to shop alone. He hesitated then half-raised his hand but they just walked past. Didn't they recognise him? Didn't they – no, they just didn't see him. That was all. Don't be paranoid, Mark. He watched them walk away, laughing and nudging each other, disappearing amongst the other shoppers. Probably for the best. He didn't want to be tongue-tied, unable to think of anything witty to say if they had stopped to chat.

The worst wasn't over. Barber next. The words "short crop" scared him, but when he'd seen his floppy, greasy fringe in the mirror that afternoon he'd decided it was maybe time to say goodbye to his Shaun Ryder centre parting. The only consolation was that Shaun Ryder got his hair cut in 1991 for the release of Judge Fudge. That was it. Just change, progression. It wasn't the end of anything.

By the time he got home both his head and wallet felt uncomfortably light. The overdraught had become a gale force wind and blown away. Budget beans every night from now on. He wondered what his flat would smell like by payday.

After dumping the stuff on his bed he checked himself out in the bathroom mirror. It didn't look like him. The lack of fringe revealed a few spots on his forehead that he hadn't been aware of. Weren't new haircuts meant to make you feel more confident? Too late to get his money back on that one.

For the rest of the evening he caught himself trying to brush non-existent hair out of his eyes, like a phantom limb. But it would be worth it if it helped him fit in.

...ned by an ex-factory employ...

...rt was St. Etienne. They were going places...

Yet they remained a down-to-earth band, humble even. Paris Angels were regulars at the Boardwalk and Haçienda. Young music fanatics, well-known to all (Clint Boon from Inspiral Carpets used to go shopping for records with Paris Angels drummer Simon Worrall). Perhaps the band's genuine love for and knowledge of the music scene is part of the reason they were respected by other Manchester musicians and got on with so many other bands.

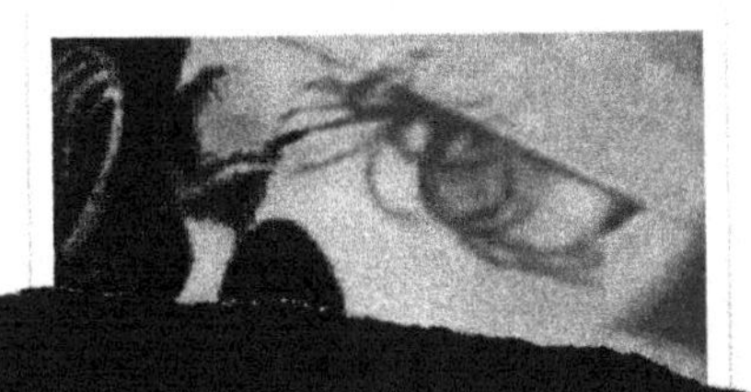

Emily dragged her from shop to shop. Sometimes literally. It was all a blur. Next had been first, Top Shop had been next. And now Em was holding a fluorescent pink TK Maxx swimsuit against her body.

"I know it's summer, but you don't have to go stupid."

"The colour would make me stand out at the pool though, wouldn't it?" She turned left and right in front of a long mirror.

"Yes. Like a walking puke. Put it back."

They browsed along the racks, practiced hand flicks skimming through each line of items noting colour, size, price. "Maybe we should go to the sea-side, do some real bathing. Blackpool?" Em suggested.

"No one swims there, do they? I heard the water was dirty, people just go for the funfair and fancy lights."

"Oh yeah, I suppose the beaches back home are all perfect? Fussy faggot." Em checked a price tag, shook her head and dropped it dismissively. A tooth-grinding squeal as hangers scraped along the rail. "Where next then?"

"Dorothy Perkins? Or BHS? Only over the road."

"Booooring."

"I just want to have a look see."

Em grinned. "You're such a Welshie."

"Sod off, Manc."

They walked round the legs of a miserable-looking guy whose girlfriend was holding up three different skirts for him to comment on. Sam knew how he felt. Time to go.

They rejoined the crowds. Music pulsed from the shops, forceful, encroaching, and too mixed up with the sounds blaring from their neighbours to be recognisable. Sometimes city life was just one big noise.

"Seriously though, I promised we'd get you something sexy," Em said.

"I haven't got the budget for that."

"Some things are important enough to open your purse. How was the sex last time?"

"The usual."

"What's *that* supposed to mean?"

"Just what I said. Y'know: not great, not crap."

Emily laughed. "No searing endorsement there."

"It doesn't have to be a choreographed gymnastic routine every time."

"Never should be. Sex is like breathing. You just do it."

"Thanks for the advice. I really don't want to waste money."

"But you'll be sexier, seduce the lucky dimwit."

"If I'm going to do anything then maybe I just need to work out a bit more. That's *free*. I've not even done the fitness video that's been on my shelf since I moved here."

"Well you should get up off your lazy arse and sit down to watch it and get up and do it." They had their arms around each other's waists as they walked. Sam noted envious stares from passers-by. "Please? Loads easier to look good in sexy lingerie than work out every night for months. He'd be putty in your hand." Em made a vague wanking gesture.

Sam sighed. "Where were you thinking?"

"Ann Summers, then that hot stall in the market with all the rubber and kinky gear –"

"No! I take it back!"

"What about La Senza then?"

"But we're going the wrong way for that! I know you mean well but I'm knackered. And I'm meeting Russell later. Time to go home."

Em stared at her. Sam stared back. Em stared some more, then snorted, pushed away from Sam and veered off to a mini-doughnut stall sat between vendors selling handbags and plastic bubble throwers. Warmth carried the sweet, fried smell from the sizzling oil. It was mouthwatering. Sam could almost feel the airy texture, with the crunch from being dipped in tubs of sugar. Em bought a handful in a paper bag which bloomed where it touched the greasy confectionery. She waved it in front of Sam's nose.

"Best not." But Sam kept her eyes on the bag. "Workouts, remember?" She swallowed.

Em stuffed one into her mouth as they walked on.

"How come you eat like a pig but stay so slim?"

A shrug. "If you're bothered about looks we could get a leg wax and bikini line, that'd be fun, wouldn't it?" Another doughnut stuffed in, chewed, swallowed. Fingers fastidiously licked. "Beverly Hills Nails has a special on."

"I don't like pain."

"Don't like fun either." Em ate the last doughnuts with a challenging glare on her face, jaws chomping as if Sam was next.

"Oh for… Okay, one more shop. Look, we're nearly at Debenhams, let's go in there."

"It'll have to do, I suppose." Em crunched up the now-empty doughnut bag and dropping it into a bin. Sam was glad to see temptation disappear.

"How come I always end up doing what *you* want?" Sam asked.

"Because it's always the *right* thing."

Emily's strength seemed to come from the fact that she knew what she liked, and she knew what she *was* like. Sureness and self-understanding in one feisty package.

"You should bottle it," Sam muttered to herself. "You'd make a fortune."

A wave of shoppers swept them into the department store's shiny perfume and make-up section which formed a bright, disorientating, logo-splashed smelly maze. It was dominated by a huge poster, suspended from the ceiling, part of a perfume advertising campaign you couldn't escape from as it permeated radio, TV, magazines and bus shelters like a bad smell. A striking woman with green-painted skin stared out at you. Hair slicked back. A human snake of temptation, surrounded by the curly-lettered words: "Follow heart. Follow love. One love." You read them in the sultry voice they used in the TV adverts.

"That crazy bitch model is everywhere," Em said.

"Dana Furlow."

"Yeah. So cheesy."

"Tell me about it. 'Follow love'," Sam impersonated, fluttering her eyelashes at Em. "Colour me cynical on that."

"I think that bit of Welsh you kept mumbling when we were on E said it all about the important bit of relationships."

"Which bit of Welsh?"

"Marr … no. Miaw? Miaw called? Shit, you told me it meant 'big, thick and hard'. Silly language."

Sam laughed. "*Mawr, trwchus, caled?* I must have been out of it."
"You were."
"Most important bit of a relationship? No." Sam tried to pull Emily on, stop her gawking at all the stalls. She'd be there all day otherwise. "It just helps."
"Hey, you're grinning. That means you're happy with Russell's package."
Sam ignored her. Wanted to rush past these outer fortifications, get to the clothes. Unfortunately, Em stopped at every bottle-topped sample stall. Painted assistants in their red blazers or white lab coats fawned over her in the hopes of a sale. Squirt squirt, sniff sniff. Hopes dashed as Em sauntered on.
She held her wrist up to Sam's nose. Sam flinched, eyes watering from the chemical weapon's vapours. "You stink, Em. I don't think you should mix more than nine perfumes at once."
"You're just jealous because of all the charisma power it gives me. It'll have the blokes running."
"Yes. Running away." They were leaving the stink zone at last. Onwards and upwards. Sam always wanted to sprint up escalators, not be forced into the same slow pace as everyone else. She made do with jumping off at the top as the metal teeth sank into the floor.
The lingerie section.
"Where are the peep-hole bras?" Emily muttered. Last time they'd been looking at lingerie Emily had asked a male shop assistant if they sold edible crotchless knickers. She never stopped.
Faceless shop dummies in frilly underwear stood guard over display racks of tidy boxes. Blacks, reds, creams. Thongs, boyshorts, briefs. Underwired, sports, boosters. Sam wandered. Let her eyes and fingertips explore the offerings but didn't see anything she liked. Her breasts weren't huge but it always seemed like the smaller bras were prettier.
"What about this?" Emily asked, holding up a black bra and knicker set. Satin-effect, bit of lace. Small bows.
"I don't know. Not what I'd normally buy."
"It's stylish. Less is more. Not racy enough for me but I think it'd suit you. What size?"
"34D."

"Lucky bitch. I'd give anything to move up from A cup." She rummaged through the items on display.

"You're lovely as you are."

"Thanks babe." Em produced a set in Sam's size and shoved her towards a cubicle. Easier to acquiesce. She closed the rough-textured curtain, stripped her top off, tried the bra. No flesh bulge, squeeze, stretch or pinch. The underwire didn't cut in. She turned from side to side with her arms in the air, taking in every angle.

"How is it?" asked Emily from the other side of the curtains.

"Thinking."

"Lemme see."

Before Sam could say anything there was a swish of curtain and Emily's elfin features popped through a gap. She held them closed around her pretty, heart-shaped face.

"Em!"

"What? Just shut up and turn around, supermodel. Let me look."

"I'm not turning round for you!"

"Prima-fucking-donna." Em eyed her breasts. "You look great anyway. Storm in a D-cup."

"It's a lot of money for something I don't need."

"A lot? Listen, love. Spend, and you shall receive. You *do* need this. You want it, oooh, can't you feel your womanly desires..."

Sam gave in. Paid while Em explored the make-up section again. Sam joined her with the dinky little plastic bag.

"You should put them on now, in the toilets," suggested Em.

"Pleasure deferred is pleasure preferred."

"I wouldn't know. I want ice cream." Em led the way back towards the Arndale. "Hey, I'm out tonight, date with a guy from Sale, but tell me how it goes. Updates 'n' stuff."

"You're creepy."

"Yeah, but you love it." She gave Sam a kiss on the cheek. Then looked at Sam with a cheeky grin she recognised. Sam rubbed her cheek where it had been kissed and examined her fingers. Yep. Lipstick red. It was like shopping with a kid. A precocious, sex-obsessed hyperactive one.

"This is it, Claudia. You and me, together at last."

Sam held the VHS tape. Claudia Schiffer's Perfectly Fit, Volume 1.

Time to *work that body.*

Leigh and Robin had gone to the cinema. Sam didn't care about their exclusive friendship any more, just glad to have the living room to herself for once. No chance of Robin coming in and sighing at Sam's choice of TV programme until Sam gave up and went back to her room to smoke and listen to music; no chance that Leigh would start a stilted passive-aggressive conversation. No one to laugh at Sam's shorts and T-shirt combo with a cheeky twist: leg warmers. Sam had loved the films Flashdance and Fame back in the day, and it made her smile to slip on these woolly fashion disasters in secret. There was nothing practical about them; they were like her frog teddy, loved because of their soft cuddliness and innate silliness.

Bonus: she could whip them off and hide them under a cushion in seconds if the front door opened. She'd done it before.

She straightened the fraying rug to avoid tripping dangers then placed the tape in the old player that came with the house. The fuzzy snowstorm transformed into images of Claudia talking about the routines they'd do. Fast forward to the main event and it was time to kick off. The tracking on the video wasn't perfect, silvery lines crossed the bottom but she could still see the smiling energetic blondness working out. Step, step, to the left … copy, 2, 3, 4, 5 … *how did Claudia look so good in a black bodysuit and early 90s walking boots? Normally only Neneh Cherry had got away with that* ... slow again … side to side, stretches … step step … oh no, quicker … Sam concentrated on her knees over toes but it had moved on to a side stretch already, almost fell over as she switched too quickly … it looked so much more glamorous doing this on decking on a tropical beach than a worn Chorlton living room … oops, legwarmers falling down again, swiftly yanked up ... pumping her body, trying to imagine she looked like Jennifer Beals from Flashdance (and knowing she didn't) … oh no, more squats, contract that abdomen … it was starting to hurt a bit and she wanted to laugh … got to keep pumping that body … argh, don't think about pumping, not with the abdomen going like this … more pulsing … arms sweeping up over her head and back down, bird's wings floating on air, she could be graceful too!

Sam finished drying her hair, unplugged the dryer, replaced it with her phone charger. There was only one electricity socket in her room, so it did shared duty for those devices plus the lamp and hi-fi. The plugs and cables there were always getting in a tangle. But it didn't annoy her today.

She ran her hands down her waist, straightening the dress as she looked in the mirror which was balanced on the wicker basket she used for overflow clothes.

She had good skin. Enough of a waist to call herself curvy. Don't worry about the rest.

"I'm beautiful today, I am, I'm beautiful today," she chanted at her reflection as she put on eye shadow and grinned at the silliness of that mantra of self-affirmation. A bit of mascara, even though her lashes were dark and thick of their own accord. Lipstick. One last long view.

Good enough … oh. The effect was ruined slightly by the fluffy frog slippers she wore. One of the frogs had lost an eye. The other one had a red tongue which was about to fall off. She kicked them under her bed.

Oh again: smells. She sprayed some perfume on, two little puffs from a Parisian bottle, each squeeze of the atomizer bulb pushing her into glamour territory.

I am so sweet.

I smell so sweet.

I look like a vamp.

She was just reaching for her phone to call a taxi when it buzzed, an insect with a message.

A text.

Off Russell.

`Sorry babe got to work. Next time?`

She stared at the blocky letters.

"That's *it*?" She gripped the phone like a scrawny neck, then jabbed at numbers, muttering, "You'd better answer, you bastard."

Twelve rings and he picked up.

"Hi babe, sorry I –"

"Don't fucking 'babe' me! I've been looking forward to tonight. Really looking forward to it. Don't let me down again."

"Shit, I feel bad, but Gary's ill and I owe him a covered shift, gotta pay my debt."

"I don't give a fuck, get someone *else* to cover." She paced up and down her teeny cage.

"There *is* no one else. I'm the only one who's free."

"You're not free. You had arranged something with *me*."

"This is my job."

"And I'm your girlfriend!" He didn't reply. She bit her lip. "Please, Russ. You don't know how much I need to spend time with you tonight."

He sighed. The lengthening silence gave her hope.

"I can't." Hope smashed, slate-like shards. "Come on, we were only going for a drink, I don't see what's the big deal. Can't tomorrow, but what about Saturday? I'm out with the lads but could leave them early, meet you? I feel bad too. I wanted to see ya, y'know. I said sorry."

"And I said *please*."

Silence.

"How about if I come to Kicks, at least see you then, go back to yours after?"

"I'll be too tired, I'm dead on my feet as it is." He yawned, as if to reinforce his statement.

"I don't mind."

"Nah, not fair on you."

"I want to see you!"

"Tonight's no good. Don't nag, I've got enough on my plate."

It was a no hoper. "Oh, fuck off to the gym and take your steroids," she snarled.

"I don't take –"

She hung up, threw the phone in the bin where it clanged against the metal rim.

Remembered the yoghurt pot in there, rescued the phone and wiped it.

She was tamping mad, kicked the chipped white chest of drawers which never opened or closed properly. Then picked up one of her green slippers, the big floppy mouth which protected her toes grinning at her; lobbed it at the window where it just missed the ailing spider plant.

She couldn't ring Em. She probably already had her tongue down her date's throat, lucky cow.

"It's just you and me, boys," she told the bottles of vodka and cider she lined up on the chest of drawers, wiping her eyes with the heel of her hand. The only escape on offer. This had been the worst week. Oh boy, she was going to get epic plastered and smoke like a chimney. Just wished Em had given her a spare tab to complete the holy trinity.

loose fit

style defined a type of music, an attitude. Loose Fit – yeah, it's the whole thing. Clothes match personality, all in one package, you get what you're seein'. And if you don't like it – well, the door's over there. It's all perfectly carried by their "don't

found it like slack clothes. Just be yourself he says. "Sounds good to me."

Loose Fit, Kinky Afro, and Step On form the stoned gold triumvirate of baggy. Everything's a bit loose if you feel this way, including the law. We only have to look

It felt peculiar walking in the new clothes. He was used to a proper Manchester loose fit, and this was all tight and rubby in the wrong places. The shoes pinched his feet and squeaked like loose floorboards in a bedroom.

Taffy the grey-haired porter looked up from his crossword and cup of tea. He wore a blue jumper, even on hot days like this. Mark assumed it was some kind of weird pride at work.

"Over here please, sir," Taffy said, beckoning. Mark gave him a puzzled look, took an uncertain step towards reception, then recognition dawned on Taffy's face. "Bloody hell, nearly asked you for ID! Thought you were new."

"It's still me."

"I know that, just a shock. You tarted up for an interview?"

"No. Well, yes."

"I thought you must be. Or for a wedding. Or a camp funeral."

Mark jiggled with impatience but stopped when the squeak caused Taffy to look down at Mark's footwear and raise an eyebrow. Best to be like a statue.

"What's the job?"

"I don't want to talk about it."

"Touchy fucker, eh?"

"Just change the subject, Taffy."

"Okay." Taffy pointed his teaspoon at Mark. "What team do you support?" A splash of tea plinked onto the newspaper. "I had you for a blue, but with that pink shirt you must be a light red…" Taffy sniggered.

"You can't just ask what team I support without saying what sport you mean."

"Well it's obvious!"

"No it isn't."

"Football!"

"Just 'cos I live here doesn't mean I have any interest in kicking a bull's testicles around."

"For fuck's sake, you're a bundle of fun today."

"I'm just sick of everyone always twistin' my melon," Mark snapped, heading off to the stairs.

"Don't walk round with a rod up your arse then," Taffy called after him. "Every Englishman an arsehole!"

"Shove Manchester Shitty and Poonited up your back letterbox!" Mark replied, squeaking on with as much dignity as he could muster.

Which wasn't much, really.

Mark tried to act as if nothing was different. Went to his locker, ignored a few bemused looks and a possible smirk. Used the bit of privacy while the locker door was open to compose himself, gather as much confidence as he could. He had to think of power.

Power lines, converging. It happened in places. It happened in music. Power. Electronic, the band. Lines ran into it from the New Order timeline. Also from The Smiths timeline. More, need more. Quick. Okay. Third line. Three. Third album. Electronic's third album, included the bassist from Doves. Doves members met in The Haçienda. Yes. But not a band line, try again. Quick. Third album also included the drummer from Black Grape. That connects to the Happy Mondays power line. Yes. All three ran in, charged him.

Mark closed the locker door. He was ready now. He tried to walk with more sureness, looked ahead. The next challenge: Rene saw him and came over.

"You look good, Mark," she said, nodding. "Very smart."

"Uh, thanks Rene."

She was still smiling at him. He scratched his neck.

"I really approve."

"Yeah, thanks." Her smile was disconcerting. He wasn't used to it. He gestured vaguely to the processing section. "Best go … papers." He escaped. Maybe he was over-reacting?

He was scheduled to do the outgoing post. Ben was there, scooting back and forth on Russian Roulette while tapping out a fingertip beat on the scarred worktable. He froze when he saw Mark.

"Wow! Tidy haircut. But pink shirt? Not a good look."

"It's a *pastel hue*."

"It's *pink*, Mark. With the tight trousers it makes you look like you're cruising."

"Smart people dress like this, so why the big lady-lemons deal?" Mark could feel his face inflaming.

"Correction. *Roger* dresses like that," said Ben with a shake of the head.

Oh. Most ultimate of insults. Mark was trying to think of a retort – while keeping his feet still – when Dave appeared.

"Who's this?" Dave asked in mock surprise. "A male model straight from a clothes catalogue?"

"Shut up, Dave," Mark muttered, not wanting to attract more attention. He might have got away with just that but Dave noticed the new shoes.

"Jee-sus!" he said loudly. "Look at those flip flops! No one has feet that long! Unless the bus drove over your feet this morning? Poor guy, you shouldn't be walking."

"Crazy fashion follower," said Ben.

"Crazy circus act, more like," said Dave. "Here come the clowns. I'm sure you gents have heard the legend of my 'Andrex Dong' – it's soft, strong, and very, very long. But this is the first time I've ever seen Andrex shoes. Hey, girls, over here!" Dave beckoned to some of the keyboarders. "Come and cop a look at Mark!"

This was not the plan.

Mark dropped the post and rushed over to the warehouse door, squeaky feet slapping the carpet tiles to punctuate his retreat.

"Will you stop pulling your top down? I can't concentrate on these numbers!" Sam rubbed a palm across her brow, trying to alleviate the headache that was banging to be let in.

"I'm not pulling my top down, I'm wafting it," replied Em. "It's so friggin' hot in here I'm overheating."

"No one needs reminding of that. Though you could go and tell Rene, ask her to send us home. Can't fail: just quote *health and safety*."

Em glared back, but didn't make any rebuke.

"Anyway, you'd better stop it because Roger is on his way back. If he sees what I just saw his eyes will pop out."

"Something would pop out, but not his eyes."

Sam suppressed a snigger as Roger plopped himself down at their desk. There was space for about six people, but the downsized book orders team only consisted of the three currently sat there, and sometimes a temp. The spaces where others would have sat were piled with papers.

"Hello my dears, hot isn't it?" He took a swig from the bottle of Sunny Delight he always seemed to have with him.

"We were just saying that," said Em. She twanged impatiently at some elastic bands she wore on her left wrist like a postman's fashion accessory. Then she spoke in a soft voice, "Roger, would you be a love and go to the newsagent's during the break? Buy us an ice cream or a lolly?"

"Okay ... if you both ask me very nicely."

"Pretty please, Roger?" asked Emily, fluttering her eyelashes.

Then Roger turned to face Sam, expectant.

"It's okay. I'll just get a glass of water."

"Suit yourself." He spread the contents of two brightly-coloured folders in front of him, and started ticking things on a third sheet with more pressure than necessary.

"Uh oh, Mama Bear approaching," Em warned.

The three of them turned to Rene, who seemed to be suffering from the heat too: the omnipresent blazer had been left in the office and she had undone the top button on her blouse. She had a pad of paper in her hand.

"Monday, bank holiday – but we've got the college orders to catch up on, otherwise we'll be in breach. Who'll come in to help out? Time and a half?" Always straight to business.

Em snorted. Roger looked down.

"Maybe people who have been taking annual leave at short notice?" Rene asked, looking only at Sam.

Shit. And she needed the money. "I'll come in," she said.

"Good." Rene scribbled on her pad; Sam was back on the good girl page. "I only need a few: if you work closely together you should get it all processed."

"I suppose I could too," Roger said. "I'm not too busy after all."

"Okay, thanks Roger." Rene jotted another note.

"Always happy to help out," Roger replied. "Packham green, we're the team."

"Quite. Oh, Samantha, can I have a quick word?"

Sam got up and joined her by the filing cabinets. There was a layer of dust on them. Relics from the time before Packham Green went hi-tech.

"Thank you for showing my visitors through earlier," Rene said.

"No problem. I could tell they were bigwigs."

"Exactly. Don't take this the wrong way, but I just wanted to say you could have made more of an effort, Samantha." Rene looked at Sam's clothes.

"Excuse me?"

"Wearing flip flops and baggy clothes."

"They're mules, not flip flops. And the clothes aren't baggy."

"No need to get defensive, I'm not going to argue, just wanted to make a friendly point. Just … look in the mirror before you come out?" She strode off before Sam could respond.

Sam looked down at her clothes. A roaring in her ears, burning urge to shout out that she wore good stuff, all bought from *What The Fuck?*, *How Fucking Dare You?*, and the superstore *Why Don't You Look At Your Fucking Self?*

Grit her teeth. *Heat.* We all get tetchy. Just chill out.

After returning to her seat she snapped a pencil in half and dropped the bits into the bin. Roger and Em looked at her. She widened her eyes and jutted her head towards them. They went back to work.

The *carroting* airless heat in the *curranting* office. Mark sniffed for the hundredth time. It was like having flu but you still had to come to work.

He stared at the screen. He was meant to be inputting paper-based orders so that another team could fulfil them. Keyboarding afternoons were okay sometimes, when he could chat with Dave and Ben, but today he sat alone after he'd completely ignored their apologies. They'd gone off to the warehouse, shunting boxes of books. Sweaty work, but obviously preferable to being around Mark.

His phone buzzed. He scrambled it out of his pocket eagerly. Could it be Mandy wanting to say sorry?

`U fuckr. Reply. Bizness to sort out, U know.`

Not Mandy then.

Mark deleted the text. It joined all the others from Denny. Words like that were a trap. Reply and he would just keep at you. Comply and he'd be nice for a while, but it wouldn't be the end of it – you'd get asked to do something else later. "You've done it once, what's the problem?" A slippery, snotty slope. Got to avoid taking that first step.

Thanks to drinking too much and sleeping too little – again – Mark's head was also banging like a bass. A really kicking one. Annoyingly irregular rhythm though, rough irritation under the scratches of pain. Like another reality behind his eyes. You couldn't see it, but it was there anyway. Seemed to affect his perception, because the words on the screen made no sense.

And it was so *hot*. His new shirt was stuck to his back. Sweat trickled down his sideburns, a horrible wet tickle. He wiped them against his biceps. He discovered that if he rested his hands on the desk and counted to ten, then lifted them away, there were damp silhouettes of fingertips and a palm. They slowly faded as the sweat evaporated.

He found he was doing that more than working.

Need air.

He approached the nearest window. Tried yanking it open but it was jammed too tight in the groove from disuse. Another bum note in the gig of his life. Why couldn't a hinge turn smoothly just for once? People steamed at their desks nearby, ignoring him in their own worlds of boring discomfort. He spied a footstool and picked it up in one hand. If he held it by the legs and struck the window with the padded seat it should knock out the stiffness, make it loose so that it could be opened. Sweat was springing out on his exposed forehead. It was worth a try.

He began thumping the window. Ground his teeth to the rhythm. Thunk thunk thunk, squeak squeak squeak. People observed him. If he gave up he'd look like a pillock. Thunk thunk. Nothing seemed to be happening so he gave it a whack as an encore.

With a bang glass exploded outwards, small pieces catching the sunlight, sparkling diamonds tumbling through the sky, tinkling and crashing their big rock ending as they ran out of air in the car park two floors below, shards skidding along the ground amongst the bins and tyres. He stared in surprise at the unobstructed view in front of him, letting the stool drop out of his limp hand with a bang.

Breeze cooled his face.

That breeze had travelled from far away. Shaded islands of green.

Then a large piece of glass swayed and fell to the inside, cracking into fragments all over one of the computers.

Oh.

There was a moment of shocked silence, post-blast aural vacuum. And then … a laugh. A sarcastic jeer. Hoots and hollers. Just like the time when he'd dropped a tray of food and drink in the school canteen, an echoing clatter followed by a chaos of screeches and shouted ridicule.

Oh sweet frowning coconuts.

Sam jumped in surprise at the nearby crash, turning to see a tall and slightly gaunt bloke standing in front of a smashed window, jagged pieces of glass still attached at the crooked edge of the frame.

The second thing she noticed was the cool air blowing in through the frame, like a kiss from an angel.

The third thing was that Emily leaped up and started clapping and laughing. Others in the office began to cheer good-naturedly. Suddenly she was laughing too.

The bloke looked round as if dazed, vulnerable. He looked familiar but she couldn't remember his name.

The clapping and whooping stopped when Rene slammed her office door open, face purpling with anger, and stood eyeing them all before fixing on the guy by the window.

"Mark! Get into my office NOW!"

Mark. Yes, that was it. Only then did she recognise him as the shy starey-eyed guy who delivered post and rarely spoke in the staff room. He used to have wild dark hair but had cut it short, and his normally casual dress, bordering on scruffy, had been replaced with a smart pink shirt today. It was no wonder she didn't recognise him at first.

Emily was wiping tears from her blue eyes. Tears of laughter. Something had broken, more than just a window.

Everyone had been looking at him. Laughing. The floppy foot clown, a source of amusement, pink-shirted buffoon, a bad piss ugly thing with stubble-backed spike hair. Claps and jeers, Rene shouting, the words made no sense amongst the cacophony, the letters typed on the sound-screen were just pounding drums and wailing guitars flooding his body with too much feedback. He had to shut it all down.

So he'd walked straight out the office doors, leaving the shouting and chaos behind him. Piddle on it all.

Now he was sat alone at the bus stop. Teeth gritted, he tried to grab the hair on the top of his head and yank it, as if he could make it grow back longer again. He couldn't face going back to work. Not today.

He was scraping about for money because of *this*? Clothes he couldn't even wear again? He looked down at the shoes and could now only see them through the eyes of others. He was no suave James Bond. He was a crabcaking circus freak.

The clothes were going straight to a charity shop. He hated them. Vein-throb anger pulsed.

His phone buzzed. Dave, trying to ring him. He turned it off.

This had been the worst week ever.

At least it was a Friday. A few days before he'd have to face the music.

Everyone had been looking at him. Laughing. The floppy foot clown [illegible]

That's appropriate

Who's the album for?

- Literary types. First track is the harsh and drilling Atrocity Exhibition, named after a J.G. Ballard novel. Ian Curtis didn't just sing, he wrote the lyrics, and was rarely seen without a book in his hand that informed their creation.

- The proletariat. Like many of these Manchester bands, there's a working class sensibility. In the midst of millions we still feel Isolation as we grind away at A Means To An End, losing our Heart And Soul in the process.

- Goths. Joy Division perfected melancholy and darkness in songs about sorrow and pain, loneliness, desolation, emptiness, urban decay. This album helped establish the gothic rock genre.

Closer is also Joy Division's final album. An LP to end their story. A closer to a career. Ian Curtis, so talented, young, on the verge of success, about to tour America, could see what they were on the edge of, what waited only one step away ... yet he chose to hang himself in a Manchester kitchen in May 1980. This album was released after his death. He never saw what he'd created. You get grabbed by circumstances, life, the things you create and the things you thought you wanted. It's easy to see that as the whole picture, to feel there's no escape from the atrocity exhibition.

Yet it's also about getting closer – to our goals, to each other. The album cover may portray a mausoleum but after the pain of love there can be hope. Don't give up, ever. Don't walk away.

The surviving band members didn't, and New Order was born.

Russell, fussel, fuck his muscles. Useless rat, brat, letting me down like that…

Sam jostled her way through the city centre crowd, trying to stub out the fuse that fizzed atop her skull.

"Jerry's depressed about his ex, so I've got to stay out with him," he'd said on the phone that morning.

"Oh, for fuck's sake!"

"It's true!"

"I never said it wasn't." Grit teeth. "After, then?"

"I'll be knackered."

"Why are you always so tired when I want to meet up?"

"'Cos I work hard."

"So do I! But I'd stay awake for you." She could feel it building up inside, that urge to explode, a word bang to shatter his eardrums.

"I know. It's crap," he said, and there was something in his voice, some sorrow that released part of her steam, hinted that he was genuine. "I'll make it up to you," he added, sealing the deal.

"Yes?"

"Yeah. Promise. Something special. We'll do something really nice."

"It'd better be pretty, amazingly, extravagantly special," she'd said, eyeing the phone suspiciously.

"Will be. Honour."

She was thinking holiday. Had to be. Their first one together. That kept the bomb in check but she was still fuming in the aftermath. Teeth clenched, striding, focussed on one thing: a big bag of Thornton's chocolates.

Forget *big*, it needed to be *massive*.

Saturday afternoon. Mark was in town to enact The Masterplan. He did his best to sidle past shoppers with his head down but once you were near Piccadilly it wasn't safe to do that any more – you had to look both ways or risk double death from trams and buses. The trams usually tooted but sometimes they'd already trundled up your rear end in near silence and you had to leap out of the way like a floppy plonker.

He wasn't fully with it. Had slept badly. Someone playing music in the flat above, bassline and kick drum so loud it was like they wanted to break through the floor. A tune that got into your brain and kept tapping on the inside of your skull looking for a way out again – it could only be Blue Monday. A good choice but a bit nobbish to be playing it in the middle of the night. Must be another music nut, though Mark had thought that flat was empty. Maybe swaggering shaggy mop-top guy inhabited it now.

There was a woman ahead of him, hair of black coal which defied even today's blazing sun, walking quickly, an impression of Amazonian toughness inherent in the hunch of her shoulders. He watched, followed the hint of familiarity to see her face, solve the puzzle once and for all. Caught a glimpse of determined jaw, and he knew.

Samantha – *"It's just Sam"* – Rees. He knew surnames from doing the post. He should have recognised her sooner, she was so striking, stood out in a crowd – literally – always would, a girl like that, the kind you stare at on buses because they're in a different league.

After a moment's hesitation he followed her. You only stride like that when you've got a purpose (or you're angry). He wanted to see what that purpose was. How the other half live.

She was walking at an angle to the tram tracks, and a shape loomed to her right. A tram. She was just looking ahead. Its weight, its metallic presence affected others, they held back, got out of the way, it cut through the crowd like a knife, but Sam continued, just looked irritated by the people blocking her; grinding wheels rolled nearer and he could see the trajectory, the ominous mass approaching the same target as her, lines of oblivious and oblivion intersecting as the dirty wheels rolled nearer; he started shoving past people, stopped apologising when he could hear the *ka-chunk!* of metal on rails, elbowed forward, shouting "Sam!" just before she stepped out (*she wouldn't have done that?*), then yelling out her name in panic (*she would!*); at the urgency of it she stopped and turned and looked lost until she saw him. The tram emerged from the crowd that had obscured it, trundled on. It was close enough to whip her hair about. She watched it disappear, blank. Tucked her hair back.

He slowed as he reached her. "You weren't looking where you were going!" he said, surprised to find his heart was beating too fast.

"I saw it. Hi ... Mark." She looked dazed. The tram tooted its high-pitched horn cheerily as it turned the corner. "Oh no. I didn't really, did I?"

"You okay?"

"Yes. No. Maybe."

People nudged them, a surge of rushing bodies forced to flow around two obstructions, blockages, forms not fitting the pattern, the direction they were meant to move in.

"You don't look okay."

She inhaled deeply through her nose. "Maybe I need to sit down." Exhale, almost a sigh.

"Want to have a hot drink? There's a place over there."

She nodded. They walked, side by side, almost touching, and his hands felt wrong, dangled falsely, pendulum weights attached directly to his mind in distracting motion.

"I should laugh, shouldn't I?" she asked, breaking their silence.

"Why?"

"I always liked the way each tram has its own name. Did you see that one though? The brass plaque said 'Prince Albert'. It would've been twice as embarrassing getting knocked down by a genital piercing."

"It's not funny. You coulda been splatted."

"You look like you can be serious enough for me. Sorry. I'm not with it yet."

She wasn't hysterical but Mark picked up an edge to her voice. She wasn't okay.

"Just remembered: you broke that window yesterday!" she said.

He squinted his eyes shut, nodded. "Yeah. I'm plopping it about going back to work. If Rene doesn't sack me on the spot then she'll probably kick my 'nads in. I'll be a Jaffa afterwards."

"Jaffa?"

"Seedless."

"Oh. But it was brilliant! I've not laughed so much since… You'll have to really apologise to her. She was livid. It'd be horrible if you were sacked. I've got to admit I was glad I wasn't the only one in trouble."

"You? You're like a boss or something."

"Ha ha, not really. Team leader's just a name."

"Still…"

"I couldn't believe it, the way you just ignored her and walked out."

"Don't remind me."

"A legend," she said as they entered the café. A young woman at the till asked Mark what he wanted. She wore a baseball cap. It was some coffee store chain. Although he preferred a proper cup of tea, especially when he was gasping, he knew Sam always had coffee.

"Two coffees."

"What kind?" At his blank stare the assistant added, "Espresso, Latte, Americano?"

"Erm, just normal ones. Britishio. In mugs." He looked down, confused. It wasn't simple like asking for a beer.

"Americano," Sam interrupted. "Two. To drink in."

The assistant nodded and grabbed the cups, took them to a complicated-looking metal machine, all pipes and steamy taps.

"I'll pay," said Mark, scrambling for his wallet.

"No, it's alright. Go Dutch."

"No! No more countries."

They sat at a table outside. An umbrella kept the worst of the sun from hammering on their brows. He lined up sachets of sugar and a wooden stirrer.

"You're from Wales, right?" he asked.

"How'd you know?"

"Your accent's funny."

"Thanks. And yours is pretty incomprehensible."

"Sorry. I didn't mean it that way."

"It's alright. Men always mention my accent first when they're hitting on me."

"I wasn't!"

"Don't look so worried, I was just pulling your leg."

The coffees arrived and Mark dumped all the sugars in. Sam widened her eyes but only poured one into hers.

"I've never been to Wales."

"You should."

"We never really did holidays. Other countries. I don't know what it's like."

"What do you think Wales is like?"

"Dunno. Stone Roses recorded albums there. So it must be a bit funky. They took pictures of stone angels. Apart from that … green hills? Miners?"

"Not any more. It's just another place. But home."

"Do you speak Welsh then?"

"Yes. It's not my first language, not like Mam, but my family use it."

"I can't imagine that. I can't even remember French from school. Say something in Welsh."

"What?"

"Anything."

"*Fel y bo'r dyn y bydd ei lwdn.*"

"Wow. What's that?"

"Like father, like son. I guess that's nearest in English. Something my gran used to say."

He took a gulp of his coffee, cup gripped in both hands. Tried not to grimace. It was rubbish compared to a good cuppa. Too bitter at the back of the tongue. "You reckon that's true?"

"Don't know. You can't read too much into folklore."

"I hope it's not true."

"I'm like my mam. Too much, sometimes. Makes it hard to be yourself."

"Are your family close?"

"Yes." She smiled, sipped. "Always in each other's business."

"Like mine."

"It's suffocating sometimes. But they really care, there's love underneath – I like that. Wouldn't swap it for anything else. So yours are close?"

"Not like that. Yours sound lovely."

"Isn't yours?"

Mark gulped more coffee. Lovely wasn't the first word in his mind. "Well, my granddad sounded ace, but I never met him. A real good guy, like a hero. He was in a war. Survived mustard gas *and* pepper spray."

"Oh no."
"He was a seasoned veteran."
He watched her expression change from concern to realisation to a smile as she almost splurted her coffee.
"You're a sly one," she told him, nodding her head. "It's always the quiet ones."
"How come you're here? In Manchester? Not stayed in Wales?"
"Uni. Came here to study history. Maybe a little bit to escape, get a change of scene. I like the industrial heritage, reminds me a bit of the valleys, like some massive version of Neath in the future but one where people have regressed. Then when I finished the degree it made sense to stay for a bit. A bit became more. It always does. It's been about five years since I finished the degree. You stay long enough in one place you stop rolling. Habit instead of excitement. What did you study?"
"I've never been to uni."
"Oh. Sorry."
"You planning on moving on then?"
"I like the idea of something better. We're all capable of more, aren't we?"
"*You* are. Brainy and stuff. More mature."
"Older, you mean?"
"You teasing me again?"
"No."
"You're not older."
"Born in '72."
"Nah."
"Yes. You?"
"1976."
"Ha, I'm four years older."
"Age dunt matter though, does it?"
She finished her drink. Slid the cup away. "Thanks for the coffee. And talking. I feel better."
"No probs."
"Why're you in town?"
He tried to brush a nonextistent fringe with his fingers. Frowned. "Me hair, innit?"

"I noticed you'd cut it. I like it."

"Too short."

"Suits you. Nothing to hide behind now. Stare the world in the eye." She wiggled her fingers in front of her nose.

"Stare at people and you get a black eye."

"Why'd you get it cut then?"

Mark just shrugged.

"Was it to do with a job? Are you applying for something else?"

"No, it wasn't that."

She looked at him, as if expecting an answer. He finished the last mouthful of his coffee.

"Okay, I'll change the subject. You pointing at your head doesn't tell me *why* you're here."

"I thought I'd get a hat somewhere. Kangol, maybe."

"Nice. Where you going to look?"

"Afflecks Palace. Bound to be some there."

"I've never been."

"How come? You said you were a student here."

"Ooh, now the prejudices surface." But she was smiling, not attacking.

"Sorry."

"So you want help? I like shopping."

"What, with me?"

"Yes."

"Up to you."

"You could sound positive."

"Sorry. It'd be cool."

"Great. Let's get you a hat. This might be fun."

Piccadilly was as noisy as ever. Pan pipes from Aztec performers were amplified through loudspeakers; a "Sex is sin!" speech was being yelled by a God-squad evangelist with a microphone; over the road someone was playing a flute; and a drummer with a full kit was pounding his way to a sweat. More than noise, this was cacophony.

They passed a Big Issue vendor. He was thin-faced and smiley, didn't seem upset by the well-dressed crowds ignoring him. There was a dog by his side, a ratty terrier, sat on a folded black donkey jacket.

"Hold on," Mark told Sam as he checked in his pocket, dug out some coins, and handed them over in exchange for a copy of the mag. He liked the music section. The guy seemed really grateful for the sale. More than he needed to be.

"There's a good article about GM crops in there," he told Mark, jabbing at the cover. "Scottish farmers accidentally planting them, seed stock was polluted. Got to destroy it all. Nasty business. Can't even trust your food nowadays, can you?"

Mark knew there should be social interaction, not just a financial one. But why were Greater Manchester buses selling plants to Scottish farmers? He was out of his depth. Struggled to think of a response.

The dog was now sat with its legs open, licking its penis.

"Wish I could do that," Mark said, tilting his head.

"Ask him nicely, maybe he'll let you," the vendor replied.

As they walked away Mark looked down at his trainers. Sam started laughing. "I can't believe you said that!"

"I didn't mean I wanted to lick –"

"I *know* what you meant! You're funny."

It was okay. She was laughing *with*, not *at*. And they'd reached the corner-dominating Afflecks Palace. They walked past mosaics which decorated the wall, intricate pieces making a whole when you step back and view things from a distance. Over the road the new Tib Street Horn coiled around the remains of a Victorian hat factory. Mark took that to be a lucky omen for his quest. Sam said it looked like a dragon.

Sam was fascinated by the place as they wandered between stalls and boutiques. It was an assault of styles. Army clothes and slogan T-shirts jostled for space with retro dresses and corsets. Evening dresses and tutus gave way to greebo tights and jumpers. Sam spent ages looking at clubwear in Strawberri Peach, wondering what Russell would say if she turned up in a sequinned bodice. Maybe *that* would make him skip work for the night. Still, it didn't feel like her. Too flamboyant for her body, only desirable for dreams.

Mark was patient, hanging around at the edges while she stroked material and checked price tags. She browsed some bags and cat-collar jewellery. A studded bracelet fit nicely on her wrist. She put it back, and her eyes stayed on it after her fingers let go.

"You could buy it," Mark said. She hadn't realised he was looking over her shoulder.

"Not me. And not here for that anyway. Sorry to be holding you up."

"I'm in no hurry. We can go all round, look at everything if you want."

"You sure? That might take all day!"

"I've got all day." A moment of silence followed his shy smile. "It's fun watching you. Like it's all new."

"It is. For some reason I thought it would just be a market hall. One big open place, like the ones I used to go shopping in with my mam when I was a kid. You'd go up and down the lines, ignore the smell of fish, then you were done. This…" She gestured vaguely. "It's like chaos."

"It's freedom. Indie. Everyone likes it. Tourists, students, schoolkids. Goths, punks, trannies, metalheads, bodybuilders. Everyone shares this space. Safe ground."

"No hats though."

"There's more upstairs."

He led her through twisting corridors that smelt of joss sticks and perfumes, while trance, rock, and indie music played in different areas, on different staircases. An eclectic funhouse maze where every inch was filled, liberatingly inconsistent. Band posters covered walls next to high art pictures in frames. Cartoons merged into graffiti reflected back in mirrors. Death metal insignia and cutesy Japanese cats all inhabited the building, and above them racks were bolted onto the building's structure, a visible sign of the place being repurposed, adapted, recovered. Beauty and chaos, all decorated, rebuilt and used with the same sense of creativity and mix-it-up mayhem.

They passed through an area with retro kitsch gadgets and ornaments. Old-style sweet dispensers were surrounded by aged lamps, vintage jackets, yellowed books, vinyls, VHS tapes, 50s clocks, 60s phones, 70s keyboards and 80s cameras. It was the ultimate recycling centre, where everything was being resold.

Up another staircase. Sunglasses stands gave way to hair extensions, tattoos and piercings, Pagan and fortune-telling paraphernalia. One shop sold rubber, bondage and dressing up items:

the display mixed furry handcuffs with false eyelashes. They both walked past without saying anything, or indicating any desire to go in.

Sam had wandered off on her own to look at gift cards and postcards so Mark hung round near one of the staircases. She'd turned too quickly at one point and bumped into Mark.

"Sorry," she'd said, moving back and restoring the empty air barrier between them.

"Me too. It's cramped…" He had gestured vaguely, petered out when it didn't look like she was going to slap him.

It was good to have a few minutes to get his head straight. Then he felt a pang of nostalgia on seeing an old Street Fighter 2 arcade machine. He used to play the one in his local launderette, always choosing the same character: the outsider, a Brazilian werewolf. Eventually he could last for ages on just one credit, perfecting the timing for his electric shock attack. Come to think of it, Blanka wouldn't look out of place in Afflecks. He gave the red joystick an experimental waggle. Nice and loose. Back, hold for a second, then hammer to the right and tap heavy punch, so Blanka curled up in a ball and spun through the air accompanied by a jungle roar of defiance.

Then one day he had turned up with a pocketful of coins and the arcade game was gone, replaced with a cigarette machine.

Out of the corner of his eye he saw Sam looking pleased. He abandoned Blanka, Ryu and Dhalsim to their never-ending tournament.

"Come on." She tugged his jacket eagerly. He followed until she gestured with both arms, a big smile on her face. The sign said Neo Hatbocks and the shelves were lined with baseball caps, granddad caps, beanies, dyed straw hats, deerhunters, scarves, riding hats, and even a few helmets. "I found them for you."

He looked at all the choices, suddenly self-conscious. Sam watched him dithering then went to the girl who worked there. She had one ear lobe stretched by a big flesh plug, but on her other ear two flaps of skin hung like amputee's limbs, a collapsed flesh arch. He tried not to stare.

"Got any Kangols?" Sam asked, before being directed round the corner.

Mark followed her, watched her examining the pile.

"How big's your head?"

"Normal."

She laughed, took a black one from the stack, handed it to him. He slipped it on and turned to the mirror.

A stranger looked back at him.

"What do you think?" she asked.

"It's… Wow. I look like I'm in The Stone Roses." He lowered his forehead, tried to look moody. "Yeah. I'm 'avin' it."

She laughed again, a good sound, and he paid gladly. It would hide his head while the hair grew back, sure, but it did more than that. It was as if he could be a new person.

"You found me this, and it's perfect. I owe you, big style. Do you wanna get something to eat?"

She nodded, so he took her to the third floor café. The table's surface was laminated with pages from superhero comics.

"You like salad?" he asked.

"Sure."

"They do good salad here. I know I should eat more veg, so I usually get that."

"I can't see it on the menu."

"No, you have to ask for it. Chip salad."

She laughed. "Chip salad?"

"Yeah. Chips and some slices of tomato. It's good if you put loads of brown sauce on."

"I'm sure it's good, but look – they have strawberries and cream."

"I've never had strawberries."

"I don't believe you!"

"Swears it. I've had strawberry flavour stuff though. Jam and that."

"How come you've never had them?"

"Dunno. Just didn't. Dad wasn't into fruit."

"You should try them."

"Okay."

"My treat though," she told him as he stood. "You bought me coffee."

He hesitated, then nodded. Better than arguing about American and Dutch things.

There was an old jukebox in here. He went up to it. Popped in some coins, entered five digits from memory, sat down again. Music swelled, perforated by drums that sounded like heartbeats. Ian Curtis began to sing as Sam returned, sliding into her seat with a questioning look.

"It's my favourite song. Atmosphere. Joy Division."

"Yes, I know this. It's good."

"Better than good."

"Yes. Better than," she conceded, looking straight at him. Her dark eyes made him uncomfortable.

He looked over at the jukebox instead. "This is one of their most famous songs, but it's not even on an album. Same with Love Will Tear Us Apart. Everyone knows it. Ripped raw feelings. Joy Division were so brimming with talent they could drop singles like emotion bombs. Amazing. You get the same with New Order. Blue Monday was their superhit, and it was only ever a single, not a proper album song. New Order didn't like putting their singles onto albums. I've got a copy of their Power, Corruption & Lies album that has a huge sticker saying 'Does Not Contain Blue Monday', since there were so many complaints about it."

Two bowls of strawberries and cream were brought, and they ate in silence for a while until the song ended. Mark liked that. It was respectful.

"What do you think?" she asked.

"Gorgeous. Like strawberry sweets, but better." He resisted the urge to lick the bowl clean.

"They remind me of home. Dad's strawberries, from the greenhouse. And the small wild ones at the bottom of the garden."

Sam reached into her bag, took out a packet of cigarettes and a lighter. Lifted the lid on the packet, offered it to Mark. He shook his head. She nodded, hesitated; put the packet away. Left her bag on its side on the table, things partly spilled out. Mark felt like he shouldn't look; women's bags were something secret.

"I didn't know you smoked. I don't mind though," Mark added.

"Trying not to. Only if I'm stressed. But I feel kind of good now."

"I'm glad. Me too. And you don't want to get addicted to those things."

"No. But I have an addictive personality, I guess. So, you're really into music then?"

"It's my favourite thing."

"Why's that?"

"You can rely on it," he said, without hesitation. "It's always there. Even when the singers die, it stays behind. A message in a bottle."

"Like a ghost."

"Yeah."

She looked out of the window, giving Mark a view of her from the side. She looked so strong. Confident. Yet thoughtful too. "Do you believe in ghosts?" she asked, turning back.

"I don't know. This sounds weird, but I heard about this thing called hauntology once, a real thing. When I was reading about Joy Division." He leaned forward, excited. "Something about how the past lives on in the present. It's all around us. The buildings and streets, the history. And like the music too, it's still there if you listen. Maybe ghosts are like that? You wouldn't think of ghosts today, y'know, all modern and stuff, but if you think about it, all the history: it keeps adding up, there's always more of it, so why not more ghosts too? And anyway, this guy in an interview, when he was talking about Joy Division, he said technology makes us all ghosts, and it was something in Joy Division's music." Mark sat back, folded his arms. "But what do I know? I don't understand all that stuff."

"Sounds like you do."

He shrugged. "What about you? You believe in ghosts?"

"Maybe. I like the idea of it. That someone you care about could come back, interact with you in some way. Make things better, reassure you."

"If it don't hurt anyone then believe it. Sounds nice. Like guardian angels."

"Yes. That's how I think about it. It's just so attractive, that idea that even though someone's gone you could still spend some time with them, even if only for seconds. A chance to say goodbye."

They both looked out of the window, across the roofs and car parks and roads. Grey and brown below the blue.

"What are you doing now?" she asked.

"My favourite shop, then home. Want to come?"

"Mystery. Okay."

As she picked up her bag a pen fell out. She used it to doodle on the serviette: a smiley face in a Kangol hat. She folded it over and rested it on the plant pot's edge in the shade of a spider plant's leaves.

We were here, once.

"Let's go," she said.

"Is that your favourite shop?" asked Sam, pointing at an adult movie store as they crossed a road.

"No! Next to it!" Then he realised she'd just been pulling his leg. Again.

He'd brought her to Vinyl Revival, its comforting green and blue sign above windows full of albums and posters. "RECORDS. C.D.s. VIDEOS. MEMORABILIA. BOUGHT, SOLD & EXCHANGED" a second sign read.

"There's Piccadilly Records round the corner too. That's bigger but I prefer VR." He fitted in better here. As they entered music was playing, punk overtones: Buzzcocks.

"Hi, Colin," Mark said to the owner.

"Alright, Mark. We haven't got any new tapes in."

"It's fine, I'm just looking today."

Colin raised an eyebrow towards Sam while she had her back turned, looking at T-shirts. Mark shook his head.

There were wide racks for flicking through hundreds of LPs in plastic sleeves, genre labels stuck up. Mark was at the Factory section, had tenderly touched the joint Joy Division / New Order label, when he realised Sam was by his side.

"I should have known your fave place would be full of music."

"Not just music. *Manchester* music. Look at all the pictures." She looked up, following the sweep of his arm across the framed posters for The Stone Roses, The Haçienda, New Order, Joy Division, Happy Mondays, The Smiths, The Fall, Oasis, Inspiral Carpets. All the legends, set proudly against a red wall.

"But haven't you got it all already?"

"There's always the chance of something you've not come across before. Years ago I found an unopened copy of The Fall Live In London here; it's a 1980 album that only came out on tape. And it's not just the albums anyway, y'know. Mugs, posters, VHS tapes. If I had a DVD player there'd be more again."

"I see. I love music too. Do you wanna check out the CDs?"

He glanced over at the racks of tacky shiny plastic.

"Nah. I don't like them."

"Why not?"

"It's not legit. I mean, people listen to them on random, don't they? It's wrong. The bands put the songs in an order on purpose. We should respect that. You don't get that issue with tapes, it's always start to end."

"I've never thought of it that way before. It doesn't surprise me that you have."

"Sorry. I don't normally tell people all the stuff that bothers me."

"It's nice. I'm glad you trust me."

"As long as you don't think I'm mad. And there *were* a few times where something was only on CD. I bought it then."

"Well done."

"But I recorded it straight onto tape when I got home. I've got this big stock of blanks for the future, in case they stop making them. Piles of the things."

She shook her head, grinning.

"I just love the feel and rattle of them. You ever wound them back with a pencil through the hole while watching TV? You can spin them like a rattle."

"I've done that! Years ago."

"It lives on in my flat."

"You're a connoisseur."

"Thanks. Most people just call me a weirdo."

She laughed, browsed the CDs anyway, while he flipped through the goth albums, turning the paperboard sleeves over to see what was on sides one and two, when it was released, which label: the origins that defined them. But he couldn't focus, wasn't able to memorise much today. He kept looking up, watching her. She was so down-to-earth and real. Maybe something to do with being from Wales. He wasn't sure what living there was like but despite what she'd said he still associated it with sheep and getting up early. Nothing poncy about that.

Her face was strong, a tough jaw and dark brows, but not like a man, just that it had possible thunder clouds behind it. Scary but exhilarating, like a summer storm. Her eyes and nose and mouth softened it all though. Shook out some of the solidity.

She was a legend.

They neared his bus stop. She was going to walk on, catch the Metro.

"Careful near the tracks this time," he said.

"I will. I feel alert now. Spider senses on max. What are you doing later?"

"Just listening to music." Then he wished he could have said something else. Something that would surprise her. He had no idea what though. Playing football in a team? Juggling cabbages? Naked hang gliding? "What about you?"

"I might see Emily if she's not on a date. Better than stewing on my own about Russell."

"Russell? Is he your boyfriend."

"Yes. When he can be bothered."

A silence. They looked at each other, and he couldn't think of anything to say. He'd amazed himself by having no problem coming up with topics earlier, but now she was going his tongue was tied. Nothing good lasts.

She suddenly gave him a hug. He froze. She smelt really good, her hair in his face; her own atmosphere, pulling gravity. He was about to spread his arms round her when she pulled back, a mildly surprised look on her face.

"Bye, Mark. Thanks for the afternoon. It was nice."

"Yeah. Thanks for helping me out." He tapped the brim of his new hat, and she was gone.

Her face was strong, a tough jaw and dark brows, but not like a

Blue monday

juxtaposed with bombers and missiles synched to the beat and clap machine. 1983's finest Cold War computerised imagery, recalling lives lived in fear, mixed with industrial desolation of cities, motorways, car fetishism, and riots. Question: Where'd all that come from? Answer: Salford.

New Order formed from the remaining members of Joy Division: Bernard S... Hook and Stephen Mo... Order minimal... FAC 73. The band and song title were encoded as coloured blocks in a system used on a few of their works. The sleeve was designed by Peter Saville, who also created the waveform cover for Joy Division's iconic Unknown Pleasures. The original Blue Monday cover had a silvery inner sleeve that was so expensive to manufacture that Factory lost money every time they sold a copy (£1.10 to produce, but they sold them for £1, never expecting the song to be such a hit).

They were the pride of Factory Records, the most well-known Manchester indie record label. Factory gave their bands unprecedented freedom – New Order didn't even have a formal contract with Factory, so the band rather than the label owned all the New Order music. As Tony Wilson, the TV personality and co-founder of Factory, said: "All our bands are free to fuck off whenever they please."

Going back to Bl... ...w Order were no strangers to long songs. ... 22 minutes long, written to celebrate the opening of Haçienda in 1982. The band were partners in financing the UK's first superclub, ...y using proceeds from Blue Monday's success. Without Joy Division, no New Order; without New Order, no Blue Monday; without Blue Monday, no Haçienda; without the Haçienda, no Madchester scene. DNA connects this musical family. Dig deep and you find the roots.

Later we'll look at some of New Order's key albums, including Brotherhood. After all, brotherhood and family is the key theme in

Mark skulked into work. Best word for it. Head down, staying at the edges, putting things into his locker quietly. Maybe he could breeze through the day that way. Get through the job that way. Shuffle through life that way. It had been the safest thing to do growing up. Not to attract the attention of the big kids, the cocky groups, the alcies on the estate … or his dad. He liked the word skulk. A safe word. A safe thing to do. The best option when hiding isn't possible. Skulk, sneak, and skulk some more until the trail goes cold.

The workplace was quieter than usual. Mark wondered if there was a meeting he didn't know about. He could get his head down and sort the publishers' catalogues into piles of "keep" or "bin". He was carrying the heavy box full of them when Rene saw him at the same time he spotted her. Eyes clicked, fire flickered under her brow; she left the woman she'd been flapping with and approached Mark.

"Office," she said, then turned her stout body and paced ahead of him, every movement betraying agitation. He was in the poo. But best to get it over with at the start: roll around in it then get a shower and move on.

He closed the door softly, didn't pull up a chair, made no eye contact, careful to be submissive. Sometimes that had been enough to prevent a belted ear. Worth trying again.

"What the hell was that about on Friday?"

"I'm sorry. The window was stiff and –"

"I don't just mean about the window. And take your hat off."

He reached up in surprise – he'd forgotten it was on. It felt like part of him. Slipped it off and held it between his hands. Maybe he could wring it if he wanted to look really contrite.

"I meant you ignoring me," she continued. "Walking out in front of everyone."

"Yeah, I'm sorry about that too –"

"It *undermines* my authority! Did you intend to make me look stupid?"

"No, it wasn't that, I just –"

"Stop interrupting me! It's clear you have no interest in this job. It's been obvious for some time. And you know why?"

He shook his head, still looking down at his feet. He had his Adidas Sambas on today. Focus on them. That calmed him.

"Because you've got the wrong attitude. A *bad* attitude."

She'd gone quiet. Was he supposed to speak yet? He looked up for a clue. She was squeezing her hands. Kneading them, like when cooks made bread on the telly. She caught his gaze on her hands, stopped them moving. Looked even more irritated.

"It's as if you want to be sacked," she added.

He resisted the urge to shrug. That always seemed to make people angrier. Best to let her blow over rather than blow up.

"Well, you've succeeded. You can empty your locker and go. You're out of here."

In his mind a kick drum followed her statement, dch-dch-dch-dch, New Order combined with the punctuating beat at the end of Eastenders. But it was really silence, apart from the creak of her chair as she sat, apparently exhausted.

Freedom.

A sudden urge to grin. To cheer. To do a little baggy dance. It was one of those points when life can turn. The end of a chorus: what comes next? End of the song? A new verse? An unexpected break, Hammond organ kicking in, or a snare drum fill, or a lead guitar's dextrous riff to make you throw your fist in the air? It was anticipation. It was potential. It was … *no job, a chance to join Denny* … an escape, it … maybe he *had* wanted to be sacked, but…

He held his body still, looked through the glass of Rene's office, into the open-plan area where the better-paid teams worked. And Sam was there … (*Denny reacted on instinct, reacted, didn't plan, didn't think ahead, you have to realise something right now*) … and Sam was frowning at the PC, didn't know he was looking, and there was something so sweet about how she looked, even though he saw her lips form a word that had to be a bad swear, still it was fascinating, the detail of her face, the mystery in the darkness that he'd never understand … (*Denny's attitude could make you a slave just as much as a shitty job could*) … but maybe looking was enough because it made him want to be here in this moment, seeing was enough, wanting something could be better than getting it, he'd always told himself this, the words made him feel better, like looking at albums in a shop and you know you'll never listen to them all but you *imagine* them all, how they might sound, the feel of them in your mind, a sensation that stays with you on the bus, in the shower, in bed, always, and for a few minutes the imagined sounds make you better than you are. Be better than … (*Denny*) … you are.

"I have an idea," Mark said, turning to Rene and fishing in his pocket. His fingers found the scrap of paper with relief. "Been thinking about it in breaks." He took out the crumpled sheet and unfolded it, laid it on her desk reverently, careful to make sure it faced her, smoothed it down with his fingers.

Sometimes when the shiny thing's taken out of the shop window, and you hold it in your eager hands, it turns out the thing don't look so good up close and in yer face.

"Signage, in here. See the blocks? That's the shelving. We can colour code it, like I did in felt tip. And the red arrow shows the flowline now. The green is what it could be if we swapped the contents of bays 2, 3 and 7 a bit. Smoother. Quicker. And that word you like…" he racked his brains and it paid off for once. "Efficient."

She looked at the paper in surprise, then up at Mark.

"It's like the new clothes. The haircut. I'm *trying* to change. The only reason I've not got them on today is because I'm going to be moving mucky books later. Don't wanna wear best for that."

She nodded, not looking angry any more. Listening to him. To *him*. Expectant.

"And I'm sorry about what happened. It was a hanging bogey of a day. Family stuff. But I won't let it happen again. I'll go round the office and say I was out of order if you want."

"That … won't be necessary," she said. Was she dazed? Seemed it. Like Denny had sometimes left Mark. But Mark had done it just with words.

"I've got other ideas too. Still thinkin' 'em out right now."

"This puts a new perspective on things."

"Am I still sacked, Rene?" He'd never addressed her by name before.

"I think we've both been hasty." She slipped the bit of paper into her notebook. "I'm willing to give you another chance."

And there it was. It had all been one moment, balanced on a point. Could have gone any way. And something important had happened.

He'd *chosen* what way to go. He knew he was thick, yet he'd talked his way out of the sack. The mother of all blags. He'd *made it happen.*

Sam had rebooted the PC twice, trying to get rid of the warnings about updating crucial files. Now she frowned at an error message on the screen that popped up while she was logging in. Clicked cancel. After a fidget-inducing age the Windows NT desktop appeared, but it looked different. The icons were too large, and weren't the ones she normally used; there was a weird blue and black bar on the left. She tried to open Internet Explorer but it gave an error.

"Oh fuck." She dialled the number for technical support, even though they just spoke gibberish half the time, and patronised her the other half. She tried to explain the problem.

"Ah, that'll be a roaming profile issue."

"Right."

"Do you know about roaming profiles?"

"Not really, but I –"

"Well it downloads when you login, and uploads when you logoff. Straightforward, but if it stored things it shouldn't, like temp net files, browse history, datagunk, then the profile gets bigger."

"*Datagunk*?"

"Yeah. And if it adds itself to the local backup profile, instead of overwriting it, you get profile bloat. Instead of four meg you end up with 40 megs, or more –"

"Great, yes, nightmare."

"– so the C drive gets too full to download profiles and switches to a dodgy local profile, which then overwrites your nicely set up roaming profile and –"

"Look, fascinating, but I just want you to fix it."

Silence.

"Hello?" she said.

"I'm here." He sounded miffed. "Maybe I'll get a chance to do it later."

"Maybe I'll remind my boss that there are other companies offering support contracts."

Another pause. "I'll need to check if the graph is full, so you'll have to get the hostname via ipconfig forward slash all. Then unplug the network and logout, and we can start deleting files."

"Eye pee *what*?"

"Do you even know how to get a DOS prompt?"

Sam inhaled deeply through her nostrils as she handed Roger the phone, pleased to hear the wasp-like buzzing continue from the earpiece. "Roger, can you sort it out please. Sounds like noise to me."

"Anything you ask." He grinned and slid into her seat. She moved to his place and gathered up invoices to compare with the printed-out orders before passing the lot on to finance. Roger was joking with the technical support guy, apparently about what files Sam had on her PC. When he pretended to discover porn she snatched up the completed sheets and left the table.

It was crazy how much of the work had to be done on the computer now. She was cut off without the bloody thing. It seemed like only a year or two ago she didn't even have to use it every day.

Ah, happy times.

She dropped the paperwork onto another team's table, now vacant. Hot drink first though. Be productive with fruit tea and paper, not keyboard and mouse.

Mark saw her go into the staffroom. He was pretty sure she was alone. He hesitated. Couldn't just follow her in. Too creepy. His phone buzzed again. Two texts. One off Denny. No asking – it *told* Mark to meet him at McDonald's after work. The other was off Dave.

`Where are you?`

That was a weird one.

"In work," he banged out. Then turned the phone off. It never brought good news.

Looked at the door to the staffroom. Remembered how he'd seized the day earlier. He could be a heavenly person today: he just had to make it happen. Impulse.

Sam was stood by the kettle rapping her fingertips on the counter and she looked round as the fire door closed behind him with a clunk. She seemed surprised then smiled. That was good. But he suddenly felt nervous, unsure what his excuse was for going into the staffroom. He always needed *reasons*, words to escape from a situation when people started to look bored or annoyed.

"What are you doing here?" she asked, amused.

"The radio," he said, pointing. "Listen. While I work. Now Rene's left for the day I can use it. Only chance." He snatched the radio up, unplugged it, hugged it to his chest. Lame.

She laughed. "You are a joker. No, I meant working here today. Bank holiday. I didn't see your name on the list?"

He liked the way she always thought he was being funny on purpose.

"Oh. I didn't know it was bank holiday."

"You're kidding me? There was an email about it on Friday afternoon."

He raised an eyebrow and she suddenly understood, nodded.

"Still, you don't have to stay," she told him.

"I do. As punishment for what I did. Rene said I had to work today. I won't get double time, but she'll let me off for the window."

"Sucks."

"Better than sacked."

"She wouldn't do *that*."

Sam was too busy pouring water in her cup to see him frown. It'd been close. Closer than ever before.

He realised there was a funny smell, like shampoo. He looked over her shoulder. Her tea was *red*. What witchery was this? She picked up the cup and faced him.

"Welcome to the naughty club then. We saddos in here on a sunny bank holiday."

"You're naughty too?"

"Can be." She took a sip of her drink while he clutched the radio, and suddenly they were joined by his nemesis: Embarrassed Silence.

He looked at her.

She looked at him.

He adjusted his stance, struggling to expel the image of Sam being naughty in the staffroom.

She blew her cup.

He wanted to scratch his nose.

She made a click sound with her mouth.

And then Roger stuck his head round the door. "All fixed," he told Sam, ignoring Mark completely, then letting the door bang shut again.

The spell was broken. Mark walked off with as much cool as he could. Which, as usual, wasn't much when a power cord dangled between his legs.

"Just make sure you're on best behaviour for a while. No hats on during meetings," Sam called after him.

He rolled his eyes up, saw the edge of the brim, grinned: he'd forgotten it was on his head again. A true second skin. "Oh yeah. I got in trouble for that too," Mark said, walking backwards now so he could speak to her. "She made me take it off."

"What, you wore it for your bollocking?"

"Yes."

"Wish I'd seen it! Precious!"

"It was funny, I guess."

"Well I'm glad you're still around. You make me see the bright side."

And so do you, he thought.

Mark was slitting tape with scissors, tearing rough cardboard, dragging out crumpled paper and polystyrene to get to the books. He removed them from the box, wiped packing dust off the covers, ticked them off the invoice one by one before putting them onto a pallet. Pulped wood smells and sneezes accompanied the task.

Mark enjoyed stabbing scissors into the boxes with more force than was necessary, especially when it came time to flatten them for packing. Normally he'd be bored but he'd tuned the radio to Key 103. The music wasn't great but it made a change from the normal hushed tones of the office, and he got caught up in the great cardboard destruction event of 2000.

"Hello."

Mark stood up and stretched, surprised to see Dave and Ben looking shifty. Mark grunted.

"How you doing?" asked Ben. "Y'know, after the other day." His normal cocky pose had melted.

"Fine. What you doing in work?"

"We wanted to say we're sorry," Dave chipped in, hands in pockets. He didn't look comfortable either. "Went to your flat. Obviously you weren't there, that's why I texted. Why are you *here*?"

"Doesn't matter. So you came all the way to work? On a bank holiday?"

They both nodded.

"So – sorry for winding you up so much on Friday," Dave said. "I know there's a lot going on in your noggin. It's just our way, we don't mean anything by it."

"Yeah, we was out of order," added Ben. "Even though it was joshing, we took it too far. Sorry, mate."

"I wasn't bothered," said Mark.

Dave and Ben looked at each other.

Mark sighed. "Maybe a little then. Yeah, I'm sorry too, I suppose. I shouldn't have got so narked."

"Glad to see you're not blue," said Dave. "You seen Rene yet?"

He nodded.

"I hope she wasn't too heavy on you."

Mark sniggered; Dave and Ben realised why, joined in. It was enough. The ice was melted, and the water washed the slate clean.

Late afternoon. Sam nipped out for a fag, propping the fire door ajar with a brick and standing at the top of the rusting fire escape. She was tired. Had slept badly. She deserved her only vice. But as with all escapes it was over all too soon before she was caught again and forced back into Packham Prison. She crushed the dimp underfoot and re-entered the building.

As the door clunked behind her she noticed Mark was sat alone, hunched over something in the receipt and despatch area. The black Kangol contrasted with the white shirt which pulled taut against his back as he leaned forward, piles of post to each side of him. His body was lean and strong-looking.

What would it feel like to put her palms against his back?

"Hey you," she said.

He flinched slightly, closed something, but smiled when he saw it was her. "You made me jump."

"Guilty conscience?"

"No."

"What are you reading?"

"A book."

"About?"

"Anti-gravity. I can't put it down."

"And the truth?"

"It's something Rene ordered for herself."

Sam lifted it so she could see the cover. "A *management* book?"

He shrugged. "I don't want to be doing the post forever."

"Well … that's cool. Just surprised."

"You thought it would be a comic book?" He could have been joking, but she noticed a flash in his eyes. Pain or irritation, maybe.

"No. I could do with reading it myself. I haven't a clue half the time."

"Ah, you know this stuff."

"I wish." She handed it back.

"Really? You always seem in control of everything."

"You don't know me well do you?"

"A bit, maybe." He tipped his hat to her.

"Okay. A bit," she conceded.

Mark hesitated, looked at his phone again. *McDonald's.* He could turn right, then cut down Portland Street. Denny would probably want Mark to buy him a burger. Bollock him for not replying. Then smooth it over, move on, talk about what Mark should do for his family. It would only take a few minutes to get there. Mark glanced up that easy road, the one he'd taken so many times before. Pictured an impatient Denny staring at the door.

Just one step. A foot moves and you've made a decision, chosen which direction to fall in and gone partway down a road. Turning back gets less likely. Momentum keeps you going. A step to the right. To Denny. It would be so easy. One moment, balanced on a point.

Mark turned left instead.

He walked down the slope to Bridgewater Canal. There was a lock here; the water in the chamber between the gates was at its minimum level, revealing algae-covered walls. Under the low bridge. Mould and old spiderweb dangled in his face even though he ducked his head. He was now following the canal, running at 90 degrees to the main roads, below them in an echoing channel. A place to get away from people and be on his own. His space. A place where you're less likely to be spotted by angry brothers. It took him the way he wanted to go.

Be better.

Weeds and poppies grew between old stones on one side, dogdirt and broken glass punctuated the other. Despite the mess he found it peaceful down here. It was like an old and lost part of Manchester, undercity beneath bustling streets. History left to rot. Jagged bits of metal and pipes jutted out of walls, remnants of something practical, now just mysteries. Over the water he could see the remains of a building, with a new one being constructed nearby. New and old girders, steel frames, arches, pillars – you got that a lot in Manchester, seeing how things were made, the bones laid bare, skeletons out of the closet.

Pigeons strutted on the mossy ground. They took it easy. He needed to calm down too. He sat by a metal ring embedded in the stone, orange lichen spreading nearby, giving even the stone the appearance of rust. The whole city was slowly rotting away. He wiped his nose. He was part of it too.

Things slowed down. The dirty water was still. And for a minute he remembered another time. Same canal, but many years before.

It was night. Dark and cold. Streetlights reflected off the water. Mark shuddered, pulled his jacket tighter, but it was too thin to do much. Denny didn't seem to notice the cold though. Too tough for that. Denny was 18 to Mark's 12. Big brother. Denny wore his new tan Caterpillar boots, and stamped them occasionally, but it was an unconscious habit, not from the cold. Mark tried to control his traitorous shaking muscles.

"Fox," said Denny, pointing across the black water which resembled oil.

Mark squinted, thought he could see something skulking along the base of a wall.

"I like foxes. Are they related to dogs, or cats?"

"Related to mangy disease carriers," Denny said. "Kill 'em all. They're just animals." Denny took a swig from his bottle and lobbed it over the water. It shattered against the wall and the dark shape dashed off, leaving things emptier, both outside and within. Mark wished he'd been on his own, could have watched

the fox in peace, maybe shared a burger with it if he'd had one. But saying something to Denny would just make him worse.

"Dad gets out again next week," Denny told him.

"I know."

"He'll want to get the fuckers who grassed on him. Probably get me to help." A stamp of the feet again, possibly meaning something more ominous this time.

"Shouldn't Dad ignore them? He might get put in jail again."

"Fuck that. He's got to make a point. I'll tell you how I see it," Denny mused.

Mark nodded, encouraging his brother to carry on. He felt like a confidante when Denny started talking like that. Felt like a brother, even.

"There's us, and there's cunts," Denny continued. "A world full of 'em. Us against the cunts."

"'Us' is you, me and Dad?'"

"Yeah. It's a philosophy, and I've not even been to university. I call it the cunts' philosophy."

"What about any good people though? There must be some?"

Denny glared. "Some fucking chance."

A crazy trigger flipped in Mark's head, rebellion against the world being so bleak. He spoke without thinking it through. "What if it works both ways?" Mark ventured. "How do we know that it's not really us that's the … cunts?*" The word made his mouth feel dirty, like he'd drunk canal water.*

Denny eyeballed Mark with his coldest "You lookin' at me are yer?" stare, and Mark tensed himself in case Denny swung a fist at his head. Older brothers could be unpredictable.

"I hope you're not serious. Maybe you're half-serious. Maybe you're half a cunt yerself." Then he grinned, like he'd said something witty.

Denny looked across the water again. Mark joined him, in silence.

It was bound to stick in his mind. It was one of the last times Denny could walk properly. The next night Denny was critically ill in hospital, kicked to unconsciousness outside a nightclub over a girl, both his legs broken in multiple places. And after that he got worse.

You've got to make your peace and move on. Every action a decision. You have to get your priorities right, and the people you spend time with say something about you. Denny was still waiting. It wouldn't be too late.

Mark took out his phone, started typing a new text. Tap tap tap, each key pressed multiple times for a single letter.

```
Dave, u want to do somthin?
```

"I'm going to go now in a minute," Sam said, turning her PC off. She looked around the office. She hadn't noticed everyone else leaving too, caught up in drafting a summary report for Rene, but apparently there was only herself and Roger left.

The clock above the door to Rene's office said 6.17pm. That was why.

"Scoot your doogle," Roger said absent-mindedly.

"What?"

"Oh, scoot your doogle." He looked up. "Just something I used to say. Don't worry, it isn't anything rude, it just means to go away. I haven't said it for ages."

"Right. You're weird, Roger. But not totally detestable." She winked so he'd know she was joking. There would be a bus in fifteen minutes. Perfect timing. Then pop in to Unicorn Grocery to stock up. She loved the Unicorn ever since she discovered it: an all-veggie wholefood supermarket on her doorstep in Chorlton. Huge displays of seasonal fruit and veg that would be great to cook with if you didn't have a shared kitchen. So much healthy stuff to choose from. She usually just bought cakes and chocolate.

"Sam, do you fancy going for a drink?" Roger's voice was quieter than usual.

She bit her lip.

"Just as friends," he added hurriedly. Unconvincingly. "You know, owe me a favour."

"A favour?"

"Fixed your PC."

She gave him a weak smile and said, "Remember to fill in the statistics sheet before you go. Don't stay too late. There are no gold stars in this place."

"Yes. Yes, of course. I'll finish up soon."

the ONLY ONE i KNOW

...nt straight to #1 in the UK.

wasn't all smooth sailing though. The song was recorded in Wrexham, Wales, and was roblematic: there were arguments with the studio and equipment got smashed. The /elsh and Mancunians have long had a strained relationship. More trouble when Rob ...ho gave the band part of its signature sound with his Hammond organ, was charged with armed robbery in 1992 (eventually doing a short stint in prison – it turned out he hadn't robbed an off-licence, ...

... An...
...a drug user for a long time – the classic "How High" was one of the band's biggest funky hits.

None of this stopped the rise of The Charlatans. They supported Oasis i... 1996 at the Knebworth gigs, an...

216

1

Mark was on the early bus to work. He watched the same streets slide and judder by every day. The only thing that changed was the graffiti on the approach to Moss Side.

He checked his phone again. Still no reply to his most recent texts trying to confirm a meeting time, and Dave was off work today. Mark spent the distance between three bus stops typing in his great creation.

`knowing of you slovenly ways bet u still in bed`

This time there was a buzz of a reply only a few minutes later.

`Slovenly my arse. I wake up early, 2 hrs of hot lovin in bed, then ready for action.`

Mark: `u didn't say suzannah was away and u wos alone today?`

Dave: `Ha ha. Then it wouldve been three hours. Will visit you at 7.`

Dave: `You arse.`

Mark grinned, hunched over his phone, using the periphery of his vision to see if anyone was watching him, seeing how popular he was. He had a *friend* coming round after work. Things were looking up.

The end of May should be the time of cuckoospit and caterpillars, blue borage flowers and sun-basking hours. Sam couldn't stop to savour the sunshine today because she was walking at a sweat-generating pace to get to work on time, thanks to the GM bus breaking down three stops from the city centre. She'd worn Capri pants thinking they'd be cooler, but their tightness caused friction and more heat. She fantasised about a loose, floaty skirt.

Crowds of stiff-necked commuters fast-walking to boring destinations: filter this way and that, occasional shoulder barges received and lucky if you find it accompanied by a muttered, condensed apology; sometimes forced to step into the road, armpits and forehead hot.

She cut across the grass in the small park near Sackville Street, surprised to find it squelching under her black plastic sandals. Moments later an unseen sprinkler restarted with a putt and a hiss, lazy lines of water quickly soaking her feet. She sped up to get away from the rotating streams and slipped gracelessly, only just regained her balance, noticed some Chinese people on the corner who had stopped to point at her.

The rest of the way she had to cope with the yucky sensation of feet slipping around inside the sandals. Wet feet in a heatwave? Not as nice as it sounded.

In the toilets she used paper towels to dry her feet and discovered mud splashes on her ankles and grassy muck underneath. She rubbed grumpily and hurriedly with further damp towels then burst out of the toilet, not wanting another lecture from Rene about punctuality, feeling her shoulders tense up already.

"You don't look happy," Mark said. She hadn't noticed him as she rushed by because he was bent over. She stopped. Followed his gaze. He was staring intently at a cactus in a large pot that prevented a line of dusty lever-arch files from toppling over.

"No. A bit stressed."

"If it's about Rene then don't worry. She's not in. Got a meeting on the other side of town."

Sam's muscles relaxed a fraction. "Good. What are you doing?"

"Just trying to work out if this plant is dead." He nodded towards its place on the sun-bleached window ledge. "Does anyone water them?"

Sam tried not to laugh. The cactus was so shrivelled and dusty-brown that there couldn't possibly be any question of life remaining but Mark seemed serious. "I'd say that one was dead."

"But it's a cactus, innit? It should be happy with all the burning sun. With the dust it must be something like a desert so you'd think it would grow well. Like being home. Morocco or Saudi Arabia or somewhere. Everything wants to be reminded of home."

"I think it's *cooked.*" She prodded the spikes warily. "Maybe nothing can grow in this environment. The office, I mean."

Mark nodded, and seemed resigned to the fate of the spiky relic. He rubbed at the dirty glass, as if that would make a difference. "Hey, I know what might bring it to life. Music. The cactus and the heat makes me think Oasis. I'll sing it some B sides."

"That would be nice. Do that."

She turned to go, still smiling, and Mark sang after her, "Step outside, the summertime's in bloom."

Yes, it was. She shouldn't forget that. So easy to let life's little spikes get you down instead of seeing the big picture. Breathe. Take in the music and appreciate friends who can turn things round.

With Dave being on leave Mark had got the warehouse liaison jobs and pushed the book trolley down aisles centre-lined with faded black and yellow markings. He liked them. They made him think of the pillars in The Haçienda.

He liked being in the warehouse for other reasons too. It made a change from the monkey work upstairs, where there were always people watching you, gossiping, judging. And it was cooler and darker down here, as he navigated grey steel racks housing stacks of books, surrounded by piles of boxes and sacks of crinkling packing material. Under the high roof hung criss-cross bars supporting ventilation pipes and striplights. He only turned on a few lights, to keep it more mysterious. It was a spaceship full of books, and he was out of cryosleep for a while so he could catalogue them. Pick up a title, look at the cover, try and guess what it was about. Despite Dave's tough appearance he'd been to university to do psychology and was always reading books, some of which he "borrowed" from the warehouse. Maybe if Mark did the same he'd end up smart.

As he pushed the trolley he sang quietly to himself, words he made up and applied to a Charlatans tune.

"Everyone has read books before, anybody can turn the page."

Footsteps. He put a book back on the shelf and returned to his list guiltily, hoping they'd go away, not notice him. Possibly just a porter checking on things. He avoided making any noise but they got closer, came towards him down this aisle, approaching from behind.

"Mark, would you mind doing me a favour?"

He looked up from his inventory list then, straight into Sam's eyes. Warm brown, the colour of a chocolate bar melting in the sun.

"Sure." He popped his short biro pen behind his ear. Her eyes flicked to it for a second and he realised that it looked stupid. He hastily fumbled it into a pocket instead.

"We've been checking the stock of the remainder titles, and there's lots of dead wood Rene wants us to clear for the new books we'll need at the start of term. I've got a list here, would you mind going through it and making sure all the titles get recycled?"

Mark knew about the remainder books – they were normally sold for pennies to wholesalers when the publishers had overestimated demand. Sometimes even those cheap wholesalers weren't interested. Maybe it wasn't just Mark, and no one read enough books any more.

"No problem. How much is there to shift?"

"About thirty shelves' worth. Don't worry, I don't expect you to shift it all! You could get someone in House Services to help. I just wanted you to organise it, to make sure it gets done."

Wow. He didn't normally get asked to *organise* anything, let alone other staff. Maybe she hadn't realised he was just a chimp and it was only Dave who organised things? He wasn't going to put her straight on that.

"I'll make sure it's done. The recycling's the green skips in Receipt and Despatch?"

"Yes. At least that way they'll go on to be something new. Before I started here PG just used to pulp them! That's why I put the recycle bins in the staffroom, try and take things out of the stone ages."

Mark had noticed the new bins but not wondered what their function might be. He hadn't realised *Sam* had put them there. "So, you into this recycling stuff?"

"Yes, I hate waste. There's a landfill site back home, just mountains of junk. It breaks my heart, seeing it pile up like that, all thrown away, then it gets shoved in a hole like burying your shame. We do our bit and the bad kind of mountains are just a little bit smaller."

Her eyelashes seemed really long. Was that mascara? If so, how could black ink make them longer? The mysteries of women.

"You okay? Anyway, I'm sorry to pass on a shit job."

"It'll be great. Honest."

"What you were doing must have been boring if you think that!"

"It was. I'd do anything for a change."

She cocked her head to one side. "I was just thinking about the book you were looking at the other day. Rene does fuck all about upskilling most people here. But maybe … oh, I don't know, you might not want this." She looked at his face, expecting something. He smiled, showed his teeth, then stopped abruptly in case it scared her.

"But if you were interested," she continued, "maybe I could get her to let you shadow my team a bit, learn more about what we do? You might pick up some skills and if there's ever an opening, who knows?"

"You'd do that?"

"Don't seem so surprised, course I would. It's no biggie."

He couldn't stop grinning. He felt like Mark Collins must've, when he moved from being the Inspiral Carpets' van driver to being a key member of The Charlatans in '91. Having friends was good, and the day's beat was suddenly twice as funky.

It was grubby under the sink. Mark eyed up the dusty cobwebs slung between ancient cleaners and mysterious powders that were already there when he'd started renting the flat. With a sweep of his arm they clattered over to one side, previous locations marked with oval stains, and in their place he pushed a cardboard box. From his back pocket he took the marker pen he'd nicked from work. He wrote resycling on the lid, in his neatest handwriting, then started crushing empty beer cans and tossing them into the waiting maw. He'd found empties hidden all round the flat – behind chairs, on bookshelves, under the bed, in the bin, and even next to the toilet. As they rattled on top of each other he wondered if the box would be big enough. Old Mark just drank tinnies; New Mark recycled them.

"There are 24 beers in a case and 24 hours in a day for a reason," Dave had once joked. He'd probably nicked the quote from somewhere: he read so much you couldn't keep up, and a fair chunk of it seemed to get reprocessed as Dave's own wit. It just showed that everyone was into recycling. Mark was catching up.

Mark hummed happily and tackled the dirty dishes next. They'd built up into a tottering pile that looked ready to fall if he so much as sneezed near it. A sign to roll up his sleeves and get his hands clean. He took a wooden spoon and spun it in his hand, a rough-textured blur of revolutions: a treat for the spoon in reward for all its hard work stirring tins of food as they heated in the pan. Then he chucked it into the sink in a splash of suds. This Hopton would cease to be a slob.

He peeped out of his window nervously. No, it wasn't for him. It was Mandy, in leggings and trainers. He'd seen her going for a run other times; he was nearly late for his bus once as he waited for her to get out of sight before he left his flat. He didn't want to get burned again.

She bounced on the spot. Stretched each leg out in turn, heel on the railing in front of her. Then side bends. Then she rotated each foot. Finally she was off, bounding down the steps. He didn't get it, this exercise thing. If you were seen running on the estate where Mark grew up it was assumed you were chasing someone, or being chased. You didn't run for *fun*.

The place seemed too quiet. Mark realised there was no music coming from the flat above for once, so he put a tape into the aged hi-fi. It was one he'd compiled himself, old baggy hits that always chilled him out. Happy Mondays one side, Charlatans on the other. When he pressed play it was The Only One I Know. Mark toyed with the idea that the song was about having a best friend. Everybody needs one.

Next he tilted the white plastic garden chairs to shake crumbs off the seats, arranged them facing each other. Looked confrontational. Put them at 45 degrees to the TV. That was better. His throat felt dry. It was complicated having a friend around.

Mark was dusting with an old sock when there was a bang on the door.

"Make yourself at home," he said, letting Dave in.

"Ta."

"You found the place okay?"

"Course."

"Give me your jacket, I'll hang it up –"

"Stop acting like my mother!" said Dave, twitching away from Mark's outstretched hands.

"I wasn't going to let you suck my tit."

"Good one. For you."

Dave wandered off, exploring, occasionally nodding. Living room. Kitchen. Mark followed in silence.

"Not a bad pad," Dave commented, inspection over. "You're lucky, having a place to yourself,"

"Costs a bomb but I can play music whenever I want. And have friends round any time too."

Dave shook his head as he opened the fridge. "Got any beer?"

"I think there's a couple of cans in the bathroom."

"What?" A puzzled look on his bulldog face.

"I'd been experimenting with having a beer in the shower, y'know, like in adverts where a woman has a glass of wine in the bath. It says *luxury* to me."

"It says *loony* to me. Didn't you get water in the can? Shampoo?"

"It didn't work out like I planned."

"You'd never get away with that if you lived with a woman. Suzannah would go mental."

Mark took a box out of his carrier bag and unwrapped the cellophane. The box was quite pretty. "I didn't want a beer yet anyway. Going to have one of these fruit-tea things."

"Those are lady drinks!"

"I don't care. It's my flat and I'm gonna have one."

Dave took one out of the box. Each teabag was wrapped in its own paper pouch. "'Sweet Berry Swirl'? Where'd you get this crap from?"

"Health shop in the Arndale. They're supposed to be good for you."

"In what way?"

"I don't know, do I? You're the clever one. Prob'ly stop you turning into a fat wader, or have vitamin C in or something."

"Sam drinks these in work sometimes."

"Didn't notice." Mark looked away. "I assume you don't want one if you're just going to take the mick."

"I do want one. Never said I wouldn't." Dave was now looking through the cupboards.

"How long do you brew them for? Like tea? Hold on, the box says 'steep'. What's that? Does it mean leave in, or dangle?"

Dave laughed. "Leave it in, you dildo. For a few mins."

"Ah, like a pot noodle." Mark filled the kettle and switched it on, then lined up squeaky clean cups and spoons. "How's your dad?"

"A bit better after the last tests. Knowing helps. But there's other family stuff and … ah, never mind. Touchy subject. What about yours?"

"The usual."

"How long's he in for?"

"Five for GBH."

"Keeps him off your back a bit, anyway?"

Mark finished the teas, poured milk in. Then he looked at the resulting mess with disgust. "Oh bongos – I think the milk's off – it's all curdled. I'd best pop out and get more from the corner shop. What are you laughing at?"

"I see the fuck-up fairy has visited us again. You don't put milk in, you cock! They're *fruit* teas."

"It's all leaves, innit?"

"God, you Stretford tossers are like barbarians. Anyway, a man's got to do what a man's got to do. I'll go toilet while you brew new ones."

"Don't rush to flush."

"Huh?"

"Landlord's put the place on a water meter. If it's yellow, let it mellow. If it's brown, flush it down."

"What if a miracle happened and you brought a girl back?"

"I'd flush *then*. I'm not a skeg."

"Do you want another drink?" Emily asked.

"Nah. Trying to stick to the health and fitness thing"

Emily gave a sneer of distaste but said nothing.

The greater part of the crowd let out a roaring cheer – which quickly turned into a pained groan as David Beckham's free kick went wide, shown in full slow-mo glory on large TV screens.

Sam grinned.

Joshua Brooks wasn't Sam's favourite bar but it could be nice to sit outside by the river Medlock on hot evenings, despite occasional whiffs of sour gas from the water leading to wrinkled noses and accusatory glances. There was no way she'd be outside right now, though. Her order of priority in TV sport was:

- Watching Wales play rugby
- Watching England play rugby (in the hopes that they would lose at Wales' national game)
- Watching Wales play football

- Watching England play football (in the hopes that they would lose at their own poncy game)

This was the last category: England versus Ukraine in a friendly at Wembley. Seeing England get beaten before the start of Euro 2000 would be almost as good as seeing The Ospreys play live. Top nuts.

She was leaning against the bare brick walls at the back of the pub, behind the main crush of bodies, in her red and white rugby shirt with "Cymru" written in huge letters below the Welsh flag. Most of the crowd had white England football tops on. Emily didn't though – she was wearing a green halter top with a keyhole at the bust. As usual she had tied the straps behind the neck too tight, leaving little to the imagination. It was no wonder that Emily referred to it as one of her "all-time top tops". Even though Sam sported a Welsh dragon it was still Emily that got the most looks.

Further groans as Ukraine's continuous attacks gave way to an England goal attempt which failed miserably.

"You look like the Cheshire Cat," Emily said.

"I feel like it. I just wish Wales was touring this summer. Then I'd be teaching you the words to the Welsh national anthem after each game."

"Urgh, no thanks." Emily wrinkled her nose. "If I wanted to spit on everyone, I'd just do it."

It was so noisy that Sam only noticed her phone was ringing by the buzzy vibration. Uncle Joe.

"Hey, whatcha doing?" he asked. She had to put a hand over one ear to hear him properly.

"Hopefully watching the Saes getting beaten," she shouted. "Can't you hear all the moaning?"

"I just assumed you were at an orgy."

"Very funny."

"I thought they weren't touring until June?"

"It's football. Just a friendly."

"Sissy sport," he shouted back.

"What about you?"

"Just out with the lads. Thought I'd give you a ring."

"That's nice of you."

"And I was thinking … remember when I mentioned you working for me? I just wanted you to know it was genuine."

"You don't want me skivvying around."

"I wouldn't've said it if I didn't mean it. Business is really taking off."

"I don't want charity."

"It's not! You'd *manage* the shop."

She blinked. He *was* serious. "I've not done that before."

"Neither had I when I started. And I've not even been university. You're smart, it's just common sense, I'd show you how I do it. Order stock, some accounts, manage staff, persuade people to buy… What else? Advertising? Y'know: stuff."

"Anyone in Neath or Swansea can do that. You don't need me. That's what I meant about charity."

"I prefer family running things. Then I sleep well knowing I won't be ripped off, see? That's why Pred's on the case, and Stacey's part-time."

"What will you do if you run out of family to employ?"

"Keeps me awake at night, that. So if you won't work for me you'd better get busy, eh? Start a new generation."

"Fuck off!"

"Charming!"

"Look, I'll think about it, that's all."

"Just remember, it's only selling stuff. Which reminds me: this English fuckwit asked Tomos, right, swear to God, he told me last night. Asked him, 'Why are so many Welsh houses called *Ar Werth*?'"

"Ha ha. Look, it's hard to hear anything and Ukraine's in the box, I need to watch this!" she said excitedly.

"Okay, see you *cariad*. Think on it."

"Miss you all. *Hwyl*."

"Don't they ever stop ringing?" Emily asked as Sam slipped the phone into her bag.

"It's nice. Hold on, let me..." Sam threw a fist into the air, ignoring the angry glances. Then lowered it gloomily when the Ukrainian attack failed. There was still hope.

Dave leaned against the doorway. "Had to flush: turned out my arse wanted to go to splashville."

"I hope you didn't stink out my toilet," moaned Mark.

"I'd leave it a few minutes, mate. The stig was so big it made my bum bleed. I think that's what they call stigmata."

Mark glared at him; negativity ignored as Dave came over and tapped on the massive plywood cable spool that served as a coffee table. "Nice."

"Found it on a building site when I was drunk," Mark explained. "Wheeled it all the way home. It was a squashed banana to roll up the stairs. Anyway, got us KitKats when I bought the tea. Thought it'd be nice for dipping in."

"Maybe you do have some style after all," Dave said, kicking of his shoes and sitting, legs stretched out, drinks and chocolate on his lap. "Reminds me, Ben wants us to go out with him tomorrow for his birthday. Told me it'll be a combination of the bees knees and the dog's bollocks. What do you think?"

"That image'll be stuck in my mind forever. Thanks."

"Thing is, I don't know if I fancy going out until God-knows-when, hitting every pub in town then on to 42nd Street or 5th Avenue or whatever road the crazy fucker sees women heading down. It's getting to the point where I'd rather stay in and watch a film with Suzannah." He sipped his drink. "Don't tell anyone."

"Who would I tell?"

"Good point."

"You know Ben's motto – he isn't happy unless he has a smoke, a toke, and a poke."

"Talking of which: after your sterling performance last time, maybe you could give him a run for his money on the lady stakes? Up for a repeat?"

Mark groaned. "No women for me."

"Why? What happened?"

"It didn't work out, let's just drop it. My own touchy subject." Mark dipped a finger of his KitKat into the fruity tea. *Women.* Swirled it round lazily. *Best stick to friends.* Sucked on the softening stick, a new experience. *New friends.* Savoured the way it combined with the melting chocolate to make him think of Black Forest gateau. Sweetness. *Nice things*. "What if we invited other people from work?" he suggested innocently.

"Who?"

"Oh, I don't know. Maybe some girls, to calm things down. Sam and Emily are nice."

"Yeah, right! They – wait, do you fancy one of them?" Dave leaned forward, eyes sparkling with interest. "Which one? Oh, this should be a laugh for Ben!"

"No! I don't even know them properly, I was just throwing an idea out there, Ben said they've got boyfriends, out of my league anyway, just thinking of getting Ben to calm down, that's what we want, yeah? Forget inviting anyone, we'll just go out, the three of us. How's your drink?" Mark's palms felt sweaty, as if he'd nearly been hit by a tram.

"Not tried it yet." Dave sipped. Relief that Dave dropped the subject. Mark wouldn't be trying that approach again. Too stressful. "Fruity," Dave added. "A bit hot. I'll try it again when it cools. Then I'll be able to tell you if it has woody undertones, or the sharp, crisp bite of mountain berries."

"It's a fruit tea, not a wine."

"I know that, numbnuts. Jesus, I thought Ben was the only one who didn't comprehend satire." He sighed in mock-disgust and began looking through the stuff on the spool – mostly unopened letters and takeaway flyers that had been shoved through the letter box – while Mark inhaled steam that smelt of fruit. So different from what he'd been brought up on. There was new stuff all around you if you took the time to look; new opportunities down the road you never took, on the shelves you never looked at, in the people you never spoke to.

"What's this?" Dave asked, picking up The Book. "2000 Jokes? A kid's book?"

Mark leaned forward to take it off Dave but he was too slow; Dave snatched it out of reach, flicked through the pages.

"How old are you?" he asked Mark, shaking his head.

"Ah, it's nothing. I was going to get rid of it."

Dave read. Suddenly chuckled to himself. "A fish swims into a wall. Dam," he said aloud.

"Yeah, I like that one," said Mark.

"Conjunctivitis.com... Now that's a site for sore eyes. Oh, this tickles me: if a man is alone in the forest, without any women, is he still wrong?" Dave looked up over the cover, saw Mark's lips moving to the punchline. "You've read all these?" he asked.

Mark nodded.

Dave flicked to another page. "Dad says to his child, 'Son, if you don't stop masturbating you'll go blind.'" Dave waited.

Mark sighed, then: "The son shouted, 'Dad, I'm over here!'"

"What's blue and smells like red paint?" Dave asked.

"Blue paint."

Dave threw the book down. "Shit, you've got hidden talents. I wondered why you were wittier than usual."

"It's what I like reading."

"Fine." There was a weird look on Dave's face. Maybe a little sad.

"Hey, you hungry?" Mark asked. "I can do chips, peas and fish fingers in the microwave. Soggy, but doesn't take long."

"Urgh. Can't you make proper food?"

"It's all I know how to do," Mark said quietly.

"Fuck. There I go again, putting my big clodhoppers in it. Sorry. Your family should've taught you but I know what yours is like. Tell you what, I'll teach you to cook if I come again."

"Really? That'd be wonderwall! You could tell me what to get, I'd buy the stuff in."

"Yeah, we'll do that." Dave leaned forward, squeezed Mark's shoulder. It felt brotherly. But in a good way. "And I'm not hungry right now. But I see you've got a Playstation." Dave was pointing to the dusty gadget under the TV.

"Yeah, second-hand on the market. It works. I play it when I get in from work sometimes."

"What games have you got?"

"There's a scary one with big spiders in. Resident Evil, I think."

"Nah, don't want to play that. Zombies are rubbish, just one of them fads that'll blow over soon enough. But there used to be a game I liked which was a racing one, spaceships or something, with trippy music."

"Wipeout? I've got that. Bought it 'cos it included a Chemical Brothers song from Exit Planet Dust, it was the sec–"

"Cool! Have you got two controllers? We could play that."

Mark nodded, unravelled the game pads and plugged them in, handed one to Dave. "The triangle's worn off the button but it still works."

"This will bring back some memories. Hey, I meant to say, you seem a bit happier at the moment. Is it the new hat?"

Mark reached up, realised he still had it on, even indoors. He hardly took it off. He grinned. "Sort of." It was part of the truth, and that's enough.

He turned on the power. Bass notes came from the speaker as the red P logo filled the screen. The two of them moved to the edge of their seats. It was game on.

Typical. Bloody *typical.* Two nil to England. The beer left a bad taste in her mouth.

There were fewer people in the pub now but it was still noisy, so when her phone rang again Sam quickly made her way outside to the wooden balcony, squeezing past hot bodies that smelt of beer and sweat. Finally she leaned over the knobby metal railings above the treacle-black water, pleased to see it was Russell.

"Hey you," she smiled. "I was wondering if you would ring. Are you out in town?"

"Yeah."

"Whereabouts? Could we meet up later?"

"I'm not sure. I'm out with the lads from football, boys only."

"Damn. I would have liked to meet up with you. It'd be good to have something nice tonight."

"Sorry. Another night."

"What about coming back to mine when you've finished? I don't mind being *tired* in work tomorrow." Enough of a hint there.

A definite pause before he answered. "Can't."

"What's up?"

"Look, I don't know how to say this."

Her smile faded on hearing the Seven Deadly Words. Instincts clicked into place, small signs interpreted differently: now he seemed reserved, the conversation around him sounded like it included male and female voices. Suspicions rose with her hackles.

"Go on."

Background noise getting fainter. He was moving to a quieter corner. "I don't think it's working out is it? Not as a long term thing. You think the same, don't you?"

"I hadn't thought about it," she said flatly.

"Don't get me wrong, it's been fun," he said, sounding like he was smiling.

Smiling?

"You don't even have the courage to dump me to my face?" A woman to her right in a tight pink dress was also leaning over the balcony, and glanced at Sam. Sam turned her back. Russell didn't answer. A few thudding heartbeats and further suspicions pinged at her like pinpricks in her flesh. "Is there someone else?" she asked.

"Well..."

"That woman you were talking to on the phone when we last went out?"

A sigh. No smiling this time. "Yes."

"I should have known. I'm so fucking stupid. Just tell me this: were you two-timing me?"

"Oh Sam..."

"Just fucking tell me," she hissed.

"Well, I never said we were monogam– omin– well, just the two of us."

She hung up and gripped the phone tight, squeezing it like a throat. A momentary impulse to let it drop into the sludgy river 30 feet below; to let it sink into dark water as if she could drop Russell in there too.

But she didn't. It was new.

She jabbed at the number pad and called him back, teeth gritted.

It rang.

And rang.

He knew it was her.

End call. Try again.

Held to her ear, she ran through what she was going to say. Most of the words would be four letters.

He still didn't answer.

End call and jab jab jab again.

This time a message said he wasn't available.

The bastard.

Em was near the front door laughing and flirting with one of the bomber-jacketed bouncers. Sam fumbled in her bag, found a cigarette, and lit up with fingers that trembled with fist-hard anger. Puffed furiously, not enjoying any of it.

Eventually Em came over, impractical heels clicking on the wooden floor, and frowned when she saw Sam's expression.

"Who lit the fuse on your tampon?"

Sam's look must have said "I'm in no mood for jokes" with a growly undercurrent, because Em apologised and started again in a more concerned manner.

Sam told her exactly what the fucking matter was.

"The cowardly little bastard!" Em fumed. She pressed buttons on her own phone, held it to her ear. They'd moved to a table on the river-side terrace, the umbrella above still open from the heat of the day.

"No, don't ring him," Sam told her, but Em twisted away, kept her phone in a death grip. "He's not answering," she said. Then Em starting pressing keys again, furious jabs, apparently a message this time, before tossing the phone onto the table. "No one can text faster than a pissed off woman," Em muttered. Then her small fist banged onto the beer-damp surface, surprising Sam. "I'd kick him in the bollocks if he was here now! The little prick! Fucking you around! You! You're worth a hundred of him!"

"Thanks."

"I mean it. Shit!" Em shook her head in disbelief, then her eyes brightened and she tilted her face to one side slyly. "What we'll do is this: go over the road to 5th Avenue. Look for the most gorgeous hunk around, and fix you up."

"No. Just stop there. Fuck gorgeous hunks. I should have known Russell was too good-looking to be true."

"He has a weasel face."

"He does not! He has a model's face. The prick."

Em snatched up her phone again, started another text while mumbling, "Pig. Bastard. Cunt."

Sam watched. Something was sinking inside. "Wait – you've got his number in your phone?"

"So what?" Em's eyes gave nothing away.

"Why would you know his number?"

"I introduced you, remember?"

"But you have his number in your phone *now*."

"It's not so weird. I knew him first."

"How well did you know him?"

"Don't dig up bones, this isn't Time Team."

Em wasn't looking her in the eye.

Fucking great.

Sam looked around. Strangers. Aliens. It felt like she wasn't on firm ground any more.

Well, technically this was a balcony suspended over the river, but she didn't mean –

She put her face in her hands.

"Stop it!" said Em, trying to pull her hands away. "It was just once, a looong time before I introduced you. I swear on my life."

"I don't even care about that."

"Well stop letting him get to you!"

"It's not *just* that," said Sam, wiping her eyes.

Em shoved her drink in front of Sam. Something with a mixer. Who knew what it was? Sam downed it in one.

"Good girl," Em told her, moving round the table and throwing her arms round Sam's shoulders, hugging her tightly. "He's just a bloke. Wasn't even great in bed from what you said."

"And what you know," Sam muttered.

"It was before I even met you! That dick is no loss." Em wiggled her little finger obscenely in front of Sam's face. "I bet you had to ask, 'Is it in yet?' Hey, was that the start of a smile but you're trying to hide it?"

Sam shook her head, but Em wasn't giving in.

"The prick has lost a gorgeous woman. I bet the slapper he went with is a muffin top. Ooh, you're struggling not to grin. You know what, I heard she's got bingo wings too. Whereas you are *hot stuff.* I bet you used to have him gasping for breath in bed, repeating your name.

Of course, that just meant you didn't hold the pillow down on his weasel face for long enough."

Sam couldn't help it, a smile flickered in place of some of the anger. She hugged Emily's arms in return, and Em kissed the top of her head then lay her cheek there, holding Sam. They stayed like that for a while until Em said, "I'm getting us more drinks. It's what friends are for. We're going to get effing slaughtered."

get the message

a summer evening sound – the ... Bernard and Johnny mooning
und the Maldives – even if the song gets barbed later ("Hark the herald angels
ng"). Johnny told Melody Maker he nearly fell into a volcano during the shoot. A
taphor for how this song mixes reality into the beauty, hurt into the love. Danger in
most lovely of things.

...ns. ...

...ark, the reflection after the storm. Then the prog...med drums ...
in and slap you. Pressure, yes, but they deal with it easily. This is confidence: a polished,
flawless gem of a song that doesn't dull with time.

The song was recorded in Johnny Marr's Manchester home during that key year, 1990.
Get The Message was Johnny Marr's favourite Electronic song. No wonder Electronic's
first British gig was performing it in the Haçienda.

Th...

shedlo...
synthesizers, ...ers, drum... ...ines, ...
workstations, computers. It's that continuity and
eye for detail which distinguished Electronic from many of their peers. And the album
continued after Factory went bankrupt in 1992, reissued on another label. Not
everything was turned to ashes when the Factory burnt down.

Sam kept glancing at the glass of Rene's office. The meeting between Rene and one of the partners had been going on for over an hour. Hometime had come, Sam had not gone. A handy chance to finish the electronic orders without distractions, get to grips with the updated EDI system they were meant to use, to look good when asking Rene for favours; and to distract Sam from her banging hangover. All so good it must be right.

She had almost finished the task when he left, striding past in a suit and face that looked lived-in but with eyes that didn't light up, even when he gave her a formal smile.

Rene was already logging out of her PC, sweeping things into a bag, turning out her desk light. Sam hurried to the doorway, rapped on the frame.

"Hi Rene, was your meeting okay?"

"Not the best. But we do what we're told."

"I just wondered if I could have a minute before you go?"

"If it's really a minute, then yes." She was locking her filing cabinet and desk drawers. The only person who did that.

The office had a window on one side with the city classic view over a car park and some yellow rubbish skips. The other window, internal, looked onto the large open-plan office and processing section. It needed a clean. The stains on the glass made the office look worse than it was. Boss's view.

"It's just an idea I had. I was thinking about how people can gain skills, without costing us anything, and maybe be able to cover for each other better, which would make us more…" Sam racked her brain, buzzword please, and it came. "Agile."

Rene put the bag down and flopped into her chair. "You've got my interest. One minute."

"Great. Well, I was thinking about how people could sit in on other teams, learn more about what they do."

"I'm not convinced. Who? What? It needs detail."

"Okay, just an example off the top of my head: Mark could shadow my team. Experience of higher level work would be good for him. He's got promise, and it would help us out, farm off a bit of the work so we can get on top of things. It's a win-win."

"None of those are compelling."

"Why?"

"One. Your team is overstaffed. I don't want *more* people doing that job. Two. He's in my bad books, written in bold. So not good reasons."

"How about 'being nice' as a reason?"

Rene snorted, stood, picked up her bag, moved towards the doorway which Sam currently blocked.

"Oh come on, we've got lots of good workers, and he's one of them, he –"

"We've got to lose some people to keep the rest. It's hardly a time to be bothered by more training. Hardly a time for jobs to be left undone. No. Ask me in six months if we're still here." Rene brushed past Sam, forcing her back from the doorway which wasn't wide enough for both of them. "And lock up when you leave."

It was like walking into a brick wall; like having a conversation with someone who didn't speak English. Sam hit the back of her head against the frame twice, rattled her brain. It didn't help. She felt like crying. Like a kid. It was stupid. She never used to get so upset by Rene's obtuseness. By anything, really.

Maybe it was because this time it was about someone else.

She grabbed her coat and left, slamming the doors as hard as she could.

Sam used her foot to push the bedroom door open, arms full with her day bag, a wad of junkmail and bills, and a binbag of clothes she'd left in the bathroom for washing but which Leigh or Robin had taken offence at and dumped outside her room. Threw the stuff onto her bed. Shoes off. Heard her flatmates laughing in the kitchen. One of them sounded like a donkey braying. She realised that in her angry rush home she'd forgotten to buy anything for her evening meal. She really should do the clothes wash too, but suspected she was out of laundry liquid. And there was a precarious pile of ironing from last time that still needed some *smoothio* action. As she moved round to pick it up she yelped, grabbed her foot and hugged it, hopping to the bed with tears of pain. It was one of the plugs that lay face up and partially hidden: she'd trodden on the prongs with all her weight, and it hurt like hell. She rubbed the sole of her foot and cursed until it stopped throbbing.

The room was a mess. Never enough space to put anything in this poxy hole. That's another thing that could do with tidying. An evening's worth of jobs. Best get started, eh?

She seized the phone, texted. When the reply came she made a call, locked her room and limped out, waiting for the taxi to Emily's.

Evening at the Thirsty Scholar, a little pub with a big character built under the railway arches off Oxford Road. Trains occasionally rumbled overhead and buses hiss-farted past on the busy main road. Mark came for the music which was live a few nights a week; Dave went for the real ale; Ben for the women. Tonight they sat on the drinking terrace under the arch. It was marginally cooler here, as a pitiful breeze filtered past.

"I saw you before, you dirty dog," Dave said to Mark, while Ben was smoking on the wooden railing.

"What you on about?" Mark asked.

"That woman you escorted over from All Saints. Don't play innocent, she was sexy in that skirt suit. A classy older lady."

"The acquisitions librarian from Man Met? I was just showing her over because Rene told me to."

"Since when did people have trouble finding our place?"

"I dunno. Maybe it was Rene giving me more responsibility. To test me."

Dave burst out laughing.

"Don't big it up, Dave," Mark said, grumpily. "And don't blame me, blame Sam."

"Sam?" Dave raised an eyebrow.

"I mean Rene."

"Wow. Freudian Slip."

"Froydian Slip?"

"Yep. When you say the wrong thing, but it's really what was in your subconscious and it gives itself away. So it's like the truth."

"Dave, you may be clever, but it's *you* who's always so obsessed, thinkin' everyone else fancies each other; it's just your dirty little mind seeing sleaze where it isn't."

Dave applauded. "Bravo, it bites! Encore! Anyway, glasses are empty lads."

Mark knew it was his turn anyway so dug through his pockets for a note or handful of coins, when Dave interrupted him, said, "You know I'm just winding you up, eh?"

"Yeah, I know that," Mark replied with a smile. "Still, it's nice that you checked. You never used to."

"No worries. I don't want people misunderstanding me. Especially not a sensitive soul like yerself. Though talkin' of misunderstandings, I saw that fucking nonce Alex again last night."

"What's he done this time?" asked Ben, rolling up another cigarette. Dave liked to tell tales about his future cousin-in-law.

"I started on some subject – some erudite observation, obviously – and the fucker doesn't get it. It's like he can't have a normal conversation with a bloke. He's up his own arse." A shudder. "Honestly, five minutes with him is worse than having teeth pulled."

"Why does Suzannah leave you with him then?" Mark asked.

"Well, his family all love him, even though they know he's a boring twat. Problem is, as soon as I say he's a mummy's boy, Suzannah jumps in to defend him. Typical family, sheltering the hopeless. I'm not surprised he's got no girlfriend. He's so uptight. Shit, you should see the hot girl living in his house though – Natalie, a right little minx. I swear she was givin' me the eye – stop smirkin'! Bet she'd be really slutty in bed too."

"Did you tell Suzannah that?" asked Mark, stretching his legs out.

"I'm just saying I reckon she knows the score, whereas that Alex hasn't a foo-kin clue. She could probably walk up to him with her jubblies out and he'd just talk about Star Trek or something. God, I won't really be able to marry Suzannah, just can't face having super-dork for a relative. Stop laughin' you guys."

Mark checked that Ben and Dave were still outside then ordered a pint of beer, a Metz, and a shandy. The last was for himself. He'd say it was foreign lager if they asked. He'd seen a programme on the telly which compared the UK with other countries in Europe. Here, everything revolved around alcohol; there, it was cafes, talking, and people spent time with each other without getting wasted. Mark had turned it off but could imagine the BBC's conclusion: we were a nation of pissheads. So he decided to cut down or water down. He was going *continental.*

While the barwoman sorted out the drinks Mark noticed he was being watched. By the cook. He was leaning against the wall at the gap in the bar that led to the kitchens, had his arms folded, wore an electric-blue short-sleeved shirt. Maybe he was waiting for food orders, but he was definitely giving Mark a funny look.

Then he snapped his fingers. "I know you! You're that guy who had an argument during the quiz, couple of weeks ago."

The cook had him bang to rights. Mark had felt down so came out on his own for the music quiz, drank a few too many, and when there'd been a question about the bands Bernard Sumner had played in Mark had stood up and argued with the results. They'd missed out the pre-Joy Division name Warsaw. At the time he'd felt righteous. Now he was nearly sober and his behaviour seemed nobbish. "Yeah. Sorry about that. I hate it when people get facts wrong."

"Don't apologise, it was funny. Anyone with an obsession, puts time into it, brilliant. I'm impressed with that. Your team beat mine. You should've won."

"I was a team of one. Lowered my chances a bit."

"I thought you were with someone? Sure I saw you talking."

"No. On my own."

"Oh. Anyway, what's your name?"

"Mark Hopton."

"I'm Martin the Mod."

"Why you called that?"

"I'm mates with the scooter crowd, aren't I?" Martin reached into his shirt pocket, took out some Blues Brothers shades, slipped them on and made a "Ta-da!" gesture with his hands before returning the sunglasses to his pocket. "I got the Martin the Mod nickname off a girl on the bus, 1980s. And I DJ."

"I thought you were the cook?"

"Let these words sink in: *you can be more than one thing.*" The last words were said slowly, as if to a kid.

"Well, I know *that.*"

"I sometimes DJ here. Did the first night when the Scholar opened in '92. I DJ at Band On The Wall as well. So not just the chef at both places. But we all need a fuckin' day job."

"Wow." Mark paid for the drinks but didn't walk off with them. Now that he thought of it, Martin resembled Bernard Sumner – similar age, dark intense eyes, his way of speaking and accent, his nose. Except Martin was a bit craggier, with a chipped tooth.

"Was DJing last night." Martin held his head, forced his hair up into spikes. "Heavy night," he said, with bleary eyes.

"What's a mod?"

"Fuck off."

"I don't know!"

"A music scene."

"What, modern stuff? Like Oasis?"

"Oasis are over-rated. I play northern soul, mostly."

"What's that?"

"You fuckin' talk the talk but you don't really know about music do you? Or you wouldn't be mitherin' me."

"I do know about music. The types I'm into."

"Which is?"

"Indie. Madchester. Baggy."

"Oh. The regulars. *Boring.* That was only – what? – six bands, one summer? So you DJ, do a Manchester night: once you've played three or four tracks from each that's it, you're fucked."

"That's not true!"

"I get it all the time, mate. 'Oy, Martin, put us on some Stone Roses.' 'See that?' I tell them. 'Big doors, left, right and centre'." He gestured with his hands. "'Fuck off. I play original stuff, not well-known crap. Don't like it, don't come in.' I chuck 'em out myself, the bunch of numpties, I'm not fuckin' bothered."

Okay, maybe a bit more sweary than Bernard Sumner. Street Sumner.

"Well-known *crap*?"

"People have this myth of it but they were just all out of their heads for two years. Then it all fucked up, apart from the Inspirals."

"No! It's all going on still. And Joy Division were getting together in the 70s, that's not two years!"

"Maybe. But it's still only a hint of what goes on. Don't get so red in the face, just 'cos it's not my cup of tea."

"You shouldn't say stuff when you don't know about it!"

"Don't know? I used to knock about with Martin, the bassist from The Charlatans. And he was a mod. Bet you didn't know that? A mod from Dudley." Martin gesticulated as he talked, cutting up concepts with palm chops. "And I've DJd at Band On The Wall since the 80s, done that for *three decades*. I'm the longest running Wall DJ. And my band's played there and other places since we got together in '95. We 'ad a really good, powerful sound. Saturday soul and blues night. Friday too, sometimes. In the olden days you got off your head just from audience's spliffs on a Friday, you'd be fuckin' trollied at the end of the night."

"You're in a band too?"

"So I know nowt, eh?"

Mark chewed his cheek. "Alright. Wrong words. But I don't like it when people diss my music."

"I can see you're well into it. We all listen to what we listen to. But you really should learn more about where it all comes from if you're into Manchester music. I mean: northern soul! There's a whole history just there! It was invented in Manchester at The Twisted Wheel. You had massive global bands like The Hollies. That stuff *ruled the world*, 60s on. And the music was all connected to the city. It all comes down to northern soul anyway. All of 'em. Happy Mondays, Oasis, it all ties back. That's where you should look. Go north, find the soul."

This could be big. As if he'd climbed the last block of flats, stood on the roof to finally comprehend the whole city, then realised there were other tower blocks, bigger ones he'd not known existed, stretching off across the flat grey horizon, cornered by roads that lived in the shadows. He needed a new compass. Work to do. "I thought I'd gone back all the way already."

"You thought wrong then."

"It's a whole new thing for me to look into."

"Course. You've got to go back to causes, foundations. Then you understand something properly. Northern soul was the start of it. Like Band On The Wall. Long history. They've had music there since the '30s, always an important live venue. Soulfinger were a regular local northern soul band, they played live in Manchester once or twice a week for *years*. Their keyboardist was in my band for a bit, she was a crackin' player. I know 'em all there. The soundie, he's a mate o' mine. Monksie. You see him in here of a Saturday. He's got great ears for tone. They've always had a good sound system there but it's not ideally placed – to the side under the stairs. Monksie has to do the stage sound then go back and twiddle, put up with everyone peckin' his 'ed while he's workin'. Good place. You should come over early doors when it's quiet."

"That'd be cool. Can I get you a drink? I'd like to know more about all this."

"Best not. Been overdoing it for a while." He blew his nose on a black and white checked hankie. "For about 30 years." He nodded at Mark's drinks. "You too, by the looks of it."

"I'm not a scholar but I sure am thirsty."

"Hey, Martin, order," the barwoman said.

"Give it us," he replied, holding out his hand to take the slip of paper. "Dragged back to work," he told Mark. "I'll catch you again. You'll find your way."

"I hope so," Mark said, as Martin headed into the kitchen squinting at the order.

Back outside. More glasses and bottles on the table, though Ben was off chatting to a group of laughing girls nearby.

"Took your time. Stop off for a shit did ya?" Dave asked.

"No, just got chatting to someone about music."

"Surprised you could tear yourself away."

As Mark sat the place vibrated from a train passing overhead. He could feel the motion in his arse as it pressed on the seat, thumps reverberating through the floor, like a bass drum from a god, just saying "Hey guys, I know you're there, dig this". Trains. Such a cool idea. He wished he'd been on one.

His nose was tickling again. Mark had a pocketful of toilet paper he'd collected on his last trip to the bog, gave it a good blow.

"Don't let a girl catch you looking into the hankie afterwards," Dave warned him.

Mark scrunched the tissues up, put them back in his pocket, embarrassed.

"Just saying it as a tip," Dave added, kindly.

"You're right though. Trampy, innit?"

"You subconscious probably wonders what shapes it makes. Snot Rorschach."

"What's that?"

"A psychology test. You see shapes in inkblots. What do you see?"

"I see angels sometimes."

They both laughed. "Bet you do. What about the future? Can you read your snot like tea leaves?"

"Yeah. It said I'm gonna get a promotion."

"No chance. Redundancy, more like." Dave seemed serious all of a sudden.

"What do you mean? I apologised to Rene. I'll be okay as long as I keep my nose clean."

Dave ignored the lead-in. "Come on, you must've heard the rumours? Haven't you been following it in the Manchester Evening News?"

"No. I don't read the MEN. Just NME."

"Our place is going to the dogs. The company that owns us is in trouble and will probably sell off sub-companies to stay afloat. Or might just go under."

"I didn't know that."

"You would if you stepped outside your obsessions once in a while. I'd keep an eye open for other jobs. *I* do. That's another tip."

Sugar. Mark thought companies like that stayed round – they seemed solid, cemented into the city's business, nothing had changed there for donkey's years. It was scary to think it might. Twice in one night he'd discovered his beliefs were only fragments of a story.

"Maybe I could be self-employed? Do something like that?"

"You!" Dave laughed. "No offence mate, but you've not got the nous. You'd be selling second-hand dildos on a market stall."

"We could team up: you, me, Ben. You could be the business guy. Ben the smooth seller."

"And you?"

Mark realised he had no answer, hadn't taken the thought that far. Luckily Ben returned.

"She said she's a Breton." Ben indicated one of the girls in the group he'd left. It was getting dark now, streetlights kicking in and the crowd growing thicker.

"What's that?" asked Mark, only half paying attention as he still wondered about what he'd contribute the company he imagined them making.

"It mean's she's from Brittany," said Dave sagely.

"Yeah, she's foreign," Ben confirmed.

"Don't mess with her then, Mr Smoothie."

"Why not?"

"Everyone knows they're dangerous with weapons. Part of their national service. They specialise in fighting with long stabbing implements." Dave took a swig of his beer, managed to surreptitiously wink at Mark.

"Really? I hadn't heard that," Ben said.

"Course. There's lots of things you don't know about. Haven't you ever heard of the Brittany Spears unit?"

"No. Why's Mark laughing? Oh..."

"Stab me baby, one more time." Dave sniggered while acting out a spearing motion.

"Yes, very funny, Dave. You keep making the sad jokes, and I'll keep chatting to the gorgeous European women." Ben sauntered back over to the girls' table.

"Gotta say this. Never let a man rule your life. Someone walks over you, it's 'cos you're acting like a doormat." Emily wagged a slender finger, long nail painted in a pink that almost matched the colour of the bold lettering on her T-shirt:

You say I'm a

FREAK

like it's a bad thing

They were sat on the floor, leaning back against the sofa.

"Not everyone's like you, Em. Super-powered."

"You've just gotta tell yourself this: no one can make you do anything. You rule the world. Girls do." Pause. "Of course, I'm the *leader*. But men in general are pathetic, just dangle bits and hangups. Silly to waste thought on any that aren't worth it."

Em passed the bottle of vodka back to Sam, and she took a swig, enjoying the way the room shifted in the aftermath. It was the only drink Emily had in, and neither could be bothered going out for anything different. Without a mixer the first swigs tasted foul, but you soon got used to it. They were down to the last quarter.

"Amen," said Sam.

"You okay? Your head swayed."

"No it didn't. It's your eyes. You're pissed."

Emily snatched the bottle and took a double gulp before returning it.

Sam downed the rest. "That was harsh. On my throat," she said hoarsely.

"Feel good now though?"

"Better than I did before. You're a lifesaver."

"Yeah, I know. Mother Theresa. I'll throw some lasagnes in the oven. Even got a veggie one for you. Hey, fancy something else, go wild with a proper pick-me-up?"

"What you got?"

"A bit of coke. Not much, but enough for a couple of lines each. No fun on my own."

"Is it like speed?"

"Better. It's all natural. Makes you confident, calm, a bit horny. Not really any comedown, and doesn't interfere with sleep."

Sam must have looked dubious, because Em added: "Everyone should do it, at least once. Otherwise how do you know it isn't for you?"

"I suppose."

"Honestly. Draw can be worse. Ever seen a newbie having a whiteout? Pukers."

"Fuck it. Why not."

Em got up, straightened the short skirt that had ridden almost up to her arse. While she was out of the room Sam headed to the hi-fi, a slight wobble to her steps, and pressed play. George Michael erupted from the speakers. "Thank you for the music," she muttered.

Phone buzz. A text. Her Mam.

`Hope your well. Nice flowers in Mamgu's back garden right now. Lots of privacy.`

Em returned with a bag and a spatula. Sam raised an eyebrow.

"I keep drugs in the kitchen."

"Yes, but a spatula?"

"Is that what it is? I just use it to cut coke."

Em tipped the contents of a folded paper envelope onto the glass table top. Yellowish grains, like ground almonds. She used the spatula to crush lumps to powder; then wielded the shovel end with fine control to split it into four lines. Two small lines for Sam, each the length of half her thumb, albino cabbage caterpillars. Em's were bigger. She took a small plastic tube, like a straw – "I don't use rolled-up money, it's dirty" – and she snorted a line up each nostril. Tilted her head back, took deeper sniffs. Handed the tube to Sam.

"Just copy what I did. Sniff it all up, breathe out through your mouth, careful. Don't sneeze, for Christ's sake. Child's play."

Sam eyed it nervously. Moistened a fingertip and dabbed a few grains. It was bitter, like speed.

"It's okay. As long as you aren't psychotic, have high blood pressure, or heart problems, you'll be fine."

"Heart like an ox."

"Sweet. Don't worry, I'll look after you." Em was looking up at the ceiling. "Always," she added, quieter.

Sam did her best to follow the instructions. She didn't quite manage to inhale it all first time. There was burning in her nostril. She did better on the other side. In fact, it was easier to hoover up than she expected. Still not as tidy as Em though: orphaned crumbs littered a few inches of tabletop. Mild burning on both sides now.

"There you go. Like a rock star." Em dabbed the rest on her finger and sucked it.

Sam nodded. Chemical smell, like dentists.

"How you feel?"

"Not sure. Same. No, a bit different. A bit shaky."

"It won't blow you away, you've not had enough. Play it safe first time. But if you do more it tips over into something euphoric. Then you get it."

"Get what?"

"Get cocaine. As in, understand it."

"Oh."

"First time is like shaking hands. Some contact, reassuring. Next time you get a hug. After that you get a snog, then a fuck. After that: always a fuck. Like anything, it gets better with practice."

"If there is a next time."

Em gave her a sidelong glance, smirked, rubbed a finger across Sam's nostrils. "Powder," she explained.

"Nice." Sam swallowed. "Hey, back of my tongue is going numb. Slight burn. Throat too."

"Relax and let it kick in."

A muscle in her cheek twitched. She moved her head, her neck felt more oiled, looser. She gulped. "Should I swallow so much?"

"If you want."

"Feels like my ears are popping. Like when you go in the Channel Tunnel."

"Wouldn't know." Em lay back, relaxed.

"I feel alright." Sniff.

"Good."

"Kinda numb."

"Good."

Sam looked round. The room moved slightly faster than her head. Running, like her nose. She kept sniffing. The burn at the back of her throat wasn't unpleasant, just weird. She hummed, start of a song. Sounded nice in her ears. "Hear that?" she asked.

"Uh-huh. Pretty."

Thumb and forefinger to nostrils. Sniff. "Like meditating."

"Wouldn't know that either."

"I was nervous but feel fine now. Just buzz." Sam looked at the clock. Felt her heart. All was normal. "Not bad, am I?"

"No. An angel."

"Feels naughtier than E. Or speed. Don't know why."

"Nothing's naughty."

"I can imagine that now."

"Not if it feels good."

Instinctive snort, then little crystals and liquid on the back of her tongue. "Urgh. I think I just got stuff from my nose in my mouth," she said.

"Everything's connected."

"Do you swallow it?"

"Yeah. Don't waste it. I always swallow if it's good stuff."

A look and they both started laughing, chest vibrations going on past what was normal and eyes needing wiping. "Don't, I'll piss myself," Sam said.

"Do it if it makes you feel good. I'll mop it up tomorrow." That just set them off again.

"Nose stuff is gross."

"Life. Bodies. Just chemicals."

Sam swallowed. It wasn't so bad. "You trying to be wise?"

"I am. Wise. Always listen to me."

"I do."

"I'm talking shit. It kicks in."

Hand on chest. "My heart is beating faster."

"Let's see." Em put her hand just above Sam's left breast. "Nah. Slow."

"Feels fast."

"Perceptions faster."

"Oh."

"Talking faster."

"Am I?"

"Yeah. Let's look at your eyes." Em leaned in. "Pupils bigger. Huh, what big eyes you have, Mrs Wolf."

"Yours too."

"Not as dark as yours I bet. So pretty."

"I feel like writing poetry."

"Nutcase."

Sam scrabbled in her bag. Took out an address book with a narrow pencil sheathed in the spine. Wrote on a blank page. "My writing's wobbly," she muttered.

No answer.

Sniff sniff. Bodies leak.

Springy spring leeks.

On Cadair I'm a poet.

Em looked over her shoulder.

"Cadair's a chair," Sam explained. "But I mean Cadair Idris. If you stay there all night –" but Em closed her eyes.

I sit to seek.

One place. In one. But not part of it.

To seek is to wander.

To wander is to return.

Oh shit. I will never win the Eisteddfod.

Sam dropped the pad, closed her eyes too, but didn't feel stable. Sniff. Swallow. Heartbeat. Repeat. Not so bad. She patted Em's head like a cat. Not tired, nice just sitting there. Not bad. Dentists with no drilling. Doctors with no waiting. Pressure in head with no headache. Sniff with no cold. Burn with no fire. Life was not so bad. Just float in the boat.

"My teeth ache a bit," Sam said.

"Yeah?"

"Or maybe my jaw. It feels swollen."

"All the fucking talking."

For some reason that made Sam crack up again. She crawled out of the room, too dizzy and full of mirth to stand. In the bathroom she blew her nose and examined it. Expected something like white powder or frothy saliva. But no. Just wet. No signs. The difference was all inside.

Despite only supping sweet shandies Mark'd had enough to drink. There was talk of going on to a club, in which case he decided to switch to water. He'd never been in a club without drinking booze before. It was an exciting prospect. Appreciate anything good in the music, and avoid making stupid mistakes. Plus he liked the idea of waking up without a furry mouth.

He also realised it was fun just to watch people. It seemed different when he wasn't drunk. Like he noticed more. Understood more. He observed the groups on the nearby tables. Nods and arm waves. People point and look, smile, hunch forward to hear. He realised it was all about humour. Smile, smile, smile, laugh, ba ba ba DUM, a pattern of music that repeats. A beat of human communication. A social pattern, everyone was aiming at it, making music together, a group thing. And the cymbal clash of a laugh was the happy affirmation of life that keeps us going. We recount jokes, tell tales with punchlines, mix words to startle; we need the reaction as much as we want to create it in others. And the music over the speakers mixed in, just an external beat to time ourselves with. But it comes down to communication that's in tune. How could he not have realised that before? Without being in tune you just have noise, and that's got no value.

He was vaguely aware of someone leaning on the wooden balustrade nearby, but didn't pay any attention until Dave went quiet and nodded. Mark turned to see his older brother's unshaven face and long dark hair. Denny was resting his chin on crossed forearms. The zip-up top he wore had burn holes near the cuffs.

"Hi, Denny." Mark had been resting his feet up on the corner of the table. He lowered them.

"How you doin', our kid?" Denny limped over, yanked out a chair and flopped onto it. "This yours?" he asked, taking Mark's glass. Mark nodded; Denny finished it off, before grimacing. "Gnat's piss. That's not proper beer, you puff! You, Mark's mate, give us a swig of yours."

"Go wild," said Dave, pushing the rest of his pint towards Denny warily.

"Got any cigs?" Denny asked them both. They shook their heads.

"How come you're here?" asked Mark.

"Charmin' way to greet me, eh?" Denny asked Dave, gesturing towards Mark with a disdainful and grubby thumb. "Came looking for you," he told Mark. "I kept texting you. Ringing you. Nowt. Changed your number or something?"

"Yeah, recently. The old phone fell out of my pocket and got ran over. I'll need to get a new one. New SIM too. I'll give you the number when I get it. This weekend."

"Right. Well I assumed you'd be getting pissed in a bar somewhere in town. Thought I'd try a few, perhaps get to trade. People are hungry tonight, you know what I mean?" Denny fiddled with his gold hoop ear-ring while he spoke. He was always one to fidget. Had to be doing something with his hands. "Where's your mate, the blackie?"

"His name's Ben."

"Yeah. Ben *Der.*" Denny squinted around, spotted Ben, and seemed smugly satisfied. "Chatting up white women. Typical."

Dave glared at Denny and he noticed.

"Look, you – what's your name?"

"Dave."

"Right. Dave. Do us a favour, fuck off out of my face and give us a few minutes will you? Family business to discuss."

"I'm not leaving Mark. He's my mate."

"You *are* leaving, son, and don't be looking at me with –"

"It's okay, Dave, just give us a few minutes," Mark interrupted, because Denny's voice had been going up a pitch and that was always bad. "Honestly, it's fine. Check up on Ben."

Dave looked from one to the other, then scraped his chair back and headed off to the bar with a glare at Denny.

"How are things with you, little bro?"

"Okay. Work's boring, but that's usual."

"Mug's game, nine-to-five for shit diddly. You always were a sap."

"What are you doing then? Dealing?"

"I've actually got a bit of a job. At a recycling centre. Get to swipe things, personal details, letters, bank statements. I've got some contacts who buy them, bit of extra cash for me, and keeps parole off my back."

"So you're working too," Mark said, with a touch of sarcasm Denny didn't expect so didn't hear.

"And what do you know, we've got something in common! Just like family should. Cosy." Denny leaned towards Mark. "Talking of family, what's this Dad says? You won't help him out with a little thing he wants? You trying to disappoint both of us?"

"No, but I'm not risking going inside. I haven't got much, and I want to keep it."

"Oh yeah?" Denny reached over, snatched the hat off Mark's head. "Shaved your head? Ha ha, Mark's gone skinhead! Yeah, that's good."

Mark tried to grab his hat back but Denny held it out of reach, then jammed it down on his own greasy hair, leaned back, swatted Mark's arm away when he tried again. Mark gave up, crossed his arms, scowled at Denny, thinking angry thoughts so he wouldn't get upset, but this was just like when he was a kid. Denny did this, always did this, dragged the past with him wherever he went, and you couldn't escape the weight of it.

"You've got nothing, Mark. And anyway, there's no risk, unless *you* fuck up. The contacts will hook you up with something foolproof so even you can do it. All you'd have to do is visit Dad and avoid shitting in your pants." Denny grinned, some joke Mark didn't understand. "Even you can do that."

"Why can't you do it?"

"Because if I get caught then I'm back in the fucking nick!" Denny jabbed a forefinger against Mark's forehead. "Use your brains."

"I *am* using my brains. That's why I don't want to be involved."

"I don't care what you want, you selfish shit. This is about *family*." Denny folded his arms, squinted at Mark, seemed to be weighing something up. "I didn't want to tell you, but Dad's not top dog, and he's got to do this. Made promises, got debts. This gets him in the clear. He wouldn't want to tell you that, 'cos he won't ever do the sympathy thing, but even if you don't care about family, *I* do. He has to do it or he's in trouble."

"What trouble?"

"This'd be a slashing at least. Maybe they'd get him in other ways. I know how these people work. Even in prison it's easy to boil up a tub of butter and throw it in someone's face. Mark them, show they can't be trusted. You wouldn't put Dad at risk of that, would you? Leave him to face the shit from people who step on you again and again until you're crushed?"

"I don't want that. I don't want anything!"

Denny sniffed impatiently. Looked around. Two women in low-cut tops on the next table had glanced over at the raised voices. Denny grabbed his crotch, asked the blonde, "Are you after this, eh?"

"Don't crack on to the 'edcase," her friend told her.

"Oh great, fucking scouse cunts!" he shouted. "Wouldn't fuck your sort with a barge pole!"

"Denny!" Mark said, trying to get his attention, distract him before things got too wild.

Denny turned back to him. "So you'll do it?"

"No … I don't know." Mark was glad to see the two women take their drinks and move to another table rather than argue back. Small mercies. "I didn't get into this, why do I have to do stuff?"

"Family. Say yes."

"I don't know."

"Say yes."

"I'll think about it."

"No, you'll say yes, and you'll follow through. You'll say yes. Say it now. Say yes."

Two boys arguing, the bigger one gets his way. The money. The sweets. The things you don't want to do. The big one *always* gets his way. Boys, men, anywhere. It was the way it was. And it wasn't *fair*.

"I'm not doing it, Denny, and that's that!" Mark shouted, surprising himself and the people around him.

"Oh, you will." Denny's voice was low. He outstared the people who were looking over until they turned back to their drinks, cowed, then focussed on Mark again. "You fucking will."

"No, I'm not." Mark's heart was beating fast. "You could talk all night. You can call me names. You can hit me. It won't change anything. I'm not doing it. *Stop trying to make me!*"

"Not *happy*? Won't *do* it? You'll let down your family? Think you're better than us?" Denny's voice was going up a pitch again. "That's the same as disrespecting Dad."

The tipping point. It always came. There'd never been a way to avoid it, never – unless…

"Two nuns are sitting on a park bench," Mark said quickly. "A man in a long coat runs up and flashes at them, shocking surprise. The first nun has a stroke. The second nun tried but she couldn't reach."

Denny's fist smacked into Mark's face, faster than he'd expected; harder too, because after some blurring of sound and vision Mark realised he was on his back next to an overturned chair blinking up at Ben and Dave, who was swearing about having left Mark.

Mark tried to raise his head but moaned. Faces swam. None of them seemed to be Denny's. That would fit. Denny usually scarpered.

"You okay?" asked Ben. "You were knocked out!"

"Shut it, Ben." Beyond them other faces looked on in concern. Ah, nice people. "How many fingers am I holding up?" asked Dave.

Mark struggled to focus. "Four."

A look of panic washed over Dave's face.

"And a thumb," Mark added.

Relief replaced the concern. "Back up folks, he's okay," said Dave, helping Mark into his righted chair. "You had us worried, tosser."

"I like the attention," said Mark. He touched his nose then examined the red on his fingers. Grabbed the toilet roll, held it against his nostrils, let the blood soak in. With his other hand he reached up, felt the absence on his head. Looked around, groaning. "Where is it?" Looks of confusion. "The hat!" he explained.

Dave and Ben helped search, but there was no sign of it.

"I'll never see it again," Mark mumbled.

"Get another," said Dave. "It's hardly the most pressing issue."

"I wanted *that* one. It meant something."

"That bastard," said Ben. "I just turned to see you get laid out. How come you didn't chin him back?"

"I don't fight!" Mark answered in a nasal voice. "Never have. Rather have peace. A big disappointment to my family, me, they've always said I let them down."

"Well, we like you just as you are," said Dave. "Fuck your family. Your head's screwed on right."

"Doesn't feel like it right now," Mark replied. "Jesus, it wrecks! And my nose is killin' me!"

It was the truth, but he couldn't help joining in with their laughter. It was good that Denny hadn't put the boot in too. More small mercies.

"Your lip's bleeding a bit," said Ben. "Split. I'll go get more toilet roll."

While he was gone Dave said, "If he bothers you again, tries to hassle you, just tell me."

"I will, Dad."

"You've got a right family, you know that, Mark?"

"Yeah."

"So how come you're smiling?"

"Because I won't see Denny again for a while." Always look on the bright side.

They didn't go on to a club with Ben and his European ladies. Dave escorted him to the bus stop as if he were a little kid, making sure he got off okay. It made Mark smile.

He walked down the road to his flat, nose throbbing and head aching. At least it wasn't caused by drinking and hay fever for once. He'd have smiled at the irony if it wouldn't have started his lip bleeding again.

Nearby, a police siren started up. A common sound since they used the main road by the flats as a fast way of getting to town. Pitch changed as it passed. Sound moving into the past and stretching. That always gives a different perspective. Curtains that had twitched fell back into place. Lives went on behind windows. How many of them were better than his?

But then he laughed, realised he didn't feel so bad after all. Pain, sure. It might not have hurt so much if he'd been drinking more, but the fact that he'd dealt with it and been sober created a first: he felt good about himself. Plus it was over with Denny and his dad. He'd taken the beats, he could move on.

When he got into the flat he took the 2000 Jokes book and put it in the recycling box. It'd had its day. The contents might not split his sides, but they definitely split his lips.

"Glad you seem happier. I've not seen you this chilled for a while," Em told her as they sat shoulder to shoulder, sinking into white pillow moments.

"Yes. It's good." She'd reached a plateau now, the effects levelled. That was reassuring. Her body was fine. Could take it. It was nothing. "Been a bad month."

"Fucking Russell the cock."

"Not even that. He's just an arse."

"A teeny cock up a big arse," Em muttered.

"It was Mamgu's funeral that really got to me."

"Mamgee?"

"It just means 'gran' in Welsh. So to me it became her name. Her going was worse than anything Russell did. It's just… You miss people more when they're gone."

"Well, yeah. Obviously."

"And it's not even just that, it's all my family. I miss the fuck out of them."

"Then why are you even here? Glad that I am that you are." Em looked puzzled. "Are those words right?"

"I think I left out of stubbornness."

"That's you."

Another buzz, another text.

PS If you come home I promise I won't say anything about boyfriends. Its your life. I just want you nearby.

Banged the phone face-down by her side. "I felt like I never had privacy. Coming here was a chance to be anonymous."

"Not someone who looks like you. You're never anonymous. Shit, that was hard to say."

"And now I miss it. Just 'cos it's irritating, doesn't mean it isn't... No, I don't know what I started there. Maybe that it's nice that they care."

Another text.

PS Wont say any more.

Sam turned the phone off and threw it into her bag. She hated people guilt-tripping her. She made decisions in her own time, her own way.

"But now you have other people. Like me. I care."

"And I worry about if I'm good enough."

"Oh, you're good enough." Emily giggled.

"I remember my gran, words she said, they keep coming into my head, it's weird. Things I hadn't thought about for years. But they make sense now. To think about them now. Like a time when she complained about this pain in her chest, said it was tight, but played it down. I was just a little girl, and I remember that, and it was years later I found out she'd been dealing with angina; she never normally complained about pain so it must have been bad that day. Dad always said Mam and Mamgu were from sturdy stock. That they'd outlast him. He was right."

"Which means you're a tough cookie too."

"Not like them."

"You don't normally talk about stuff like this."

"I know. Sorry."

"No, I like it."

"No, I meant sorry I don't… Never mind."

"I'm confused. Mind if I just listen?"

"Nah."

"Cool. Tell me more. I like listening to you."

"That day, when I was little, I was in the garden with Mamgu. She loved gardening. It was bright, a bit cold, spring day I think. We were sat on a bench together. I leaned against her."

"Like this?" Em leaned her head on Sam's shoulder.

"Yes. Like that."

"It feels nice."

"Yes. Mamgu had a shawl around her shoulders, and I snuggled up to her, and she pointed out all the different types of birds. She was telling me how to identify them, by size, and colour, and song. Fascinating all that she knew. All gone now."

"Not *all* gone. You remember it."

"You're right! Like she taught me how to recognise a male chaffinch. Pinky-brown belly and cheeks. If you're lucky and hear one sing, it's a little descending song with a flourish at the end. I got it mixed up with a house sparrow's song at first but those are more like chirps and cheeps than a proper song, she told me that. We saw the sparrow, they look like they've got a black bib on. But the top of their head is grey, just like the chaffinch."

"See, you remember what she taught you."

"When I saw him I asked Mamgu where his girlfriend was. She hugged me tighter."

Emily lifted one of Sam's arms, put it around her own shoulders so that Sam could give her a squeeze too.

"'To be held, is to be healed', she used to say. Anyway, I love birds, they're so pretty. I told my gran, she said they were but you can't love things just because they're pretty."

"It helps though."

"She told me you've got to love everything. Then you'll be a good person, and that will make you strong. I didn't understand properly then. But life throws things at you, and some of them hurt. She said you don't want pain in your heart, so you have to make it strong. And you do that by exercising it, by … by loving. And I told her that I understood and she told me that I was clever, and I felt six feet tall when she said that, and she meant it. She said that you have to love your fellow creatures, big or small, pretty or strange, and you've got to love other people too, the whole world and nature, and you've got to see beauty in a winter's day, always with love, and I said I'd try, and I don't always … I don't think I always do it."

And she was sobbing, had to wipe her eyes on her sleeve.

Emily looked at her, surprised maybe. Looked sad herself. "You do it. You're veggie too."

Sam tried not to laugh and cry at the same time. Em gave her a tissue from a box. "When I was twelve. I never realised, but I reckon it's because of what Mamgu said that day. Telling you, just now, it makes sense, doesn't it?"

"Yeah. It's like we're seeing things clearly, set free. I feel free."

"I miss Mamgu."

"She's with you."

"Yes," Sam said enthusiastically. "I sometimes feel like she's watching over me. Guardian angel."

"I mean she's with you in there." Emily put a hand to Sam's chest again, rough approximation of heart, but more realistically on her breast. "I'm amazed, you sharing this with me, it's important to you."

"It is."

Em's hand was still there, and she leaned forward, her lips were on Sam's before Sam fully realised what was happening, and she kissed back at first, Em's lips soft, tongue gentle, playful; so different from kissing Russell where bristles chafed her chin during his insistent mechanical probing. Oh, more softness please! It was tender and beautiful but … no … she moved out from under Emily, and Em resisted, tried to stay on her and keep kissing, but Sam was stronger, pulled Em's hand out from where it had sneaked up her top, sat up, wiped her eyes.

"Em, what are you doing?"

"I felt close to you, that's all."

"I'm not a lesbian."

"Neither am I! You converted me. By being you." Em looked confused too now, her face flushing. "I love being snogged to the ground. A biker I went out with when I was 17 introduced me to that pleasure. I just thought it'd be nice."

"Sort of … but … it doesn't feel right. Not with you."

A look of hurt on Em's face.

"But I do love you," Sam added quickly.

"Who's talking about love?" Em snapped. She struggled up, leaning on the sofa, and Sam stood too, stupidly hurt, then broke the eye contact first, grabbing her bag and trying to put her shoes on without falling over before heading out into the night, leaving Em's front door open.

"Hey, I'm sorry!" Em called after her.

Sam ignored her, nearly twisted her ankle as she left the pavement. Buses, there were some round here, or taxis, or whatever. Fuck trust. She was angry. Em had taken advantage of her opening up. Made her boil. Made her cry too.

Home. She had to get home.

There was half a bottle of wine waiting there.

fools gold

Hello Fools Gold [sic], the anti-drugs drugs anthem. Metaphors of a tired goldrush man, hoping for the big win. A long road, aching pains, going down, sinking, hoping for a change that won't come. Cheery stuff, eh? Yet the tune is so catchy, so repeatable. And that repetition induces déjà vu, as if you are tired and hearing things, lost and going over the same ground; you're part of the story. But you're not really going round in circles. The story just progresses at its own pace.

The official video is a microcosm of the scene at the time. Loose-limbed band members walking in an exotic location (Lanzarote), floppy fringes everywhere, trippy editing, no fitted clothes in sight, Ian Brown doing Bez-like dances. Not far off their performance of the song in 1989 on Top of the Pops – the same episode when the Happy Mondays performed Hallelujah. That broadcast put Manchester into the living rooms of the nation.

The Stone Roses were a notorious band. Fallouts, legal battles, graffiti, aw
interviews, tantrums (don't ever shout "Amateur" or m

Rough was not the word. Abrasive brain, sandpaper throat, jagged head pains, see-sawing stomach. Sam stood outside the entrance of Packham Green, black and bitter machine coffee in one hand, cigarette in the other. A sip then a puff, pungent tastes and smells that injected the terrible chemicals that were making her feel alive, brain-slapping her awake.

She was early. Waiting. One or two other people arrived and she slipped round the side until they entered the building, then returned to her vigil. Before long she saw Em walking down the road. And Em saw her. Slowed.

"You don't normally smoke outside work," Em told her coldly.

Sam held up the white plastic cup. "Not just smoking. But it's all I could face this morning."

"Whore's breakfast."

"You'd know."

Too strong, Sam thought, but Em just looked down at her feet rather than retaliate.

When Em did look up she said, "You in a bad mood?"

"You work it out. You know that old tramp I told you about on the bus, the one who calls me 'love', with the scars on his cheeks?"

"Oh, yes, the fat sweaty drinking one?"

"He sat next to me on the bus today."

"You had to put up with that fucker?"

"Not quite. He started trying to talk to me, insinuating stuff under his breath, creepy bastard. I snapped. Stood up, shouted at him to fuck off, pointed at an empty seat. He was terrified. Everyone looked, and he did it – shifted his arse like it was on fire. Didn't hassle any other women all journey. If he'd have answered me back I'd have chinned him, I think. Does *that* tell you about my mood?"

Em went quiet again. Then nodded towards the cig. "Those things will kill you."

"Says the junk food, speed and coke queen?"

"I'm not talking about me. You should look after yourself better than that."

"I should."

"You want me to get you some lunch? I could go and pick something up now."

"That would be nice."

"Veggie stuff, don't worry."

"Obviously. I wouldn't want you getting me meat. I don't know what would be in it. Some *tongue*, maybe?"

"Point taken, you win. I'm sorry. After … what happened … I was just being defensive. I made it worse."

And lo! The heavens opened, the angels sang Hallelujah, and little sheep did bleat the chorus! An apology given without sarcasm *and* Em actually looked embarrassed. Tiny wonders in the everyday. Take it, don't look a gift horse in the mouth. It might try to snog you.

"Sorry too. My reaction. I didn't expect that."

"Am I forgiven then?" asked Em. Her lips pressed tight in a sort-of smile.

"Yes. We're good." Sam stubbed out the cigarette on the floor and poured the last bit of cold, black liquid down the drain: offerings to the grid god to take her suffering away.

Sam finished off a glass of water. So dehydrated. Her head was feeling worse, temples throbbing. A bunch of teeny pissed miners clanging away at them with miniature pickaxes.

"Oh God," she moaned, hand to head.

"Not quite, but I try my best," Em told her cheerfully, sat on the worktop. "You look like shit. I always feel fine the next day, whatever I do."

"You're a freak."

"Yeah. It's great."

Sam was refilling her glass when Roger came in. "Energy, energy! Come on, chop chop!" he said, way too loud.

"You're not the boss," Em told him.

"No, but I'm Mr Motivator."

"You're motivating me to kick your arse," Sam said. "Keep your voice down."

"And please don't put images in my head of you and spandex," Em added.

"You two are so full of cheer today," he laughed, putting a bottle of Sunny Delight in the fridge. "Time of the month is it?"

"Why do men always think that?" Em asked.

"Don't periods bring women to a full stop?"

"Ooh, on the witty juice are we? Actually PMT does make *her* impossible."

"Please, both shut up. I can't take the banter this morning."

Roger looked at Sam and frowned. "You really okay? You look afflicted."

"It's self-inflicted," Sam replied. "I'll be fine."

"Well, whatever it takes. A cuppa to get uppa. A siesta resta. You'll soon be boingy again."

But something stuck in her mind, stood out from the background noise, and she left the room.

She was having trouble peeing, enclosed in the plywood walls of a toilet cubicle. Obviously dehydrated. She wiped, then examined the tissue, expecting hint of pink. No sign of that Dulux speciality though. So she used her fingers to count back; the digital abacus told her she was due about a week ago. It wasn't like her to be late; the Rees women had always been like clockwork.

Oh.

That could explain a lot.

Oh fuck.

Liam Gallagher signed Mark's ticket. "Here ya go, mate."

"Thanks!" Mark put the ticket in his back pocket, careful not to crease it. He could stick it in a scrap book later.

"You takin' in all the bands?"

"Yeah, I'm off to see Inspiral Carpets later. On the stage down by the woods."

"Lovely. I used to have one of their posters up in me bedroom years ago, venues on it." A wistful look replaced Liam's thick-eyebrowed stare of a few seconds ago. "They'd played at Oasis Leisure Centre in Swindon. That's where I got the band's name from. And our kid used to be a roadie for the Inspirals. Got a lotta time for them fuckers." Then he put some round shades on and was hustled off by smartly-dressed people that always seemed to surround rock stars.

Mark checked his phone. Didn't want to be late. He followed the stream that ran down to the woodland glade where the big festival tents had been pitched. Rabbits hopped out of the way as he approached, disappearing down their holes. It was further than he'd thought so he started running, dodged groups of people who stood chatting, felt sweat break out as his arms and legs pumped away. He eventually reached the rope-lined path which curved around the low field where those Manchester bands that usually got overlooked were going to be doing a short set: Elbow, Lamb, Puressence. Strangely for an open-air concert there were rows of chairs lined up on the grass. Mark found an empty seat, which was lucky, since the area was packed. Everyone had vacant stares. Mark hoped they'd perk up when the music started.

Ben sat to Mark's left. He was jotting messages on a pad and passing them to Emily to make her giggle. Sam was in front of Emily, on the second row. Mark idly wondered if her black hair would feel cool on fingertips, like the shade under a tree, water in the stream trickling over a palm.

Then Rene got on the stage, ruining everything. Her bushy hair was like an explosion of sand erupting from the neck of her formal blazer. Mark tried to ignore her, focus on the event … Bernard Sumner, maybe he'd do a medley of Electronic and New Order songs, if … Rene droned on: the importance of this, the importance of that. He could hardly focus on what the "this" or "that" were. Her words were peeling back the layers. He couldn't focus. The green grass faded away to rough green carpet tiles; the sky shrank to the small square framed by the window; musicians from the event that would never be popped out of existence. The sweat was real, but came from being stuck in the summer sweatbox of a training room, not from running into bliss. Something ached inside as he got pulled fully back to the staff meeting, a thing to be endured because it had no music of life. Just arse-aching repetitive waffle on rows of tubular steel and orange plastic chairs temporarily unstacked for the great event. Afterwards they would return to the 1970s where they belonged.

His nose was playing him up again, an endless tickle. He'd got through half a packet of tissues during the morning. Hell was hayfever plus heat; another degree worse after being punched on the schnozz. Then it hit like a cymbal to the face: double sneeze, eyes squeezed shut.

"Sorry."

He hoped it was over but it happened again. A tickle of an intake, an explosion of air in a trumpet of sneeze that he only just had time to put a hand over. Rene paused and looked at him.

"Sorry," he repeated. All those eyes on him, even his ears felt hot now.

He blew his nose. Another sneeze. Some people were sniggering, diverted by his monstrous noise, waiting for the next eruption. It was hopeless. He scrambled up and towards the door, managing to knock over his chair. "Sorry, need water," he said, righting the seat, feeling another pressure buildup in his head, body in rebellion.

Sam was looking too. But softness there.

As he closed the door the laughter muted, faded. Indistinct words through the wood as Rene returned to her speech. Woodland streams and shade? Only in dreams.

Sam watched. Mark was stood by the photocopier, frowning at it as if it was an alien life form. Or maybe that was just his usual intense look. Sheets of paper dangled absently from a clenched fist. He pulled a leg back as if to kick it.

Sam had been waiting for him to finish so that she could use the machine. "Be nice to it, don't kick it," she told him as she approached.

He grinned when he saw her and lowered his leg. Then he leaned over the photocopier, embracing it. "Hey baby, show me a little sexy paper lovin'," he said in an uncharacteristically deep voice.

"You want some lovin'?"

Looked down awkwardly. "No, just..."

"Don't sound so horrified, it wasn't a proposal."

"I didn't think it would be."

"That was some escape from the meeting this morning. Wish I'd thought of it."

"More black marks though. I doubt if I'll still be here on Friday."

"Get another job. I think about doing that all the time."

He pointed to his red nose. "I'm a mess. Kidding myself if I think like that."

"You're not a mess! It's just hayfever. It'll pass. Get tablets or something." He could be so serious about small things. But then again, so could she. Not so different after all.

Mark realised she didn't know his sniffy nose was swollen because of last night's brotherly action. He could tell her it didn't normally look like a strawberry, but explaining his psycho family would disgust her even more. Let her think he was just a red-nosed clown with a coldsore. "Anyway, other jobs are just as bad."

"That … may be true. Shit, that reminds me. I asked Rene about you shadowing our team. She said no. I'm really sorry. I was fuming. Still am. It must be a crappy day, having hayfever then being told that."

"It just got better."

"How?"

"I mean, knowing you asked. No one normally does anything like that."

She shook her head as if dismissing him. "Still. She's a fucking arse-clench. Makes me steam like fuck-knows-what."

He bit the inside of his lip. "You don't have to swear so much, you know." He said it quietly, worried it would seem like a criticism.

"What?"

"I'll listen to every word you say. Even if you don't swear."

"That's why you say weird things, about vegetables, right? To avoid swearing?"

He nodded.

"I'll try it." She gave him that strange look again. He couldn't hold it. Picked up his papers, riffled through them. "You're better than this, you really should be doing something totally different. A comedian or something. You make me laugh."

He mused it over, remembered what had happened last night and where 2000 Jokes had ended up. "No. Not a comedian."

"What then?"

"Rob banks, write books, or rule Britain."

"No dodging. Truth or dare. What would you want to do if you did move on from here?"

He normally avoided thinking about the future. When he did it always seemed to be a long corridor. Family hidden behind random doors waiting to kick him up the arse as a joke when he walked past. "Don't laugh."

"Promise."

"A job in the music business?"

"Perfect! You really should. What have you got to lose?"

"No idea where to start."

"I bet you do. You're really into your music. And you're smart. You'll get an idea. You must know people: ask them. *Paid â bod yn barod i roi'r ffidil yn y tô*," Sam said in a soft voice that sounded like music. Then she laughed heartily, presumably at his blank gaze. "Something my Mamgu used to say. I haven't thought of it in years. Old-fashioned. Literally it means 'Don't be ready to put the fiddle in the roof', but it's just a long-winded Welsh way of saying 'Go for it'!"

"I like it. I'll remember that."

Her words. She knew things. She was so brainy. So good. Someone worth listening to. Plus he'd had that fantasy in the meeting, a music one. It *meant* something. Had to. He didn't want to live in a world that was just random.

Muzak, the soulless blandbore played to hypnotize shoppers, was making him angry. Mark couldn't wait to finish his after-work shopping and escape from the city-centre supermarket. He picked up a tin of thick soup – good stuff, like baby food for adults – and threw it in the teeny trolley before rolling on, correcting its leftwards list.

Breakfast cereals. He looked at the boxes on offer. So many choices, colours, cartoon characters dancing like idiots leaving trails of sparkles, tracks of sugar. The word "family" repeated. All so neat, tidy, fitted together on shelves without a finger space between. Boxes for busy homes, to be shared. But family was never tidy, not really. He stared at the packets, couldn't bring himself to reach out for one. One. Single. Alone. Even with all these shoppers around.

The cold light of fridges reflected from wet floors where a miserable-looking teenager had been mopping. Mark knew how he felt. Suddenly Mark's trolley lurched left again, crashing into someone else's. He apologised and moved on as quickly as he dared. The budget supermarket had the atmosphere of a dirty hospital ward. Cramped, unfriendly, full of people who avoid eye contact.

Mark eyed the fruit and veg suspiciously. It always seemed pretentious to buy stuff from here. He saw posh people squeezing things as if they were boobs. He didn't know why they did that. He checked no one was looking then placed a punnet of strawberries in his trolley carefully. As he moved away he nearly slipped on some squashed grapes. Kicked them under the display, despite being Shaun Ryder's favourite fruit.

"Hey bro."

Denny. Mark ignored him, grabbed some spray-on deodorant, threw it in with the rest of the supplies.

"Sorry I slapped you."

"Punched."

"Hardly. I'd have knocked you into next week if I'd meant it."

"What you doing here?"

"Followed you. Got bored waiting for you outside. You can't escape, see, 'cos we're the same. Family. Like that big anchor at Salford Quays. Solid. Keeps us strong."

"Chains," said Mark, under his breath.

"Don't get lippy."

Mark snatched a few jars of rogan josh curry sauce. As they rattled with the other things Denny put a finger on the edge of the trolley and wheeled it towards himself. Looked inside.

"Mostly tinned stuff."

"Was good enough for us growing up."

"I don't mean that. I meant that you cook a lot. I prefer takeaway. Fish, chips, pizza. None of that Indian or foreign crap though."

"I like cooking. I do pasta sometimes."

"Pasta!"

"Yeah. With sauce on."

"Fuck. Jamie Oliver Hopton, eh?"

"Why're you here? Just to take the mick? We're done."

"Not done. Wanna be friends. Want you back on side."

"Where's my hat then?"

"I dunno. Someone nicked it? Thieving bastards round here, you can't have anything for long without it getting robbed."

"It was *you* that took it."

"Oh shit, yeah!" Denny started laughing, slapped his thighs at the cock up.

"Gonna give it back?"

He looked sheepish. "Can't. Soz. Threw it in the canal. Maybe I can blag you a discount on a new 'un?"

There was no point looking hurt, surprised, angry. Denny would remember it, a way to needle him. He had enough ammunition and sadistic instinct already. "Forget it."

"That's why I wanna make it up to you, be friends again. Brothers. Do stuff together."

"Yeah?"

"Course."

"What like?"

"Fun stuff. But first, we've got to sort out this business for Dad."

"Not that." Mark pushed the trolley onwards.

"Yeah. That. Dead easy, what're you worried about?"

"Prison?"

Denny picked up a bar of chocolate, ripped open the wrapper and started eating it. It wasn't worth saying anything about that either. He'd either pay for the empty wrapper at the till or wouldn't, depending on his whim and if he was seen by staff. Mention it and he'd just eat another bar to be awkward.

"Ain't so bad. When juvenile sent me to the borstal it was great. Cooked breakfast, choice of meals, pool table. Like fuckin' Butlins."

"Denny, you were only 17 and you were in prison. How can that be good?"

"It was only low-security. And it's the only stint I've done. You just don't get caught with your fingers in a pie and it's all plain sailing. Better than a wanker's 9 to 5."

"So I *could* end up in prison."

A look of realisation as Denny realised he'd mis-stepped. "No no no, hundred per cent safe."

The good thing with Denny was that if you always assumed he was lying then it was easy to see the truth.

"Do what we say, you'll be fine," he continued. "Leave the thinking out, eh? You're not known for your imagination."

"I can imagine."

"Too much, sometimes, eh?"

Mark ignored him.

"Anyway, you talk about imagination," Denny added. "Two words. Office worker. Wage slave. That's all I'll say."

"And if I still say no?"

The scary stare Denny had perfected years ago. "You can't!" He said it loud, shoppers looked over. Denny glared at a nearby woman. "What you lookin' at, sugar tits?" he asked.

Mark had to get him out of here if Denny was going to start freaking out again. He wheeled the trolley to the till, still fighting to force it in the direction *he* wanted.

"I'll get the shopping. Make it up to you." Denny was suddenly nice again, a smiley big man with an arm over Mark's shoulder. He could be like that, a summer storm blown over in seconds when it was in his interest. The empty chocolate wrapper was even added to the basket. Denny paid with crumpled notes recovered from various pockets.

"How come you're so flush?" asked Mark, shoving things into carrier bags.

"Been skimming. Good money."

"Skimming?"

"It's thanks to the gang I sell stuff to, from the recycling gig. Top scam. We set up a stall, with a proper Orange or Vodafone banner, all dressed smart, badges and shit, looks the biz. Different town each time. Pretend it's an offer, free phone, people queue up. Tell 'em there's no charge unless they sign a contract but we need their card number, just to confirm that they only enter once. Then we pretend the signal on the swiper's gone again, we just need to write it down, then we get security code too. They give us their name and address to send the phone to because they're one of the first hundred. Then we've got all the details we need. Pack up and move on before anyone gets suspicious."

They were outside the shop now, walking towards Mark's bus stop.

"What do you do with all those details you stole?"

"Pass them on to the gang," he said proudly. "They're all set up for it. They get the details while we're on the stall. I assume they order shitloads of stuff online, or print cashcards with the details on to buy stuff in shops. Sell it on later, maybe in them rigged auctions that move round. Piece of piss, rent a hall, have loads of stuff, plant the first bidders, get a fortune for crap."

"So, in a way, you just work for other people too? Same as me? Just that you work for scammers and crims?"

"Something's changed about you. I can't put my finger on it, but I will. And I don't think I like it." Denny sniffed, shook his shoulders like he thought he was a boxer warming up, but really he just looked like a shaking boxer dog. "Thing is, it's good money. You do the job for Dad, you'll get a taste too."

I'm no clown and I won't back down.

"Denny, I said –"

"Nowt. Nowt! You useless shit!"

"I'm not useless. I can do things. I will."

"Yeah, right. Fucking fantasy land again, is it?" Denny rotated his finger by his temple.

"I'm not a nutter."

"You are! Was always you, Marky. I *remember.*"

"Shut up about that."

"Don't tell me to shut up! I've had it up to here with you!" Denny went to cuff Mark's head, Mark ducked.

"Don't lay a finger on me –"

At which point Mark's phone rang.

"What's that, in your pocket?" asked Denny.

"Phone."

Mark tried to turn away as he cancelled the call – Dave, he noticed. And Denny's hand clamped on his wrist, squeezing, while the other pried the phone loose, a scuffle, twist and turn and shout, tried to elbow Denny away and nearly got head-butted in return. And suddenly his elbow was locked out across Denny's chest, fingers weakening as Denny bent them back one at a time despite body pulls, Denny was stronger, Mark yelled in frustration, and his shopping got kicked around. Then it was over. Denny had the phone and they stood panting, facing each other, always that same outcome.

"I knew it! It's the same one, you liar," Denny said as Mark picked up jars and tins, put them back in his carrier bag. The strawberries had been trodden on in the scrap and the punnet leaked fruit blood. Mark reluctantly dropped it into the bin. "I could tell. That's why I was so angry. I should be even madder now! But I'll forgive you. I'll forget it all if you agree. Just this one thing, this teeny thing. 'Cos I won't give up. There's pressure on me too y'know."

Mark knew that look. That dogged face. The stare. Denny wasn't fibbing. Mark snatched his phone back and looked away. Denny seemed to take that as some form of weakening. Moved in for the kill.

"And we'll be good. We'll be brothers." Denny hugged him awkwardly. "We'll spend more time together. Good times," he said.

They used to exist. In isolated spots. The times when Mark *felt* like he was Denny's brother. There was the occasion when Denny beat up a lad who was picking on Mark at school: though Denny laid in too hard, broken bones, police came round, led to lots of trouble. Still, no one at school ever touched Mark again, which was almost worth the nightmares about Denny's ferocious temper. And another time, when he was small, Dad was on a drunken bender, shouting and hitting things; Denny grabbed Mark's hand and dragged him out of Dad's way, took him to the common and they stayed there until it was safe to go home. Mark missed holding hands. With anyone. It had always felt good leading, or being led. One of them took a wrong turn somewhere. Mark would like a way back.

"Alright," he said quietly.

"You'll do it?"

"I said it, didn't I?" Ignore the sinking feeling inside. Don't pay attention to fear.

"Nice one. I'm sorry for the hassle," Denny said. "You've come up good."

"No problem," Mark said flatly.

Denny's grin said he thought he'd won.

Mark wanted a way back, but remembered the translation of something that Mark E. Smith added to his version of Lost In Music: it's useless to look behind you. Mark had agreed just to shut Denny up, postpone the breakdown, put it somewhere round the next bend, blow him off later or make a real effort to avoid him. Denny calmed down if you could stay out of his ambling way for long enough. Not a great option, but the other – saying no at every encounter – was just as bleak. Both options went down, down, down, but when had life ever been easy? Unlike Denny, who always got that glint in his eye, always thought there was an easy fix for things, Mark knew: there never had been, and never would be.

The entrance was like a fenced and canopied traffic island leading under the ground.

"You sure about this?" asked Sam.

"Course. My kinda place. Yours too. I've gotta make it up to you. You wanna get off your head or what?"

Em's tight T-shirt said

`My liver is EVIL`
`And I must PUNISH it`

The choice had already been made.

The bar might have a middle of the road location but it was not a middle of the road venue. It was called The Temple of Convenience and had a pleasing honesty to it: it *was* a converted toilet. Tiny. Dark. Seated faces illuminated by candles flickering in red jars. From down here you couldn't hear any street noise. You were below the streets, beneath reality, under the light: it felt like you were part of a select club, rather than some seedy privacy palace. An escape into another world. In fact, it was like Emily herself: unconventional, rock, cool, all in a tidy package.

They got drinks and sat in the red alcove facing the juke box which was on continuous play, churning through the city's music whether people were there to appreciate it or not.

"You always show me new things," Sam said, clinking her lager against Em's and making eye contact like her dad always taught. "Iechyd da."

"Good health?"

Sam nodded, pleased.

"Screw that. Live life to the full. But cheers, m'dear. Anyway, what is it? Russell?" she asked, without missing a beat. "Just forget him."

"I would if people didn't remind me."

"Is it 'cos he dumped you? Or because he was cheating?"

"Thanks for cheering me up." A big swig of lager. Cold, bitter, refreshing. She liked that bitterness. More lifelike than sweet liqueurs.

"I suppose it's because I didn't get my say. It just happened, his choice. Over the phone."

"He's slime."

"Slime…"

"So you want closure. And I'm your girl. Got you presents." She rooted in her bag, removed a CD, held it out. "Here. I'll want it back though."

"What's it for?" Sam asked, taking the album. Alanis Morissette's Jagged Little Pill.

"A ritual. Just knowing that Russell is a dick isn't enough. This is what you have to do. I order you to play it. Learn the words, then sing along at full volume. Smash stuff if you have to. You'll feel better."

"Thanks, but I don't feel that bad."

"Hey, you're talking to me, remember? I know you. I know that temper you've got. Not so mild as you look. And believe me, Jagged Little Pill is *the* album when you have to do a ritual purge of man-hate from your system. Fact. I discovered it many years ago." Em gave her a quick hug, silky hair brushing Sam's cheek with a faint floral conditioner smell.

"You're good, Em."

"No, I'm not. But I'll do anything for you." Em disengaged herself to arm's length. "You're the last great innocent, and that's why I love you. That's from the album – you'll see. It shows what an effect it had on me. I know every word. Proper girl power, not The Spice Girls' version. And something else." Em slipped a packet into her palm. "Present to make up for upsetting you."

"Coke?"

"Not some crappy 50% pure shit. This is a special delivery I scavved off Rob. It's a few grams so spread it out, don't go mad. Best to start small – you can't rewind if you take too much."

"Erm … great. Thanks."

"Want to try it?"

They downed their drinks and went into a damp-floored cubicle together. Crude words and chaotic drawings crawled around them. One poem read:

here i sit
Broken hearted

tried to Shit
But merely farted
Nearby someone had drawn a circle, which contained the words:
Insert glory hole here
The rest of that wall was full of over-eager drawings of cocks.
"I thought this bar was a bit like you. And here I find that the toilet graffiti isn't far off your filthy mind."
"This is tame."
"I believe you."
Emily rolled up a fiver, took out a cashcard, lowered the toilet lid. She was about to tip some coke onto it.
"Urgh, no, not off that!" Sam said.
"You're right."
Em sat on the lid. Parted her legs slightly. "You can do it off my thigh."
"Forget that. I'm not kneeling in front of you with your legs open." Sam realised she was staring at the darkness up Em's miniskirt. Snapped her eyes away.
"It was a joke, y'know."
"Oh."
"We'll do key bumps. Can always do more later to top up."
Em held a nostril, stuck the tip of her housekey into the plastic bag, took up a small pile, shoved it up her other nostril and inhaled hard. Then it was Sam's turn to toot.
"Wow," said Sam, after pinching her nostrils and sniffing to make sure it was all back. It hit harder this time. She rested her palms on the cubicle wall to steady herself. "That's. Something. Else."
"Uh. Huh," said. Emily.
"Need to sit down." Needed to let things flow normally.
"I need a piss." Em's knickers came down, no debate about it, so Sam squatted against the door, focussed on her hands.
"Want to get food after this?" she asked, ignoring the water splashing. The throat burn kicked in after the first high, then the back-throat trickle started. "I fancy a pizza. And garlic bread?"
"Urgh, no. Just no."
"Why?"
"Don't you know I hate garlic?"

"First I've heard."

"It's because of a guy I went out with."

"You surprise me."

The rattle of toilet paper. She was finished at last.

"He used to eat raw garlic every day. Was convinced it was good for him. But he always stunk of it; kissing him was like kissing wet garlic bread." A flush and it was over.

"Let me look at you," said Em.

Sam let her examine her nose. Em flicked it with a fingertip.

"Fine. And mine?"

"Clean."

A nod. They could get out of the cubicle.

Em washed her hands and used the dryer, hot noisy air blasting away so she had to raise her voice. "I also had to put up with the farts and him moaning about diarrhoea. I just couldn't cope with it any more."

That set Sam off, laughter trapdoor in her gut wide open.

"Sometimes I ate a bit myself so I wouldn't notice it on him, but it made me feel sick. I can't have anything with garlic now."

"I never knew," Sam said between gasps, feeling her body reacting to words, expelling air, blood rushing, all flowing, and under it the heart beating. She wasn't aware of it normally; we don't notice we're alive, and it felt good to be reminded of it. She smiled as they went back to the bar, switched to spirits.

"Stop sniffing,"Em hissed.

"I wasn't!"

"You were. Beginner's habit. Don't do it so much. Too obvious."

"Sorry."

"Fucking noobs."

"Sweet leeks."

"What?"

"You can say that. Instead of swearing."

Em gave her a funny look. "Fuck that shit."

When they staggered up the stairwell a few hours later Sam was surprised to find it was still light and the evening sun was yet to make its final dip below the horizon of high building tops. It was still light, and she was renewed.

And totally off her face, as Em had promised.

Back in her room, trying to focus on the clock, but the numbers swayed as froggy's arms pointed at them. A dance. Probably late then. Her nose felt hard, crusty. As she put the remains of the coke into her bedside drawer she took a small amount, rubbed it on her gums. "Boring, am I?" she asked. But he wasn't there to hear her.

Flatmates asleep. Safe to go into the kitchen. Sam had not got round to buying pizza: they'd drunk more instead. Hunger and a mind full of ideas both told her she needed to do something before sleep.

The kitchen was not that of her mam. This one had unwashed plates stacked up in the sink, coffee cup rings, a part-eaten cake left open to the heat, a fruit bowl with more fuzz than fructose. Robin had made a runny mess which was perhaps meant to approximate scrambled egg. Russell had once complained that Sam didn't clean up enough. Sam took a dirty knife and scraped the leftovers into a jar by the sink. Stared at the yellowed gloop. Then she cut off a corner of cheese and added that to the jar, where it sat like a smelly jewel on a bed of yellow velvet.

She shoved some dry crackers into her mouth, went back to her room munching them, jar in hand.

lost in music

rawls and lyrics abo… efurbishing pubs, excess lea… shagg…
nd dodgy French randomness. Yet it retains as much positive feeling as Mark E. Smith
s able to muster: there is still the optimism of that chorus, "Lost in music / Feel so
live".

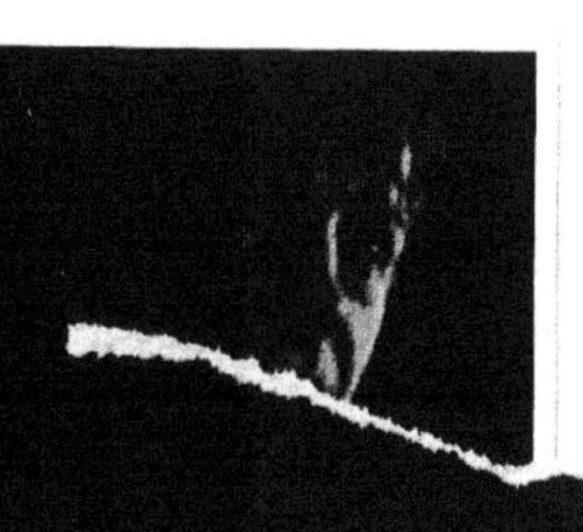

The original's lyrics mentioned quitting the 9-5 job to become lost in music (in The Fall's version it's a 10-5 job; rock stars don't get up so early). The line is relevant since Mark E. Smith quit his job at Salford Docks to devote himself to the band. This song therefore symbolises something about The Fall and all bands, all creatives: the sacrifice required.

Buzzcocks' manage…
performing on a Tony Wilson-hosted Granada TV programme. Since then they've maintained a prolific output (no surprise when their first album was recorded in a single day). Yet the band have been subject to ever-changing lineups. Mark E. Smith is the only constant. He's another Salfordian poet. An earlier version of Shaun Ryder. And their influence has been fel…
…irate with their con…

The Thirsty Scholar. Inside this time. Stone floor, wooden benches, peripheral shadows: like a rockin' church for music and beer. Head to the lights to get your communion lager. The side doors were open, bringing in some much-needed air.

Mark sat at a table in the corner, nervously watching the long-haired man on a high stool at the end of the bar. The man talked to the barmaid whilst making a roll-up without looking down at his nimble fingers. Mark took another sip of his drink. It tasted wrong. Then he remembered – it was lemonade, not beer. He wiped his forehead on the back of his hand. He'd asked for "That low-alcohol stuff Billy Connolly drinks" and just got a funny look, so fell back on lemonade. Mark had pronounced it with a French accent, so that it sounded like Mark E. Smith saying "Le money". There always had to be music.

The barmaid moved off to serve someone.

Oh boy. Caught in a trap. He picked up his glass and moved to the bar, sat next to the guy who was now fiddling with a Zippo lighter. Clink, spin, flame; close again and repeat. He didn't have a drink. Just contemplated his tobacco tin. The man's scruffy sandy hair reached his shoulders. He was skinny, late 30s, wearing faded-arse drainpipes held up by a rainbow-coloured elastic belt and an old T-shirt which said "Perverted By Language".

"Hi," Mark said.

Long hair turned his head slowly. "Hi," he eventually replied.

"I've seen you here before. You're the sound guy aren't you?"

"Yeah, I'm the resident. Here and Band On The Wall."

Mark offered his hand. "Mark Hopton. Can I get you a beer?"

Long hair ignored the hand. "Are you chatting me up?" he asked, face impassive.

"Am I 'eck! No. I was..." He let his voice trail off when the guy started laughing.

"Sorry mate, just joshing. Ignore me. Thanks for the offer but I don't drink when I'll be working, and there's a band on later. Jeff Monks. Call me Monksie. Sorry for being an arse."

Monksie held his hand out and Mark shook it with relief. Monksie had a surprisingly strong grip for a skinny bloke.

"You must love your job."

"Yeah. I do. It's a laugh, even when the musicians play up a bit. Check this out: the other week I was trying to sort out the soundchecks. You always start with the headlining band that are gonna play last, then go in reverse order. But that night all three bands wanted to play first so they could get shitfaced after, fuck the kudos of being last, fuck the etiquette. Nutters. Even when the pressure's on and you're dealing with a nervous band or misbehaving equipment, you just do your best and enjoy the scene. There's nothing better than being this close to music. Last year I went on tour with Monaco. Great music each night, and paid for it!"

"Wow! What was Hooky like?"

"What you'd expect: down-to-earth, will call a ginger-haired twat a spade. Still lives here, not fucked off like some of the others, only want to get famous so they can escape to London. He's a lifelong legend."

"Still playing the high bass."

"I like you kiddo." Monksie's teeth looked yellow in the light from the bar. "Makes up for all the people who can't recognise good sound when they hear it. You get that a lot. Pisses me off no end when punters tell me, 'That sounded shit mate, what are you doing?' or 'Don't give up your day job'. Fuckers. Still, you always get those, can't please everyone. Sound's art, not science."

Mark nodded.

"That's a shiner you got there," Monksie said, looking at Mark's eye, which had started to go purple the afternoon before, now matching his bruised nose.

"Yeah. Brother got carried away."

"Bummer."

"Don't worry. His knuckles were probably sore for days."

A monkey noise from nowhere. Monksie took a phone from his back pocket, silenced the "ooh ooh mook!" sounds. "Ayup… Yeah, that's the plan… Nah, it's fine… Can you rustle up some mates? I want people in and drinking at the start. Ta." Put the phone away. "Look, I'd better shifty. Got some gear to lug. Nice meeting you though."

A voice whispered in Mark's head. Female. The *Go For It* voice that had led him here tonight: it urged him on.

"You know what … is there any way I could help?" Mark could hardly believe he'd said those words.

"You know sound?"

"Not technically."

"Equipment?"

"Not really."

Monksie sighed, but there was sympathy in his voice. "Sorry mate. Music's not a hobby thing, pick up and drop. I appreciate you've got some interest, but I don't want hangers-on who know fuck all about it and don't have any real passion for it, just thinking it's somehow cool." He did double air quotes for the last word. They were like bull's horns. Mark saw red.

"*Hobby*?" He looked up for strength. "Hobby?" Then back at Monksie. "Music is my beating *life*. As a kid I heard Atmosphere, by Joy Division. It took me to another world. Helped me deal with things. When I got older, I couldn't get enough of them. I knew they were meant for me. *You* check *this* out: I was born in 1976, same year they got together; I grew up in Salford and that's where they're from too. And Tony Wilson who set up Factory Records is from there. That all says something, right? Their music echoes down through time. It was meant for *me*. Ian killed himself at 77 Barton Street. Macclesfield. Another town, sure, but I live near Barton Road in Stretford. And Ian Curtis was born in Stretford. It's like a pattern for me, it's all connected. *All* of it. 'Cos that ain't the end."

"Oooooookay," Monksie said nervously.

"The rest of Joy Division formed New Order, carrying on the work, but different. Sumner even got Curtis' guitar, played it in early New Order songs. Connected, see? Obviously I only found this out later, I was too young at the time, but I've been digging, I join the dots, I *remember* this stuff."

"Uh-huh. I think it's about –"

"Connections. New Order blew the world away in 1983 when they released Blue Monday. Same year Inspiral Carpets formed. Their big hit was This Is How It Feels – and their next single was She Comes In The Fall. Is it a coincidence that a few years later they do a song with Mark E. Smith from The Fall? I Want You was Mark E.'s first appearance on Top Of The Pops, all chaotic, disinterested, reading scraps of paper, brilliant."

"Look..."

"I do, yeah. You know something else spooky? New Order formed in 1980. Factory Records had another band get together then too: The Happy Mondays. Tony Wilson discovered them at a battle of the bands in The Haçienda. Haçienda *again*. Tony Wilson *again*. The Happies influenced others: Oasis, The Charlatans, The Stone Roses. Legacies down through time. If New Order described Manchester, it was The Happies that gave it the attitude. Lived it. And both bands folded in 1993. And both bands have got back together recently. Isn't that weird? Like a pattern?"

"Yeah. Right. This is just facts, man. I hate to break it to ya, but it isn't the same thing as life."

"It is. For me. Not just facts. Take The Smiths. Like their name says, they made stuff, painted pictures with words that spoke to the people about what life's like. *Really* like. But I was just about to go to comprehensive school when they split. I was gutted. But then, you know when it rains and all the dusty grey shines for a bit, all the concrete catching the sun, shining like it wouldn't if there hadn't been rain? Well I felt like that in 1988 when Electronic formed. Because it was bringing things together. Johnny Marr was guitar in The Smiths; Bernard Sumner was guitar and singer in New Order. Wham, two lines of music being fused, right there. Factory Records, again. Magic. Kept me going in the shit jobs. This ain't just a hobby for me, Monksie."

"So I see."

"The same day The Stone Roses' first album came out I got beaten up by some lads in the year above at school. I thought about Ian Brown's attitude, that confident arrogance, and managed not to cry. Just went home and listened to music. And recently Ian Brown went solo for some monkey magic. And other bands got back together. As if everything can come back. As if you can go back, change stuff the second time round. Don't you wish you could do that? Maybe it'll all happen. Maybe The Haçienda will open again. Second chances. Maybe ... maybe music can change stuff. It has for me. It isn't a *hobby*. It's my *life*. It's the only thing I get up for in the mornings. It's the only thing that gets me through. It's just ... the only thing. If I didn't have it I think I'd be dead. Everything is connected, and this is the only thing I care about. The only flapping thing."

"Hallelujah!"

"It's not a *hobby*!"

"Okay, relax, I take it back. You're obsessed! A proper Manchoonian. Fuck, you should write a book."

"I did want to. About the best tunes from Manchester. Singles, albums, what influenced what. Got to wait until there are enough songs though. Things aren't moving at the same rate, slowed down in the 90s. The flood of good music became a trickle."

"Got anything written down?"

"No, it's just in my head. I've got to learn to read first." Mark kept a straight face, and could tell he had Monksie for just a second.

"Funny guy," said Monksie.

"It's really to do with the numbers. Probably about 1,500 things I'd talk about right now. So will take a few years for another 500. I keep an eye on things."

"Well, you have passion for music, and I respect that." Monksie tapped his fingers on the bar, gave Mark a calculating look. "You still want to help?"

"Does Ed Blaney play the guitar left-handed?"

Monksie looked puzzled.

"Never mind. Thing is, I have this shit job. It grinds me down. And I've felt that I could do much more than wasting my time like that. I mean, life's too short. I know that. When you love somethin' you should go for it. So I'd love to be involved in some way, somehow..."

"You really want to help out?" Monksie asked, bemused. "I can't pay you."

"That's okay. *I'll* pay. Yeah, I'll pay just to watch."

"No need. But there's not much glamour in working with a sound engineer. Even I don't get any rock star status. We're short staffed, paid next to fuck all, do long hours."

"I don't mind," Mark said quietly.

"My nephew normally acts as helper but he's in Spain for a bit. Idiot! It's scorching here, why go away?"

Mark kept quiet. Couldn't imagine Spain.

"You'd have to realise it's mostly donkey work if you haven't got a music background. Lug gear. Make tea. Work in gopher mode. Try to be ready with the next thing. Like a trainee. There's lots of hanging around and it can be boring."

"I don't mind."

"It'd be me that stayed behind the desk mixing the sound for the audience and bands. And you have to follow instructions right sharp. I mean, plug something in the wrong socket and you can blow two grand's worth of amp. The kit is easy to break and expensive to repair."

"I'd learn. I'd pick it up. I'd watch. Not hassle you."

"Well, you're keen. And you can learn a heck of a lot from just observing, even short-term. I've gotta tell you though. When it comes to having some sort of assistant, there's two things I'm after. And the top of the list is not being a pisshead. When we work we have to be professional and polite, to get a good rep. So no drink or drugs on the job. Feel free to get pissed once the gig's a success, but not before."

"I can do that. I won't touch a drop on nights when you need help. I promise. See, I'm on lemonade tonight."

"The second thing is being reliable. You have to turn up when you say you will. Generally the sound engineer is the first person there and the last to leave. It's the way of it."

"I wouldn't let you down. I could help you tonight if you want?"

"Nah, the band's got their own guy. Driver and sound engineer. Free on Wednesday?"

Mark could imagine his dad laughing at the idea of being a gopher for a "puffy sound engineer"; Denny sneering that there'd be no money in it so it was pointless.

"Yes. You can count on me."

No turning back. He had found the music.

Another pint of water, swallowed as quickly as possible, trying not to gag. Then Sam lay back on her bed, hands on her tummy, just above the bladder. So much water, oceans of it, and she was adrift. There were no stable points. She felt bloated.

It was just all the water.

It wasn't just the water.

She felt sick too.

Nervousness, that was all it was. Nervousness that her imagination grabbed on to and ran away with. Or just a stomach that was upset. That happens when you get pissed a lot and don't eat enough. Last night she'd woken to dizziness, pale and cold. Into the bathroom, hated being sick but a body in revolt cannot be ignored. And it *was* revolting as she knelt and spat into the toilet, shivering.

See, there was an explanation for it. She had to stop overthinking every bodily sensation.

She turned to her side, pulled her knees up, pressure on her bladder. Soon. On the bedside unit was the rest of the plastic baggie Em had given her, off-white powder like fairy dust. Sam reached over, touched it: then put it in the drawer, at the back. There couldn't be any of that for a while. Depending on how the next half hour went, there might not be any of that for a fucking long time.

She closed her eyes and fell asleep.

Woke to a bladder bursting to the point of pain. Like the buses, nothing when you want one, then all at once. She stood, but slowly, and genuinely wondered if she would even make it to the toilet without wetting herself.

Diw! She couldn't even get this right.

Snatched the paper bag from the chemist and shuffled into the bathroom, thankfully empty. There was no debating with her bladder now, all she could think of was bursting balloons and cracking dams. Once on the toilet she removed the irritatingly pink plastic pen-like test and sighed with relief as she was able to pee at last. Held the tip of the test in the stream for a few seconds.

It couldn't be positive. She knew that. She was careful to the point of paranoia. At one point even condoms weren't enough, there'd had to be sperm-killing cream too. Her first boyfriend accused her of being a "spermicidal maniac" when they'd started sleeping together. And she'd always checked the condoms for splits. So it couldn't be positive. Not *now*. Not *him*. Except … well, she'd been pretty drunk sometimes. Hadn't been going out with Russell for long, but at the start she'd been a bit wild… No. Surely not.

She hadn't checked every condom.

She should have gone on the pill as well.

She washed up, took everything back into her room. Lay on the bed. Only another minute to go and she could look. Again, hands on her tummy, and this time she couldn't pretend it was because of her bladder.

She wasn't ready for this. It could change everything.

It was nothing.

It was everything.

She was hardly breathing. A part of her *knew* why she was like this. She didn't want to look. Didn't want to see the lines stating that her life had shifted, that she'd have to be proper responsible, she'd have to … protect. That was what mothers did.

She wiped her eyes. Picked up her phone, dialled. Needed to speak to the person she missed. And it was answered.

"Mam. It's me."

"I wondered when I'd speak to you. You're always so busy."

"I know. I'm sorry. Not much of a daughter, eh?"

"I'd never say that."

Sam stifled a sob, needing to hear those words and more.

"Why are you ringing now?

"I just wanted to hear your voice."

"Are you crying?"

"No."

"Are you drunk again?"

"No!"

"Hung over? Because if so I've not a shred of sympathy."

"No!"

"I can't tell nowadays."

"What do you mean?"

"Just that you seem to be drinking a lot of the time. Like father, like daughter."

"I don't drink a lot!"

"I just mean when I ring you. Don't get defensive, it must be coincidence. I'm just saying. I care. And you never used to be like that."

"Mam, this isn't the … I was, anyway. I always liked a drink."

"Not like now. Sometimes I don't feel like I know you so well as I used to."

"You know me."

"I know, it just doesn't feel like it sometimes. That's all. Like you've changed."

"Nothing's changed!" Christ!

Silence for a few seconds before her mam said "Sorry, here you are ringing me, and I'm being mean. It's good to hear your voice too."

Sam let her mam talk, tried to keep the hurt out of her voice, inject it with *normal* instead, but she felt guilty relief when her mam had to go because someone was at the door.

She tossed the mobile down the bed. Phonecalls were disappointing. You have words when you don't want any; you have no contact when what you really need is a hug that says everything will be okay. Even if it isn't true you can believe a hug for the time it lasts, that warmth, that unconditional simplicity, that honesty. That was what she wanted to communicate to her mam. And she failed miserably. Doing it at a distance wasn't the same.

She couldn't put it off any longer. She took took the piece of plastic and looked.

A dark line on the display.

A single dark line.

She squinted at it, but there was no second line.

Negative. She was not pregnant.

And she was stomach-punched by a sense of loss for something she'd never had and didn't want, something that would have derailed her life, and something she suddenly realised she'd also perversely wanted. She moaned and curled up, and cried, deep sobs, bottom of the sea sobs, and she was drifting again, no fixed point.

Kits could be wrong. They made mistakes.

Everyone made mistakes. It didn't help, and the crying didn't stop.

Later. Sam hummed along to the CD Em had lent her. There were bitter words about being taken for granted, patronised, objectified. Once again Emily was right. Sam jabbed her finger at empty space in front of her, accused the air with a sneer. Robin and Leigh were out and she could have the music playing in the kitchen as loudly as she fucking wished while she finally washed the dishes.

"I see right through you!" she yelled, then gritted her teeth. The music was altering her moods, lifting them one minute and firing a sharp barb of anger into her the next. A rollercoaster by the sink. One she rode alone.

There was poetry in the album. The words, the music, Alanis Morissette's voice – they fitted perfectly and she accepted the illusion that it was written for her. She never read poetry, not the boring formal kind they'd taught at school, but today she could see what an effect putting the right words in the right places could have. And it fulfilled the role of vital distraction.

She finished up, took a pen and paper from by the phone and started a shopping list. First she scanned the contents of her cupboard to see what she might need. Quite a lot. The half bag of pasta and jar of sauce wouldn't go far. And the block of grating chocolate might be perfect for cocoa but it wouldn't count as a meal.

Oh, this was the best one. The energy built as Sam sang along, feeling the fine hairs on her forearms tickle as her skin contracted. "Are you thinking of me when you *fuck* her?" she asked the empty kitchen, yelling as she kicked the cupboards. A pain contracted in her pelvis and she gripped it for a second, but it passed and she could straighten up again.

Thanks Alanis. Thanks Emily.

The fridge light buzzed on as she opened the door. Rooting around she identified some vegetables that were hers and a yoghurt and pasty that were both within date. She also found the source of the pong that made her wrinkle her nose – it turned out that what she had thought of as Leigh's blue cheese was actually old Cheshire that had gone furry. Inside the cellophane was a disgusting squidge of liquid at the bottom.

Sam got her jar which was more than half full of gunk now, then carefully poured in the mouldy cheese liquid. An offering: put all bad stuff in one place. It was greening horribly. She screwed the lid back on quickly, unable to endure the stink. There was a faint whiff about it even with the lid closed. It couldn't stay in her room any longer.

Instead she put it in the airing cupboard next to the boiler, double-checking that the lid was as tight as possible first.

in yer face

Their [illegible] is a statement of intent, [illegible] their favoured drum machine. They were formed by a record store owner and two of his favourite customers in 1987, and are still going strong. (Tip: always be nice to people who own record shops).

They're well-known as remixers, re-users, replayers and creators: their acid house remix of Blue Monday was a popular track when they DJ'd at The Haçienda's Hot Nights. They used the bassline from Joy Division's She's Lost Control in th[illegible] [illegible] radio show in the [illegible]'s on Sunset [illegible]

[illegible] connected via collaborating wit[illegible] with Bernard Sumner (from Joy Division/New Order/Electronic) in Spanish Heart; [illegible]orked MC Tunes, the Manchester rapper, on various projects, the best-known being The Only Rhyme That Bites; with the lovely Lou Rhodes from Lamb in the track Azura; with Guy Garvey of Elbow in the song Lemonsoul; and, breaking the Manchester lineup for a second, James Dean Bradfield of the Manic Street Preach[illegible] [illegible]pez (the Welsh and Mancunians can get on, see).

That morning she'd taken her coffee into the lounge. Then another pang hit. She rushed to the bathroom.

There was blood in her knickers.

Over-indulgence causing body damage.

Miscarriage.

No, it was just the period starting.

It was normal. She should be glad. No need to try a second pregnancy kit.

It's more than that. It's a bad sign.

She couldn't help it, scrunched a fist against her eyes and started crying. The kit and blood said she wasn't pregnant. That's what she wanted. This feeling that she really was: it was just paranoia. That spiteful little *bwci* that loved to chase good feelings away.

The boom of an explosion. A star shooting away, space dust trail. Dots, separate then joined up by jagged lines. Swirls of the pen, circling and looping across a spoiled order sheet. Then letters rambling on the page. They were random, Mark thought, but he had spelt S A M amongst the other letters, which then took on the appearance of distraction around those central three, orbiting them as if they were the densest things in the paperverse.

He was bored, alone in the post area waiting for the day's delivery. He'd seen people go into the staffroom, watched who went in, didn't feel like joining them today. Doodling was a good pastime in those circumstances. It looked like you were working if Rene happened to be watching.

Ess to the *Ey* to the *Em.*

He liked those letters, that rhythm.

He started to sketch a face. A random face. With dark eyes and hair. Just any old face. He made the chin too small and drew over it, but then it looked like a double chin. That wasn't appropriate for...

Ah. He had been drawing Sam.

In that case the nose needed to be slightly softer.

He smoothed his pen up and down, lines of different density. The new version emerged on the page, better than the previous.

He could look at this face as much as he wanted. No one would be angry or repulsed. Girl like that. Boyfriend. Mark on the outside. The pieces didn't fit. Never had.

His stomach fluttered. Maybe he was hungry.

Sam was like a catchy riff that fills your head when you're trying to sleep, preventing any other tune from getting in. He began to draw in the neck, making sure some dark hair overlapped it –

"What's that?"

Surprised, Mark flung his arms over the paper and glared up, not sure if Roger had been watching him draw, spying over his shoulder.

"Nothing!" he snapped reflexively. "Just work!"

"That's not work. Let me see." Roger reached out, tried to brush Mark's arm aside.

Mark scrunched the paper up and crammed it into his pocket. "It was nowt to do with you!" he said.

"It didn't look like work to me. Looked like a drawing of someone. Who?"

"Your mum."

"Maybe I should tell Rene to keep an eye on you."

"Tell her what you want, if you wanna be a creep." Mark stood, and was surprised to see Roger twitch and shrink back. Mark hadn't meant it as a threat – he just wanted to head downstairs and wait for the post, get some peace away from Roger. But Roger backed away, gesturing with two fingers from his own eyes to Mark's. "One false move…" Then he turned away.

Mark took the paper from his pocket, smoothed it out, wondered if it could be salvaged. Maybe even pass it to Sam when no one else was around. Wouldn't that be a nice thing to do? Then he realised how it might look: the office weirdo sketching a pretty woman. Lock your doors, ladies! Close your curtains! Mark's on the prowl!

No. Stick to jokes, not something as intimate as a drawing, that required attention and care and observation. Good things like appreciation and friendship always got twisted in places like this, just as the crinkles and lines meant his sketch was ruined. Unworthy of what it was meant to represent.

Rows of plastic seats, with empty ones between each person if possible, mental barriers to the diseases everyone obviously carried. People watching each other surreptitiously but avoiding open eye contact. Impatient eyes flicking back and forth to the red scrolling L.E.D. display, hoping for their name to appear in lights. Magazines were flicked through listlessly, words not read, because everyone was obsessed with their own worries.

Who ever likes going to see a doctor?

Bong.

CRAIG POOLE, DR STEVENS, RM 6

Sam had rung work, left a message for Rene saying she had to go to see her G.P. and would be in as soon as she could after that.

She had to know.

Bong.

SAMANTHA REES, DR SMITH, RM 4

Oh. Doctor Smith. He was not her favourite. But you got no choice with the emergency surgery. Luck of the draw, and hers had been pretty slim recently. Sam's normal doctor was a considerate woman, who listened and understood. Sam always felt there was sympathy behind the professionalism: it didn't matter whether it was true or not, the belief alone made baring yourself to a near-stranger that little bit easier.

Time to face the Parade of Stares. People watched her walk to the corridor from which the doctors' rooms led off. All eyes, jealous that they were still waiting; eyes wondering why she was there, what dirty secrets her body held; eyes weighing her up. She was glad to knock on the door, hear the invitation to come in, the sacred protocol that got her out of their prying sight.

He was reading a medical record on his monitor, presumably hers, didn't look up, just gestured at a seat. Greying hair, glasses, round face, hadn't shaved that morning. There was a crumpled look to him that she didn't like. Still, she was probably no better after last night's lack of sleep. She took the chair, kept her bag on her lap. A familiar thing to hold, to save her hands from fidgeting.

He looked up and smiled. A professional smile. "Hello Samantha. What can I do for you today?"

She explained the situation. She had to drag out each sentence, worrying that it now sounded somehow trivial when spoken aloud: smaller when freed from her mind where it had seemed to fill the space. "And whatever the test said, I *felt* pregnant. I've never felt that before. And it might be related, but I've been emotional and tired recently. Not felt like eating. Out of sorts." He carried on looking at her. Assessing her. "Run down," she added feebly. "So I just want to know that … well, that things are okay, I suppose."

He leaned forward, and for a moment she was worried that he was going to place a hand on hers, but then she realised it was just a pose he used, to look more concerned. "How heavy was the bleeding? Was it just light spotting?"

"More than that."

"Like a normal period?"

She was hesitant. "No, I think … more blood. And it *feels* different."

"We can't always trust our feelings though, can we? Have you been under any stress recently?"

She gave a nervous laugh. "I always feel stress. That's normal." Damn. Her laugh had sounded mad, not reassuring.

"But anything out of the ordinary? Have you experienced any big life changes? Anything different that upset you?"

"I lost a family member recently."

He nodded, apparently satisfied that he'd found the answer already. It was why she'd been reluctant to mention it. "Someone you cared about?"

"Yes! They were *family*." Surely it was obvious she would care? Where did they get these people?

"Anything else?"

"Well, me and my boyfriend split up. But maybe that's a good thing." She wanted him to know that she'd had a boyfriend. She felt pressure to justify herself. If she had been pregnant it was from being in a *relationship*.

"And have you been sleeping alright?"

"Not great, a few late nights… Nothing too bad though," she added quickly.

"Eating?"

"Normal."

"I see. Well, I could examine you. If you want to get onto the bed I can have a look."

She glanced over at the raised medical bed, disposable blue paper cover stretched over the top. Felt surprising revulsion at the idea. Doctor or not, she just didn't like him. And she couldn't have someone she felt uncomfortable with prodding about in her vagina. She licked her lips. "Could the nurse do that?"

He sighed. "If you want. She's busy this morning though. Wart clinic. You'd need to come back this afternoon." There was an edge to his voice. This was not what she'd hoped for. Not what she'd needed. "She could check you for anything obvious, and if you want definite answers we could do a test. But let's be grown up: there's little point. Nothing here sounds worrying. It's probably just your period being late, and that's common. Is it worth it?"

I'm so common.

"It *feels* worrying."

"Did you have unsafe sex?"

"I don't know." She hated saying those words, facing that judgement. But it was true.

"I see." He paused again, thinking, picked up a ballpoint pen from his messy desk. "Look. Either it's your period – which is most likely if you've already tested yourself negative. It's possible to get a false negative with a home kit, but unlikely." Pause. He clicked the point in and out once. "You followed the instructions properly?"

"Yes! I followed them properly!"

"Okay. Or it could be an early miscarriage. A silent miscarriage we call them, almost symptomless. They're very common too."

So common, again.

"But there's not much that can be done afterwards. Nothing, really. So why not just go with the simplest explanation? It's pointless to worry yourself now. Best to forget it ever happened."

Simple. Common. Pointless. He could have said, "Pointless to worry your silly pretty head" – it would be the same patronising dismissal. Why couldn't she forget? Because if she'd been pregnant she *needed to know!* Didn't she? To fill the hole formed by the question. Or it would always be empty.

"Are you okay?" he asked with another click. He wanted her gone.

And maybe leaving the hole empty was better after all. Seeing a coffin lowered was the worst thing in the world. She knew that.

"Yes. I'm okay. It's a common thing. Just a period."

"That's it. Don't worry. There's worse things happening to people every day."

And that was it. *Right there*. He'd undermined it. He wouldn't have said that if he didn't think a miscarriage was a distinct possibility. But he didn't want to do anything about it. And there was nothing *to* do. Except find out for sure. But that was just for her peace of mind. What was that worth?

"Is there anything else?" His professional smile again. It was not reassuring. "If you're having trouble sleeping there are pills that can help."

Pills. Huh. "At the moment there's nothing you could help with."

He didn't shake her hand. Just turned to his keyboard, started typing notes, no doubt about her inability to deal with stress, or her bad personal habits.

She left, closed the door behind her with relief. Put a hand to her tummy, empty now except for hurt. Empty of the thing she didn't want; and, she now realised, also empty of the thing she wanted totally.

She knew. She *knew*.

The only teeny thing she could focus on, a hint of light in the gloom, was that the last tie to Russell was broken.

Nearly.

"Oh, I'm sorry. That doesn't sound like the kind of thing we'd normally send out."

As Sam listened she made notes and doodled with a pencil, curvy lines around the words.

"Yes. Absolutely. I understand. How about a 20% reduction? Or would you prefer replacements?"

Some more listening. She did a doctor's professional smile, hoped it was recognisable in her voice. "No problem at all. We'll do that. Sorry again." Finally they hung up. She checked her notes, crossed out words, added a reminder to apply the discount.

The curved lines around the words resembled hills. She squiggled down one. A stream.

Then scribbled all that out too, with cross-hatched finality.

Sam had rushed back from the GP, not wanting to be any later than necessary and risk the Wrath of Rene, only to find that her boss had just left to take the afternoon off sick. "Isn't it ironic?" Alanis would ask, incorrectly.

She leaned back. Stretched. Saw Mark approaching.

"Post. I saw you were back. Thought it might cheer you up."

"What makes you think I need cheering up?"

"You look proper grumpy." He said it with a shy smile and she couldn't help joining him. He could do cute.

"I doubt the post will do anything about it."

"We'll see."

"Are you alright? Your eye –"

"Oh, that's nothing." He put the envelopes near her hand. Retreated a few steps, still smiling, a teeny handwave, then turned.

Roger came back from the toilet. Looked from her to Mark while she sifted the envelopes.

Aha. A yellow sticky note with scruffy handwriting on.

Hey baby. I'm your post. Show me a little paper lovin.

She had trouble stifling her giggles. Read it again.

"What's that?" asked Roger.

"Just the post. I'm learning to appreciate it."

The note went in her drawer, an artefact to examine again; words and paper that added up to something bigger, because of intention, because of secrecy, because of a curving of the lips that makes us feel so much lighter. Someone thought about her enough to replace emptiness with that curve.

The job.

Top job.

Most *important* job. It was Mark's this week.

1. Go into the staffroom 15 minutes before break time.

2. Fill the big water boiler and turn it on (button, not sexy dance).

3. Get jars of coffee and teabags and sugar out. Line them up smallest to largest (feels like at least something has progressed that day).

4. Check there's milk in the fridge and it ain't whiffy (quick sniff test).

5. Optional. Put the radio on (not classical).

Ben was rinsing cups, another high-grade task undertaken by The Musketeers: Porthole, Aroma, and the other one.

Mark started task 5. A serious voice talking about an earthquake in Sumatra. 120 people had died in the quake, the panic, and the hundreds of aftershocks that followed. Too much sadness. He twiddled the dial, didn't want to think about death, not in front of other people, he wanted life – and found a music station.

"Turn it up," Ben commanded.

Mark jiggled the wonky dial, sound cutting out completely then coming back louder due to the loose connection. He had the knack though, tamed the cronky twister.

One song ended and another began. Relaxing strings before a cool drum kicked in, while the voiceover said, "And this is Frank Wilson's almost-lost 1965 Motown classic, the northern soul staple 'Do I Love You (Indeed I Do)'."

"Northern soul!" Mark tapped his feet.

"And?"

"Northern soul!" repeated Mark.

Ben shuffled at the sink. "Do I love you?" he sang.

It was as infectious as office flu. Next time the chorus came round Mark joined him, singing to a teaspoon. And dancing. They were both *dancing*, and the room wasn't a worn-out kitchen any more: it was a spangle-balled groovy northern boogie palace. Mark did a funky foot shuffle.

"Yeah, this is the shit! Soul, white boy!" Ben said, making his way over to join Mark at the fridge and waving a towel exuberantly.

"Do I love you?" they sang. No way to be still.

The door opened. It was Sam. Ben didn't stop so Mark didn't either. She folded her arms and leaned against the wall to watch. Ben danced over to her with a strut, gesturing heart beat flutters with his palm, "Do I love you? Indeed I do!" he sang, and she cracked up, and

Mark felt a twinge inside, and the tambourine faded out with the song, and he was flushed, and Ben kissed Sam's hand then left to get crisps.

"You've got the moves," Sam told Mark after the door closed.

"Nah, just shuffle, throw in some Bez arms, Brown strut, Bernard shake."

"I don't know what you're talking about but it makes me laugh."

"As long as I make you laugh."

"Your arms moved like you were swimming. Badly."

"Close. I normally aim for drowning."

"I should make an effort to come to breaks early. Always up for a floor show."

"Do I get a tip?" He pretended to pull a suspender, turned his leg towards her.

"Sure. Invest in dance lessons."

"You're no fun."

"You'd be surprised."

"Hey, I'll be back in a minute. Something from my locker." She didn't move, he had to detour around her.

"Shake a leg."

The staffroom was full now. Smells of coffee and tea, pie heating in the microwave, and a pong from the bin that needed emptying, all rarefied by heat.

"Take one. And don't grub about in the bag, just take something, the first thing. I don't want fingerprints on all the sweets."

"What are you so cheery about?" asked Dave, hand diving into the paper bag. He came out with a red gummy bear, and didn't look too pleased.

"Nothing. Everything. Life's not always a brown smelly thing."

Mark had popped out at dinner time, Woolworths, gathered a jumbo Pick 'n' Mix. Now he was offering them round.

One of the keyboarders selected a cola bottle; Taffy took a white chocolate drop with hundreds and thousands on. Emily got cheers when she pulled out one of the bright yellow banana chews.

"That's better than mine," moaned Dave as she popped it into her mouth with a satisfied grin.

"Got any allsorts?" asked Ben.

Mark grimaced. "No. I hate licorice. Why would I want to put burnt rubber in my mouth?"

Ben ended up with a cola bottle too.

"Sam?"

She smiled, dipped in. She had freckles on her forearm. She received a white chocolate milk bottle.

"You really are in a good mood today," she told him.

He wanted to tell her about last night. He wanted to tell her what the *Go For It* voice had been whispering. He wanted to say that just seeing her freckles made him happy. So many things he'd like to say. But not sure how to do it safely. Not in this environment.

He shrugged instead. Sat and enjoyed the remains of the bag himself. Watched Sam eat the milk bottle. He dug one out himself, enjoyed the way the powdery chocolate melted on his tongue, and when he sniffed his fingertips surreptitiously they smelt of vanilla.

Would her mouth taste of vanilla?

Indeed it would. And now, so did Mark's. There was a connection only he knew about. He leaned back and smiled.

"Your mind's wandering. What the piss are you staring at?" Emily followed Sam's gaze. "Oh," she added with a grin.

Sam shook her head to wake herself up. "Sorry, I wasn't paying attention. And what do you mean by 'oh'?"

"You don't have to be so obvious you know."

Sam gave her a quizzical look.

"You're always staring at him."

"No way! I was just looking over there because that's where my chair is facing. Get your facts right."

"No, you get yours right. I *know* what I'm talking about." She looked so smug. "At first I wondered if it was Dave you looked at. You know, since you like the thuggish look. As Russell proved."

"You're on thin ice."

"Hey, if you fancied him, maybe that's why you resisted me? Only room for one in your head? Oh, sorry, forgot. I won't mention *that* again."

"Better fucking not. You're wrong. And I'll prove you wrong. I won't look at him again today," Sam stated with assurance.

A good word, a smile and a bit of banter to get through the day. That was all it was. She sulked for a bit as she checked over the work of a temp who was dealing with the filing system for invoices. Then she was thirsty, still had a bit of a headache, got a drink of water, poured some on the plants. Gathered paper clips from another desk. And while she was there she moved to a calendar to check a date. And from there she could see the post section, and after she had glanced a few times she realised she was watching Mark work from a position where he couldn't see her.

Her palms felt sweaty. Em was a monster. And this wasn't a good time.

Mark left work with Dave and Ben, savouring the open feel as they escaped out of the double doors. There were view-blocking buildings on every side, but when you looked up you could still see the sky, and its permanence meant something. It was magnificent tonight, a bold blue with scattered white dunes of wispy cotton wool. Up there was another world, peaceful, alien, mystical. He would spend hours looking up if he could find a quiet space to do it in without distractions.

"No, honestly, I reckon I'm a sex addict," Ben said, breaking into his thoughts. "I can't help it, think I'll explode sometimes. Hardly anyone can keep up with me. Maybe I need to see a doctor."

"Yeah, right. That's like passive-aggressive fantasy bragging tied to an inferiority complex," Dave told him.

"There's nothing inferior about me."

"Point proven. Go and see your GP then. But you know you won't. Because it's all in your head. All mouth, no trousers. You don't pull *that* often, so if what you say is true, you'd have exploded long ago. Unless you whack off all the time?"

"Don't start that again. It's you who's always going toilet in work time. That's suspicious."

"Nothing suspicious about holding it in until break's over so I can dump in work time. Otherwise you lose out. It's the law of men. Was practically supernatural today though. Double flusher. The kraken. Like the spear of destiny staring up at me."

"How come all conversations with you end up involving shit?"

"I was fixated at the stage of psychosexual development that catches so many wobbly two-year-olds out."

A lank figure detached itself from the shade of a doorway and did a quick step towards them.

"Wotcher," said Denny.

The banter ended. It was like Denny had a bubble of life-suppression round him.

"Mark, say bye to your little friends. You're comin' with me."

Oh super poop. So much for hiding from Denny until it blew over. Mark's plans normally fell to pieces, but not this quickly.

"I said I'd go pub with Ben and Dave," Mark told him. As the words came out he knew they were wasted breath.

"Unsay it then." Denny glared at Mark's companions. "I said BYE, BOYS."

"Mark doesn't have to go with you," Dave stated, calmly. He didn't clench his fists or step forward, or give any aggressive signals that could set Denny off, but Mark still didn't like how it was going. Last thing he wanted was for his friends to get hurt. Dave might look scary but Mark doubted he'd win a fight with Denny. Denny was sly. Denny would happily fight dirty. And Denny usually carried a screwdriver, still attached to packaging, "In case I get pulled – I could say I just bought it. Smart, eh?"

"It's fine, Dave," Mark said, trying to move between them without being too obvious.

"Yeah, keep out of it, squash face. This is family business."

"Oh, like punching him?" Dave asked.

"You some stuck up uni student?"

"Not any more."

"Then don't lecture me. That's all sorted. He don't need you."

"It's fine, honest," Mark added quickly. "I'll see you tomorrow."

Dave seemed reluctant but had no remit to help. He hesitated a few more seconds, where time seemed to creak with tension; then he nodded at Mark and walked on with Ben, who looked relieved to leave Denny behind.

"Toerags. We don't need them," Denny muttered, watching them go. Once they turned the corner he smiled at Mark, face altering. "It was a bit of a shiner, wa'n't it?"

"What do you want, Denny?"

"You. Coming with me. We're got people to meet in the arches. They're waiting, and they're not people to say no to."

"What if we did, though?" Mark swallowed. "Just supposing?"

"They'll come to your flat, and it won't be nice. An' I wouldn't be there to step in. So don't anger them. But hey, why the long face? They're not mad with us. The opposite. They just wanna talk, so don't make somethin' out of nothin'. Come on, we've got a tram to catch. Don't wanna walk all that way."

At Piccadilly Gardens Denny bought a tray of chips and gravy. Took the plastic ketchup dispenser and smothered everything in red gloop. He always did that. Made the food look like blood.

When the Metro arrived Mark got his wallet out, assuming he'd have to pay for two tickets but Denny just scoffed. "What you buying a ticket for? Idiot. There's no need when it's only a few stops."

It wasn't worth arguing, so Mark stood in silence, shaking his head when Denny offered some chips, plastic fork stuck out the top of the mound like a fresh war memorial. When the tram pulled to a stop Denny pushed on first. There were no free seats; rarely were if you caught it after work. Mark gripped a hanging strap but caught Denny's derisive sneer and let go. Denny offered his chips to a pair of schoolgirls. They made the right choice and ignored him. Mark let his body sway with the movements of the carriage. Tram surfing, Denny called it when they were younger. One of the many things you practised until it became effortless, so you looked like you belonged in the city, and it belonged to you. People didn't mess with you then. So many lessons learned. And always some sharp punishment if you didn't pay attention. No wonder school sometimes seemed like an escape.

They had only been trundling for a while when Denny muttered, mouth full, "Oh, fuckin' 'ell."

Mark turned to see what he was looking at. *Ah.* Inspectors had got on at the last stop, and were working their way through the carriages checking tickets. And there was no way off until the next station. Typical Denny, making trouble when it didn't need to exist. Yet if Mark had argued about it back on the platform he'd have just received a slap for being sissy.

"There's a big fine if we're caught," Mark told him.

"Shut up." Denny kept his eyes on the inspectors. He was calculating, Mark could tell. Counting how many people they'd check before reaching this spot. He looked back, Mark did too, but it was the end carriage. No way to add time by retreating.

"Come on," said Denny, putting the tray with the remaining congealed chips on the floor. He started walking towards the inspectors and nearest door. He took his phone out, held it to his ear without dialling.

"Yeah, yeah, here now, will be with you in five, just don't leave, I promise, on me way. Tell her to keep her legs crossed. No, just get a doctor, it's happened before, fucking hell, it's serious man!" He continued with stuff like that – urgent-sounding nonsense to no one. He put on an air of snappy impatience, a mental Do Not Effing Disturb sign, and he pushed past an inspector to get to the door as the train decelerated, ignoring an attempt to speak to him.

"Yeah, I said I'm nearly there!" he yelled, banging the door-release button and diving through the gap as soon as it appeared, yanking Mark after him by the sleeve and half-dragging him as he quickly made his way across the platform to the slope down to street level.

No one followed. The tram pulled out. A sign said "Shudehill".

Denny put his phone away. "We'll walk. And don't look at me like that, it cost nowt."

As if money was the only issue.

The packet in the drawer called to her. "No," she'd said, with some strength, as she continued to work down the bank statement to its depressing conclusion.

Later, a plaintive call. *Numbness.* She took it out. *Comfort.* Held the pouch of powdery particles. *Anaesthetic.* "No," she said. But she held the packet still. It had been put away for a reason. There was no reason now. It would take a lot of powder to fill that hole though.

She lay her handmirror on the bedside table. Took a straw from an empty juice carton in the bin, trimmed it to size with her nail scissors. Tipped the coke onto the reflection. More than Em had done. Tried to create lines with her bank card but they weren't straight because her hand was shaking slightly. Fuck it. Life isn't straight. Nothing is. She added more, curved the line, and it became a bent smile.

Her own was crooked too, leering up at her, unnaturally close. She snorted, swallowing that smile inside her mind. Dipped a finger in a glass of water and sniffed a few drops of that up too, one of Emily's tips after Sam had complained of a dry nose. Then sank into it, slow-mo style, like a soft, white cushion.

Wow. Sniff and swallow. Nice pattern. Sniff, get that bitter grit in your mouth. Part of life, swallow it down. She looked left and right, head back and forth, so smooth, she could hear her neck, gristly noise in her ear but it felt nice, left and right, nice. Pressure in head, weight to it. Lie down. Release the pressure.

Just this time. Worries gone poof world gone poof people gone poof.

Just this time.

And it was just her, revealed, alone in her skin. Her skin.

Lonely but that's good, right, her skin. She touched it and it felt like a stranger. This was more than she'd done before. It came in waves. Floated in waves.

Her hands were strangers touching her skin. She was alone. And so fucking sexually-frustrated-horny. One to the other, flip flop, bare feet, bare skin, fingertips on it. Oh, she needed to get rid of that tension, couldn't focus. Needed a fantasy. Words, words sent tension, no, relieved it, sentences, grab onto something in those word waves. Dirtier the better.

She patted her knickers lightly, pitter patter, flip flop fingertips tapping her lips. Pat tap pat tap.

She was in a room. Wearing a dress. A light, blowy, flowy summer dress, high up her legs, high. Sun through the window made it transparent.

Tap. Pat.

Not alone. A man watching. No, needs to be dirtier. Men. A group of men. In suits. Watching. No, telling. Word commands. She had to undress for them

(fuck you, won't do what man tells me)

(shut the fuck up you need to get off)

and she took her dress off, over her head, in her underwear, best underwear   shimmer   slimmer body and they watched

her fingers inside her knickers, middle finger slide

up

and

down

then circled the clit, bud, budding wetness

no, dirtier, they were wanking too dicks out   she was making them hard

making her wet

making them

naked now she knelt and took it in turns to suck each guy she was the *focus* of everything centre

in the centre

focus on the clit, rub, spiral, all it takes is the slightest touch but we spiral up

down on hands and knees, one at each end

to something that spreads warm

(never want to do that in real life, why's fantasy so different, so slutty)

they were swapping

yes it felt

warm inside

her head was abuzz

got to clear it out to escape fully, can't be held back

but it was fading, those men had no faces

no no   No

grab on and float

one man now, face hidden, tall   dark

yes

She was on a bed.

He was behind her

yes

not rough, not gang bang

he loved her

in and out and in and out he

up and down finger
he told her he loved her
he told her
if he said it   yes yesyes   it was true
not good-looking but she liked his face
heat flooding up her body, her finger moved faster
she knew who he was, who he represented
pushthatbutton, push it girl
pushed her hips back, oh silly love, Mills & Boon with a dick
it was all it took, it was here
and she clenched her teeth and spasmed her hips
so silly we move, so fully
she came in waves, floated in waves
and when she took her hand out of her knickers a last tickle of wiry hair, reluctant
in waves
she turned on her side and stared at the wall.

Around them soared even taller buildings than those near Mark's workplace. Some were being constructed. It was a zone in transition. Office blocks or flats, it wasn't clear. They all reached up away from him. It was too hot in the direct sun, but a warm breeze made Mark grateful whenever they were in the shade of the lofty structures. The brightest sun was always paired with the deepest shadows.

"You could see the whole city from the toppa them, couldn't you?" Mark asked, pointing.

"Yeah. Know everythin'."

"It'd be like being the god of the city."

"See it all. Then rob the rich cunts blind."

As they walked the area became more drab. A place you didn't stay in for long. Just passing through, a different type of transition zone, everyone wanting to be somewhere else. Car parks, car show rooms, car repairs. Lorries and dirty white vans roared past down the wide road. Billboards advertised chicken, perfect smiles, expensive running shoes that were better than ever before (if that was true every time a new running shoe came out, why couldn't people run any faster than they used to?), insurance, new homes.

"I don't think I've ever been round here," Mark said.

Denny just grunted. They walked by a wasteland separated from them by railings, piles of earth and brick and sickly brown weeds.

"Not far now. Down here," Denny told him after a while.

They turned off down side roads that went lower, a kind of under-city. The sun kept being blocked out as they passed beneath riveted iron bridges that echoed with traffic. Denny kicked through rubbish from a tipped-over wheelie bin.

"I wanted to tell you something," Mark said, eager to break the atmosphere which felt strangely funereal. "Good news."

"What?"

"A music guy gave me a job. Just a trial thing, but working with bands. Like I've always wanted."

"How come? You let him bum ya?"

"No. Because I'm into music. Know stuff. He was impressed."

"Yeah. I know those types. Waste of time."

"But this is what I've wanted to do for yonks!"

No answer.

"That's why I'm not sure about this. Can we talk about it a bit more?"

"For fuck's sake..." But Denny stopped.

They were in an arch underneath one of the bridges. There was no one else around. It smelt of wee and damp.

"You see, if I'm getting a shot at good stuff, at last, like, after all these years – maybe I shouldn't risk it."

"I *told* you. There's nowt to worry about. Even if you got caught, *which you wouldn't*. I know this guy, right, works for the people we're meeting, and he only got three years for beating up a copper so bad he needed his face stitching up. And this is nothing compared to that. And you only do half the time they give you anyway: less if it's a first offence and your nose was clean. So don't fuck up, and it's all sweet, eh?"

There was no point. No last minute reprieve. Nothing he could say that would change Denny's mind. Or his dad's. "Fine."

Denny squeezed his shoulder. Hard, brief: not much of a reassurance, but the best he'd get.

Everywhere seemed shut. And falling apart. Filled-in arches, steps leading to bricked-up doorways. Corroding metal, collapsing fences, crumbling brickwork. The only sign of life was the plants growing out of the disintegrating bricks. Up above a huge bush whose flowers were purple spears managed to sustain a precarious existence over a small empty parking area that had

PRiVATE
LAND

spray painted onto the cement. A stack of flyers for a long-past event blew along the gutter. Everything here was forgotten. Madchester was a distant memory. This was Badchester.

They reached a line of security fences with rusting barbed wire on top, set back down yet another side street. A dead-end road, in permanent shade from the bridges above where the only indications of life rolled past.

There was an intercom but the spiked gates were open. Within there were cars in various states of disrepair. Stacks of tyres, bumpers leaning against the wall like half a metal tepee, junk yard feel. A steel pipe ran up the side of the building, some kind of foil-wrapped chimney. Grinding noises from the darkness beyond two sliding doors within the compound, that led to an enclosed arch. There was barking from round the back.

"A garage?"

"The top gangs have all sorts of handy businesses under the thumb. Taxi firms, massage parlours, clubs, strippergrams, fast-food delivery. This garage is run by the Connors. They may work for another gang, but they're bad enough themselves. I think they've got lots of legit stuff going on too, but they patch up stolen cars to sell on as a cushy sideline." They walked through the gates and approached the dark sliding doors that the noises came from. "Don't tell them I said anything about that," Denny added quickly, and just so Mark could hear. Then louder: "Hey, it's Denny and Mark. Hold your fire!"

Cope. Cope. She could coke. And edges are the best places to fly from. She flew.

Couldn't fly away home, not yet. So much to do, and so much time to do it in that nothing got done. The curse of the working lasses in a strange city that was stranger now than when she first came here. Oh bright eyes, they burnt like fire, but less so now, too grimy, maaaaan, as the natives said when they were restless, and they were always restless, no rest for the wicked, and some were wickeder than others, but she could repay that, be something wicked herself, something that this way comes with a chance to get one up, one back, no back answers, barley, oh yes.

She had to turn Alanis off. You Oughta Know rattled in her head after so many listens that it was stuck there, and her current floating mind magnified it, must shut down that avenue before overload. She had enough righteous indignation for the night. As she reached for the stop button her hand knocked the water glass over, splashing liquid down the side of the unit, a dark wet patch forming at its base. "Chaos follows you around," her mam said. It would dry.

She grabbed a carrier bag, put in the things she needed, because she was going out, out and away. Would text Em later, see her too, a posse of two, to light the world and set it on fire. She had it all. Except she wasn't dressed for it. What then?

A rattle of hangars, and she nearly went for her black dress – all women have them don't they? – the big guns, show the bastards what they're missing, and that seemed right in a way but she couldn't be arsed doing the face and hair to go with it, why half measures when she wanted a pint? No, he didn't deserve her black dress. Lower rung. Denim skirt, running top. Hardly rock night out but then again it was only Wednesday … Tuesday. Whatever. Wouldn't even need a jacket, it was sticky hot and clammy. Couldn't go barefoot. Could she? Liked the idea, amazon striding along with a Tesco bag clutched tight, enough to strike fear in all the blackhearts' hearts, strike a flame, hot red top to match her mood, but no, what if she trod on glass or in some dogshit? And heels were out, too wobbly, wouldn't go, that was black-dress woman talking, better in flats, better for running. Ha ha, run, feeling like this, when the world wobbled at the edge of vision? Still, stick with that plan. A pair of trainers. Best bet. Kelly Holmes, not Zola Budd. Even in her current state she could be practical.

All was done, packed up and ready to go, leave the prison cell, and leave behind the warders, Ray and … no, Robin and Leigh … fuck it, the Lobon and Ray of Darkness, her flatenemies. *Hwyl fawr my uglies.*

The sky was only just darkening, the hint of a breeze blessing her face, but beauty shattered as she nearly tripped over some litter dumped on the pavement outside the flat, Mancunian scummers, never forget the stuff that'll trip you up if you don't watch it like a hawk. The bus would take her to severance, and she would then maybe think about it again, why she felt like this, but probably not, because that hurt, that knot inside, better numbed and ignored with action not words, and the action was coming.

There was a steely clang, a muttered curse, voices, then an oil-stained young man in overalls appeared in the doorway. He had a scar on his forehead and didn't look amused by Denny's nervous joke. He held a rag in one hand and a wrench in the other.

"You always got a gob on you?" he asked.

"Guy wanted us to come. Is he here?"

The mechanic gestured behind him with the tool, an action that didn't reassure Mark. Denny led the way and Mark stayed close, trying not to look intimidated. He kept an eye on the wrench.

Inside smelt of oil, work; things put together and taken apart again by big hands. There was solidity to the machinery and the people. One bloke with a beard was in a pit below a car, staring at Mark, and was joined by wrench man. They kept watching their visitors until a door opened at the back and a man in a suit came out. He had short hair and three gold hoops in his left ear; the suit was tight on his large frame. Maybe he chose a size too small to emphasise his muscles and solidity, to intimidate. It worked. The man walked with assurance and weight. Mark noted his hands, something he always checked, a habit from childhood where spotting if they were open or fists made the difference between a slap or getting out of the way quickly. This man's hands weren't fists but they were big and the knuckles looked hard. Punches from them would break things.

"Alright, Guy," Denny said.

"Mr Connor to you." The reply came without humour.

"Yeah. Sorry."

"About time," he said to Denny. "So, this your brother?"

"Yeah. I said I'd bring him. See, I stick to my word."

"So you do. Now fuck off."

"What?" Denny asked, surprised.

"You heard. Don't make me repeat it. It's your brother I want to speak to, not you. You've done your bit now get the fuck out of here before I decide you're trespassing and set the dogs on you."

Denny was about to open his mouth when Guy leaned forward and raised an eyebrow. Denny closed his mouth again, nodded. Licked his lips nervously, said, "See ya, Mark. You'll be fine," then left, at a fair pace considering his gammy leg.

Beardie and wrench man were laughing, making cat calls after Denny, who reddened but said nothing. No doubt he'd take it out on someone else later. And he was gone. So much for being a brother, sticking with Mark through thick and thin. A train rolled overhead, creating metallic echoes in the workspace.

"I don't know what you're laughing for," Guy said to the two mechanics, his voice not loud, yet seeming to carry every word clearly and with a brick-like finality. "Leave that for now. Go for a brew."

"But I've nearly finished doing the cut 'n' shut, just the VIN plate to do!" said the young bloke with the wrench. "I can get it done in five, why don't I–"

"Please don't make me repeat myself, Mikey."

Mikey put down the wrench, held his hands up, oily palms out. Beardie man threw down a rag then clambered out from under the car, and both mechanics walked off. Only when they were out of sight did Guy – no, Mr Connor – turn to Mark.

"You want a drink?"

"I'm trying to give it up, so –"

"I meant a cup of tea."

"Oh. No, I'm fine. Thanks. Mr Connor."

Mr Connor picked a chair up in each hand, plonked them down facing each other next to a wheeled rack of dirty tools. He sat in one, just as big and intimidating when he wasn't towering over you. Mark waited until he was invited to sit in the other chair, just in case. Don't presume anything with people like this. He'd learnt that long ago. Mr Connor nodded at the chair.

"Thanks," Mark said, sitting and trying not to look too tense.

"We can keep this brief. I just wanted to see you and make sure you know what's going to happen. You can just say yes and no. You know you're gonna be a mule?"

"Does that mean smuggle drugs into the prison for me dad?"

Mr Connor sighed wearily and nodded.

"Yes, I got told that."

"Anyone discussed how you do it?"

"No."

"It's pretty straightforward. The drugs will be wrapped up. You'll put the package up yer arse. Visit your dad. Go toilet, get it out – it'll have string – wash it, pass it your dad under the table. If it's your first time that's easier than bothering with slipping it into a cup of coffee. He'll take it from there."

"What if the guards search me or scan it?"

"Scanners only pick up phones, electrical stuff. There's like, what, 30,000 people a year passing through? They hardly have time to check more than a sample. Have you ever been body cavity searched?"

"No."

"There you go. The only thing that would cause problems is if you acted funny, drew attention to yourself. I recommend you visit your dad without the package first, get used to the idea of it. So do that as your next step."

"Yes."

"You look uptight. Gotta get better at hiding it." He leaned back, one large arm over the rear of the chair, the other hand on the wheeled tray, tapping his fingers as he sized Mark up. "You're not into this are you?"

"No."

"But you *are* into it now, son. You've got to follow instructions. This is a one-off as far as I've been told – and I don't get told everything either, we all get our instructions – but don't think about doing anything stupid."

"I won't. Denny would go mad."

"If you fuck up then you can forget about your brother – we'll do you ourselves. Thing is, there's two types of law-breaker. Criminals; and violent criminals. Currently we're the former. You are too. Help us and we won't become the other type."

"Okay, Mr Connor."

"You're sweating."

"I'm fine."

"This should be obvious, but don't tell anyone. You will get a call at some point, then you'll get the package. Do the delivery. Then you're clear."

"Yes."

"Okay, that's the business instructions over. The things I was told to pass on. Any questions?"

"No, sir."

"Don't you wonder why it was you, and not Denny?"

"It's because he'll go down for longer if he got caught."

Suddenly Mr Connor roared, or at least that's what Mark thought it was, almost falling off his chair in fright, but then he realised it was a huge laugh, and there was a shark-like grin on that ferocious face.

"As if anyone gives a shit about that arsehole! Nah, the real reason is that he can't be trusted. My bosses know that. If he was given a package he'd use it, sell it. We know you're a safe bet though: you don't do drugs. I mean, with Denny we'd have to fucking shove it up his arse ourselves and drop him off in a van, collect him afterwards and check he'd passed it on. More shit than you could imagine. That's a joke, by the way."

Mark tried to smile politely, but it was pretty weak.

"Nah, always take the easy route, use a goody goody. Far higher chance of Denny having a torch shone up his arse than with you. You done anything like this before?"

"Never."

"Why now then?"

"My dad and brother are all I've got, really."

"I see. You got a job?"

"Yes."

Mr Connor leaned forward, making the chair creak, and folded his hands. Mark could see the wiry hair that grew from the back of those big fingers. "You're a good lad. I'd rather you weren't involved but we all follow the instructions we're given, even me. One word of advice though, because I like you: your brother's a fucking toerag. After this I'd rip him out of your life and never see him again. I never met your dad, maybe he's better, who knows? Right, that's enough of me being a nice guy for the day, I don't want to start getting a reputation for being soft. But please don't make me get heavy with anything."

"I won't."

"Good. Just be cool. You'll do fine. Okay, you're done."

Mark stood. Wasn't sure if he should shake hands, but Mr Connor didn't offer one, and that was kind of a relief, since those rock crushers probably wouldn't be kind to bones.

"Oh, and if you see the monkeys having a smoke, tell them they can get back to work."

"I will," Mark replied. He was glad to get back into the sun. He passed on the message, ignored their snide stares and walked out of the spiked gates, still in one piece. Life goes on.

She stomped towards Kicks – that cheesy disco bar she hated so much – which sat below ground level under the grimy sandstone frontage of the Brittania Hotel. She squatted on the pavement, looked down through the windows. A subterranean crowd, mostly strangers, but she saw who was working, as she knew he would be on a Tuesday. In his checked short-sleeved shirt, muscles showing, and he seemed to be aiming the guns at a blonde sat on a high chrome stool, who laughed brashly at the moronic things he was no doubt saying, in a super-short skirt that showed her tanned legs. Was this a potential shag, or Sam's replacement? Fuck it, Blondie was welcome to him, muscles, good looks, tattoos and all. Alanis was in Sam tonight. She would bug him. Right in the middle of serving.

She passed two smokers standing outside and had to push hard on the stiff door to enter. A glitter ball hung from the ceiling, a reminder that this was a disco bar, and later there would be dancing, and smooching, and groping all over that floor which was so sad-looking by day and magical when you were drunk at night. It had worked magic on her, but she saw through it now, saw through it all.

She strode straight across to the open end of the bar, fierce-faced, people who saw her stepped out of the way. Sam opened the bag, removed the jar, and unscrewed the lid as she moved next to her target. Only now did Russell look up, confused expression crossing the model features, but it was too late and the process was in motion. She leaned forward and threw the sour stinking fermented and mouldy slop of revenge she had nurtured in his face. The smell made her want to gag. The blonde nearly fell off her stool trying to get away from the splashes, people stared in surprise as some eggy drips fell from Russell's chin into a pint he was pulling, a plish plosh that clouded the yellowness immediately. It was a mess, a dripping horror. Someone gagged at the rotted cheese smell which resembled vomit and drifted in the hot air.

All eyes in the pub were on her now; someone was yelling "Aye aye!" to get the attention of herself or a bouncer. Russell was pulling gunk out of his eyes with slippery fingertips, maybe not even aware of who she was yet. Who was she? Well, he oughta know that.

"It's called 'cheating slime'!" she yelled, almost a scream.

Russell spluttered, "Sam?"

She turned and walked out quickly, expecting to be grabbed by someone, a bouncer maybe, but it was as if she was charmed and no one laid a hand on her.

Or maybe it was just the still-open stinking jar containing the remains of a sloshing rancid sick substitute that she held in her hand.

Behind her there were a few cheers and laughter broke out once people realised the action was over and there was no violence involved. She walked tall (but quickly), making her own path to somewhere quieter.

"Where are you?" Sam was breathing hard as she spoke into her phone while moving at a brisk pace, glancing back from time to time to make sure no one was coming after her. She dropped the carrier bag and jar into a litter bin as she passed.

"The Garratt. The others are going in to 5th Ave but I'm being a good girl tonight," Emily replied. "I was about to head to Monsoons for takeout with chilli sauce. What about you? You sound like you're ringing me while you're in action. You're not are you? Not on the job while you talk to me? You wouldn't ring me while a guy was putting–"

"Dream on, I'm just walking, but I'm not far from there. Wait for me?"

"Okay. Do you want me to get you a drink?"

"Please. Anything."

"You might regret saying that. See you soon."

She got there three roads, one junction, two crossings and a tooted horn later. The Garratt's sign shone in blue neon curly writing. It was facing the 5th Avenue nightclub on the corner. There were wooden benches and tables outside amongst a few trees with lights in them. A favoured place to get pissed on a night as hot as this. She spotted Emily at a bench on her own beyond the diamond shapes of the blue metal rails, there to keep the drinkers in one place as a discrete herd. Em's face lit up with a wide smile when she saw Sam. "Hey, girlfriend."

"Hey you."

They kissed on the cheek. Emily was wearing a pink vest top that Sam suspected was meant to be an item of underwear. Still, it was so sweltering that it didn't seem too crazy. Latin American fashion in a pore-opening jungle of buildings.

"I got you Sambuca."

"Vile," said Sam, downing half of it. "Thanks."

"What are you doing in town tonight? If I'd known you wanted to go out I'd have invited you to join us."

Sam looked round, but there was no sign of Russell. There wouldn't be. He couldn't follow her when he was working. But she still felt like she couldn't relax out here, right by the pavement. Maybe coke made her paranoid. "Can we go in?"

"If you want. It's like an oven in there though."

"Just for a bit."

They found a corner table facing the bar. Sam could see the door from there too. She relaxed a bit. Her heart was racing. Not just the excitement of the evening. Enjoy it, don't sweat it.

"Okay, what's got into you?" Em asked. She leaned forward, looked into Sam's eyes. "Dilated a bit, you been on the coke?"

"A bit. And I've been a bad girl."

"Ooh, I like the sound of that." Em rubbed her hands together in childish glee. "What have you done?"

Sam told her. "Urgh, just remembering the smell makes me want to retch."

Em was laughing, leaned over the table to give Sam a hug. "Way to go!" She said, wiping her eyes. "It's not like you. I applaud. I shoulda suggested something like that, but I didn't think you'd go for it."

"No. It had to be my own idea. I'm starting to realise that. I'm tired of other people's choices affecting my life. I'm now single."

"Just for info, you already were."

"He'd told me it was over. I hadn't done the same. *Now* it's official."

"Fair play. Remind me never to piss you off."

"I wouldn't throw slime on you."

"What then?"

"Vodka."

"What a waste. Pour me the vodka, throw water on me."

"Not in that top, it'd go see-through."

"And?"

"You're as bad as me."

"We're a team. Your turn to buy one."

"What do you want?"

"Vodka and a glass of water."

Sam shook her head, but complied. Got the same for herself.

"We've got to do something tomorrow," Emily said. "How about Overdraught, get wasted on cheap shots, then into 5th Ave to dance?"

"The crowd's too young in 5th Avenue. 18 if you're lucky."

"Okay. Option two: there's a house party in Withington. Would be cheaper, and on your side of town."

"Whose party?"

"Rob's. He's cool."

Sam had met him a few times. He was a small-time dealer, just for friends. "On your radar?"

"Maybe."

"So if you're going to be batting eyelids at your supplier all night, what will I do?" Sam asked.

"You'll know *some* of the people there. Larky, Will, the gang from Rusholme. You could always pull one of them and we'd have a double date."

"I'm not interested in any of that lot."

"It was just an idea. What about inviting a certain someone who works in the office then? Then at least you won't be bored."

"No! If you invite someone to a house party it always looks like you want to get off with them."

"Not always. Don't worry. I don't give a shit what he thinks. I'll do it."

"If you've not invited him out before he's bound to suspect something."

"Nah, he's too slow. Haven't you noticed? Borderline retard. More like a team mascot than a functioning worker."

"No he isn't! He'd surprise you."

"Doubt it. But you've settled it – he's coming. Then we'll both be entertained."

Sam knocked back the rest of the vodka. Her mind was racing with possibilities. She was *now* a free agent. The dotted line had been signed in vomit-like ink. Life could move on.

WONDERWALL

...song, recorded in Wales, which achieved platinum status and Gold in the US, topping the charts in a number of countries? The video reinforces those band messages. Firstly, we see the band's name rotating on scratchy vinyl. The video is black-and-white (the only colour is the guitars – you can't suppress the music). So we're talking about connections to the musical past. Then we see that the video is full of circles: dartboards, the sound hole in an acoustic guitar, a hand-mirror. You see, what goes around comes around and we reconnect with where we come from. We rotate around a central force. Could that be the wonderwall? Noel said the it was "an imaginary friend who's gonna come and save you from yourself". So we're empowered. Go after your dream, best friend, love. It will save you.

... Oh, there's a floppy-footed clown in the video too, for example during the mid-song four-beat introspective silence. Maybe it appears because we connect them with our pasts. Maybe for no purpose. Or maybe just because we all sympathise with them. Anyway, the video did somethi...

Oasis, the adopted sound of Manchester. The ultimate proof is when they were used as the soundtrack to the most accurate portrayal of Manchester lives. No, not Coronation Street, but The Royle Family. The Gallaghers and band are princes behind the castle wonderwalls. Before we finish we'll be learning more about the monkeys, kings, and Godlike geniuses that also live there.

Mark finished loading the van with Dave. Ran a forearm over his sweaty forehead. He'd be glad to get back under the shutter's shade.

"Good to go, mate."

"Yep. Hey, Mark. Do you want to talk about last night?" There was concern in Dave's voice. "About Denny?"

"No. It's all fine. Thanks though. I know you've got my back."

Dave's gaze lingered a moment longer, then he nodded. "No problem. But let me know if you ever want to talk. No piss-taking, just … properly."

"I will."

He watched Dave drive off in a belch of blue smoke. Deliveries to colleges would take him all morning. Dave gave a quick wave out the window, without looking back, but it was still a message to Mark. One more glance at the sky, last he'd see for a while, then back into work.

"You alright?" Taffy the porter asked, as he shifted some parcels into his office.

"No, half left," Mark replied.

Rote response to a stupid question. Words used every day that had no music in them, no poetry, just wasted air. Hello would do. A wave or smile would do. Better than communications done on reflex that neither person cared about.

"Lankybollocks," the porter mumbled.

"Taffyapple," Mark called back.

Mark had walked on when he had the idea. Words had meanings and so did names. It all came down to words. He turned around, went back, and asked Taffy some questions.

Sam rooted through her bag looking for her phone as the PC booted up. Items spilled across the desk. Her hands were a bit shaky this morning.

"Hey. Let me get you a caffix." It was the first thing Em had said to Sam. That didn't bode well. Normally there'd be a joke.

"Thanks."

"You look like you've not slept for a week," Em whispered in her ear as she passed.

"I haven't."

Her attack alarm rolled onto the floor. Sam squatted, collected it from under the desk, and bumped her head as she stood. Crammed things back into the bag, snatched it up and went to the toilets.

Bag in her hand, looked in the mirror. Bags under her eyes too. She fumbled out eyeshadow, put some on. It wasn't necessarily an improvement.

Please, let this day be over.

When she got back the cup of coffee steamed aromatically by her keyboard. Grateful smile to Em. A sip with her eyes closed. If she could just stay awake until lunch she'd be fine.

Third cup of coffee. 11.25am. She was winning.

Mark brought the post. Didn't say much today, presumably because Sam wasn't working alone. As he left Em whispered, "Nice arse", then laughed her dirty laugh. Mark looked back in curiosity, then frowned as he moved to the next team.

"Stop it, Em. You make people paranoid."

"Sorry. True though. About the arse."

"What's the joke?" asked Roger, looking up.

"Nothing I can share," Em told him. He didn't seem put out by being left out. Just went back to reading something on the screen. He'd been in an uncharacteristically good mood all morning, in fact.

Footsteps approached. Sam ignored them and stretched. Dry-wiped her face with hot palms. *She was winning.* Maybe another cup of coffee next.

A tap on her shoulder.

"See me," Rene said, and stalked off to her office without waiting.

Sam looked at Roger and Emily, confused.

"Ideas?"

They both shook their heads. Sam gazed after Rene, who had already banged her office door closed.

Shit. Scratch the win.

"The priority order for West Trafford College. Why hasn't it been fulfilled?" Rene jabbed at a printout on her cluttered desk. She didn't ask Sam to sit.

Sam tried to pull up details in her mind. The order was outstanding. Some graphic novels and lots of physics books. No reason why it should be marked as priority this far ahead of term. Yes, she remembered chasing this up.

"Supplier problem," Sam answered. "I'm not sure why it hasn't come yet. I'll ring them now."

"You should have rung them already!" Rene shouted, leaning forward aggressively, blazer stretching at the seams. "I don't want to have to grovel to a client; I don't want our company to look unprofessional. If we want to keep important customers then we can't have this slapdash approach."

Sam tried to control her anger. Remember: Rene's not happy either. No one is in this office. Or most jobs. Remember what she studied in sociology A level. *We're all unhappy because we have no stake in it. We work out of desperation to survive. Other people have power over our lives and jobs. We're disenfranchised, we don't know or care about the people we work for and they don't care about us. Faceless people own companies and get rich. Try and stay calm. It's not her fault. Stay calm. Be proud that you remember anything from your A levels. Nothing's wasted. Be cool.*

"It's not slapdash, Rene. I've chased this up already, I have, but no reply. It's on my list of things to do. It doesn't help when PCs break down and you can't get on with your work. Let me go back to my desk and get the details."

"Or make up dates and excuses."

Be calm. "I'll ring them up and sort it out, find out why the order hasn't come."

"You should have done that *already*, Samantha." Rene crumpled up the order into a ball and threw it in Sam's direction. Whether she intended to or not it hit Sam on the chest with a crinkling rattle.

It didn't hurt, of course. Not physically. But the knowledge that any nosy eyes in the open-plan area would be watching her getting upbraided through the glass of Rene's office was too much.

"It's not..." Sam started, but had to stop, her voice wasn't under control. She hated feeling weak. She took a deep breath. "It's not my fault," she whispered, to avoid her voice breaking.

"Oh yes it is!" Rene shouted again, making Sam start. "It *is* your fault. You're the one in charge of orders so it is your responsibility.

Why didn't you chase it up properly in advance? This is one of our most important contracts, not some corner shop! If we want to keep preferred supplier status for the educational institutions we can't act like some amateur... You're always having a joke with the others, I've seen that, don't think..." Rene seemed unable to finish her sentences either, so angry. "And you're looking shabby, not like a team leader. Careless." Sam felt near to tears. Bit them back. "You're out of line, Sam. That's all I want to say. Think about your future. Isn't tomorrow your performance review? You can go."

So Sam got out, avoiding the curious stares of the other office workers. She grabbed her bag, rooted – ah, a couple of cigs left in a crumpled packet and some pills in her emergency purse. She walked out of the office, popped two bitter painkillers dry. Standing in the sun at the front of the building with a cig was better than bashing her already-banging head against a desk. Which was what she felt like doing.

No win, pure fail.

Afternoon, staffroom. Idle chatter kept her awake.

Mark was here too. He'd been quiet, reading NME. She picked up a magazine off the pile, didn't look at the title, turned pages without seeing, just used them to pass time. Metronomic paper. Flick the seconds away. If only you could do that with problems.

She stayed when the others drifted out. At last. So casual. So unmanipulative. So *Cool Cymru*. She pointed at his mag. "Obsessed."

"Got to keep an ear to the ground. Look out for signs."

"Of what?"

"The next big thing. The next band that continues the good work. The *vibe*. I know it's not over."

"So music's more important than anything else, for you?"

"Not *anything* else."

Sam was about to pursue that, ask him what things he'd put first – a girlfriend, maybe? – when he said, "Anyway, what's that rubbish you've got?"

The magazine Sam had picked up off the pile without thinking was Good Housekeeping. "Yes, well, I don't normally read this," Sam replied as she slung the magazine back onto the low coffee table, trying to be casual. She flung it a bit too hard and it skidded across the smooth plastic surface and onto the floor near Mark's feet. He picked it up by the corner as if it was toxic and put it back on the table.

"Didn't realise you hated the magazine that much," he said quietly.

"Nor did I," she muttered, smiling.

"You looked a bit down again before. You okay?" he asked, leaning slightly towards her.

"Yes. It's nothing. Just work." Mark was still looking at her. Eyes calm and curious. No need for tension. "Rene had a go at me," she explained. "It wasn't really my fault. Or maybe it was. It leaves me feeling bad either way."

"Had a go at you? You should tell her to bounce off and stick her job up her back-radar." Mark flung the words as if suddenly angry. "She must be out of order. Don't take it to heart."

"I won't. Thanks. You're my Kangol-helmeted protector. Though I notice you've stopped wearing it to work."

He touched his head gently, but kept his eyes on her. "Sorry. I haven't –"

"I don't mind. You look good either way. You out tonight?" she asked, over-riding her decision to play it cool. But this moment was too delicious. Keep piling on the sugar.

"Yes." He grinned shyly. "I've been looking forward to it."

Just then the door opened, Dave Chambers came in. They sat upright, probably looking guilty for no reason. But a soft conspiracy of connection wasn't illegal. She went back to her desk with a smile.

Mark dragged the bin bag up to his flat, hoping it wouldn't tear. Past the door to Mandy's place, which he avoided looking at. Inside his home, where he could finally tip everything onto the sofa. Masses of socks, trousers, shirts, underwear: it had been a while since his last visit to the launderette. He rooted through, found a top and some trousers, cleared the kitchen table so he could use it as an ironing board, remembering to wipe up the spilt HP Sauce first.

He was really pushing the boat out.

Poured a glass of water, drank most of it and used the remainder to fill the iron.

Tonight was going to be special, he knew it. He was leaving nothing to chance. Drink water, don't talk bollocks, look smart, be relaxed.

He felt nervous but happy. Energised. He'd slept well – in fact, there'd been no noise from upstairs for a while. Anxious excitement trembled his muscles. His armpits were sweating. He'd wash them again before putting the clean top on. More underarm deodorant.

One night, away from the normal daily grind. It had to be perfect.

At home she made herself a sandwich. Then found she wasn't hungry.

Leigh was shagging her boyfriend upstairs and Robin was out, so Sam went into the living room and put the TV on for a bit, tried to relax. She channel hopped impatiently, but it was just coloured lights and noise. Nothing connected or made sense. She turned it off, irritated.

Get dressed. That would help.

Her wardrobe was open, long mirror balanced on a chair. Even though it was still light she closed the curtains to stop people gawping in as they walked past. A hazard of having the ground-floor bedroom.

A simple black dress. She smoothed it down. Held tights against one leg, comparing them to the pale skin on the other. Yes, tights. Pulled on a patterned pair and stood in front of the mirror. Turned to take in all angles. She didn't like the slight bulge at her tummy when you looked from the side. She breathed in and it nearly disappeared, but she couldn't do that all night.

The dress came over her head, flung onto the bed, hangers consulted.

A black skirt. A shell top with a Peter Pan collar. Heels. But when she looked in the mirror it was too formal. As if she was going to an interview, not a party. Back down to underwear. What else?

A denim skirt, she liked them. Found a brown buttoned top, nothing flashy. Took the tights off. Put a trainer on one foot, flat shoe on the other. Pointed each forward in turn. Was happy until she turned to look at her arse, realised the denim had faded at the back where she sat. Why should that bother her now? She didn't know. But once she'd spotted it she was too aware of it. Clothes off, flung onto the pile.

Tried another dress but it was tight at the hips. Had she put on weight? Or had it shrunk? Either way, it was a no.

Took jeans out of a drawer. Didn't try them on. Too scruffy. Onto the bed. Black culottes? No, she wore them to work sometimes, and didn't want any reminders of that hole of a place.

She continued to look at items, try them, fling them. The pile grew. It was the Discard Monster.

Fuckity fuck. She was normally the girl who just put on the first clean thing she found.

She wanted a drink. Or a snort. *Really* wanted them. As if they had voices, called to her, offering confidence and an end to desperation. They wheedled but she ignored them, and felt good that she could do that.

She did go outside for a cig though. In the back yard, letting the smoke calm her with every deep inhale, each longer than the last. She blocked out the suburban sensations: traffic, TV from next door accompanied by the smell of chips, shouts in the streets, and instead stared up at the sky. The sun was fading. Pink last light on a bed of blue, fading to black. Slow motions, but inevitable. Maybe even the same sky she'd see if she was back in Wales, a connection there. Calmness spread.

She had it.

She dug out a glittery blue top, not far off the sky's shade. She hadn't worn it for some time. It was close-fitting but comfy, didn't make her tits look huge. A long black skirt with a split up the side. Smart and casual. Then she opened her jewellery box and took out a silver necklace with a pink stone, something she'd begged for many years ago on a family visit to a mine. That one thing in the gift shop caught her eye, despite pink not normally being her colour. Something about the solidity of the crystal. Beauty and strength. And now it hung on her neck. She was the colours of the calming sky.

A bit of lippy, a smear of eye shadow, and she'd be ready to go.

Sam paid the taxi driver and stood in the neglected front garden of the house in Withington, that town of hospitals and ex-students. An old cement sack was partly overgrown by brambles. She shook her head. *Mancunians*. She would have loved a bit of garden to call her own. As a child she'd always helped her mother and Mamgu, holding the basket of freshly-picked vegetables, or squatting in the mud and making small holes for seeds with a dibber.

She could hear music blaring out of the house: Little Green Bag. Not the original, but the version from Tom Jones' recent Reload album. Maybe they thought they were being ironic, but it made her smile. Wales followed her round.

Ding dong.

Some lads were sat on a wall opposite and sidled over while she waited for someone to answer the door. They wore baseball caps and dirty Kappa jackets. "Hey, can we come in with you?" one of them called out. She ignored them.

DING DONG.

"You're tasty for an older woman," another yelled.

"Older woman"? When had she become that?

She pushed the door, just in case. Yale lock. Rang again, felt relief when it was answered by Larky, one of Em's followers. He gave her an affectionate bear hug. "Chuffed that you've come," he told her, brushing his long fringe out of his eyes.

"Stop fiddling with your hair and get it cut."

"Never. Oy, lads, fuck off!" he yelled past her ear.

"Come and make me, you streak o' piss."

He let her in and shut the door. Shook his head. "I'm keeping an eye on them dodgy shits for Rob, they keep throwing litter in his garden."

"Charming." She held up the bottle of cider she'd brought.

"Ta, just put it in the kitchen," he said. "Emily's in there making cocktails."

"*Quelle surprise.*"

"The only surprise is that she stopped flirting with Rob for five minutes."

Sam recognised a lot of faces as she walked through the house. All connections through Emily. You could almost draw the dots. Maybe that was why she couldn't remember names to go with the faces.

Emily was cackling and tipping the contents of different bottles into a jug, then sloshed pineapple juice into the red-coloured liquid.

"What cocktail's that supposed to be?" Sam asked.

"Hey! You came!" A big hug. Sam inhaled and smiled. Emily was wearing her favourite perfume, Body Shop White Musk.

"Course."

"Do you want sex on the beach?"

"I'll stick with cider in the glass."

Sam opened cupboards until she found a clean tumbler and poured out a cider. A very small one.

"You look great," Em told her.

"Thanks. It took ages to get ready."

"I know what you're like when you do your make-up. Little Miss Cleanse-and-start-again."

"I'm not that bad. And it wasn't the make-up, it was… Never mind. It would've been more fun with you there. A bit of your giddiness and energy."

"Yeah, sorry babes. I'd promised to help get the party going."

"That's your specialty."

Emily mixed the jug's contents and poured herself some, leaving the rest for other people. She took Sam's hand, led her through the brightly-lit living room with the loud music and into a dark back room where Massive Attack was coming from a smaller hi-fi. The only glow came from lava lamps, colouring the room with reds and greens like Santa's sinful grotto.

Emily zeroed in on Rob, obviously her next victim. He was leaning forward in an armchair and rolling out a spliff on the coffee table. Emily sat on the arm of his chair and rested against his shoulder, watching him roll with dextrous finger motions. He was a snappy dresser, always smart clothes, and into the details – black shoes polished to a shine, trousers ironed, some kind of curved pendant hanging around his neck outside his smart jumper. Even his hair was perfectly styled. Sam understood why Em fancied him. Sam also suspected he was gay, and it would be amusing to see Em's frustration if her many charms failed for once.

Sam knelt on a cushion next to the coffee table as Rob licked the Rizla and sparked up, getting first drag. He offered it to Emily.

"No blow-back?" she asked with a fake pout.

He just grinned and kept the joint extended until she took it and inhaled deeply, holding the smoke in for an impressive amount of time. She offered the joint to Sam; seeing the red glow of the end, the pale smoke drifting up ghostlike, and smelling the good quality weed meant Sam could almost taste it. It would be so calming, so mellow, like melting herb butter on the tongue. Warmth that could pass inside, drawn into your core, your lungs, and from there into the circles of a bloodstream, riding the flow, passengers of peace.

But she shook her head. Had a sip of cider instead. And the spliff got passed to someone else.

By now Sam's eyes had adjusted to the sensuous gloom and she checked each face in the room, but there wasn't the one she hoped to see. Maybe he hadn't arrived.

Em was fiddling with Rob's pendant, and Sam felt a tinge of pity for her. "Don't get too mellow," Sam said, "I want to see what's going on next door."

"Okay." Em slid off the arm, and her skirt was so short that it didn't leave much to the imagination. It made her slender legs seem to be even longer than usual. "You'll see me later, Rob."

He just smiled and nodded, opening his bag of hash and rolling up another spliff.

Through a hall and into the other room which was bright by contrast. Furniture had been moved to the edges to create a space for dancing, and a few people were doing that self-consciously, others stood or sat around talking. Someone had got Christmas decorations out and put up tinsel and brightly coloured globes. Gaudy but cheery, if incongruous for June.

She was surprised to spot one face where she knew the name: Roger. He hung awkwardly by the sidelines with a bottle of beer, wearing a horrible Bermuda shirt and white jeans. The poor guy probably thought it looked retro-cool but it was more Timmy Mallett than Miami Vice. Sam pointed him out and Emily laughed, headed straight over to him.

"Holy shit, look at you!" she said loudly.

Roger seemed relieved when he saw them. "Hi ladies."

Urgh. Sam was glad he didn't use that term in work.

"What's this?" asked Em, feeling the collar of his shirt.

"Something new. Summery."

"Wow. It's certainly bright," said Sam.

"Didn't you know? The 80s rang," Em added. "They want their shirt back."
"It's good quality. Cost me £40."
"That doesn't make it any easier on the eye," Em told him. "But never mind that, Sonny, wanna dance?" She grabbed Roger and Sam's wrists, pulled them both, but Sam twisted free, didn't feel like dancing yet, preferred to lean on a wall in view of the door. Watched Emily and Roger laughing as they danced to the B-52's Love Shack.
Every time the doorbell rang and someone came in she watched eagerly ... then it would be someone else whose name she didn't know.

It had gone 10 o'clock but no one else from work had showed up. Still, she didn't always come to a party at the start of the night so there was no reason why anyone else should. She tried not to compulsively door-watch. Did it anyway.
"You okay?"
It was Roger, looking quizzical. Serious, even. Something that completely failed in that flowery shirt.
"Sure. Why do you ask?"
"Emily said you looked bored; told me I should talk to you."
Sam scratched her eyelid.
"I would have done anyway. If you seemed lonely," he added. "Don't need Emily to tell me to do that."
"Well, I'm fine. Thanks for the concern."
"No problem. Do you want some more drink?"
She looked at her glass. It had been empty for a while and she hadn't refilled it.
"No thanks."
"Dance?" He held out a hand.
"Not in the dancing mood, sorry. Though you two looked like you were having fun."
"Emily's mad. But cool. Nice party, isn't it?" he asked.
"Yes. I've not been to one for a while."
Pause. She looked round the room.
"Hey, supposed to be hot again Friday onwards," he added, not giving up.
"Right."

"Are you doing anything this weekend?"

"Not really."

"That can't be true. You must have *something* planned."

"Why?"

"You know, good-looking woman, dates or something?"

"Yeah, right. A toss-up between shopping, watching TV, or spending the day with Em. Or possibly combining two of those at once for super excitement. What about you, got something lined up?"

"Oh, all sorts of things. You know me: work hard, play hard, rest hard."

She nodded.

"That was a joke," he added.

"You're too subtle for me."

He smiled, taking it as a compliment. "Well, do you fancy doing something with me? Maybe we could go to the Odeon, see a film or something like that?" he asked.

"Thanks, but I've got things I need to do." Sleep, for one. She felt so tired. She was really fighting the urge to yawn.

"You said you had nothing to do?"

"I didn't want to bore you with every little detail."

"Maybe next weekend then? It would be good to go and see a film."

"I'm more into music, really."

"Oh, you should have said! I have loads. I could lend you some."

"I meant live music."

"Me too. Wanna go and see a tribute band?"

He really wasn't going to give up. "Good idea," she said, with a hint of fridge. "That would be nice. A gang from work, get lots of people together. I'll look into it. Thanks."

"That's not..." He sighed. "Yeah, sure. Bring the idiots along. I'm getting a top up." He headed off towards the kitchen.

That was weird.

The room was heaving now. The music had changed to drum 'n' bass and was giving her a headache. She wouldn't even know how to dance to that kind of thing.

Rob tried to sell her some speed. "A bargain." She declined.

The urge to drink was still there, but she switched to water. It made her puritanically proud. And miserable.

Someone put their arms around her waist from behind and rested their chin on her shoulder. She could tell by the perfume and easy touch that it was Em, not some drunken male groper on their way to a knee in the bollocks.

"Hi darling," Emily whispered in her ear.

"Hello *cariad.* What do you want? I thought you were with Rob?" Sam untangled the arms and turned round to face Em.

"I've got Rob under control, don't worry about that. Well, I think so. He's always so cool."

"Maybe you can't win them all."

"We'll see. I just wanted to check how you were getting on. You seem a bit edgy. Why not help me put away a bottle of Cava with your name on it? Or join me for a smoke?"

"Nah."

"Or just have some *fun.*"

"I'm fine enough."

"Roger said you blew him out."

"I didn't blow him out at all, I just didn't... Well, he was maybe coming on to me a bit. Or not. Who can tell with him?" She shuddered.

"Yeah, he is a creep. His weirdness makes me laugh though, even if it's unintentional. I won't send him over again."

"Good ... hold on a minute, have you been talking to him?" Sam asked suspiciously.

"Only a bit." Em giggled. "Don't worry, he'll be okay. I won't say anything again."

Prickly annoyance flushed Sam. "Fucking hell, stop doing things like that, it's not as clever as you think it is."

"I'm sorry. I'd been mean to Roger. I told him that whatever kind of look he was aiming for, he missed. Then his face was so long I felt sorry for him. I just sent him to you to make up for it. Being round you is like a reward."

Sam sighed. "Sorry. I'm over-reacting. It doesn't look like Mark's turning up either."

"What do you mean?"

"I thought he was coming?"

"Why?"

"Don't wind me up!"

"I'm not," Em replied, apparently serious.

"You said you were going to invite him when we were in The Garratt, remember? I thought you did, since it seemed like people in the office were talking about a party today?"

Emily laughed and the prickles became spikes. "Oh, I'd forgotten about that, we'd had quite a few drinks. Wasn't I talking about Roger? Or was it that you said no, so I respected that? I didn't think you really wanted him to come. Anyway, no, I didn't invite him. Did I make another boo-boo?"

"Oh, just forget it!" Sam snapped. A few people looked over but she didn't give a shit as frustration twisted her insides. "I'm going home. I'm not in the mood for partying. Don't think I ever was."

Em lost her silly smirk. She tried to take Sam's hand but Sam shook it off. "Tell you what, I'll text Ben Lawrence," Em said. "Mark's usually out with him I think, find out where they are, get us a taxi and we could head off –"

"No. Not the right frame of mind for that now. I just want to go home."

"I'll come with you then. Let me grab my coat, we'll leave straight away."

"No, it's okay. I can get a taxi from the rank up the road. Look, I need to go. Stay here and have fun."

Emily got hold of Sam's hand this time but then seemed unsure what to do with it. She spoke earnestly. Softly. Un-Emily-ly. "I really *am* sorry, I didn't realise you would be upset ... that you were serious."

"I don't want to talk about it."

"But I upset you again. It hurts me that I've done that. I'd do anything for you. To make you happy."

"Just forget it. It's not you, it's me." And her own fucking fault for relying on someone else instead of doing things herself.

"Men tell me that when they never want to see me again." Emily suddenly hugged Sam, her short hair brushing Sam's cheek and the scent of her perfume mingling with the smell of alcohol and it was a tight squeeze like she'd never let go. Sam eventually had to free herself, face the concerned look in Em's eyes.

"I'll be fine," Sam said. "I'm acting like a kid. It's been a shit day. I'm exhausted. Let me get some sleep. You get back to Rob, he'll be missing you. Speak tomorrow."

"I'll make it up to you. I promise. I'll get you two together," Em told her.

"If you want to help, just leave me to do things my way."

She left. Pushing through people oblivious to the ache that suddenly crackled in her ribs. A cage to keep stuff out, why was it inside, how'd it get past that bony barrier? The light was now fading. She let the gate clack shut behind her and was pleased when the music faded as she strode down the road. Leave that shit behind. She hoped the bad mood would be left behind too. It wasn't though. Never did work. Perhaps because most of all she was annoyed at herself, for being bothered about such small things.

"Hey, it's the witch again!"

The lads with their caps were still there, drinking from cans now. A quick glance showed empties on the pavement. She walked faster, noticed them slipping off the wall and following her.

The *witch*?

Usually there were taxis around the corner near the shops. If not she'd have to ring for one. Should have done it from back at the house.

"Hey, where you going?" asked one of them, gaining despite her brisk walk. She reached for the pocket with her attack alarm in, just in case, then realised she hadn't put her jacket on. It had seemed too hot to bother with that. The orange streetlights gave everything a hellish glow, each pool of discoloured light surrounded by dark shadows of bushy gardens, walls and alleys.

No one else on the road, no one looking out of windows. She didn't want to yell for help, not yet, just wanted safety, to be left alone. Knew the worst thing would be to stop, respond; bad people took that as a twisted invitation.

"Stuck up bitch!" she heard, different voice.

Her heels clacked, multiple footsteps behind, getting nearer.

Round the corner … and there it was, a taxi near the bus stop, the driver with a newspaper open. She rushed over to it, got into the back seat gratefully, only then aware of how fast she was breathing.

There was no sign of the lads on the road.

"Where to, love?"

"Home."

"Where's that?"

Across the border from England, that's for sure. But she just said, "Chorlton."

Mark was sweating uncomfortably, heat rippling beneath the skin, but he didn't mind. He'd just been helping a roadie unload gear from the band's van out back, running back and forth, helping to set things up before the doors opened. The roadie's black shaved head glistened with perspiration too. He grinned at Mark and sat on one of the boxes.

"I don't even know what band this is," Mark admitted.

The roadie laughed. "Vigilantes of Love. It's Bill's band."

"What kind of music is it?" The name immediately brought New Order's song Love Vigilantes to mind.

"Americana," the roadie told him when a yell from Monksie across the room diverted his attention to a new type of cable.

The multi-core was a long, fat red worm with lots of plugs in its mouth and arse. One of many pieces of equipment he was getting familiar with. He had to double check the connections; Monksie thought one had come loose.

He'd no sooner done that than his name was yelled again and he joined Monksie at the main sound station. Mark was reminded of the old comedy film Airplane! as he looked at the deck controls which seemed to go on forever, a mysterious console a mile long made up of what looked like hi-fi pieces, some silver, some grey, but all with a complex array of dials and needle gauges and knobs and plugs and sliders and sprouting a chaotic spaghetti cable junction. He'd only ever seen it from the audience side before – a counter with a head bobbing up and down behind it. Seeing things from this side felt special.

"I can't go into much detail tonight, but I've got a few mins spare so here's the basics – worth knowing," Monksie said while pointing to pieces of gadgetry with one hand, and scratching his arse with the other. "That's the 32 channel sound mixer desk above the amplifier. More than we need but the manager got a bargain there. Each column on the deck is a channel and we can plug one mic or sound source into each. So basically we get the sound from the singer and instruments; the boxes fiddle with the signals, optimising and compressing and maximising – that's my magic bit – then we pump the mixes back to the audience and the band.

"The main ones on this side are the DRC kit: compressors. They squash the dynamic range, so that the quiet sounds are more audible and the fucking loud sounds – technical term – don't deafen anyone. I use it for boosting the vocals usually. Most of the time we only have to fiddle with the attack and release controls a bit. It helps to know a bit about basic acoustics for this."

Mark vowed to himself that he would read up on this arcane science. The public library was bound to have some music books.

"That's the reverb unit. Some nights I have to fiddle with it a lot. For example, I might put a bit of reverb on the vocals if the band wants that effect, but it's got to be turned off at the end of the song so when the singer speaks he doesn't sound like Stephen Hawking. Always got to be monitoring stuff like that."

"I'd be lying if I said it looked simple," Mark said.

"You get a handle on it eventually. Like anything else, it all clicks into place, boom! Happy ending. I remember I got wasted once – wasn't working that night, just at a gig – and I was so out of it I thought I could see how signals went round the system in my head. All these coloured lines, and splitters, and changers. It was a freakshow revelation, all visual. Since then I've felt an affinity for the kit. Like I can see inside it. Make it go smooth. Hey, don't look at me like that, rookie! Everyone's entitled to trip now and again!"

Mark laughed, trying to picture the lines and colours, but it was just a fluorescent mess of a mental image, the distorted book flowline of Packham Green.

Later he was just as confused by the foldback principle. He was positioning speakers on the stage, Monksie called them wedges, pointing back towards the drums and other instruments. They had been fiddling with positions in order to stop things feeding back to each other: all the speakers and mics in close proximity were a balancing act. He'd been told it was so Monksie could send a particular mix back to each musician. It seemed to get complicated quickly.

Mark waited until the band members weren't around and he wouldn't look stupid before squatting next to Monksie. "I know I said I wouldn't ask many questions – but why? Can't the band just hear the noise they're making without you having to do all this? And why is it different for each, surely they know the song, how it should sound?"

Monksie repositioned the wedge he'd been connecting before he answered. "Well, quite often it's hard to hear what's going on if you're playing, believe it or not. The guitar might not need to hear the vocals but she definitely needs to hear the drums, and not have it all drowned out by the trumpet player stood next to her. Every member of the band has different sounds that are more important to their performance. So you always have some foldback – at least one by the drummer so he can hear things over his racket. And what the band hears is different to the audience. Though the audience is always the primary thing. Sometimes the band has to lump it."

"Oh," replied Mark, trying to imagine how different the music would sound when you were on the stage. That perspective he'd never experienced. But tonight he was close enough to touch it.

And once the gig got going he joined Monksie behind the mixing desk, now close enough to touch the backs of the audience members bobbing up and down to the music, facing the stage and feeling every twang of guitar in his bones, every bending wail of harmonica. The music had hints of what he normally liked, but also an interesting alien nature to it, a difference, a newness, an itch he was tempted to scratch. His feet tapped, his head dipped with the rhythm and chord changes, and he *appreciated.*

Monksie seemed to be at one with the kit, occasionally holding a single earpiece from the headphones against his ear, frowning, making some change to the equipment, nodding, smiling, then letting the headphones hang loosely from his scrawny hand again. Mystical gestures by the wizard of sound, connecting the seemingly unconnected. Above the gadgetry Mark could see the crowd watching the stage, bopping and bouncing as if electrified, people crammed together within personal space zones, even within the *intimate* space zone that so often acts as a repelling barrier between two foreign bodies. Tonight they were colliding and impacting. Was this the physics of molecules in the books he processed for a local college? Monksie was the master of lives unknown as he played around, fine tuning sounds, trying to mix things right, his actions running through cables and pumping out of speakers, crossing space and entering ears then brains, affecting moods and behaviours and connecting things. Connecting people. Unseen contacts, but no less real.

Being a sound engineer was a fridgeload more secret power than Mark had realised.

The band were all smiles backstage after the gig. Monksie was pleased too, everything had gone well, and he praised Mark for getting on with what he was told quickly and efficiently, but also for getting on with *the people*. All the human parts had to be greased to run smoothly, trust built by showing you were into it too, enthusiasm given, professional helpfulness shared with tour managers, stage managers, performers, lighting, staging.

"Do what you can to make people feel good, make the band feel better. Then they play better. It's all tied together. Getting on with people is just as important as the technical skills. And you've got the former down good. Patience and attention to detail – that brings the rest."

The praise from Monksie repeated as Mark travelled home, sonic echoes in his ears on the bus, through the door, even into bed.

Yes, it was only helping out in-house at a small venue. Yes, it took a while to get used to the faders. Yes, he shat himself when he turned the vocal mic up too far while it was close to the foldback wedge and it started squealing with feedback and nearly deafened someone ("You've made a mistake – just learn from it. It's all experience, mate," Monksie had said.)

But he'd done good. On his own.

He'd *Gone For It.*

corpses in their mouths

singing. It accuses its target of being a habitual liar and a drug user, then Ian tells them to slip their neck into a rope (the last bit an unpleasant reminder of another Ian, 1980). It's been claimed that a number of this album's songs are aimed at The Stone Roses guitarist John Squire, who Ian had accused of being a selfish, unreliable, cocaine abuser. We'll get to Squire

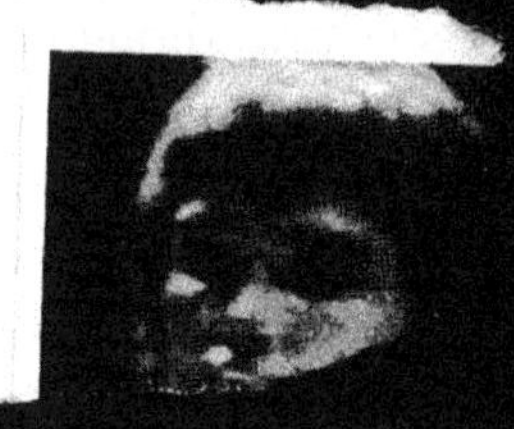

video starts with monkeys, then Ian jiggling round with his trademark heavy-browed ape-like stare. That iconic Ian Brown appearance also graces the cover of this, his debut solo album. The album's name is a further nod to the simian analogy: Ian said he'd been called a monkey so much over the years that he adopted it as part of his persona. So what if his arms are long compared to his body? It just means he can reach that bit farther. And as he swivels in a rotating chair, headphones on, he is even more

The Roses, then lost it all. Then he started again in a council flat with nothing, launched his solo career, and got it all again. There's always hope of improvement and escape. "The reason I was in a group was to get out of Manchester, because it rains every day, it's industrial, there's nothing to do," he once said.

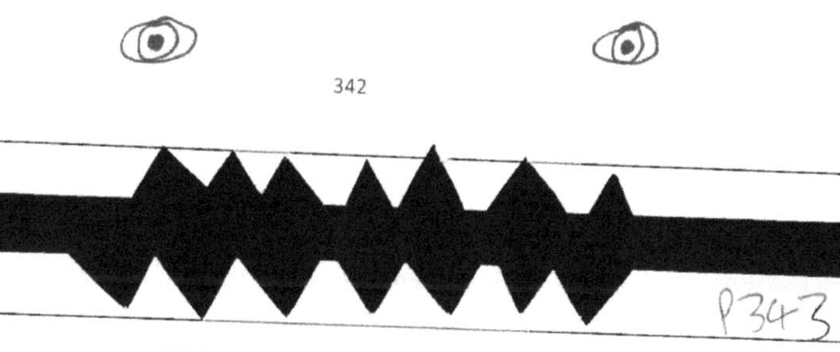

P343

Background drives character. Pre-Stone Roses Ian was into northern soul, going to all-night dance and music events. He doesn't like fighting, despite taking beatings from others on many infamous occasions. And in December 1999 he was sent to Strangeways for two months, and while there he wrote three of the songs for his album.

"You're Aquarius, right?" asked Emily, a pen tapping on her cheek as she scanned through the newspaper. It was break time but they sat at the work desk with coffees. Emily had been reading out the headlines prior to her question: yesterday Tony Blair had been heckled when he gave a talk to the Women's Institute. When Sam had not paid proper attention to Emily's reciting of the highlights she'd received a slap on the arse. One of Em's attention-getters. It was hard to hold on to negative thoughts for long. And not worth ignoring her again.

"Yes. Why?"

"'A holiday could be rewarding to you. You are on the cusp of important decisions so this is a favourable time to overcome or reinforce the past. A life-changing event may take place on a busy street in a few weeks. Your advice to someone close to you was helpful'," Emily read out, before looking up with a smile. "Not a bad one there. Holiday? Lucky bitch."

"I don't believe in that kind of thing. It's all too vague," replied Sam, sitting back from the keyboard and stretching. "What's yours?"

"Why'd you ask if you don't believe in it?" Emily teased, winking at Roger. "Mine says I'm going to meet a tall, dark stranger."

"Rubbish!"

Emily shoved the paper across the desk to Sam and tapped the circled horoscope. "See. I might have already met him. Did you see the new estates guy that came round before? He was tall, black and sexy, and I don't know his name yet."

"He was fit," Sam conceded. "He'd better be careful next time he comes here." Sam tried to make a sexy tiger purr, but it came out more like a froggy gargle. "But what about Rob?"

Em shook her head, went back to examining horoscopes.

After a while Sam yawned, collected some parcels. "I need to stretch my legs."

"Give them to *Mark*, eh?" Em asked.

"No, they're for Dave, *actually*."

Roger looked up from the scribblings in his pad, frowned from Sam to Em as if disturbed by their interruptions.

"Sorry," Sam told him with a smile. She moved off, boxes tucked under each arm.

An armful of packages were dropped onto his desk. "Sorry," said Sam, as Mark looked up. "These are for collecting. For Dave. Is he around?"

Eyes dark. Proto-goth, almost. But shining inside.

"He will be. He's doing his performance review with Rene."

"Oh crap. I've got mine today."

"Me too."

"I'm in Rene's bad books."

"Me too." That brought a smile to her face. Being naughty kids in detention always made people more equal. Though it would've been better to be equal at the top than the bottom.

"I don't think she wants to sack you though."

"Is it that bad?" Mark asked, surprised.

"Could be." She sat on the edge of the table. She had a smart skirt on. It hugged her bare legs. Eye-height, side-on. Such lovely curves in the lines, reminding him of musical notes on paper, the curls in that alien language of notation; those interesting shapes, fascinating, he could stare but he didn't understand them. And a scary moment, an urge to reach out and touch her leg by the knee, to check it was really solid, and that made his heart beat faster at the enormity of it, the inevitable reaction of horror, a slap maybe, eternal ribbing probably, bad reputation definitely. Perfection wasn't for him.

"You look zonked. Did you go out last night?" she asked, picking at a mark on her skirt.

"Yes. And it was amazing," he said with energy, glad of the chance to change where his mind had been going.

"Oh?" She didn't smile. "Something good happen?"

"I helped out at a gig. Real bands. It was unbelievable."

"Oh!" She smiled. "I didn't know you were doing that!"

"I kept it quiet." He looked down, happy. "Didn't want to jinx it. I didn't get paid or nothing, but the experience is good. Monksie – he's the guy who let me help, he's the best – he told me I did well. And the bands were brilliant too. Hopefully it's a foot in the door. I'll do it again."

"That is so great! I'm really happy for you."

And she leaned forward as if to kiss him on the cheek, and he froze, and it seemed suddenly awkward as she stopped and put a hand on his shoulder instead then withdrew it quickly like she was shocked, or repulsed, and her smile was unsettled, something was there but wasn't in words, it was like music, confused music he didn't understand but which filled him with longing, sickly dizzying, and he wanted to listen to it again.

Oh sweet potatoes. But no, it could be good. This was it. This was the moment he'd been waiting for.

"Shoo ducky, Sam?"

"What?"

Holy Hooky, Taffy the porter must have been pulling his leg when he taught him that one. The busker.

"I thought it was Welsh... Sorry, you probably wonder what I'm on about."

"Oh, *sut dych chi*, no – you're right!" She laughed. "It is Welsh. 'How are you?' I love hearing Welsh in Manchester, especially in your accent! That's really sweet! Do you know any more?"

Mark wasn't sure if he was more embarrassed when he thought he'd said the wrong thing, or when she'd said he was sweet. "No, that's it. I'd like to know more, it sounds so different. Rhythmic."

"Ha. The sensibilities of a bard. *Sut dych chi* – I love it! So you've got hidden talents as well as good looks, anything else I should know?"

Good looks? Was she being sarky?

If she said it's sexy, she doesn't fancy you. That's the way with offices.

"Erm … no … that's it." Mark saw Dave approaching, grabbed the parcels and shuffled them to the side, moving slightly away from Sam as he did it. "Just finish this – Dave, got parcels for you. Can you drop 'em off on the run? – For Sam – I said you'd do it."

"Hi, Dave," she said, slipping off the table. "How'd the review go?"

"I aced it. She thinks my arse is golden. And she's right. Buttocks firm as metal. Feel 'em if you want?"

"No thanks," said Sam.

"I nearly squatted on her desk and laid a golden egg. In the shape of a book."

"That would make your eyes water," Mark added, not wanting to be left out and feeling a strange stab of annoyance at Dave's invitation to Sam.

"And what's Marky Mark been doing? Regaling you with tales of his music industry breakthrough?"

"A bit."

Mark waited for the punchline – maybe something about sucking a producer's cock, or having drugs pumped up his arse. But Dave just said, "He did well. Proud of him. I think we should all go next time. Support."

"Yes. We should," Sam added.

They were both looking at Mark. It felt weird. Like he was a foot taller.

She skimmed the subjects of new emails. One caught her eye. She read it eagerly.

Supplier procedures ... paper-based ... no trace of her order ... temporary staff ... possible printer problem – all irrelevant compared to the sincere apology at the end from the manager, and a promise that the books were now on their way.

It wasn't her fault.

Of course she'd known that. She'd followed all the procedures, had chased up flagged orders, had done everything right. But ever since Rene's outburst her confidence had been shaken, she couldn't just shrug off the feeling that she'd failed. This email – seeing words written by someone else, someone who didn't know her personally, apologising – *that* made a difference. She clicked print and the ancient inkjet on their desk rattled to life.

The desk phone went. Em beat her to it. The paper churned out. She stapled the sheets together. Her mobile buzzed. A text. Russell again.

`Soz you got hurt, I understand that, can we at least talk?`

Yes. Talk to the ignore button you low-life bastard.

Okay, papers neat, past controlled. Looked at the clock. She was ready for the future.

Emily was shaking her head at the receiver. "I don't know who you think you're talking to, but I'm not the complaints department," she interrupted in her most melodious voice and put the phone down. She returned to the list in front of her, ticking items off and muttering either "Completed" or "Not important any more".

"Emily, did you just hang up on a client?" Sam asked with a frown.

"Huh? No. Supplier. He needs to calm down. Used the word 'portfolio'."

"I've told you before about being so abrupt! It's me who gets the flak if they complain."

Emily sighed. "Sorry. Will. Try. Harder." She batted her eyelashes as punctuation. Today it infuriated Sam.

She was going to swear when she remembered Mark. So instead she thought, "Carrot, carrot, moron." And the anger dissipated. Instead she felt like smiling. Maybe there was something in Mark's methods after all. Things shouldn't be so serious. Sam never had liked giving orders anyway.

Rene beckoned to Sam through the glass of her office. Sam gathered up her paperwork. This might take more than a carrot to get her through.

"Anything I need to know?" she asked.

Emily shook her head. Roger shrugged.

"Great. Wish me luck."

Inhale deeply. It's just work. Carrot.

"I've always wanted this to be like a family business. Like it was when it started," Rene told her. "I was assistant manager back then, for Mr Packham. Before he sold up to Eduteach Services."

Sam nodded. They'd got through the preliminary sections on the performance review form. Then Rene had got a wistful look in her eyes.

"I've tried to keep things the same. But nothing stays that way, does it?"

"I suppose not."

"I've been here thirty years, you know." Rene stood up slowly, stretched up to take a framed photo off the wall, separating blouse from skirt in a flash of pale waist flesh. When she sank back into her chair it creaked. Handed the photo to Sam.

Sam had never seen it up close before. As with all the things in Rene's office, you noticed them peripherally, but never paid attention to the detail. You were rarely in here for long enough. A group photo. In the car park by the side of the building. Mostly young people. Sun shone on them. They looked happy. In 70s clothes, browns and khakis, flared trousers and collars. The men had moustaches and big hair.

And then she recognised some of the faces. The fresh-looking woman in a low-cut top – that was Jean, the keyboarder, who complained about her back. The grinning young man with arms folded cockily – that was Scotch Stu, from the warehouse, who now seemed quiet and withdrawn. And the slim woman in glasses with long dark hair – Marie, in finance. Who was now silver-grey and tired-looking. And then she spotted Rene. In the front row, to the right of a tall man in a suit. She was slightly plump but not rounded like now. Smiling at the camera. They'd all given their lives to this place. Sam's eyes widened in horror.

Rene leaned forward. There was a whiff of peppermint about her. She took the photo back and gazed at it for a few seconds before hanging it up again.

Sam glanced through the office glass. She could see Emily frowning at the computer screen and tapping away at the keyboard. Would *she* end up withering here too? It was hard to imagine. Em was surely a James Dean, a Jim Morrison, fuck and check out. But maybe the people in that photo were once the same.

"There's changes coming. Got to be," Rene told her. "And I've got to take it seriously. Because I'm told to. We've *all* got to take it seriously. The family days are past."

"I am serious."

"Good." Rene pulled some papers over. "I checked the invoices from the last month. There's money down. See here." She slid a page to Sam, who scanned it quickly.

"That's fine. I just gave them a discount."

"What for?"

"Some books in the last order were missing and one was damaged."

"Did you see them?"

"No, but they're a good customer."

"We don't just apply 20% discounts here and there."

"I know. It was a goodwill gesture." No hint of understanding. "A one-off," she added.

"But they might have been lying."

"No, I can tell. Why is it a big issue? We want people to come back to us."

"The issue is you overstepping what you're allowed to do. This is what I mean when I say there's got to be changes. Some people will be leaving. Others might have to reapply for their jobs."

"That's ridiculous."

"I don't make the rules."

Sam took a deep breath. "Fine. I won't do it again."

"I'll hold you to that."

"Why do you have such a low opinion of me?"

"It's based on performance."

Ouch. Sam separated out the sheet of printout she'd brought with her. Slid it in front of Rene, careful to rotate it the correct way to be read. "I've just got this," Sam said.

Rene didn't look down at it. "And?" There seemed to be more distaste than curiosity in Rene's voice, but that would change.

"It's about order 1082, for West Trafford College. It's from the supplier." Rene's unblinking stare was unnerving. "It explains what went wrong," Sam finished weakly.

"I don't particularly care. As long as the order gets fulfilled yesterday."

Sam faltered, but then decided to press on. She deserved to be heard. "Please will you read it? It shows that it wasn't my fault, that they made a mistake, that I *had* followed it up. It's all in there."

"I'm busy with other things, and not particularly interested." Rene picked up the sheet of paper, making a point of not letting her gaze cross the words, and moved it towards the bin by her desk. After a moment's hesitation she added it to a pile of paperwork instead. "Now let's get back to the review."

When Sam had got this job in a new city she'd been proud. When she got the minor promotion to team leader her family had been even more proud, blowing it out of proportion. It was as if she'd been knighted. Always supportive. The way people should be. The way she used to think people were. Now it felt as if, outside of your circle of family and closest friends, the rest of the world was an alien and hostile place. Things made no sense. Why were most people so mean? Uncle Joe would never have treated her like that.

Sam looked up. Blinked hard, opened her eyes wide, willing them to stay dry. Lowered her gaze to Rene. "This is because of the water bottle thing, isn't it?" she asked.

"No. I'm helping you out here. If I don't point out your problems then I wouldn't be a good manager, would I? And there's the fact that you're always wandering off."

"Yes, for *work*. Passing something on, or checking something. Or if it's break time. It's not shirking."

"That's not what I heard."

"Who have you been talking to?" Sam asked, suspicious.

"No one. I meant 'that's not how it looks'. Out of my window."

Sam looked at her in disbelief. The walls were crumbling. "I can't do this. Sorry." Sam stood, picked up her papers. "It's not worth it."

"But we've got to do training requirements and SMART targets!"

Sam shook her head, mute with disappointment, and left, only just over-riding her impulse to slam the door.

Rene's padded-shoulder blazer was over the back of her chair because of the heat, and instead she sweated in some sort of white blouse that made her face seem redder by comparison. She studied paperwork in front of her. Mark felt like he was at the doctors having his tool examined.

"In the year's achievements section you put 'doing my job properly'."

"I couldn't think of anything else. That's a good one though, right?"

"They'll expect a bit more." She looked at him. She was waiting. Why'd people always want *more*? Wouldn't it be nice if they sometimes wanted *less*, just for a change? Then everyone would be satisfied and happy more often.

"I'm usually on time for work," he tried. "Unless the bus doesn't turn up. Or breaks down."

"Okay, let's add 'Maintained punctuality under difficult circumstances'."

"That sounds fancy."

"And you've smartened up recently. The hair. Shirts. We could also include 'Takes pride in appearance'."

"Yeah. Ta."

"Okay. The section on what you enjoyed most and least this year. For least, you've put 'paper cuts'."

"I always get loads. After work on Fridays I have chips for tea. I get salt and vinegar in the cuts. It kills."

"Erm … okay. We'll leave that. The thing you enjoyed *most* was the Christmas party?"

Mark glanced out of the window. From this angle he could only see blue skies. It was like being in one of them posh tower blocks. His attention went back to Rene, sensing her gaze on him.

"Yeah. 'Cos I did the music."

"It would be nice if we could add something more impressive-sounding."

"There's nothing impressive about my job though. A monkey could do it."

"Do you really want to say that to head office?"

"I guess not. I liked it when I got to do the warehouse liaison for the day."

"Ah! Extra responsibility."

"It was cooler in there."

"But we'll put that you liked the task and enjoyed the extra challenge." She wrote on the form, looping lines deceptively graceful compared to the pudgy fingers doing the work. "The only other bit I'm not sure about is the 'Future Plans and Objectives' section. You can't put 'Get a new job in the music biz'."

"But I don't see much future here. That's my new plan."

Rene laughed. "You've got to pay the mortgage, Mark. You can't do that on dreams."

"I did a gig."

"How much did it pay?"

He didn't answer.

She put her fingertips to her lips. Thinking. He saw the blue veins on her hands. There was a glisten of sweat on the meaty forearms.

"Do you have any career aspirations, Mark?"

"I'm generally happy enough doing what I do."

She stared at him. He felt he had to say something extra. *Again.*

"I suppose it would be good to have more responsibility." She seemed to like those words. She smiled and nodded her head when she heard him say them. "Look at moving up. More pay would be nice."

"The latter is difficult in these conditions, but more tasks might be an option. So I'll put something in about increased responsibilities again, eh?"

"Why's it important though? At the end of the day it's just paper 'n' forms, innit? Just fancy words to make someone you don't know tick a box."

She put down her pen. Looked down her nose at him as if he was an escaped and deformed bogey.

"It's more than that. There are threats to jobs left, right and centre," Rene told Mark.

When he didn't reply she looked down at the paperwork in front of her and moved some of it into his folder. "We're under pressure from head office. They say we're overstaffed and we under-perform."

"Overstaffed?"

"Yes." She paused. "You do well. Get on with your job. Apart from the window incident, but we've moved on from that. And leaving work without authorisation. And the meeting disruption –"

"I had hayfever."

"– and interrupting me."

"Sorry."

"As I said, we've moved on. I hope you will stay. But I'm not sure that we need so many delineated teams. Three in your team – we may need to look at that. Three in orders. Extra staff in the warehouse, finance, keyboarders. If I'm forced to let people go then we might have to reassign duties to those remaining. On the plus side, that could mean more responsibility for you, as we discussed. It won't immediately affect pay but might eventually, and would look good on your CV. I could see you doing some more acquisitions-related work."

"You mean, I'd work in the ordering team?"

"Perhaps, some of the time. I do pay attention, you know. I got the impression you'd like that."

"What about Sam and Emily and Roger?"

"The team may have to be re-sized."

It suddenly struck Mark that things might really change here. He'd heard the talk before, but it had always ended up with business as usual. Now however... He needed to say something. Chewed his lip.

"It's down to Sam," he blurted.

"What is?"

"Me doing well. Everyone looks up to her." *Where in the world of raisins did that come from?* It was like jamming though, go with the flow, lay one sound on top of another and see what builds up. "If jobs go then you should definitely keep Sam. Being team leader and everything."

"Sometimes people aren't happy in their position. Things don't have to stay as they are."

Mark remembered watching Sam and Rene argue, saw their body language through the glass. He needed to bring in some keyboards. "Well, the heat makes everyone snappy, might make things seem like problems when they're not. But Sam is really good. She doesn't just run her team, she helps make sure we stay organised."

"Does she?" Rene asked, surprised.

"Yes, she works closely with Dave. She always has her team working hard, it sort of sets an example to the others in the office." This was easier than he'd expected. Almost fun. "They're so well organised. I overheard Sam the other day too, with one of the suppliers. They were messing her about and she was dead firm with them, it was … erm … inspiring? I wouldn't have wanted to cross her. She got them to backtrack. Yeah, she can be impressive."

Rene scribbled some notes on her pad. Mark hoped he wasn't overdoing it.

"She keeps the ship tight. Without her things would be looser than a choirboy's rectum."

Rene frowned.

"Sorry."

"Whatever happens, some of us will go."

"Yeah, but some are worth keeping more than others. Look at it this way, if it was a choice, someone like Sam is more important than me. And I could do other stuff anyway, like music. If I was a boss, I'd keep her." Oh great, now he was doing himself out of a job. Then

Inspiration struck like a crashing power chord. "If anyone in the team had to go, I'd say it would have to be Roger. Sam and Emily definitely get the most work done. Roger is, erm, a good guy, I've nothing against him, but I reckon I could do some of his work, with the right training."

More notes scribbled. Rene seemed pleased when she looked up. "Well, this has been useful. As to your hayfever, you should try something from your doctor."

"I'll look into it."

Pause.

"It doesn't affect my work," he added hastily.

"I'm sure it doesn't. Thanks, Mark."

"S'okay."

He was excused.

As he left he grinned to himself. His dad would approve that he had lied to the boss. His conscience approved that he had done a good deed. And the bonus was that no one would find out, so he wouldn't have to deal with a ribbing from the lads or the embarrassment of Sam knowing.

Everything was going right. He was learning about people. He was gaining friends. Respect, even. He was doing the right thing. If his life kept improving like this then *anything* could happen. Before he knew it, The Haçienda would be re-opening. Today the world shone like diamonds.

The staffroom was full of people, chatter and laughing, radio voices, horseplay; the usual serious atmosphere banished in Rene's temporary lunchtime absence.

Emily was heating up a floury bean tortilla she'd bought to share with Sam. The microwave hummed and vibrated. Dave and Taffy the porter almost knocked the kettle over as they used a battered tangerine to demonstrate some football goal. Mark was explaining to Ben and the temp why Ian Brown was a God-like genius and music from Manchester rated as the best in the world. Others joined in to form a good-natured argument that made Sam smile, glad to just listen as Mark tried to imitate some wah-wah guitar intro by Johnny Marr.

A car revved its engine in the street outside then sped around the corner with a loud screech. Roger peered out of the window, perhaps eyeing the inevitable rubber marks on the road. "I think he's making up for having a very small penis," he said.

"What about you?" Emily asked.

"I don't drive in town. I've got a bicycle."

"Good one," Emily said. "Almost funny. You're not yourself today, Roger, I noticed the improvement straight away."

A ping. Emily halved the wrap onto two plates, thrust one into Sam's lap. "Eat." Em had already told Sam off for skipping breakfast. Then she wriggled her hips to squeeze in between Sam and the woman who dealt with staffing, receiving a glare for jostling her Financial Times. Em didn't notice it.

"I prefer a kebab," said Ben, staring at the plates.

"And I prefer Cordon Vert to Cordon BLURGH!" Sam replied.

"But they're nice."

"Don't go there," Em told him. "She's beyond help. Won't even touch bacon butties."

On the news there was a piece about an appeal for people who lost homes during the recent Indonesian earthquake.

"Charity begins at home," muttered Roger, picking up a magazine. "Come on, it does, right?" he asked again, shrinking down into his seat.

Emily leaned forward. "Hey! We should get a collection organised here."

"Yes. Pay money for Roger to come into work without gel on his hair," said Dave.

"Charity diets," Roger muttered. "Rene to lose five stone." He seemed surprised when people laughed at his joke.

"What's your idea, Mark?" asked Emily.

"Charity 'listen to music' event? Battle of the bands?"

People groaned. Mark just shrugged.

"No, I've got it. Charity kiss. People pay to kiss Sam," Emily said, turning to Sam but speaking to the room. Sam felt uncomfortable as everyone looked at her, as if assessing. "I know I'd pay. For a big wet tonguey tango."

Guffaws, whilst Sam almost spilt her drink.

"Me too," added Ben, and suddenly there were lots of claims shouted about how much people would pay to kiss her. Sam shook her head but the embarrassment was almost delicious, full of the flavour of smiles and compliments.

"What about you, Mark, you haven't said what you'd pay for this great honour?" Emily asked.

Mark looked at Sam, something weird there – distaste or fear, or just surprise? – then quickly stared at his lap, mumbling that he didn't know, didn't do stuff like that.

Now all stares were on him, along with puzzled expressions. The room was silent apart from the bubbling of the kettle. Mark's face reddened as if he was boiling inside too.

He won't even look at me, Sam thought. *What the fuck?* The sunshine moment was over. Then she decided it was probably shyness. He wasn't shy when alone with her, but in a group he always did seem quieter if the conversation was about anything other than music. No boasts from him, no cockiness. That was probably it. He was just *shy*.

Sam felt genuine gratitude to Ben when he broke the silence with "I'm going to add my own offer too: girls can pay to kiss me, as sloppy as they want."

"I see you've set aside this special time to humiliate yourself in public," Emily told him, and everyone but Sam and Mark laughed.

Roger had been looking out of window. "Hey, Rene's back. Manic stations, everyone." There were sighs. Lunch was over.

"Have you asked Mark out yet?" Emily shaded her eyes from the sun and glanced at Sam. It was the afternoon break. Only a few hours and the work day could end. Sam and Emily were stood outside with coffees, leaning against a wall that overlooked the canal. There was a warm breeze. It rustled the branches of a lonely street tree, at the base of which litter had gusted into a pile.

"That wasn't necessarily my plan. I've had other stuff on my mind today."

"Forget the performance review shit. You need a positive. Mark should sweep you off your feet and into Rene's office for a wham-bam-thank-you-Sam."

"With you lot looking in through the glass? Yeah, right."

"You need to do *something*."

"You're blowing this out of proportion."

"No I'm not." Emily balanced her cup on the top of the wall. Folded her arms. "Maybe the answer is simple – make him jealous. You'll know soon enough if he likes you then. Flirt with the people round him."

"I don't think this is good advice."

"Do you think I'm successful with men?"

Sam snorted.

"No rude comments please. My point is, I must be doing something that works, right?"

Sam nodded. Finished off her coffee in a bitter energy burst.

"So listen to me and do as I say. We needn't make a big song and dance out of this, you don't have to become the workplace slapper – no jokes please – but just a little. After all, flirting is just what people do when they get on well. Trust me."

"I never trust anyone who says 'trust me'."

"Then don't trust me, just do as I say."

"Look, I know you mean well, but I'd feel better if you just left me. I do things in my own time. My own way. None of this game-playing."

"But I want to see you happy!"

"I know."

"So let me give a few nudges, or I could –"

Sam thunked down her cup. "No. Please, just leave it. You went far enough at dinnertime."

Em fluttered her hand in a sinuous gesture like a bird taking off, but Sam suspected it wasn't a proper capitulation. Em was going to keep interfering. The whole thing could end up a mess. What was Sam stalling for anyway? She liked him. That was it. She would just go and ask Mark out before it all got silly.

Back inside. Sam sent Em off to print a list of every outstanding order. It was less than thirty seconds before Emily gave the printer a thump and yelled to the office, "How do I set a laser printer to stun?" That would keep her busy for a while. Sam slowed down as she approached the post and processing area.

"What do you mean, you don't fancy her? Are you out of your mind?"

"No, I just don't go for women that are too bouncy. Lively. And her smile seems too wide. It scares me."

She'd hoped Mark would be alone, but his was the second voice in the conversation. The first was Ben's. So instead of going ahead with her plan she held back, pretended she needed some headed paper from a free-standing bay of shelving nearby, where the stationery was kept. It was out of the way and she was on the opposite side of the bay to them. No one seemed to notice her, so she stopped rummaging and listened. It wasn't anything out of the ordinary: she often overheard bits of conversations when she was collecting supplies. They seemed to get caught up in their nonsense while doing some boring job that didn't require thought.

"So you're telling me that if Zoë came on to you, you'd say no?"

"Yeah. Prob'ly," replied Mark. Sam had no idea who this Zoë was – certainly not someone at work, maybe they were talking about someone famous?

Ben laughed, then spoke more softly, "What about this then: you're lay in bed, it's 4 o' clock in the morning..."

Sam heard a third male voice – Dave Chambers? – say "Oh no, not the 4 am test!" but Ben ignored the interruption.

"You've been asleep but have woken up, something's roused you, you don't know what. But you notice that you've got a huge throbbing erection. You need release." Sam could hear them chuckling quietly. Like schoolboys. "So you reach down and begin to pleasure yourself, as you naturally would in the circumstances. Suddenly the door opens and in walks Zoë! She's wearing some slinky black night-dress, and you can make out the shape of her thighs and breasts. She climbs onto the bed and begins sucking you off –"

"We wouldn't, she's married."

"Shut up, imagine she's single again. And you stroke her head. Her mouth is hot and eager and she moans as she swallows your throbbing love missile. Now," and here he paused for effect, "are you telling me that in that situation you wouldn't poke her?"

Sam could tell Mark was struggling to think of a response, then he just sighed then said, "Well, I would then..." It sounded like he was smiling. Sam felt a stab of jealousy.

"So there you go! You would sleep with her. Case closed." All three were giggling now. Sam wondered how they ever got any work done if they were like this all day.

"It's not a proper test though: according to that I would sleep with Rene!"

"You said it, Mark. You're irrepressible." More quiet snorting laughter. "Whereas me," continued Ben, "I'm choosy. I'd only poke Little Miss Rees or Emily. No one else here is quality enough, but either of the Rees and Garfield duo would do a man proud." The third voice, the one that was probably Dave, agreed.

Sam flushed when she heard her surname. She had no idea where the "Little Miss" came from. She felt mildly thrilled at being praised above the other women, but was also angry at being talked about in that way behind her back. Then again she was listening so it wasn't really behind her back. It reminded her briefly of something Mamgu used to say, about eavesdroppers only hearing bad things as a punishment for being nosy.

"You got worked up at dinnertime or something?" asked Dave. "All that stuff about kissing?"

"As if! Okay, here's the question," Ben continued. "Who's your favourite? Samantha or Emily? And why? You first, Dave."

"Well, I'm spoken for. It's irrelevant."

"If you were single."

"Alright. I'd choose Sam. Deeper personality. Sexy accent. Down-to-earth. Chocolate-box pretty, my gran would have said. And I like dark hair."

"But isn't your Suzannah blonde?"

"Sandy. Darkish. Anyway, shut up, Ben! I can guess which you'd pick."

"Yeah, both!"

"You can't have Sam *and* Emily."

"S and Em. I wouldn't mind a bit of that kind of S&M," Ben laughed. "Only kidding, real answer is easy: Emily. She's got a dirty laugh. I like that. And she shows her legs off. Short temper like the skirts, but I like a bit of spirit. Okay, Mark, your turn."

Sam felt her heart skip a beat.

"I don't want to play this game," he said, sounding disinterested.

"Why are you being all coy?" asked Dave. "Emily or Sam?"

"Heads up, Gel Head," Mark said.

Sam had noticed a figure passing her shelves. She hoped he didn't see her, felt the guilt of the amateur spy. But no, she should have been out of his sight here if he wasn't looking directly at her. She didn't want to go yet.

They'd been unpacking the afternoon delivery, arms deep in packaging and inventories and clean-smelling books, checking things off then sorting them onto trollies. Normally it was a chance for fun banter but Mark didn't like the current topic. He was glad of the chance to change it.

"What are you doing over here where the real work gets done?" Dave asked Roger.

"We do real work too."

"Yeah. Roger the Dodger more like. This your latest skive, come to join the lads?"

"Just on a wander. I was looking for Sam."

"Not seen her."

"I thought I heard her name."

Ben laughed. "We were just talking about who's the fittest."

"What, out of you lot?"

"No, you pillock," said Dave. "Out of Sam and Emily."

"And what was your conclusion?" Roger was looking through the new items.

"Stop messing with those, I've sorted them."

"Sorry." Roger put them back hurriedly.

"Well, for me it was Sam. Ben prefers Emily. And Mark is being mysterious."

"I just don't think it's right to talk about people like that," he muttered.

"Don't give me that, they're both gorgeous, smart women, we're not dissing them," Dave told him. "Which one?"

Mark shrugged. "Dunno."

Dave slapped his own forehead. "Come on! That's a crap answer. Don't be such a demic."

"And you always just shrug when you don't want to say anything," Ben added.

"It's like my catchphrase."

"It's a shit one," Dave told him.

"I bet I know who it is," Roger said, interrupting with a sneer. "It's Sam. And he more than fancies her. You can tell by his face."

"That's not true!" snapped Mark.

"That proves my point."

"Ah! That explains why he smartened up," Ben jibed. "Making himself look good, impress her."

Dave nodded slowly. "They did look shifty in the staffroom the other day."

"Shit, him fancying Sam?" Ben whistled. "That's material for a *year* of wind-ups. Does Emily know?"

"And there's no point, she wouldn't go out with a berk," Roger said.

It was the closest Mark had felt to punching someone in years. He tried to force tension out of his bunched muscles. He couldn't trust the people at work. He didn't want this getting around. He'd be ribbed about it forever. And worse: Sam would hear. She'd never talk to him again. He wanted to just run off, except then they'd assume they were right and it would be worse than ever. He was trapped. Unless … well, possibly they were still just joking, didn't really believe it yet. Maybe he could put them off.

It's one of those things about life. Always keep a bit back, son, whatever it takes to keep the bastards guessing. But never give the game away. It's only used as evidence against ya.

"Oh shut it!" Mark said. "I don't fancy her. Too much eye make-up."

This caused another uproar. "You're either blind or daft or gay," said Dave. "Or even all three!"

"No, it's true. There's something about her face that seems a bit weird. She doesn't smile enough. And she dyes her hair, and I prefer natural."

"Shame you're so perfect, huh?"

"I'm not saying that, Ben. I guess it'd be Emily for me. She's more like my ideal woman: a super-slim Caroline Aherne … crossed with the lonely elfishness of Louise Rhodes from Lamb, and … and the expressive eyes of Jacqui Abbott – who took over from Brianna Corrigan as The Beautiful South singer around '94 when Heaton heard her sing at a party – and the … erm … classy style of Corinne Drewery from Swing Out Sister, and I like how she was influenced by northern soul, it's all a bit out of my normal area, especially the jazzy stuff, but I remember loving Breakout back when I was at school, y'know, the fun angle of it –"

"Fucking hell, put a sock in it," said Dave.

"Well, you wanted to know what I like, it's that. I go for girls like the lawyer one I was seeing, or girls with some music connection."

"Oh. Well, if you're that specific, then you probably are right," Dave said, seeming bored now.

"Yeah. Bit of a let-down, though," Ben added. "Way to put a dampener on a conversation."

"I don't understand," said Roger. "How come you know all those names? Were they bands or singers?"

"Drop it," muttered Dave under his breath. "Please don't get him started."

And it *was* dropped. Mark had swung out and broken out, brother.

Sam was outside. Lighting up a cig with shaking hands.

Too much eye make-up. Weird face.

She took a huge drag, walked round the corner so no one would see her if they came out.

She wasn't even good enough to get on the first rung of the ladder.

Doesn't smile enough. Unnatural hair.

She did dye her hair sometimes. Just a bit darker. He'd once asked her if she did, and it had annoyed her, since it made her think that she must do it badly. But she'd just thought he was a bit free with his comments, tried not to take offence. Now though … looking back, maybe he was being critical of her even then.

So obvious now. Like how he was uncomfortable when she hugged him outside the record shop that time. Didn't enjoy it. He criticised her for swearing, thought she was vulgar. He didn't want to joke about kissing her in the staff room. So obvious *now*. She was just someone he passed the time with.

She was so stupid. She slumped, eyes shut and head forward, thumb on one eye and forefinger on other. There was a throbbing behind them.

Maybe he was right. Maybe she wasn't pretty, or gorgeous, or desirable. Maybe she was even weird-looking. Still, he had no right to talk about her like that in front of others. No right to be such a male chauvinist cocky pig bastard fuck. No right to hurt her confidence; to twist a knife in her gut when she could have felt something for him.

She realised she was grinding her teeth. On a collision course with violence if she didn't calm down.

She sniffed then wiped her eyes on her sleeve. Which was probably a mistake. She didn't have a mirror on her. Looked in one of the warehouse windows. The sun shining down made it reflect. Yep. Eye make-up smeared. She was frowning. She tried to straighten her hair with her fingers, and it felt dry.

She stubbed the cigarette out on her reflection and turned away.

Her granddad had owned a miniature steam engine. Only a foot long, always kept polished. On special occasions he would get it out, put it on the big kitchen table, oil parts, buff it up some more. Sam and her cousins would all peep over the top of the table, watching the old man work patiently, lovingly, on that marvel of miniature engineering. Eventually he would stoke up its boiler with fuel, add water to the tank, and wait. All the children would go quiet. And after tense minutes steam would appear, and he would pull a small lever, letting it out in a whistle that made them smile, before he flicked a little switch and the steam would start driving the wheels, the force of it great enough to move shafts and gears and create forward motion, even from that little frame.

And fuck: she needed to blow off steam and get some forward motion.

First she took the bottle of vodka from its carrier bag. She'd picked it up at the corner shop on the way home. Couldn't be bothered getting any juice from the kitchen. Necked a mouthful of the clear liquid from the bottle. Grimaced.

"Rehab is for quitters," she muttered.

Then she yanked the old 70s-style brown and cream curtains closed. It was rough fabric, horrible to touch, and not thick enough to keep morning sun out. They didn't close properly, the plastic hooks on the rail were too stiff, but she could overlap one piece of material on another as an approximation of privacy.

The drawers on the chipped white laminate furniture were stiff too. Nothing moving with tended precision here. Nothing made to last. She found the plastic bag of powder at the back of the drawer, behind a torch and some necklaces. She couldn't find her hand mirror. She was sure it had been left on her bed or on the bedside unit, but it wasn't there now. She lifted the clothes off the floor; it wasn't under them. Pulled out drawers, looked behind the curtains. Bit back the frustration.

A Taz Mania postcard was stuck out from a pile of LPs she couldn't play any more. Duran Duran were at the front of the line, Rio. "Save a prayer for me," she said, then tossed the album onto the bed. That would do.

She couldn't find a straw or bit of cardboard in the drawers. She thought she'd kept some aside? Knelt by the small wicker bin. It was full. Rooted through, letting wrappers and make-up darkened cotton wool fall onto the carpet. Came across a tampon applicator. Would that work? It would stretch her nostrils. No, she wasn't that low yet. Found a cardboard box from a packet of biscuits. Tore off part of the lid.

Onto the bed. Tipped coke onto the LP sleeve. Used the cardboard to move the particles round, stray lumps herded together like sheep, to form two lines, fat worms of anaesthetic, then rolled the cardboard into a tight tube. Hold her left nostril, snort up the right, then sniff a few more times, getting it up to the back. Same on the other side.

She'd forgotten to bring a glass of water into her room so dipped a finger in the vodka bottle, tipped it up to wet the end, inhaled that up each nostril instead.

On the floor she spotted a large, worn cushion. She grabbed it, propped herself up against the headboard, and relaxed. Familiar sensation. Nostrils cold, bitterness but not bad. Pleasant numbness setting in. Like an ice diamond on her brain, cold water rushing in her bloodstream, heart pushing the rapids with clarity and speed, she could almost hear the beat in her ears, at one with her body, maybe; her mind was escaping down the chute.

The plant on her TV was wilting. She knew how it felt.

Should have put music on. Couldn't be bothered now. Stay still. The bed could hold her. A friend. Not a trap. The trap was the location, the situation that had lost its novelty.

Hot. Hands felt clammy. She pressed her palm to her cheek then pulled it away. Cold stickiness. Again. It wanted to cling to her. Body happy, joints smooth. "It's okay," she told the room. "I'm not lonely."

She'd wanted independence. University had been an escape from living at home, escape from everything. And then it just continued.

She hummed a few notes, an old song from somewhere, it echoed in her ears.

But her past was important. It had shaped her. Now it pulled at her as strongly as the boyos in the annual village tug-of-war.

She licked her lips. Bitterness there, too.

Teddy The Frog sat on the wicker clothes basket in his best blue jumper. "Get outta this shit hole," he told her. She murmured agreement.

If she went back it would be different. Her own place. What Mamgu wanted. What did Sam want?

She wanted her mam. She had looked older when she'd last seen her.

Sam stared at the bedspread. It had fine detail and was calming.

"Say fuck it," Teddy The Frog told her.

Today I was this close to quitting.

"That close?"

Just one more thing to push me.

"Then why don't you? Instead of bending my fluffy ear about it?"

You sound like … oh, I don't know.

"Fuck and check out."

She looked at the white walls. She did want to get out.

It takes weeks, sort things out.

"It doesn't. Just go when you want. Who gives a stuff about a deposit? Why are you even here?"

You're so wise, Teddy The Frog.

"Yes. The puffy white shit I'm full of is wisdom fluff."

I want wisdom fluff.

"I think you've got enough of that in your bloodstream already."

Wish there was more.

Her head floated, the bed enveloped her. It had never been so soft. A drink of vodka to keep things ticking. It tasted nice. She had a bit more.

come home

Come Home is the opening track of James' ... Mother album which was recorded in Manchester and Wrexham. Their third album, but it was th...

... a complex narrative to make a whole from but the feelings are clear. It's about dealing with pressure, separating love from rudeness, dealing with hate towards a man, ambivalent feelings and the homewards pull. It is also about coming of age and whether you can overcome the direction your personality goes in, be yourself rather than what the past and your genetics might push you towards. Resist, scream yourself hoarse, and try to find somewhere safe, wherever home actually is. The chanted ch... of "Come home" is like a command, acco...

... 1980s, even supported The Fall at one gig. In 1982 while they were playing at The Haçienda Tony Wilson persuaded them to release a few tracks with Factory. They collaborated with The Smiths around the time of the latter's Meat Is Murder tour, and there was mutual respect. James had a reputation for being a good live band with lots of fans but little money. Bank loans and volunteering for medical experiments at Manchester hospitals kept them going until their commercial success began in the 90s (Sit Down became a staple of student discos across the land). At that ...

Sandpapery eyes. Desert tongue. Throbbing, dehydrated, cactus-stabbed brain. She groaned. Didn't want to come out from under the duvet but the ringing alarm was insistent. Reached an arm out, swatted about. An empty bottle rolled off the edge and donked onto the floor before she shut off the siren of doom.

What had she done last night to feel so bad?

Dry braincells creaked. Oh. She remembered.

Well, *some* of it.

She sat up and stretched, which made her head pulse more. Not refreshed.

Her foot brushed something. A ball of paper. She reached down and unscrunched it in slow motion. Squinted blearily at the spidery words.

Dear Rene. Shove the job up your fat arse.

She stared at it in surprise. Dropped it and looked around. There was a folded over sheet just past that. She snatched it up. Another resignation notice. A bit more professional than version 1.

She rubbed her eyes wider, read it again, disbelieving. *She'd* written this? While out of it? What else could she have done if she was that blitzed? She glanced at Teddy The Frog in accusation but he said nothing. Then she grabbed her phone, brought up the list of calls she'd made. Sighed with relief when she saw that she'd made none the previous night.

She was about to scrunch this note up too, throw it in the bin, when she paused. Her body ached as if it had wrestled with itself. Her mind had been doing that for some time, fighting behind worn-out eyelids, out of sight in the background. And now there was a winner.

"Fuck it," she said in a scratchy voice she hardly recognised.

It was scary, but finally done. All along it was just a decision waiting to happen. And this was *her* choice.

First thing in the work morning, yet Mark was in a good mood. He decided to be helpful, to use … initiative. So he went round the teams with a notepad, asking what stationery they needed, making a list. He did it in his neatest handwriting, so even he could read it.

Then he saw Sam. She looked tense, so he approached her with a smile, wanted to cheer her up. Asked what her plans for the weekend were, ignoring the other people within earshot for once.

"Nothing much," she'd replied, continuing to count out carbon sheets on the stationery shelf and not looking at him. She sounded bored.

"Erm, I might go to a pub, nothing special. Or stay in. Read and listen to music. We all drink too much don't we? Well, I do sometimes. I mean in our culture." He knew he was waffling, but felt ever-more desperate to get a response. "I don't feel like drinking for a while. Just tea. Or, erm, like fruit tea. That can be nice. How about you?"

"We'll see," she'd said impatiently. That was it.

He waved his notepad. "I've been collecting lists of what things people need. Pens and stuff."

"Oh."

"Do I pass it to you? Dave's not round, he normally does it."

"Why would you give it to me?"

"Well, your team orders things…"

"We order *books*. Give it to the finance team."

And suddenly he couldn't think of anything else to say. He'd walked into a wall, and all his planned topics had fallen out of his head onto the floor. He had to get back on track. She was holding cigs and a lighter. He nodded at them. "Going for a break?"

"Yes."

"Smoking – corpses in your mouth."

"What?" she asked sharply. She was frowning.

"Erm, ash and death connections. It's just what –"

"Urgh. Thanks for screwing that up."

"I didn't mean..."

She was back to counting sheets. Obviously just wanted him to go. Something had changed. He couldn't think of anything else to say anyway. She was making it easy for him; he walked away, confused.

Sam was in the staffroom waiting for the kettle to boil.

FAO Rene Hacking, General Manager, Packham Green she wrote on the envelope in her neatest script, and then stroked a finger over it. For many good reasons she should just throw it away. Forget about the relief she felt every time she imagined handing it over to Rene.

But, to quote her favourite philosopher: fuck it.

Rene opened the envelope and read the letter slowly at arm's length. She let it fall to the desk and blinked twice before looking up at Sam. "Is this some kind of joke?" she asked.

"Not in a joking mood."

"It seems incredibly sudden."

"Believe me: it's not."

Rene looked imperiously down her nose at Sam. "I like you, Sam, despite everything. You remind me of myself when I was young and stupid."

"Of yourself?" Sam couldn't keep the incredulity out of her voice as she eyed up the padded-shoulder blazer, the bushy mop of sandy hair, the size of Rene. "Then I hope I don't end up like you," she said with delicious cruelty.

Rene stood and came around the desk, face reddening, to stand in front of Sam. "Your problem – you've got no..." She seemed to struggle for a word, couldn't find what she wanted, and spat out, "vision. Or ... or talent."

"I have plenty of talent and vision!" Sam replied angrily. "I just don't give a shit! At least, not about this poxy place, this sinking ship, and this crappy job."

"So this is for the best. When do you want to leave?"

"Right now?" Sam snapped.

"You owe six weeks' notice. But since we're looking for savings you can make it *three*."

"I'm owed a pile of annual leave, since I hardly ever take time off. About fifteen days."

"You really want to quit today?"

"I don't like to drag things out."

Rene shook her head in disgust. "Leave at the end of next week. Five days to hand over. Tidy up as best as you can."

"Great. I'll leave next Friday then."

"You must think you're so 'cool'," Rene said, bending her forefingers as sarcastic air quotes, "but really you're just damned reckless, stupid not to care about your future."

"This isn't a future, it's a dead end." Sam glared at Rene, whose glassy eyes stared back from an angry complexion, and Sam tried to think of another put-down or coolly sarcastic comment, but she noticed there was something else in Rene's expression … and then Rene started crying. Proper tears. One ran down her check. Rene turned her back on the office window in case anyone was looking, so Sam snatched a tissue from the box on Rene's desk, handed it to her. Rene wiped her eyes. Sam had been spoiling for a fight but now it dissolved, and her spite seemed ignoble.

"I'm sorry, Rene," she said quietly, not sure whether to put a hand on a padded shoulder or not.

"I'm sorry too," Rene sobbed.

"You've got nothing to apologise for."

"Oh, you're so wrong. But me being stressed shouldn't be an excuse. I always thought a boss was meant to feel powerful, but I never felt that. My own line manager, from our parent company, he's very rude on the phone. They're putting lots of pressure on me to 'innovate', and get things to 'work smarter', and to 'grow the business'." Here Rene did her air quotes again, and Sam didn't have the heart to point out how old-fashioned that was. "They always use phrases like that."

"What about, well, not that I know, but going on a management course?"

"I've been on management courses. I've spent whole evenings at home reading books on it. And I never feel like I understand half of it. Despite all the words there seems to be no plain speaking, no straightforward advice. Or maybe the advice is just lost among all the words, the fancy names. Contingency Theory? Force Field Analyses? What do they all mean? I'm sorry. You think I'm a silly old woman. You're more right than you think. Don't tell anyone this, but I bought shares. In Eduteach. I thought it would give me control. It was most of my savings. But I didn't understand how it works. It wasn't enough.

I don't get any say in things, Samantha. Worse – they've lost value somehow. I'm not good."

"Oh. That's horrible. I understand."

She was still crying, but getting some control of it now. "And I know people call me names. One develops an ear for these things. So many of you are young, with your whole lives ahead of you. Some of you are pretty. It's hard to relate to all that. From my office the nearest table I can see is yours. How can I look at Emily, all slim, wearing short skirts, then not look down at my own legs and feel bad? Look at my new skirt suit. Trying to look the part. But I had to buy it from a shop for the 'plus-sized' woman. Words again, they skirt round the real issues. I don't live alone, I'm just 'partner deficient'. Words. They say so much, and so little. And you, with your lovely skin and dark eyes, you remind me that my hair is a mess, my complexion isn't good. It makes me hate looking at you. It makes me mean. But that's wrong."

"I didn't know. That you felt like this."

"It's why I'm saying sorry. I don't really think you were bad at your job. But I can't ever like you. I feel awful."

"Don't. It's nothing. This is the right decision for me. If you helped me make it then I should thank you. So don't cry about it. It's good for you too. You have to cut staff? Well this saves you making a decision. You'll look good to your bosses."

Rene sniffed, gave a weak smile. "Thanks."

"It's not all on you. I fly off the handle. I have a mean temper."

"It's a shame we've only cleared the air now. We could have made a good team."

"We learn and we move on."

Rene wiped her eyes, conquered her sniffles. "Are you sure you still want to go? Now we've sorted this out it could be better. I could rip up the letter." She held it up. A bit of paper with a life's direction on. "Or you could leave but stay longer, not rush off so suddenly?"

"I still want to go. I know I do. Because when I made the decision to hand this in, to go back to Wales, I felt like a weight was lifted. It's the right thing to do. But thanks for double-checking. I appreciate that."

"I'm sad to see you go, Samantha. Really. You are good at your job."

This meeting was the weirdest disparity between expectation and reality Sam could ever remember having experienced.

But it was better this way.

"Can you hold back any announcements until Monday?" Sam asked at the door. "I'd like to tell certain people myself."

"Of course."

"Okay. I'll get back to it. Work to do."

"Need to speak to you tonight," Sam told Emily after leaving Rene's office. It didn't seem like anyone had been watching. Good.

"Sure, babes. A drink?"

Nod.

"Wanna invite anyone else? I'll do it. Properly, this time." Twinkle in her eye.

"No."

Roger looked up from his PC. "You mean Mark?"

"I mean none o' your business," Em told him, without malice.

Roger ignored her, and asked Sam, "You don't like Lanky Lurch, do you?"

"I don't like anyone," Sam snapped. "I've got a brain like an October cabbage and people should refrain from saying words to me today – any words – if they don't want to get their balls ripped off."

"Bad words from dirty mouths," he muttered, sinking back into his chair.

"Don't worry, it's just one of Sam's crazy sayings," Emily told him with a grin, before picking up his lunchtime orange and squeezing it in her palm in front of his eyes. He swallowed, hard.

Despite the hangover she was buzzing inside. She stepped outside the building with her phone and a cup of peppermint tea. The sun kissed her. There was noise from the tables by the canal where lunchtime drinkers chatted and laughed. She wanted to laugh. Except there was something she should have done *before* handing in her notice.

She crossed the road to a bridge over the canal. Had a sip of tea. It tasted so green. She balanced the cup on the wall. A woman went past pushing a child in a buggy. Sam waved to the kid and smiled. Then took a deep breath and dialled the numbers she knew by heart.

"Hi, Mam."

"*Shwmae, cariad.* What day is it?"

Sam laughed. "Friday. I'm in work."

"What's the matter?"

"That's a fine way to start a conversation!"

"You don't normally ring unless it's the weekend."

"This is an *exceptional* time. Do you remember what you said about Mamgu's house?"

"Of course."

"Well I'd like to come home. Live there. Is that okay?"

"Is that *okay*?" There was a sound like a pig squealing at the other end of the phone. "Of course it's okay! It's what my mam would have wanted. What *I* want."

"I'll pay rent –"

"Don't be daft. It saves me having to think of anything else to do with it! I couldn't sell it. No, it would have gone to you in my will anyway, might as well have it now. Her, to me, to you. To your kids, maybe. It's only right." Her mam was laughing and the last reservation was broken. It was all going to work out.

"I've handed in my notice."

"Well done you! When? When is all this happening? I'll have so much to do."

"It's happening fast. Turns out I can leave next Friday. Come back to Wales on Saturday." There was more laughing from the other end of the phone, and the happiness carried, kept Sam smiling, the sunlight twinkled in her eyes off the water, and now she knew she was going everything looked beautiful. "I'll need to get a job. Do you think Uncle Joe was serious about me working for him?"

"Oh yes, he'd love that. You were always his favourite. If he'd had a child he would have wanted it to be you."

"I'll ring him next."

"No need. I'll do all that. Don't worry about a thing. Do you want someone to come with a van? We could borrow one off Ianto."

"Nah. I haven't got enough stuff to be worth it. The hi-fi doesn't work properly any more and I won't need to bring any food. I'll charity shop a lot of the stuff. I can post some other things ahead. Then I'll be able to do what's left in a suitcase."

"Really?"

"Don't sound so surprised. I want a clean start."

There was a pause. It sounded like her mam was crying.

"Samantha. This makes me really happy."

"Me too, Mam." Sam sighed and it became a shudder. A letting go. "And I understand now how you feel about me. I'm sorry for the times I didn't appreciate it. I love you."

"*Dw i'n dy garu hefyd.*" I love you too.

And that was it. Sam was about to pick up her drink when she instead interlaced her fingers, remained leaning on her forearms. Closed her eyes and raised her face slightly.

"I'm sorry," she said quietly. "I've not done this for years. So I should say I'm not contacting you to ask for anything. That'd be cheeky. I'm just doing it to say thanks. I'm so lucky. And I *know* it. I really do. So thanks. Oh, and if Mamgu is anywhere up there, please look after her. And tell her we miss her. Erm, amen."

Heat-softened tarmac pulled at his trainers. Advertising signs screamed for attention. Shop doors were like hungry mouths begging to be fed. All greedy. Everything wants a piece of you.

Tunes ran through his head but they were broken up and ground to a halt with the sound of a scratched record needle not long after they started. Apparently his mind wouldn't relax any more than his face muscles would.

Striding down the busy Oxford Road throughway, Mark had his hands thrust into pockets. The traffic was piled up for some reason. Horns blasted, engines revved, muffled insults shouted behind windscreens. It reminded him of work: you crawl forward, get nowhere, end up stressed and angry, everyone you see is in a bad mood, and you just dream of the time when you can get out of the car and walk.

Someone bumped his shoulder as they passed then hurried off with a worried expression, as if Mark looked like he was going to kick off. Not that he would. Fighting's for idiots. Maybe he was scowling. He plodded on through the crowds.

He wasn't happy. Dave had once told him about people who go moody in winter. SAD, it was called. But it was June and hadn't rained for weeks. He just felt sad in small letters.

Too many people, all striding like robots, apart from one person with a cocky saunter wearing a fisherman's hat and indie clothes; but then he gave a mischievous grin and faded into the crowd.

Swaggering mop-top man?

Mark shuddered like someone had walked on his grave. Maybe he was going loopy.

He needed to get away from this mass of people. Go walkabout down at the canal. His place. Flat water instead of choking traffic. Empty paths instead of crammed pavements. The flow would come back to him down there.

A few turns and he was going down the slope to the water. The vehicle noise was already fading. He'd just catch the Metro from G-Mex instead. Hopefully he'd be calm again by then. There was no hurry tonight. It was Friday, after all.

But it seemed noisier down here today. Sounds echoing between nearby buildings, like high pressure water jets or grinders. Powerful and mysterious machinery. It made him think of garages. He tried to focus on something else.

There was no railing between him and the brown, opaque water which reflected muddy walls. He scanned any disturbance in the surface, hoping he would see his hat. It was another reason to walk this way, as he had a few times recently. But no sign of it floating like a dark jellyfish, or blown against the crumbling brick walls, or jammed under an arch.

That's life, right? Something that once existed just disappears. You can't control it, you didn't choose it, you don't understand it.

Sam had been cold. So cold. He was used to women going off him, but he'd thought she was different. A friend. His antibiotic for sick days grinding at the Green.

Sod it. It was nothing to do with how he felt now.

There. In the water. Something.

He squinted. No. Too small. He picked up a pebble, tossed it near the item which bobbed and rotated, watched the ripples spread out from even such a teeny action.

Finger shapes. It was just a glove.

He walked on.

He remembered a time when he first started at Packham Green. Sam was already working there. He'd been all excited, new job and everything. Was delivering post. Saw her. Amazing hair, almost black. He had thought he was being chatty. Asked if she dyed it. He meant it as a compliment, assumed she'd say no, then thank him. But she'd said yes, really curt, like she was offended, and she'd glared at him – only then did he see his mistake. Back then she didn't know who he was. But he thought that had all changed. That they were friends.

Some pigeons that had been waddling and feather-fluffing on the path flapped off as he approached. Flicker flack and only a feather left.

Why all these thoughts of her? It was just work. He shouldn't be taking it home with him.

Something else in the water. Near the edge. He squatted, held on to a rusting metal ring and reached out. It was at the extreme of his reach. He had to grip so tight his knuckles hurt, leaned, could see the depth of the water below him, the dirty drop to blackness just waiting … then he fished the item with his fingertips. The water that brushed them was warm. It was a wallet. He let it drip, darkening the old stone, then gave it a shake before opening it carefully.

Empty.

Strange.

There was no bin nearby, and he didn't want to put the wet thing in his pocket so he lay it at the base of the wall to his left, some kind of warehouse. Maybe whoever lost it would see it.

The situation with Sam was confusing but not altogether unexpected. Mark knew he wasn't God's gift to women. But he lived and breathed.

Why was it bothering him so much?

He kicked at the ground with the toe of his trainer.

She once told him she had an addictive personality. He could believe that now. He needed to talk to her, see her smile, have her attention on himself for a bit. They didn't have big conversations or nothing, but even just asking how she was could be enough. Something that small; yet it made a difference. Ripples in the day.

He shouldn't let things drag him down.

He approached the next lock, just before a section that passed under a dark arch, cars on the road far above. There were the remains of a fire in the shadows. Things recently burnt. A smell of acrid smoke. Over the water was a cardboard city, boxes flattened and laid out on the old brickwork at the junction of the arch and a building. Three bare-chested skinny men lay on dirty blankets. One sat up and stared at him, skin burnt red by the sun. Mark looked away.

The path was narrower under the arch. He was aware of the black oil water to his side, lapping softly against mossy stone. It was slippy under here. Something brushed his head, made him think of big spiders. He walked quickly as he could without slipping, and was glad to break out into sunshine again. He listened, thought he heard the lock behind him rattle. Maybe just the water pushing it. Maybe someone crossing it from the other side.

He broke into a run.

He realised that down here was only peaceful when you were alone. There were no safe places for him in the city any more.

The "World Famous" Lass O' Gowrie, next to the canal on Charles Street. A quiet place to go for a drink after work. Sam and Em had the snug to themselves. It was a carpeted and curtained side room with an unlit fireplace and shelves crammed with books and magazines. They had a corner seat and sticky round table on which two pints of cold cider fizzed.

"I always wonder what that means," Em said, distracting Sam from the bubbles. "It's got to be toilet-related."

"What?"

"The sign outside. The one that says the pub was a 'Pissotière'."

"Oh."

"Anyway, it's been on my mind all day, the Rob thing. He's gutted. He told me he thinks it's some scummy lads who burgled him. In baseball caps. They took his gadgets and jewellery. Probably the gold chain he's most gutted about. They even did graffiti on the walls, he's got to get it repainted. He was fuming."

"Everywhere's going downhill."

"I know! Crazy, huh? I was watching this programme the other night, might've been on ITV, and –"

"I want to tell you something," Sam interrupted.

"Why so serious?"

"It's kind of a story."

"Go on." Em picked up her pint and sat back, a wary look in her eyes.

"When I was a little girl I was a tomboy."

"You?"

"Yes. Even Mamgu called me that. She'd say it and stroke my hair, when I'd come in after climbing the weeping willow at the bottom of the garden, or after getting muddy playing football with some of the boys at the top end of the waterlogged field. She always smiled as she said it, accepted it more than my mam did. It's so vivid, even now. I loved those moments sat on her knee in a chair in the kitchen, cuddling up to her, cooking-smells in the air. I was into most boy-type things. My favourite was frogs."

"Frogs! You're pulling my leg. They're all slimy."

"No they're not. Just moist."

"Urgh."

"They fascinated me. The way they start as tadpoles then transform from one thing into another, completely different-looking thing. Like me, in a way. I used to be gawky and unattractive – stop shaking your head! – but when I hit my teens I like to think that I scrubbed up okay. It was definitely tadpole to frog rather than frog to princess, but still an improvement."

"You *are* a fucking princess."

"We had frogs in our pond. I'd watch them hop along on the grass, and loved the feel of them if you picked one up gently, its chest rising and sinking rapidly as it breathed."

"Now you're making me sick."

"I always put them back. I was careful when I played, not to tread on any in the grass. And I always helped my dad do the mowing by walking in front of the mower, looking for things to move out of the way, saving them from being sliced to death."

"Much as I like knowing about you as a kid, what's the point of this? I thought you were going to tell me you had cancer."

"Are you going to keep interrupting?"

"Probably."

"I collected any old junk if it had frogs on it. Notepads, books, a pen with an image of a frog that slid up and down in a water-filled section; a cuddly yellow frog my dad won for me at a fair."

"I've seen that! In your room!"

"No, that's a new one. I bought it from a market stall at Piccadilly."

"Oh."

"Back when I was a kid there were also two small frog pictures on my wall. Still have them in a box somewhere back in Wales, in my parent's attic. One was a drawing of a fat smiley frog in a cosy hole, looking up at the moon in the sky, with the caption 'Small but happy, that's my world'. I think it's a translated bit of Japanese wisdom. Whenever there was something I couldn't afford I would remember that message, then realise that I didn't need the thing after all."

"That's probably why you've hardly got any shit."

"No, that's because I live in a box. Anyway, the other picture was a colourful drawing of a bright green frog leaping from lily pad to lily pad in a deep pond that seemed to go on forever, shades of blue deepening to black. I swear I used to feel vertigo looking at that. I always thought frogs lived on lily pads when I was young, so I assumed this was a picture of a frog moving house. One pad wasn't really any better than another. The frog just liked the change of view."

Emily put the remains of her pint down. "Why are you staring at me?"

"I'm changing lily pads."

"You'd better be joking."

"I'm not joking. I'm going back to Wales."

"No."

"Yes."

"Since when?"

"Since I decided that is what I wanted to do. Come on, you didn't really think I'd live in Manchester forever?"

"Why not?"

"Things change in lives."

"What, you miss your *mummy*?"

"Don't be sarcastic. But, yes, I do miss my family. And my mam's lonely. I know it. She needs me."

"I do too!"

"You're tough. Indestructible, possibly. I used to think my mam was too. Not so much, anymore."

"Visit her more often then! It's not far. Wales is only a small bit of England."

"I know you're saying that because you lack any geographical knowledge, not because you mean to be offensive. But it would still be a dangerous thing to say in a pub where I come from."

"But seriously, come on," replied Emily. "We've discussed this in the past and you've always changed your mind."

"Or you've persuaded me against it. But not this time."

"You don't like your job? Get another. Though I'd prefer it if you didn't. You just have to get things in perspective. It's not many days really. Out of the year ... I don't know, 52 weeks … so like 104 days are weekends. And you get 20 days of annual leave. And there's, what, about ten days of public holidays? And then maybe ten off sick. So that means you get nearly half of the year off, right?"

"It's not just the job."

"But you're settled here." Emily pursed her lips. Had an idea. "If you move back to Wales – isn't that running away from things? Being cowardly? It's not like you."

"Do you think it will be easy? To start a new life again, have to make new friends again? To take risks? No, that is the harder option. It's not cowardly. But it's the choice that will make me happy. That's the thing, Em: this is for *me*."

"I can see your point, but I still think you're full of shit," she snapped. "And what about your job?"

"I handed in my notice this morning."

"What the *fuck*? Who else knows? Why didn't you tell me first?" Em was gesturing with her hands, hurt and agitated and close to knocking Sam's drink over.

"Only Rene. 'Cos I handed in the letter first thing. It was a one-shot deal, I had to do it then. Y'know. Before I sobered up and became sensible again. I wrote the letter while I was off my face last night."

That coaxed a grin from Em, which she tried to hide immediately.

"And leaving you?" Sam added. "Not the easy option. You're the only good thing here. But I'm not giving you up. I can't go unless I have your solemn promise that you will come and see me. I'll only be a train line away, even if it is *another country*."

"As if you even need to ask."

"So you accept it?"

"I relent." Emily pouted comically. "You have been pretty unhappy, and I do want what's best for you. But I can be selfish, and I'm in a pisser of a mood. Down that drink while the *English girl* gets us some more." She muttered to herself as she headed to the bar, and Sam made out the word "indestructible". Emily seemed pleased with that. Sam partly believed it too. The only thing that could destroy Emily was herself.

Four empty pint glasses standing in a row. Two more full ones waiting to go.

"Well, he's a shit to have said something like that," Em stated, before downing a few mouthfuls of cider. She was outraged by Sam's tale of what she'd overheard.

"It doesn't matter. It was just one more thing."

"It *does* matter."

"Let's change the subject. You know my future plans. What about yours?"

"My sole purpose in life is to serve as a warning to others. But actually, it does give me a thought. Two words."

"New job."

"No."

"Another drink?"

"Yes, but not the two words."

"I give up."

"Leaving do."

Sam groaned.

"We'll give you a proper send-off. You'll love it. You can be princess for a night. You've got to give me something to make up for the hurt."

"The idea of making a fuss puts me off. And there would be all this 'who do we invite' stuff."

"We can get round that – just invite everyone. All the creeps will refuse to come or go home early anyway. It'll be cool, and I'll do any organising. Not that we'll really need any, just choose a place and whoever comes, comes." She was leaning forward over the desk, smiling, her pretty face animated.

Sam relented. "I suppose so. I don't want to ruin your fun."

Emily's smile widened. "Oh, you're so sweet! And while you're conceding things, here's another: I'm doing stuff with you *every night* until you go. No arguments. Every night for a week. And when you go you've gotta phone me, or email me, or text me. Visit. And I will visit you in Wales."

Sam laughed. "That would be great. I don't know if Neath is ready for you, but I'd love it. And you'll be goggle-eyed at all the big hunky blokes."

"It's a deal. Let me get us another drink then. We're going to put a few more away before I let you go."

"I think I'll explode."

"Go for a piss then."

Eight empty glasses, and if one of them should fall…

"You've done it again," Sam told her as she finished her last drink. "Got me drunk. Been a bad influence."

"I'm so *sorry*," Emily recited with childish sarcasm. "But I've got to broaden your mind. You country bum-folk. Oh, I meant bumpkins. Did you hear that?"

"Yes, very funny. My mind's pretty broad you know."

"I'll miss you, really, 'cos I *do* care. Like when you were crying that night, telling me about your gran. And we kissed a bit. I felt close. That's all. Sorry it panicked you."

"Not panicked… Oh, I don't know. It was just unexpected. And I was upset. I felt like you were taking advantage of me."

"I didn't get that far – hold the daggers, just joking. I understand. I'm sorry."

"I've nothing against anyone snogging anyone. It makes no difference to me. It was just not how I thought we were."

"Oh yeah? Coming round to the idea now?" Em winked and leaned forward.

"Not really. I just love you for you." Sam said quietly.

"Me too." Emily was wearing pale eye shadow. Light to Sam's dark. "There's no one else in here," Em whispered. "Do you want to have a non-pannicky, non-surprise experiment? Everyone should do it, at least once."

"What, everyone should kiss you? Already happened, I heard."

"You know what I mean. Kiss someone of the same sex. Otherwise: how do you know it isn't for you?"

"Why do I always do what you want?" Sam tilted her head forward. Their lips touched and they kissed, held each other's faces gently. Sam had her eyes closed, just let their tongues and lips slide onto each other, taste, softness and warm wetness that reminded her of salt and apples. It was Emily who pulled back first. Sam opened her eyes, a bit dizzy. Emily was smiling at her.

"Well?" Em asked.

"It was nice."

"Yeah. Nice … but weird?"

"It was a bit weird wasn't it?"

"Just like kissing a man. But less prickly."

"Thanks."

"Sexy as you are, it didn't really get my motor running. Not like I expected," Em told her.

"Me neither."

"It was like hugging you."

"Sort of."

"Maybe stick to that? Hugging's easier."

"Yes. That's easier. Maybe we're just close."

"It might be different if we went to bed together?" Em suggested. "Would that be better?"

They looked at each other, grinning. "Nah!" they both said together. Then hugged. Zero tongue action.

"If I was into women I'd totally be into you," Em whispered in her ear.

"Thanks. That does flatter me a lot."

"And if you were into women, you wouldn't be able to resist me either."

"That's the truth."

Emily pointed at the empty glasses with the tip of her nose. “I think we’re done.”

When Sam got home she held the last of the coke in her hand. There wasn’t much, but it was enough. This would be more symbolic than anything.

Then she pushed it deep down inside the kitchen bin, amongst the food scrapings and tea bags which pressed cold and wet on her fingers. There, another thing done.

She was going to clean up her act. Change. Start again. End of the bad associations and start of the good. She smiled as she washed her hands. Going home this time would be different because she was going back as an adult. After all, nothing stays the same. Day, night. Life, death. Places and people, they all change.

She decided there was really nothing wrong with being a little bit boring.

Bitter Sweet Symphony

- **Album:** Urban Hymns
- **Year:** 1997
- **Label:** Hut

The album's opening track makes you want to be in love, as it combines hair-prickling beauty, believability and honesty. When you get down to it the whole album is about the pain and pleasure of love. It's a fragile thing and may not last long. Maybe that's why The Verve use butterfly imagery: this album has the trippily haunting song Catching That Butterfly, about a dream of finding love; their first al

love song? Bitter Swe ymphony is not a happy song. about a depressing and dark night of the soul. Can you change or not? Break the mould or not? There's irony when people use it as their "romantic" song, or a wedding song: they've never listened to the words, just the absorbed the surface, the rising and falling orchestral chords, heartbeat rhythm, and a vague understanding that it somehow relates to love and emotion. You've always got to look beyond the surface to understand something. Bitter and sweet. Life is not all good or bad, you have to navigate as best you can, even when things are difficult.

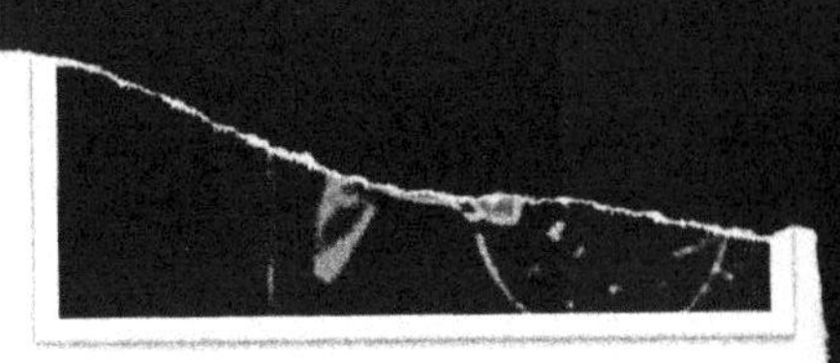

e Richards track. The law is frequently at odds with both common sense and justice.

As was Richard Ashcroft's captivating performance in the song's video, which got the band massive exposure in the 90's (appropriate, since it was based on Massive Attack's 1991 Unfinished Sympathy video). Richard Ashcroft walks down a road, he will not move or change course or acknowledge anyone else. He moves through danger, oblivious because he's really in his own mind. The song, like the official video, has an endless summer feel which touches a chord, resonates, and makes it eternally popular. Maybe it's partly the lighting, the way the sunshine washes streets (and pained souls) clean. The lighting is even more apparent in their Lucky Man video. Sunshine everywhere makes life a dream, and the brighter the shafts, the darker the shadow. It's how you perceive the world.

"Ha ha, you read this one, Mark?" Ben was reading out the headlines from a new website despite Mark's clearly-displayed lack of interest. The two were in the dusty post and processing section like good little gorillas.

"Told you, I don't read human news, only music news."

"I know, but anything which shows what dicks southerners are is worth reading. They built this fancy-arsed Millennium Bridge in London, right? About twenty million quid. Opened on Saturday. Then had to shut it because it turns out that it sways and wobbles like Rene's arse if people walk on it! The pillocks can't even put a few planks together."

This was definitely one of those days: a Blue Monday, not one of the rare Happy Mondays.

"I don't care."

Dave appeared, still drawing pencil lines in his A-Z map so he wouldn't get lost delivering to a new site that afternoon. "Guys. What's up?"

"News," Ben replied.

"Only news I care about is the shocker of Sam leaving. So fucking sudden. That ain't normal. Question is: did she fall – or was she pushed?"

"Her choice," said Ben. "Emily told me."

Mark looked past him. Sam was typing at her PC but kept stopping and conspiring with Emily, or laughing with the stream of people who were going up to her. There was a buzz going round ever since it had been announced. Looking at Sam gave him a sinking feeling. This was so out of the blue. It just shows, you never really know women. Maybe his dad was right all along.

"Yeah, it's a sad day. Gonna miss her," Ben said, wistfully. He picked up an internal newsletter, flicked through it. Then added, "Oh, Em's putting it out, there's a leaving do on Friday."

"I heard that," said Dave.

"You'll be comin', yeah?"

"Of course. It's perfect. Suzannah has an important family party at her aunt's house. Huge thing. She wants me to go, meet the rest of her cousins. But they're probably as boring as her retard cousin Alex. So this is my Get Out Of Jail Free card."

"Mark?"

"Nah. I wasn't invited."

"Everyone's invited. Emily said so."

"Dunno."

"Oh, come on! It'll be a laugh! The Three Musketeers!"

"I'll think about it."

"Regardless of Ben's sad musketeer bollocks, you'll promise to come and keep me company. Otherwise I won't come round again," Dave said.

"In that case other mates will come round."

Dave stared. Then held up his forefinger. "Pull the other one, Mark. There's me." Then he held up his thumb. "And there's Ben. And he only counts as half. So you'll come, right?"

Sigh. "Alright, don't nag. I'll come. *Jesus.* It's like you need me to hold your hands."

Ben turned back to the screen. "Talking of your geek cousin –"

"*Potential* nerd-in-law, get it right."

"Yeah, whatever, his kind of news here too. A science thing about some massive machine called a Large Hadron Caulinder or something like that, where atoms get mashed into itty bitty pieces. It says it'll be their first experiment, and no one knows what'll happen. It might be the end of the world."

"You'd have to be a mentalist to believe that. Sounds right up Alex's street."

"The world will still be here tomorrow," Mark added sourly. "I wouldn't be so lucky."

Em stuck to her word and was stuck to Sam. They'd been out in Chorlton. Even after the pub shut she was reluctant to go; wanted to come back with Sam for something to eat.

"It's nearly 1am. Go home," Sam had said.

"Not yet."

"We'll feel like shit tomorrow."

"So what?"

"Okay. Ten minute meal, then you get a taxi straight home."

"Promise."

So they were in Sam's kitchen and Emily was half-helping, half-hindering. For once Sam wasn't trying to be quiet. Robin and Leigh were asleep upstairs. Fuck them. They never considered Sam.

"What about Via Fossa for the do?" Em asked.

"Sure. It's close to work." Sam had always liked the the place because it was fun, like a decadent church interior glammed up with chandeliers, disco globes and velvet sofas; no surprise being in the heart of the gay village.

Sam was chopping veg for their ridiculous late-night stir fry and Emily was examining spice jars in the cupboard when she asked, "How do you feel about Mark now that you're going to be leaving?"

Sam was proud that her mushroom-cutting didn't halt for a second. Em didn't seem to be looking anyway – but then Sam noticed that she *was* half-looking, slyly, which immediately got her suspicious. Emily wasn't really interested in cumin and coriander.

"Why do you ask that now?"

"Just wondering." Emily picked up and looked at an unlabelled jar. "What's this?"

"Very hot chilli powder. You don't want that."

She put it back. "Well?" she persisted.

"I'm fine."

"Do you still like him though?"

"When I think of him I get angry. But…"

"But?"

"Sometimes I think about him. It's confusing. He used to be so nice."

"Do you still fancy him?"

"Just stir the noodles."

"Answer!"

Sam could feel her inner-self squirming, but thought it best to be honest. "Yes. It's a look. It grows on you."

"You know what?"

"What?"

Emily climbed up onto the kitchen counter and sat on the edge, watching side-on as Sam prepared the meal.

"I think you still care a bit. And I also think if you just go away now you'll always be bothered – sort of like you've failed something, even though you haven't."

Sam was about to respond but Emily put a finger against her lips in prevention.

"Just listen. If I fancy someone I normally go after them, and if they still seem nice I sleep with them, and that's when I really find out if I like them or not. Most often I then realise it was just lust and they're out of my system. Others I might see afterwards. There's still too much shit though, too much second-guessing, too much bother about appearances, time wasted when what you really want is a no-nonsense fuck with someone you like. God, I wish things were simpler in the UK, that I could just have a fuck buddy without it all getting emotional –"

"You're losing me."

"Sorry. The best bit is that in the long run it means I don't get left with a load of 'what ifs'."

"And?"

"And? I thought it was obvious. You should fuck Mark."

Sam nearly cut her finger as she sliced, her hand suddenly feeling shaky.

"Why? I don't want to!"

"Your body does. And I've already explained why. It's the only way to get over him and leave here without being fucked up over it."

"Nothing to get over."

"You liked him enough before."

"You're talking shit, you are."

"Never more serious."

"Anyway, he wouldn't sleep with someone who looks 'weird'."

"The very fact that you remember the exact words he used shows that you're not over him and need to sort all this out. As to him not sleeping with you ... any man will in the right circumstances, whatever they say. Give him a few drinks and be nice to him and he'd eat out of your hand – or anywhere else for that matter." She winked. "At least until he sobers up the next day."

"Sex isn't this huge important thing. You don't have to sleep with a guy to decide if you like him. It's how you get on that's more important."

"Yes, if you want to go out with them. But in this case sex *is* the important thing, because it's all your body is after and if you don't give in to it you'll be frustrated. In a way that you can't help with this..." Emily wiggled her middle finger obscenely, a mischievous glint in her eye.

Sam turned away in disgust. Looked at the carrots. They appeared obscene too now. Poor innocent, sweet carrots. Instead she looked up at the ceiling to calm herself. Emily having an answer for everything could be pretty tiring, push you into a corner.

"It's just life laundry," Em added.

Sam thought about her responses carefully. "Okay, so this is your philosophy, right? You said that you find out if you like someone when you sleep with them, and maybe you won't like them afterwards. But you might like them. What if things get reversed, and the guy decides he doesn't like you but you then like him? Wouldn't that mess everything up? Mess *you* up?"

"Yes. Could be a problem. And I'd face it if it happened. But it hasn't ever happened. And don't change the subject from what I'm suggesting *you* do to what might happen to *me*. Because that problem scenario you've created can't happen to you can it? He's a prick so won't end up liking you. If he did it'd serve him right. And you don't really like him, it's just lust, so you won't end up liking him more and being spurned. You just need to get this out of the way."

"And get a rep as the workplace slapper?"

"Don't worry what other people think. *Ever.* No one'll know, anyway, will they? And if they did no one would care. If you really think there's something wrong with sex you wouldn't sleep with anyone until you got married, and you don't believe in that, you hypocrite lapsed Catholic."

"Lapsed Presbyterian."

"Whatever. You're being annoying now! You've fucked round before. You told me. Sometimes with people you didn't even like."

Sam felt a flash of annoyance. "I was drunk, and you know I don't do it any more."

"You could do it if it's the right thing to do, and it is. And you'd have me and a drink to help you chill out. It'd be easy."

"But it's mean –"

"Oh, screw Mark! Literally! Have you heard yourself? 'It's mean to sleep with a guy' – no it's not! You're gorgeous, and far better than he deserves. You can get him out of your system and at least get some fun too. Clean slate."

"You're impossible."

"No, I'm really easy to get along with once people learn to see everything my way. And –"

"Stop," Sam said, quietly but firmly.

"No, listen. You –"

"Em, I said shut up!" Louder this time. Em seemed surprised.

"But I'm helping you!"

"No. You're not. I want you to stop interfering." She stared at Em. And Em gave in first, looked down.

"You've changed," she said softly. "You don't like me any more."

"Not true. God knows you drive me bonkers sometimes, but I love you to bits. You are half right, though. Everything I do, it's always going to be my choices from now on. If I say I'm finished with something, I mean it. Please respect that."

"Okay. It's getting to the point where *you* scare *me*, Sam."

When they hugged, that universal sign of understanding, Sam felt for the first time ever that she was Em's equal. And she felt all the closer for it.

He sat up, dry-mouthed staleness, looked round at darkened shapes, unfamiliar, lost in space and clueless about time. Prison, his mind sang, vibrating like a saw edge: he was locked in a prison cell.

With panicky hands he fumbled to put the lamp on, only calming down when the shapes and surroundings became familiar again. Everything in its right place, ordered, the wardrobe door sagging on one hinge as it should, clothes piled on the chair as was usual, a hole worn in the carpet as was meant to be.

The digital clock's glowing red letters said:

01:43
TUE 13/06

There were footsteps circling in the flat above, and subdued music filtered down.

He flopped back, sweating despite the frozen feeling of the dream he could only partly remember. Something about it being really cold; music was playing, it echoed off the hard icy floor, made him feel a stab of loneliness and loss; and then something about a tunnel, maybe on a train. Terrifying confinement that seemed like it would never end. He shuddered remembering it.

What was lost? And how could it get back?

It was just a dream.

Mark got up, his body feeling chilled. There was no way he could sleep. He'd make a cup of tea. Put some music on and read in the living room, distract his brain with words. That seemed like the right thing to do. Read more. Allow music to calm him, cleanse him; surround himself with melody, the only road he'd ever known, and let light shrink the night away.

make it happen

ould have got the message about how they formed: this is how Electronic ended.

Their third and last album. A sign off, a tactic to finish something on a high. Twisted Tenderness represents how potentially good things get destroyed if you're not careful. The murdered Russian mystic Rasputin raises a hand on the cover

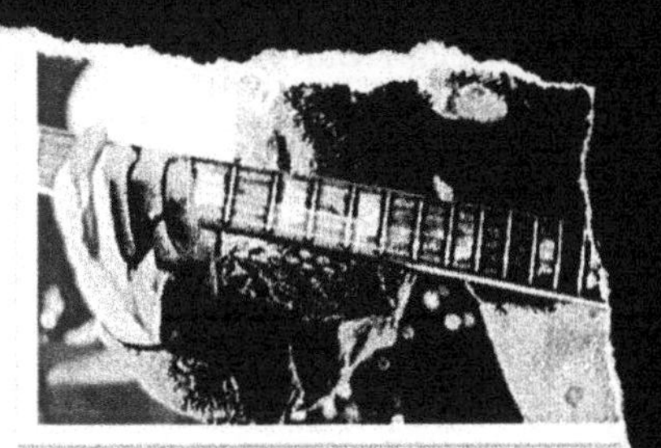

words kicks in? People who find themselves at a crossroads, looking for a way forward, something new. A song about a man who isn't whole; unsatisfactory sex and the aftershock of that. Not just one person, either, since Sumner sings "let's make it happen" to a heartbeat background. Let us. It takes two to tango. And two geniuses to

Drrrrrrring!

Sam jerked awake, torn by that irritating emergency sound from wherever her mind had been. She reached out to lock the clapper but her arm was numb from sleeping on it; she just succeeded in knocking the device onto the floor. That worked though. The bells went silent.

She'd set the alarm early to guarantee her getting first shower before Leigh or Robin hogged the bathroom. Last day in work. Celebrate in style. She was under the spray shaving her legs when Leigh began banging on the door and whingeing that she needed a shower.

"Yes, yes!" Sam shouted, and speeded up her process until it resembled hacking at her legs. She made a point of using lots of Leigh's expensive shower gel, shampoo and conditioner.

Sam padded back to her room. As she surveyed it she felt a moment of sadness. It looked so bare now. Only contained what she needed for tonight. It was transitional. Like her.

Best underwear on. A new black polo shirt which wouldn't be too hot. Her favourite skirt with a fabric tie belt. Make-up and a change of clothes into a temporary bag to take into the office. She wanted to look as good as possible tonight, let them all know what they were going to be missing.

Then she picked up her fluffy frog slippers. They were ready to fall apart at the first excuse but were something she loved, and she wouldn't abandon them. Into her suitcase. They would go home too.

Beep! Beep! Beep!

Mark bashed the button on top of the alarm clock but wasn't quite accurate enough. It skidded out of reach. He had to emerge from under the quilt to locate it and turn the beeping thing off.

One of Dave's phrases popped into his head. "Fuck-a-doodle-doo!" Dave had explained that the phrase was "Perfect for when the alarm doesn't go off and you're late for work – it combines arse-clenching panic with the first noise of the morning".

"And the fact that you're a pretentious cock," had been Ben's reply.

Peace again. He could do with another hour under the covers. Hadn't slept well. Too hot in the night. But he didn't want to risk falling back to sleep and getting blasted for being late to work just as he'd slithered into Rene's good books.

He shuffled into the kitchen. Decided to stick to proper tea that morning, rather than those fruit-tea things. Super strong steep strength to wake him up. And some jam on dry Weetabix. Quicker than making toast.

After his shower he located clean, uncreased clothes. He put a fine silver necklace on underneath. He'd bought it in Afflecks once after seeing a picture of Ian Brown wearing something similar. A quick glance in the mirror told him he was dressed good enough to go out after work for a quick polite drink to fulfil his obligations.

He felt the turning in his guts again.

Brush teeth, get fuzz off tongue. Comb hair, surrender when it just sticks up anyway. Getting it cut had been one of the daftest decisions he'd made. But at least it was growing back. It could have been worse. If he mussed it up he looked a bit like Richard Ashcroft now, and maybe that suited him more than the early Happy Mondays bowl head. It wasn't 1990 any more.

His black boots looked worse for wear. City dirt. He grabbed the duster and furniture polish, gave them a few squirts and a rub, and they looked good as new.

Again, that sinking feeling inside. Shouldn't get that on a *Friday.* Maybe it was just work. Just life. Or maybe he was going mad. Maybe his whole family was, it was just coming out differently in him. Depression rather than violence. Even so, he wouldn't swap that round.

The morning was a mixture of embarrassment and satisfaction: embarrassment during the formal presentation of leaving gifts when Rene made a short speech; satisfaction that everyone really seemed to wish her well. Many of the messages in cards made her smile. Not all, though. Mark's comment was simply "All the best, Mark". She stood the card on her table, a reminder to be realistic.

She had done the traditional thing and put a selection of treats out in the staff room: cake, sweets, fruit. She noticed Mark wasn't in there at break time. She felt a flash of anger but swallowed it down. She could be bigger than this. Bigger than pettiness. It was the new Sam.

Mark snuck into the staffroom after the break was over. He couldn't face all the talk about Sam.

Couldn't face having to look at her.

He scoffed a slice of chocolate cake that had survived the onslaught, and was picking at fruit – which hadn't been demolished like the cake – when the door opened and Emily came in.

"Those are big strawberries you've got there," she said.

"Err, yeah."

"No no no. That's not the right thing."

"What?"

"I fed you a line. Don't look so confused. You're meant to say 'Ooh, thanks, I've been waiting for a girl to say that', or 'They're bigger later in the summer' or 'Do you want one, they're juicy?' It's innuendo. It takes two people."

"Sorry."

She scooped the last bit of chocolate icing up on her finger, then put it in her mouth and sucked it clean. He looked away.

"You really need training, don't you? Hey, forget it, just a joke."

"Oh."

She put her fingers to his shoulder. Just light; the barest touch. Everyone seemed to like doing that to him. Maybe he seemed insecure. Em's touch was strange. She'd never touched him before. Her fingers seemed small. The nails were painted a bright pink. He felt nothing at the contact.

"It's Sam's last day. I want it to be all smiles."

He took a deep breath, nodded. She seemed satisfied with that, and left.

He sat down on the low sofa seat. The one where he'd occasionally joked with Sam when the staff room was nearly empty. He just wanted to curl up on it and go to sleep.

"Hi, you."

Mark jumped at the sudden voice. He'd thought he was alone with the unpacking. The place made him jumpy anyway, due to static electric shocks: about once a day he would touch a metal shelf or a metal bar under the desk and jump, hearing and feeling the sharp crack. You know it will happen sometime that day, but it always occurs when you lower your guard, forget about it. A bit like Russian Roulette, but with volts.

It was Sam. Smiling at him. The few buttons at the top of her shirt were undone.

"Erm, hi." More was needed. But she'd been so distant, her leaving was so alien, he wasn't sure he'd ever understood her. How can you talk to that? So much he'd like to say to her ... but only the superficial seemed possible now. "I saw you getting your leaving presents. Rene doing her speech."

"I told her that I wanted it to be quick. I hate a big fuss. Always have. The gifts and cards are nice though, I'm really touched."

"I haven't seen everything they got; we just pooled the money."

"Come and have a look then."

She tilted her head in the direction of her desk and he surprised himself by nodding. Swept along by her presence. And, he had to admit, pleased at the attention. He'd been annoyed at her in the last few days. She was instantly forgiven. He followed a few steps behind, able to admire. He loved the way she walked. Confident and controlled. No gangly arms.

Gel Head and Emily were at the desk, along with a few keyboarders, and they were all chatting more than working. Rene must have turned a blind eye. That corner of the room had been decorated with balloons; a ribbon ran across a filing cabinet, above a sign which said "SEE YA SAM! LOVE FROM THE CABINET OF DREAMS!" There was a pleasant scent, and he realised he'd first smelt it when Sam came over. Perfume.

"I've brought Mark over to show him my goodies," Sam explained.

Roger said "Oo-err!" and some of them laughed. Mark felt like he was the butt of a joke, but couldn't see what it was. Didn't like being exposed like this. But it was worth it to have her showing an interest.

She pointed out her cards first. Mark read them. One was jokey, the one most people had signed, and he wished he'd written something better in it. Wished he hadn't been angry at the time. Another was an old-fashioned one with some flowers on the front. That was off Rene.

"Something to remember you all by at least," said Sam, perched on the edge of her desk.

"You must be glad to be getting away from this place. I'd be gone if I got a better offer. Somewhere to go."

"Mixed feelings. Anyway, then there's this perfume, pretty expensive stuff." She had the bottle in one hand, having just taken it from the fancy box, seemed to think for a second, then held her wrist out to Mark's nose. He bent over and inhaled. It made him dizzy.

"I don't want to keep opening the bottle, Rene told me not to waste it," Sam explained. "And this dressing gown." She held it up in front of her, against her body as if to test the fit. It was a shiny green kimono thing, a strange gift he thought. For a second he had an image of her wearing it, and nothing else. He shook his head to dispel it.

"Suits you. Though it won't keep you too warm in winter," he joked lamely, then wanted to kick himself. It was fucking June. And sounded snarky. No one else seemed to notice. Sam just smiled. Then she picked up a blue-black box with gold writing, which had been on the desk under the dressing gown. It was a box of chocolates. She took the lid off.

"And I got these too, though the best ones have been scoffed already. Especially by Roger!"

Roger held his hands up, and said, "I've only had one or two, don't blame it all on me. You and Emily have eaten them all morning! Jeezus Beezus, I get the blame for everything." They were all laughing, though Mark thought Roger sounded as false as ever.

"They would only have melted anyway," said Emily.

Sam held the box out to Mark, saying, "It's not true. They're not melting."

He shook his head. "I don't really eat chocolates."

"Why not?"

"I prefer sweets."

"Oh, go on, everyone else has had one! What flavour?" She scanned the layer, thinking aloud. "Not the coffee – I don't see you drinking it at work. I know! Strawberry fondant."

He remembered a time with her. She took something in his face to be a yes, held the box out and pointed to one with a red-painted fingernail. He suddenly felt unreal, as Sam smiled and looked straight at Mark with an intensity he couldn't hold. He put the chocolate in his mouth. It felt like a bubble popped, then everyone started talking again, normality was back. There was a clack of an old label printer somewhere further down the office, and the slam of a door closing too hard somewhere else.

She seemed a bit more serious now. It was his turn to speak.

"That's all … nice stuff. You can tell you'll be missed."

"I'm 'dead chuffed' as you Mancs would say. Anyway, to the point: are you coming out tonight?"

Mark must have looked unsure, because she added, quietly, "I'd like you to."

"In that case: yes."

He hurried back to the post section. Gazed blankly at a calendar for a minute. Thought about perfumes. Mis-addressed two envelopes. Couldn't focus. Butterflies in his stomach.

People were unpredictable. No, it was more than that. It was like they weren't themselves, but you can't explain why. And it's only you who notices it.

He noticed alright.

And it didn't matter. She could be what she wanted. She liked him again, a little bit. That was enough. Yes, that was enough.

After he left Emily stared at Sam in surprise. But Sam was doing the right thing. Forgiveness. Inclusion. And it had gone well. Mark had smiled at her, for the first time in ages. It had transformed his face back into the one she'd first been attracted to. He'd made an effort to be nice, even if it was only because he knew he wouldn't have to see her weird face for much longer. The important thing was that they'd been talking again, relaxed. And when she'd held out the inside of her wrist so he could smell the perfume he'd bent over and inhaled gently, and she felt a momentary thrill.

Her favourite gift was a dressing gown. A shiny green kimono. Sam had praised one just like it a few weeks ago when she was shopping with Emily, so she knew who had chosen it, even though at the time Em described it as "a big frog costume". When Sam had held it up in front of her body something seemed to flicker behind Mark's eyes. That strange expression stayed with her all afternoon.

At 5pm Sam and Em got their bags from the lockers and commandeered the toilets. Emily changed into a short, tight T-shirt and a short, tight skirt. Bare legs and trainers. The kind of outfit you had to be super-confident or deranged to wear.

Emily also had a bottle of Lambrini.

"I can't believe you brought that. I'm not a Lambrini type of girl."

"Shut up and open your mouth."

They swigged from the bottle like naughty schoolgirls, absorbing contagious effervescence while Sam changed into a glittery black vest top, and swapped her long skirt for a shorter one. Nowhere near as short as Emily's though; this came just above the knee. Sam wore tights and switched her flat shoes for low heels. Maybe not *femme fatale*, but presentable female.

They finished the Lambrini, did matching dark-eyed make-up ("I'm a fucking panda," Em had whined), packed up, returned to the office. There were a few whistles and Sam's mood got even better. Em was bouncing all over the place and singing, Roger told rude jokes, and the giggles went round.

"That's trouble with a capital B." It was Ben speaking.

"That makes no sense," Mark replied, but he couldn't tear his gaze from Emily and Sam as they returned to their desk in new clothes.

Wow.

Snap out of it, Mark.

But he kept staring.

As Sam was packing up for the last time, Rene approached her.

"You look lovely," she said. "I like what you've done to your eyes. I wish I had that skill. And I hope you'll be really happy working for your uncle. He's lucky."

"Thanks," Sam said. And she gave Rene a hug. Such an alien thing, but it felt right. Rene was surprised but then hugged Sam in return. Tightly.

"You could come out too. It'd do you good," Sam told her, holding her arms by the elbows.

Rene shook her head. She was smiling, but sadly. "It's not for me. But thank you for asking. No one else ever has. It's 5.30. Now go."

She was free.

Mark joined a large group assembling near the cloakroom, listened to the laughing and bantering from the sidelines. There were about 20 people. He couldn't imagine such a big group if he left.

Emily and Sam led the way to the Via Fossa. Summer sun cast a golden light over the streets, washing them almost clean, and a refreshing breeze cooled Mark as he walked at the back of the group with Dave and Ben. They were joking about some sort of encounter they'd had once in the bar but Mark couldn't work out what they were getting at so ignored them and focussed on the glittering water of the canal. It didn't look so ominous from up here. A few small trees had been planted along its edge too. Mark liked trees. Dave said the UK was covered in them once: a single, massive forest. Bears. Boars. Wolves. Pretty much all gone now. Seemed weird to feel sad for something he'd never seen, only imagined. But he felt it anyway.

It was only a few minutes to the bar. Annoyingly near work: a place he couldn't escape from, he was like a moon or something, always seemed to be circling within a mile of it. Even when he couldn't see it he knew it was there, living in the back of his mind as he criss-crossed round town. It infected time and place.

Mark hadn't been in Via Fossa before. Lots of dark wood: panels, beams, balustrades, chairs and tables in thick oak. The group organised itself on the upper floor, people bought drinks, heavy tables were pulled together to make one big social area. Sam was in the middle throne-like seat, a focus for everyone. She looked the part. A dark-haired modern princess. Yeah, she could rule for the night.

At first work was the main topic of conversation, then it changed to TV, nearby bars, last weekend, mobile phones, holidays. Mark just listened and nodded absently. None of that interested him. Instead he couldn't help glancing at Sam. People wanted to be near her. Something about her was raw attraction, a flickering candle to pull them in. It must be nice having that power. To be able to live under spotlights rather than in shadows. She had a growing line of drinks in front of her as well-wishers kept buying her more, and was doing quite a good job of tackling them too, taking each one down like a rugby pro. She was pretty hardcore. Mark had to admire that. Another thing to fascinate.

It was only his bodily needs which could break the spell. It wasn't easy to find the way to the basement where the toilets were. The place was maze-like with walkways on different levels, connected by small staircases; disorienting mirrors and flashing lights added to Mark's confusion. And he kept seeing Sam in his mind's eye, her face, her smile, her gestures. Couldn't focus on mundane things like directions. It was a relief in more ways than one when he eventually got to the toilets, having survived overpowering smells of aftershave while boyband pop played in the background.

On the way back he took the opportunity to get another drink and noticed Emily leaning over the bar, arms folded, waiting to be served. There were two silver clips in her blonde hair, and she was wearing a short skirt that gave a long view of the back of her slim legs. There was a bruise near the top of her thigh, half hidden by the skirt's hem. He looked away from her body, suddenly feeling like a dirty voyeur.

"Not being served yet?" he asked as he edged in next to her.

"Huh?"

"Leaning over the bar like that … I'd have thought they'd see to you first."

"Well, they're obviously all gay in here. What are you having?"

"Don't be daft, I'll get you one. And Sam."

"I'm getting a round in. Don't try and pull any sexist shit or I'll rip your bollocks off."

"I didn't mean it that way!" Mark replied defensively.

"I know that, you pillock. You can help me carry them up. So what's it going to be?"

"A pint then. Shandy. Thanks."

"Don't be a soft lad. You're having a proper pint."

She got someone's attention and ordered the drinks. Then turned back to Mark. "Sam's having a really good time," she said with a smirk.

"That's … good. I mean, I'd hope so. On her last night. Out here. With everyone." He scratched his nose, looked around. "She's leaving for Wales in the morning, isn't she?"

"Yep, bright and early, off to the Taffs."

"You'll miss her, won't you?" Mark asked.

"I'll really miss her in work, but it's not like I'm never going to see her after this. She's got loads of friends here. She'll visit some weekends. And I can visit her in Wales." She said that proudly. "What about you? Going to miss her when she's gone?"

"Sure. The place will be less interesting without her there."

"Yet you two never really hit it off, did you?"

"Why do you say that?"

"She thinks you don't like her." The drinks had arrived now, and Emily was calmly sipping hers, yet the more relaxed she was, the tenser he became. It felt like he'd been discussed behind his back and found wanting.

"Well I do." Pause.

"Yet you keep a distance. I've seen it. Why's that?"

"That's a bit personal isn't it?"

"Why is it personal?"

He was feeling more anxious by the second. "I'm not great at talking. Can we change the topic?"

"But this is interesting! Why do you seem upset?"

"I'm not upset!"

She laughed, and he didn't know if she was laughing at him, or at something else. "Look, Mark, take my advice. Sometimes you shouldn't follow the line of 'who started it'. It gets you nowhere. You can both be stubborn. But it's her last night, and I'm sure if you make an effort, she will. Make it *nice* for her. Anyway, grab those drinks and give me a hand, lazy arse."

Mark carried three pints up in silence. His ears were hot. He really needed to go for a walk to cool down, get away from people, sit by the canal for a bit, look at the black reflective water, something he could identify with. Flight not fight. But that would just attract more attention, more discussion. All the mirrors and balconies already made him feel as if he was being watched. It was like needing to pee: you can hold it for ages if there's a toilet nearby and you can go whenever you want. But when you can't go easily, like when you're in the middle of a row at the pictures, you feel like you're bursting, desperate. Mark was trapped here. Mentally bursting.

Sam had been telling Gita from marketing how jealous she was of her gorgeous jet-black hair when Em returned with drinks, followed by Mark carrying more. Sam knew that something had gone on even before Emily winked. Earlier Mark had kept looking over whenever he thought he wouldn't be noticed. But Sam had noticed. Sudden stomach churn.

Em sat close to Sam, leg touching hers. Sam was impatient to speak to her but Roger had a new camera with a zoom lens and was taking photos of her (and everybody else). She posed for the picture, drink held up, smiling but leaning away from Em when she tried to stick a tongue in Sam's ear; Sam was glad when he finished and moved off to take a picture of a girl in a low-cut top.

"Well?" Sam whispered.

"Don't look so worried. We were only talking about you leaving. I was just surprised that he said he'd miss you."

"Really?"

"Yes. Maybe he's not such a prick after all."

Em had to reply to something from Roger at that point, and Sam could lean back, tackle one of her drinks as an excuse to not speak to anyone for a minute.

If Mark thought that now it was probably just because of the booze. Still, it felt good. She'd been right to forgive. It spreads kindness instead of anger, and everyone benefits.

Ben and Dave's conversation had devolved into football. Mark was unable to pay attention.

Sam was surrounded by people. Her smile was amazing. People had to be near her.

Dave was arguing about chances … what? … United, United's chances.

Emily had said things. They milled around in his head, a chorus, a repeating breakbeat.

In front of Sam were three glasses of clear stuff, one with coke in, a pint, and a few unidentifiables. Maybe you could measure popularity by the gifts you got.

Team formations now. Words on either side of him. Mark nodded. It wasn't worth asking what it meant, since surely footballers all just ran at the opposing goal? Back and forth, mindless, a good side and a bad side, an end you aimed at.

Roger was saying something, and Sam laughed, and Mark squinted.

The bloke to Sam's left got up.

That knife edge, that point, you risk hurt whichever way your finger slides.

Back and forth, and you look at a goal but maybe it wasn't just a white frame, it was something else people saw, something beyond it.

"Squidgegrapes!" Mark muttered. He got up quickly before his brain could impede his action, moved to the chair next to Sam.

"Have you got enough drinks there?" he asked, gesturing towards the spread, heart thudding in its box.

"Everyone just keeps buying them," Sam replied.

"You're pretty stacked," he said, mindless and flustered.

Sam snorted.

"I mean with drinks!" he added hurriedly, his timing off and content crap. He wanted to groan. He wasn't cut out for this, but then he caught a subtle thumbs up from Emily.

"I won't drink them all," Sam said. "Here, have a tequila." She handed Mark one of the glasses.

"Okay, but you have one too."

"A challenge. Down in one."

It was something beyond that. It was the look in her eye.

They knocked them back. The lovely ice-thawing liquid raced down her throat and burnt its way into her stomach; then Mark coughed.

"That hits the spot!" he said, his eyes twinkling as much as his silver chain in the flickering tea-lights.

"I could have done with those in work a few times," Sam joked. "What do you think of it in here?"

"I like it. Never been in before, but it's pretty cool. Do you come here often?"

She raised an eyebrow.

"Oh yeah, that sounds corny. I don't mean it like it sounds."

"We come in sometimes. You don't get the aggro that goes with meat market bars."

"And you wouldn't go in them anyway," he said. She must have seemed puzzled. "Meat … veggie," he added lamely. "Sorry. You should know by now. I'm rubbish at jokes."

"Only when you try too hard."

After a pause they both went to speak at once: "Later...", "Have...", then laughed.

"Go on, you first," Sam said, feeling Em's elbow poke her in the side.

"It's a shame that someone has to leave to get us all out together."

"It's all a shame."

"What were you going to say?"

"I don't know." She really didn't.

"Hey, Mark, we're thinking of going to The Conti Club later, will you come?" Em interrupted, before turning away again.

"Yes, you could," Sam added.

"I've been there before I think, really dark and seedy? Somewhere behind the Palace Theatre?"

"Yes, that's the one. Em heard they're shutting it down soon. I wanted to go once more before they do, relive some good memories of the place."

"Sure. If everyone else is going. We –"

But he was interrupted by Ben yelling at Mark from the next table: "Yo slapper, you owe me a pint!"

Mark asked Sam if she wanted a drink too. She shook her head and waved her hand towards the full glasses in front of her. Yeah, stupid question, Mark. Words were proving difficult tonight.

The place was packed now. It took nearly ten minutes to get to the bar, let alone getting served. Loud dance music blared out, a remix of something by Erasure. He ordered the drinks, nodded at a guy in a tight shirt who smiled at him. Mark was feeling hungry so got crisps too. Denny used to tell him beer and crisps counted as a pub meal. Potato was healthy.

As Mark paid he noticed Sam pass by in the direction of the toilets. He quickly tried to get to her, not knowing what he was going to say but feeling bizarrely desperate to say it, leaving the drinks temporarily unguarded. But there were too many people in the way, and as he jostled left and right and reached an arm up to wave she disappeared through the door. He was disappointed at being blocked. Then surprised at himself. What the hell was wrong with him tonight? He commanded himself to get it together and stop being weird.

Once Mark had gone Sam had made excuses about needing to go to the toilet and got up. She'd hoped to bump into him away from everyone else. Had edged through crowds, looking round for his dark hair above the height of the mob, but didn't see him. She came back disappointed.

More people had turned up. The Rusholme, Withington, Eccles crowds. She hadn't realised how many friends she'd accrued until the bodies were all crammed into a hot section of a pub and formed a sweaty mass. The group was getting louder and sillier, and Ben kept threatening to do a moony, which caused a bit of amusement. Especially when someone suggested Roger photograph it, which made Roger stutter defensively.

He carried the cluster of pints upstairs, getting wet hands from spillage as he navigated past bodies and benches. His place next to Sam was filled by someone else, so he gave them a dirty look then made an effort to chat with other people. It was difficult though. He had such little interest in the things they wanted to talk about. He would rather replace the words with lyrics; punctuation with mood; syntax with rhythm, and mouths with melodies.

He caught Sam looking at him and whispering something to Emily. They giggled. Don't feel paranoid. It was just words.

Dave and Ben were now talking about cars, another topic which Mark found incomprehensible. He checked the time on his phone – they'd been there over two hours already. A number of people had drifted off, "just the one" polite drinkers. The numbers stayed about the same though because other people Mark didn't know had turned up, friends of Sam and Emily. They hogged the girls' attention. He picked up his phone again.

"You got another date?" Dave asked.

"No."

"Stop looking at the fucking time then. You're making me nervous. Shit, I'd better ring Suzannah and find out how her gormless family party is going." He left.

Mark had drunk more than he'd intended. So much for his decision to cut down. Yet he couldn't seem to get pissed, or even giddy. All around people were losing their heads, cutting loose and getting loud, but he couldn't escape from himself.

"You okay mate?" asked Ben.

"Yeah. Why?"

"You were miles away. Seemed it all night. Though what do I know? I'm on the way to getting wasted!" He laughed and drank some more of his pint, sitting on the edge of a table. He wore a shirt that seemed too tight, but Mark realised it must be the current style if Ben was wearing it.

"I'm fine. Are you going to the club afterwards?"

"Yeah, sure. You are too. That's nothing to sulk over though, is it?"

"I've just been feeling a bit weird all night."

"Why? Is Sam scaring you?"

"What do you mean? You been talking to Emily?" Mark was too snappy. Ben looked at him vaguely amused.

"Well, you and Sam have been looking at each other all night, like you got the hots for each other." He paused, idly searching Mark's face, then something seemed to ignite in his eyes. "Well fuck me, amma right or what?"

"We're just being friendly."

"Make a move on her."

"She's got a boyfriend."

"Oh yeah? Where is he then?"

Mark frowned.

"She's been single for a while."

"Really?"

"Course! I know this shit. You should've asked me, you buffoon." Ben was louder than usual. Mark looked around to make sure no one was eavesdropping, unlikely as it was in the cacophony of voices and music. "So, you gonna try it on with her later?" Ben added, as if life was a case of simple decisions made and acted upon.

"No! It's not like that."

Ben laughed and looked over at Sam. For a second Mark thought he was going to tell her something about Mark, something embarrassing, giving away a secret part of him to the whole room for people's laughter and derision. Mark felt like a child as his heart lurched. But Ben just made a joke about the booze, and the night club, then turned back to Mark with a wide grin, like he was enjoying it all. Mark wasn't enjoying himself one bit at that moment. The headlights of a car were bearing down on him and he was a rabbit, a pigeon, wanting to move but unable to.

"Chill out mate. It's cool. Hey, Roger's put his long lens away and gone to the pisser to use his little one. There's room if we're quick, so let's sit with Sam and Emily. No pressures. But I'm behind you if you need me. Okay? After all, I am the black knight of love. Best wing-man in the world."

"We're joining you ladies," Ben said, with his usual unshakeable confidence. "So now it's time for some *real* intelligent and sexy conversation." Ben pulled two chairs round, crammed them between Sam and Em. Mark smiled shyly and took the one next to Sam. Shapes fitting into place. *Tidy*, as she'd say back home.

"I didn't tell you. You look really good," Mark said before gazing away quickly, as if he didn't have the confidence to look her in the eye – *didn't mean it* – but it was still something. A hint of flirt fuelled by pints of tipsy, but she'd take what she could.

"Thanks. As long as the outfit isn't weird."

"Huh?"

"Nothing."

"I wish I could dress like you."

"You want to wear a skirt?"

"No, I mean looking good. Fancy. No, that's not the word."

"You look fine."

He just yanked at his top in reply.

"You're strange. I like that," she said.

"What?" he asked above the noise.

"No matter. Are you going to help me drink these?"

"What?"

"Are you –" It was too loud. She leaned in to speak in his ear, repeated the question.

He spoke back into her ear. It tickled.

Sam's phone vibrated. She picked it up: a message off Em, who had only just put her own phone down.

`Go get im, sexy. ;-)`

Sam quickly turned its screen off.

Em was doing a good job of keeping attention on herself so Sam could talk to Mark without interruptions, though Roger frowned in Sam's direction once or twice – presumably because he'd lost his seat. Sam ignored him. She ruled from her chair just this once, living in the moment. Just the other person in your close zone, where you smell their skin and hair; words straight from lips to ears, privately intimate, just a tongue flick from the other's flesh. It might only be the two of them trading quirky misunderstandings, half-heard comments, but it was perfect. A delicious bubble of time.

A roar, laughing, shouting, and the bubble popped. Emily was daring Ben to really stand on a table and drop his trousers. It looked like he was going to capitulate.

"It's not Canal Street, it's Anal Street," someone yelled, and another pisshead shouted, "Get 'em off!"

Time to move on.

Their group was smaller now. Conti was officially announced. An opportunity for others to take their leave with a hug, a word, a sentiment. The remaining hardcore squirmed their way out through the thick crowd. It seemed to take forever before they could breathe what passed for fresh air in Manchester. It would be the last time for a while. This time tomorrow she'd be asleep in Wales. It was transition, something between times and places, a liminal area where you can do anything, be anyone. These times are few enough, only a fool wouldn't seize them. And her family had raised no *twpsin.*

Mark had loved the last hour. Sam was in his mind and he knew he was in hers as they leaned in to each other to whisper or giggle, easy rapport, and each time he had felt his stomach churn but in a way he liked, and he could smell her perfume, her hair; *her*. He had wanted to do it more and more but restrained himself. He didn't want her to think he was some pervert inhaling the scented air around her because the smell made him giddy.

"Come to the club with us," Ben shouted to Dave.

"Dance like you've never danced before," Mark added.

Dave left a pause, then said, "Why not? It always looks like *you've* never danced before."

Others laughed but it wasn't mean. Em gave Mark a surprise hug. There was something weird about tonight. Mark wondered if Ben had sprayed him with sex pheromones.

On the way out Mark spotted two men kissing. Watched. Dave caught where he was looking. "Better than kickin' off."

"Oh, yeah. I wasn't thinking it's bad. Love not war. Just never seen it."

"And more for us, eh?" Ben said with a laugh.

"Your mind. One track," Mark told him.

"Ever wonder about getting off with a guy?"

"I suppose they'd know what to do if they were giving you a hand shandy," Dave said as they left the building. "Insider info."

"I'd prefer to get off with myself," Ben mused. "That'd be the ultimate."

"I'm surprised you don't already." Dave made a loose fist, poked his tongue in and out of the hole.

There was a small crowd left, some from work, some Mark didn't know. A man in drag with gold skin was striding past on stilts. He seemed cool and majestic up there. Mark tried to imagine the different perspective he must have, looking down on the little people. Maybe your position in the world always determines how it appears.

"Are we all here now? Party!" yelled Ben, grabbing Emily around the waist and dragging her off. She squealed, but it was a noise that said, "Look at me!", not "Let go of me!" The group made their rowdy way along the canal. Mark was at the back. In front of him Sam was talking to Roger and some bloke he didn't recognise. Now and again he could see Sam's face, animated and alive. She caught him gazing at her and pulled faces when Roger wasn't looking, and that made Mark smile. It was good. She knew he was there. That was all he wanted.

They detoured to a fast-food van. It was on the paved area outside Cornerhouse, the cinema where they showed arty-type films that seemed like they'd be too clever for Mark. Most people got burgers but Mark bought a chip barm. The hot greasy potato mushed lusciously on the tongue. Sam had also been different, getting some salad in a pitta pocket, but she eyed Mark's chips hungrily.

"You want some?" he asked, holding out the hot wrapper.

"I love chips. But I shouldn't."

They shared anyway.

"You were staring at the canal a lot. What were you thinking?" she asked, taking some more with a rustle of paper.

"I was looking for something, but I only saw cans and bottles. It's a mess. Don't you think? Litter. All around."

"I was in Paris once, that was clean, for a city. I think they pump water from the Seine each night to flood out the gutters."

"Wow. What else was Paris like?"

"I forgot you've not been abroad. It's exciting. Different but familiar. And no one knows you. You can be who you want."

"Who were you?"

"A sophisticated Euro-lady."

"You're that anyway."

"I wish. It was good when someone thought I was English and I'd correct them. '*Non! Je suis du pays de Galles!*' And they'd laugh and turn warm. That's something about Wales. Once a French, Scots or Irish person realises you're Welsh and not English, you're one of the family."

"You'd be welcome wherever you go. I like the idea of being someone new, somewhere new. Like starting again."

She didn't reply. The chips were finished, the group moved on.

Not far from Bridgewater Canal, in back streets of unlit and crumbling warehouses, lurked the dodgy-looking Continental Club. It was like a descent; slowly, glow on glow, the city darkened. The towering and gated-off industrial remnants made his group seem small, teeny: pleasure-seeking specks burning brightly for a time. And when they were gone the buildings would remain, the city's sentinels.

The club was nicknamed the Conti because all but the first few letters had fallen off the sign. People only knew of the cramped but lively place by word of mouth. Something at the edge of society, whispered, almost underworld secrecy. They paid their subs and went down the stairs into the depths of Manchester. Music blared out, banging bass, some house-type anthem Mark knew but couldn't name. Presumably his subconscious blocked it out as not being proper music.

First stop was the bar. The place was already busy and Mark lost everyone as he sidled his way through hot bodies. He tried to get the barman's attention by leaning forwards over the counter but just earned wet sleeves from a puddle of sticky beer. Three more people got served before him, and when he eventually got a drink it was a rip-off price for a can of lager.

Despite being a small venue resembling a concrete cellar with a few fairy lights (on second thoughts, it didn't resemble that, it *was* that) he couldn't see the other side of the room, it was too dark and smoky. Fire flickers of hellish red light shone near one corner of the dance floor. Some dancers shuffled around, others had their arms in the air, mad looks on their sweaty, grinning faces. They were lost in sound and he could identify with that.

Looking for his group again was a challenge, squeezing past people whose clothes rubbed against his, different sensations each time. There was a subdued smell of sweat below everything else. So many shiny happy people. He caught a glimpse of Dave but lost him in the shadows as Mark was shoved from behind by a staggering teenager. He was glad to have beer in a can after all since it prevented the drink from spilling down the boobs of the woman in front. No more black eyes or bloody noses for him.

Sam had lost Mark almost as soon as they entered the humid heat of the packed club. She went to the cloakroom with Em and used the opportunity to spray a bit more of her new perfume on, the cheesy "One Love" by Ramadis that she'd scorned so often. Its choice as a present had to be a joke on Emily's part. But it actually smelt nice. Then she consigned the bag of leaving gifts to a raffle ticket cloakroom location.

She'd needed the toilets back in Via Fossa but hadn't wanted to fight her way there and back when everyone was ready to leave. By now she was knee-touchingly desperate. As she entered these toilets with Em though, she wished she *had* used those in the Fossa: the Conti toilets were cramped and dirty with a grey space above the sinks where there used to be a mirror.

When they'd finished they had the place to themselves. Em offered a small plastic bag of powder to Sam.

"A going-away gift. I was going to get E but Rob said there's a drought on, so it's just whizz. Don't treat it like a Rizla wrap, you'd be twatted. It's from a good batch."

Sam looked at the bag. Licked her lips. Could imagine the bitterness at the rear of her tongue, sweetness at the front. But she shook her head. "You keep it."

"What?"

"No. I'm done with it. Just thinking of it's too tempting, which suggests – stick to no. In the past I repeated mistakes; it's about time I learnt from them. I've nothing against it but it's not for me any more."

Em looked at the bag as if it had turned into a snake. "Not even a dab?"

Sam gave her a close-lipped smile. "I'll see you outside."

Mark didn't recognise Sam at first, he thought she was just another grinning demon. Her face shone with the heat and her eyes glowed, wide and wild. They fixed on him and the smile broadened as he walked over. He couldn't think of anything to say but it didn't matter – she grabbed his wrist and pulled him onto the dance floor. No words, just dancing and sweating. Her body moved sinuously, confidently. Seductively. Mark stuck to old reliable: wide steps, hunched shoulders, maraca arms and head bounces. Emily and Ben came over and the four danced together: all that was missing was the handbag. Roger watched from the edge of the dancefloor, didn't try to break in to their square of power. It was perfect.

The moves petered out when some song filled with high-pitched headache-inducing sirens began. Mark took Sam's hand, feeling nervous but trying not to show it, and led her off the floor. People pressed in on all sides. She asked him to get her a drink. At that moment he would have done anything she asked. He was getting off lightly.

The whole place was banging now. It had slipped into some kind of retro-trance session, Juno Reactor, Koxbox, stuff like that. Not his kind of thing, and tonight the swirling analogue and creepy voices sounded almost satanic. Ben and Emily weren't to be seen. Dave was chatting to some girl he'd met – judging by her body language she seemed interested in him, but Mark knew she had no chance, Dave was serious about Suzannah. Mark edged to the bar and didn't think about the cost this time.

Her heart raced, but not from powder. She missed the sniff and swallow and numbness. But she loved knowing the feeling was real. Dance and smile.

While Mark was away the Withington lot found her and tried to get her to go back to a house party. Were pretty persuasive. They needed her. They'd miss her. She was a star.

She sent them away with hugs and goodbye kisses.

Mark had held her hand. It was a sweet gesture. His palm had been hot. Her fingers had interleaved with his. She could almost feel them now, ghost presence left behind.

He returned with the drinks, was leaning against a pillar, apparently happy just soaking up the atmosphere, nodding his head at the music, smiling at the dance floor then at her, his face damp with clean-looking sweat. She suddenly realised she wanted him: to have him in any way she could for as long as she could. Screw it all. Maybe it was the drink's fault. She looked at the bottle suspiciously. It was always the great lubricant to pulling; whether in Wales or England, they used the same oil. She just wanted to kid herself this once.

Mark looked surprised as she kissed him but that soon turned into eagerness: she felt it when she pushed against his body. Liked having that effect on him. Equivalent of what he was doing to her.

He was a good kisser. Passionate without being rough or clumsy. He put a hand on the back of her neck, something she always found sexy. They touched each other gently, and it felt like they were together, and Sam was almost ready to forgive him for not liking her.

The touch of lips, soft and wet and sensual. Was it one long kiss or lots of smaller ones? Didn't matter. Something opened in him. The night had been a continuous build up of sexual energy and it came together now as a total head rush. It was beautiful, and he knew it wasn't just because he was a bit wasted. When she'd started kissing him it was like a cold water shock that only allows life back in slowly but that life was precious. He could smell her perfume and skin, taste her mouth, feel the warmth, see into her dark eyes: every sense was filled, and he was intensely aware of her presence so close, every movement. Sam was smiling when they broke off, her body an insistent pressure against his. Her eyes flashed with pupils creepily dark.

She pulled him onto the dancefloor. He was still buzzing off her kiss. As they danced they touched each other. A hand on a hot waist, or a face, or her buttocks, or lips against a sweet-smelling neck.

It was that time of night when real life is left behind and a weird nightclub abandonment takes over. People don't care what you're doing. Mark had once seen a guy being sucked off on the dance floor while everyone else just carried on, at least until the bouncers got there. The dangerous feeling that you can act on your impulses, whatever tomorrow brings.

They danced closer this time, bodies touching. He seemed bolder (*drunker?*) and slid his palms from her hips to her bottom. Normal worries about whether someone would think her arse was too big were buried underneath other feelings. The confidence of groping hands; the tune of hope, germinating in dark paces; the beat of forgiveness, even if only temporary. Anger was an insistent emotion, and required every finger to plug the dam. He was doing a good job at the moment though, maybe even enough to persuade her that Em was right again.

On a break from the dance floor. People blurred in the smoke at the edges of perception. Only Sam was in focus.

"Sam?"

"Hmmm?"

"This is kind of weird."

She moved back slightly. "Weird like you're not into it?" she asked, as if she was barely covering anger.

"No! I meant, I didn't think you liked me."

"Oh. Well, maybe I thought the same thing. It's a good job last nights are special."

Cryptic again. "This is. All of it. Well, apart from the music, maybe," he added as a joke.

"So you want to go?"

"Yeah."

"Even if I want to stay?"

"No, I meant I'd go if you did. Not that … this is confusing."

"I know how particular you are about your music."

"That doesn't matter. If you stayed then I'd stay too. Obviously."

"Obviously." She looked at her mobile and said, "It's nearly one – this place shuts down in an hour or so. What do you want to do afterwards?"

"I don't know. Whatever you want. I'd like to spend more time with you."

"Before I go."

He nodded. "The night's not over till the sun comes up."

"I like that. Well, let it carry on. And it's cheaper if we shared a taxi."

He felt suddenly inexperienced next to her. "Yeah, I'd like to go with you," he muttered.

"Good. We'll go in a bit, rather than stay till the end of the night when the music goes bad. I'll just check with Emily."

"Fine, I want to have a quick wander too. I'll be back here in a few minutes."

"Where are you going?"

"Toilet."

She smiled at him. He wasn't sure why that seemed significant.

The place was still pulsing. Mark popped into the men's and filled his latest empty beer can with water. He was so hot. Drank it all in one go. It wasn't enough to quench his thirst.

When Mark went to the toilet to buy condoms Sam thought "Good boy".

She found Em talking with Roger. He looked quite gone, and she seemed to be trying to convince him of something. Em gave a weak smile.

"I just came to say I'm leaving now in a minute."

"Why not stay out a bit longer, Sam?" Roger blurted out. "You're one of a kind – coolio, like me."

Sam declined. She started to speak to Emily but Roger interrupted again. "I was thinking of going too, want to share a taxi back?"

"Thanks, but Mark said he'd share with me."

"Bet he will," muttered Roger.

"We'll be fine, Sam, you just go. Ring me tomorrow sometime, okay?" Em asked.

"Okay."

"And you promise to visit soon?"

"I'll come for the weekend once I've settled in. A fortnight from now?"

Sam hugged her, and Emily whispered, "I love you, y'know." Sam squeezed her tighter.

Sam was waiting for him when he returned. Mark hadn't seen Ben or Dave for a while, but they could fend for themselves. More importantly: he didn't want them to know where he was going. This was just something between him and Sam. He didn't want disrespectful rumours about her going round the workplace. Sam put her arm round his waist. Up and outside, into night air which dried the sweat in cooling contractions.

They walked slowly. She leaned against him. He could look down on the top of her head. There was no need to speak. He took her to kickacars on Whitworth Street West, built into one of the many filled-in arches under the raised train track. Well, officially it was Radio Cars, but no one called them that. He kicked on the shutter a few times until a small window opened up above and a woman leaned out.

"Where to?"

Sam shouted her address up to the window.

"Five minutes."

The window slammed shut.

Mark didn't mind waiting here. It wasn't far from The Haçienda, so that was good vibes. And because they'd left before the clubs all shut there was no long queue to face, full of rowdy groups of lads in their fancy shirts and townie shoes and pants, or girls in short skirts and high shoes, flirting their way down the queue. And it felt good having Sam by his side. No pressure to speak. Words could break things.

The taxi arrived. They got into the back. As it pulled out she grabbed him, kissed him. He softened into her, reassured: it was mutual. He didn't know if the driver was looking or not, but supposed they must get used to it if they did a post-club shift. Sod it. Let him perv.

Mark paid while Sam fumbled her key into the door. The house was big, lit only by the orange glow of a street light. She turned and held a finger to her lips, "Shhh!" before leading him down the hall to a ground-floor room. They entered in darkness. When she left him for a few seconds he felt weightless and disoriented. Scrabbling sounds, a curse he didn't recognise – something Welsh? – and then the lamp beside her bed came on.

He looked around, interested to see what the room said about her … but it told him nothing. Her personal possessions had been packed into a large suitcase and a few bags. The room didn't look lived-in. Just furniture. Our spaces quickly forget us. Apart from one: she had put some piece of reddish gauze over the top of the lamp, a feminine touch that made everything look delicate and indistinct. Sam turned on an old-looking hi-fi, pressed a button, and some mellow music played. "It's a CD but it's not on random," she explained.

Ghostly haunts, bass thumps and squeaky scratches over military drumbeats. Female vocalist with a yearning voice. It sounded familiar. Bristol scene. Tricky, Portishead, or Massive Attack. Not his specialism. It fitted though.

She took a step towards him. Seemed tentative. Maybe he should make the first move. It certainly felt like the right time. Everything was spot on. He reached for her hands.

The music was trip hop but started to skip, then jump. Sam cursed. Attacked the hi-fi with a stabbing finger, moving through tracks but it seemed indifferent to her wishes, each one was jumping. She thumped the machine, went to do it again but he touched her arm.

"Be nice to it, don't kick it. You said that. I'm happy with silence."

She nodded. Pressed its power button and the display lights faded. "It's on the way out. I won't be taking this piece of shit with me." She sighed, then lay on the bed. He bit his lip then joined her, looked at her face, her eyes focussed on him – on *him* – and they kissed again. Hands came into play. And he found himself lay on top, his hips moved slowly, a life of their own. The soft wet noises of lips. Was she going to try and have sex with him? But after a minute she pushed him off and sat up.

"I just need a quick smoke. Want one? Oh, I remember. You don't."

Her eyes, such a pull. He had to look away.

"I probably couldn't with my hayfever. I'd never stop sneezing." The weak joke got no response. "Do you still smoke a lot?"

"Why, are you going to get strict and lecture me again?"

He couldn't tell if she was joking, challenging, or angry, but it almost looked like her hand shook a bit.

"No. I've no right to tell you to do anything."

"Good."

"It's not like you're smoking crack, is it?"

"God, no. Nothing like that. I can't offer you a drink. I've nothing left."

"I'm fine. Honestly. I've had enough."

"Of me?"

"No. Not enough of you. Just enough drink."

They stared at each other. *Now* it felt like a challenge.

Was he up to it? He swallowed.

"I really like you," he said, forcing himself to keep his eyes on her, even though he felt like breaking the vulnerable connection. But it was Sam who looked away. Was she disappointed? Unreadable. Like walking on ice, no way of knowing when it was going to crack.

She only smoked a bit of the cig but it gave her seconds of respite.

"Look people in the eye. Especially if you are lying to someone."

Fucking hell. He was lying.

"Rock and roll," she said quietly.

"You okay?" he asked.

"I am now."

"You were anyway."

"How'd you know?" She stubbed out the dimp.

"Your aura."

"You're strange."

He pulled a face: squinted, bent lips in and mimed a gummy gnashing that set her off, laughter the release she needed. They started kissing again. If she forgot about meaning then she could live like this for hours, just kissing in soft light, timeless indulgence. She slid her hands underneath his top, ran them over his chest, felt short hairs, muscle beneath.

She made him feel confident with her smiles, the noises she made. This wasn't too serious. He relaxed. It was just kissing. No more. Mark lifted up her top and began feeling her breasts in her bra. Warm, near her heart. It was a game, messing about, no more. He wasn't breaking resolutions. And

she removed his top, which took two attempts – the first time it got caught on his silver chain and ended up stuck over his head, which made them both giggle. They rolled around, stripping and pulling any buttons, zips or studs. Her skin felt more sensitive, tingly, heart beating fast but strong. Then he surprised her, kneeling down, taking her shoes off gently and rubbing each foot for a few seconds. His touch was surprisingly tender

her feet felt warm and soft, this was all reverential, just affectionate exploration, then

he lay on his back, completely in her hands. She unfastened his belt and trousers

and he grabbed her wrist, not hard, but he was already so close to dropping his restraint with her, she was inside his defences and he knew he was weak, hadn't felt like this with anyone before; but a needy look from her and his eyes misted, he let her wrist go

because he was hard, had been since they started kissing, turned on, maybe he was worried about coming too soon, she wouldn't touch him for long, no accidents, but she slipped her hand into his pants; his penis was smooth, not wide but long, she could imagine it up deep inside her

he stopped doing anything much as she squeezed and stroked, until she removed his trousers with a strong yet half-comic tug and slipped her top off.

and he sat up, unfastened her bra,

he got it right first time, relieved at not looking foolish, removed the bra completely. Her breasts were heavy and soft as he touched her, dark areolas attracting his eyes then lips, nipples hardening. She slipped her skirt off and sat astride him with just her knickers on, looking down the curve of her nose like sexy nobility, maybe Lady Godiva riding a horse; her hair hung down, casting her face into shade

no shame naked, none of the nervousness she expected, he smiled at her body as she sat on him; no doubt the soft pink light helped, flattering effect, hide as much as it reveals at this time of night

"You're beautiful," he told her. "So sexy, I –" but she stopped his mouth with hers, didn't let him tell her that he couldn't hold on to his principle round her, couldn't do anything except focus on her

because she couldn't believe he was sincere even though he sounded it, she knew it wasn't what he believed, what his sober mind thought, she wouldn't be taken in, no *twpsin* she, but oh his hands felt good, she leaned forward, pushing her breasts against them

and moved her hips, rubbing herself against him, the material such a thin barrier, inconsequential, they were so close, he'd never wanted anyone like he wanted her, she caused a reaction, nuclear, "No more" he whispered, but he started to pull her knickers down, she climbed off for a second to remove them properly, and he took the opportunity to remove his boxers, both naked to each other, and she leaned over and took a condom from a drawer by the bed, tore the foil with her teeth, spat the top out, rolled the rubber onto his dick, reassuring tightness as it unfurled to the base. He was glad she'd done that, he didn't agree with unsafe sex, but suspected darkly he would have gone on and done it anyway, because

she enjoyed smoothing it onto his penis, being able to touch him there, savouring what was going to come next as she straddled him again and reached down, guided the firmness inside, so wet he slid in smoothly, making her shudder, a flush of warmth

such a dark, sweet feeling, that first moment sliding in; there was a smell of her in the air; her presence filled his eyes and nostrils, a whole atmosphere that was made up of one amazing woman, and she moved alone at first but then he had to join in

and they made love, she felt herself moving towards an orgasm as he sucked her nipples whenever she forced herself deeper down onto him, this position rubbed her the right way, and he was gentle as

they moved around, across the bed to the edge and back again, rolling and switching positions like a carnal wrestling match, then Mark was on top, they kissed, grabbing and pinching skin to the point of desperate pain

her inner thighs around his hips, and he moaned, and she knew he was going to come, and felt close herself as she bit his shoulder and felt him start to spasm inside her, thrusting her hips towards him as best she could, helping him to prolong it

sensations so intense

end swollen, in out wet friction pulling him into her, into release, into her, into release, "No" he whispered

she couldn't last longer, "More" she said

he collapsed on top of her, panting, his head resting on her shoulder and she was holding on to him, her legs wrapped around him

might never let go
he didn't pull out straight away
she didn't seem to want him to
rest and recover breath
high off something good
high off each other
so high he was up above and looking down and she
made him feel like a god.

But nothing good lasts forever. Mark rolled over onto his back, with a squelch sound as his shrunken penis came out of her. He pulled the greasy condom off, tied a knot in it, asked her if she had a rubbish bin. She took it off him and dropped it in the bin by the bed. Then he lay on his side looking at her, his hand on her belly. She was still lay on her back, staring at the ceiling, an arm across her forehead and a lazy smile on her red lips.

All she could hear was their heavy breathing. She hadn't come but it had been surprisingly close, and the sensation left her feeling dizzy and close to him. She had the strange feeling that she would cry, but resisted. It wouldn't have been right. Not unless he'd really been there because he cared about her. She squeezed her eyes tight shut until the feeling passed, a hard thing broken and made soft, but it left a pain in her chest, the kind she got when she'd been shouting at someone she cared about.

"This is turning out to be one of the best nights of my life," he whispered softly.

That was exactly what she wanted to hear then, but she wanted it to be true, not just a platitude. She didn't dare think about it too much. It might ruin the fantasy. So she chose to get him talking: then she could just passively relax and not think. She asked him, "What are the others?"

"You don't really want to know, do you?" he asked, surprised.

"I wouldn't have asked."

"Okay. I suppose one was seeing 808 State at G-MEX years back – nearly 10,000 of us crammed in for this massive party, music pounding and laser rays blinding you, smoke machines pumping, MC Tunes turning up to dance and rap, then a weird frozen moment when Björk appeared and started singing, like you'd gone to this other world. And I don't even do raves! But when it ended with In Yer Face I was grinning, couldn't stop, oh *wow*. A totally mad night, blisscherries brilliant... Another night was when I got to chat to Shaun Ryder while he was DJing once. He was off his face but was sound, really down-to-earth... And the night I met Becky.... Oh, and the gig I went to in –"

"What was so special about the girl?" Sam interrupted.

Oh, applesauce ... why did he always say the wrong thing and mess stuff up? "It's a long story."

Sam had felt a twinge of jealousy. Stupid, stupid girl. If anything she should have been glad. It was a reminder that, whatever she pretended, she was just a fuck to him. And tomorrow he'd be out of her life for good. But she never could resist picking at a scab. What was so special about this woman? Was she better than Sam? Scratch that itch.

"Go on. I'm interested. Count it as pillow talk."

Sam was an even cooler person than he'd realised. She deserved respect.

"Okay. If that's what you want. Her name was Rebecca Daw. Actually, she looked quite a lot like you. Dark. Her hair was almost black. I called her Jackdaw sometimes. She said she hated it."

"When was this?"

"Few years ago. She was someone I'd known for a while, from a supermarket I worked in for a bit, but I hadn't expected anything to happen. I didn't think we were that kind of friends. Well, apart from once when she'd come back to my old flat after we'd been to a club, and we'd got off with each other after chatting for hours, but we hadn't had sex. It didn't feel right. And it was about seven o' clock in the morning, and I was knackered. So I said no. She stayed the night but we didn't talk much after that. It was kind of weird the next time I saw her."

"You surprised?"

"Well, eventually this night came. I'd met some people at The Haçienda, they were really into music. I ended up at a house party with them in Stretford, not far from where I live now. During a storm. Everyone was wasted. Rain was coming down in sheets. Rebecca was at the party, she always seemed to know lots of people, outgoing, and after a while I managed to wangle it so we were sharing a chair at the kitchen table, one cheek each, and we got chatting properly again, the first time since she'd stayed over. Like I said, things had been strained, so this was really nice, like we could go back to being friends. Only things are never exactly the same, are they? Anyway, I was in a crazy, happy mood, and some of the guys at the party were nutters too. I've always loved really powerful storms, when the wind's against you, dead strong, that kind of thing. It energises me."

"I know what you mean. There are hills where I grew up, there was nothing better than going to the top of the valley and feeling all that natural power," she said, her hand playing with the hairs on Mark's chest. "Sorry, go on."

"Well, me and this ginger guy went outside, leaving the front door open, and everyone was saying 'What are you doing, you beeping nutters!' as we ran about in the rain, doing the can-can, clowning round. It felt great with lightning shooting off, and thunder booming, and us howling the words to Singing In The Rain. We were jumping in the puddles, soaked to the skin by now, the guy even lay down in one and pretended to swim. Every time there was a roar of thunder we shouted 'Come on!' at the sky. (He shouted the B-word too.) It was totally insane, people were looking out of windows or standing in doorways, some laughing and some telling us to beep off, and other people from the party came out, one girl was shampooing her hair in the rain. It was that mad." Mark smiled as the vivid memories of that night came back.

"Anyway, Rebecca was watching from the door and shaking her head. After a bit the thunder moved away, and we went back into the house, soaking wet through. The party was winding down. I needed to dry off, it was about three in the morning anyway. I said bye to everyone, then went over to Rebecca. She was laughing, saying I was nuts. Her eyes shone, reminded me of the lightning. I said I was going home, asked her if she wanted to come around for a cuppa too, since I wasn't far. She didn't seem sure so I told her I'd be staying up for a bit anyway if she changed her mind.

"I got back to mine, a teeny ground-floor place back then, the storm pretty much died down, put the lights on, kettle on. Took my shirt off and put it on the radiator. Felt great, even though water was still trickling down my back out of my hair. There was a knock. It was her. Looked tired but sexy too, that way girls have when you let go, don't give a fig any more about what you look like. Can just be a person. She put music on then sat in my bedroom. I went to ask her how many sugars she wanted. My keks were still wet, and I was stood there with no top on asking this silly question. I felt weird, like I was in a Patrick Swayze film or something; like a movie star. I know I'm nothing special that way, but we all have our moments, and I'd been feeling great all night, I was sparkin'.

"Well, the hot drinks didn't get made until the next day. We – are you sure about this?"

"Yes. I'm not made of glass."

"Well, we kissed again and this time she started ripping my clothes off, the next thing we were on the bed and ended up having sex all night, and into the next morning. Well, that was that. It stuck in me mind."

Sam had her palm on Mark's cheek, lay on her side too now.

"Did you see her afterwards?"

"Yeah."

"How come you changed your mind? You hadn't liked her that way at first."

"Well, I did really like her when I thought about it, it had kind of crept up on me, like some things do, so after that I was hoping she'd stay interested. I didn't want a one night stand."

"How come you're not still going out? Or maybe you *are*?"

"No! We finished, but it was weird, because although there was a storm that night it was actually spring. After the storm there was this beautiful weather, we spent loads of time together, spent weekends drinking, took days off work to stay in bed or go on picnics, it was like something ideal. But it was just a summer thing. Hormones controlling us, maybe. I was just surprised at the passion, I hadn't ever felt anythin' like it. It was mad. I remember her putting her hand in my pants while I was playing Puzzle Bobble in an arcade, like we were connected, always sparks. But the passion tricked me. Into thinking it was something more permanent, I mean. I don't know if she realised or not. When I'm in a bad mood I think she did, but maybe I'm wrong. With the end of the summer it just sort of, I dunno, it all just stopped. There was a weird bit where we had a couple of arguments, then she went off with some other guy. Felt bad for a while, then I realised the summer had done it all."

He knew he was understating it. Didn't want to tell her how hurt he'd really been. Looking back, Becky had been his last real girlfriend. And he wouldn't admit it to Sam, but maybe his first, too. A gorgeous woman like Sam must have had loads of boyfriends. Why reveal what a sad case he was in comparison? She was already stronger than him. He had to hold onto any shreds of bravado he could.

Mark had said Sam reminded him of this other woman, this "Rebecca", which made Sam uncomfortable. Maybe she envied her. She'd somehow got Mark to care for her, and had chosen to give him up.

"That's a beautiful story," she said. And in some ways she meant it.

"Anyway, how about you, the best nights in your life?"

"Ah, not many to talk about. A few, it doesn't matter." A defence reaction. She didn't want to reveal much. Or rather, she would have loved to – if the situation had been different. If she had been going to see him again.

"They matter. They're what life's for," he insisted.

"Okay. Any night that makes me live."

She might not have him for the future but she had him at this moment. Sam wasn't like that other girl he'd been with. The thought of marathon sex sessions made her feel inferior. But Sam knew she could make love once more. And she wanted to.

She put her hand down and began to stroke him. With all the talking since he'd come he did feel perky again. His prick was jerking back to hardness. They started kissing, and ended up having sex once more. It took longer this time, and was nicer because of it, more gradual and cosy. Afterwards they snuggled under the covers because it was getting cold in the quiet that comes before dreams. And as he drifted off, their arms tight around each other, he felt that they'd got it right, here in this city, late at night.

Sam lay on her side watching him sleep. He was breathing deeply, his face relaxed and with a faint smile caught on it, the silver chain around his neck lax too. Everything pulled towards slumber. She was tired but determined to resist for just a while longer. To look at him for just another minute, because once the light was turned out, the next time she would see him would be a different day, a new life, and this fantasy would be over.

To be held, is to be healed.

She mused over the sex again, and it made her squirm slightly with pleasure as she relived their contact. And now they were bonded together under the covers.

She yawned. Then fantasised that the silence around them was a loving one. It was difficult to hold on to that fantasy though, it kept getting flattened under the weight of the truth, that a week from now he'd hardly remember her, unless he kept notches on his bed. Still, you have to kid yourself sometimes. For one night she could pretend it meant something more. She stifled another yawn then turned the light out. Slowly she drifted into sleep in his arms, and dreamt of butterflies.

Sunrise

- **Album:** Low-
- **Year:** 1985
- **Label:** Factory Records

Despite the optimism of a new day and all the possibilities it holds, this is a song of despair and cynicism. Are its accusations aimed at God? The insubstantial? Ian Curtis? A lover? New Order are as ambiguous as ever. But it's clear this song (which, appropriately, follows This Time Of Night) shows New Order totally in control of rising mood and power, from the ominous funere catchy guitar

New Order performing Sunrise in The Haçienda, 1985

Just as sunrise separates night from day, this, their third album, is seen as their transition into a mature form of their sound with more electronic synth and dance built into their tracks. Transitions are always worth exploring, those times when something changes forever. Maybe that's why this is
band members –

Sam woke first. Sunlight was peeping through a gap in the curtains, shining onto Mark's chest and making the silver chain glitter as he breathed deeply. He looked peaceful and huggable. As Em once said, it was unfair that men woke up as good-looking as they went to bed, but women somehow deteriorated during the night.

She slipped on her dressing gown then collected the dried condoms and wrapped them in a tissue so she could put them in the sanitary bathroom bin. The condoms were as shrivelled as she felt. Her head was aching. Dehydration and lack of sleep. A farewell to decadence. She found her underwear, slipped it on under the dressing gown, and sat on the edge of the bed, gathering the energy to move on.

He first realised he was conscious when he sensed movement in the room. Dog-tired, eyes shut. Only a few hours sleep. He would feel like birdpoop later. A faint elastic snap that must be knickers. Sam sighed, then sat on the corner of the bed. That wasn't promising.

He opened his stinging eyes. They felt like there was grit under the surface. Sam was lighting up a cig. Hadn't she said she only did that when she was stressed? Maybe she was thinking, "Oh kumquats, I was wasted, now I've got this geezer in my bed, I wish he'd left last night." What now?

He rolled onto his back and looked at the ceiling. Yawned and stretched, hoping she would turn around.

When Mark started to stir her stomach lurched. What would he be thinking? It didn't help to ask "Who cares?" because *she* cared. And now she didn't have booze to give her false confidence. As she inhaled quickly she felt a bit calmer, pulling the smoke inside, nicotine entering the bloodstream, then exhaling all the dirtiness and grime. It felt somehow purifying. She must give up one day. The thought of ash in connection with mouths, a horrible thing, horrible associations. Yes, give up one day. Soon. Not today though.

When she turned round his hair was all stuck up, and that made her grin. It was reassuring that men could deteriorate too.

She'd smiled at him. That was good. They both said "Morning" at the same time and he wanted to kiss her but it didn't feel right, not with the real world of sunlight signalling the end of last night.

"What time is it?" he asked.

"About half nine. I have to leave soon. Got an advance ticket."

"Oh yeah, the train. What a pain up the backbits."

She took her clothes into the bathroom and got dressed there. Leaving early was surely a good thing. She didn't want to prolong this part, much as she'd have loved to spend time with him if things had been different.

She had a quick wash and tidied herself up. She still looked a sight: exactly like a woman who'd been out late drinking and slept badly. But it was the best she could do without getting a shower. There wasn't time for that. Mark would probably need the bathroom too.

Leaning in towards the mirror above the sink, she forced a smile. And decided that she quite liked her face. It was strong and (*weird*) genuine. The kind of face that could go through with things. That was something to hold on to.

He put his clothes on then sat on the edge of the bed wondering if he had dog-breath that morning, knowing he needed to freshen himself up, feeling awkward and drained, looking at the floor. He would have liked to have spent the day with her. Then he had an idea. He looked around for a pen. Nothing. He peeped out into the hall. No sign of Sam. There was a pad and pen just outside her bedroom by a hall phone, so he grabbed a sheet and quickly scribbled something down, folded it, and put it into a pocket.

When she'd returned to the bedroom Mark was clothed. Neither had got dressed in front of the other. The awkwardness was significant.

"Can I borrow your toothbrush?" he asked.

"Sure, here. It's old, just chuck it in the bin there when you're done."

She packed her last things while he used the bathroom. This is how it had to end. There were no alternatives left, it was inevitable that they would say polite goodbyes and leave. She would have plenty of time later to think about it all. When he returned she would make it easy for him.

Mark had a long wee first. It was brown and smelt of Sugar Puffs. That was a bad sign. He brushed his teeth, wet his hair and tried to flatten it.

Okay. He was partway alive again.

Back in the bedroom she said, "I've got to go. I need to ring for a taxi now in a minute. Do you want one too?"

That seemed a bit cold to him. Or maybe she just felt awkward at having to rush off like this. Yeah, that could be it. He didn't want to say bye yet, and not in this way, so blurted out, "I could give you a hand taking your luggage to the station." It was a gamble. Maybe she just wanted shot of him. "If you want," he added.

But she perked up, and said, "Yes, that would be good. Big strong man to move things."

She got one on the first number she tried. He listened to the banal details. Then they moved her stuff to the hall and chatted for a bit about where she was going in Wales, what her town was like. Mark was trying to find out everything he could. She seemed excited. At the back of his mind he was wondering if he would see her again whenever she came back. Or maybe even in Wales. He knew people sometimes went out long distance, travelling back and forth at weekends. It could be done if people wanted it to work. He hoped she felt the same.

The taxi came. It was such a sunny and hopeful morning. Mark put her luggage in the boot while she locked the house door and put the keys through the letterbox. "End of an era," she told him.

He joined her in the back seat. She seemed in a better mood now. They still hadn't hugged, but there was time yet.

The day was beautiful: bright and fresh. Despite that, once she was in the back of the taxi she'd felt nervous, since the last time they'd been in that situation they'd been kissing. Her body told her it wanted to do it again, but what did bodies know? Their moment had come and gone. Kisses bring things together but she had to push things apart, say goodbye. So they just joked and talked like old friends, all the way to Piccadilly.

Mark paid for the taxi, said it saved him money anyway because he could use his Megarider ticket from the station. Her weak half said he was paying her off, but the side that tried to love saw the chivalry in his action.

They lugged her stuff across the echoing and noisy shopping and ticket plaza to the timetable screens. The whole place seemed confusing. Echoing, semi-intelligible muffled voice announcements sent people into panics. Stressed parents dragged kids and suitcases, always a sense of urgency, trolleys and cases being pushed past, hurry, hurry, bewildered-looking people asking for directions and attempting to decipher timetables and work out the train's final destination so they could identify which platform to go to. There were benches full of tired-faced individuals who'd become too exhausted trying to make sense of it all. Strong smells of coffee came from the station shops. Horrible drink, lovely smell.

"I could walk you to the platform, help you get your stuff on the train. Is that allowed?"

"I don't mind."

"No, I mean, I haven't got a ticket. Can I go on the platform?"

"Of course."

"I didn't know. Never been on a train."

"Never?"

"I don't think so."

"Wow. No trains. No holidays. Didn't your family do anything?"

"Not if it was legal."

"Huh?"

"I'm just kidding."

He followed her, pulling the suitcase to the section where trains waited, engines rumbling louder than his stomach. Decorated pillars supported a massive arched roof; a warehouse that went somewhere.

"Thanks for helping. Weighs a ton, doesn't it?" she asked.

He was going to make a joke as a reply, something like "Yeah, how much make-up have you got in here?" but he managed to stop himself in time, remembering how defensively she'd reacted when he'd once mentioned her hair colour.

She was grateful for his help, and happy to put off the moment when he said bye and walked away for good. Pigeons took off as her suitcase trundled along. She found the carriage with her reserved seat, double-checked her ticket, then they put the luggage into the shelved area just inside the doors. They bumped arms accidentally and it sent a confused thrill through her. Mark apologised. There was no one else around and they were physically close, and she just felt like grabbing him and kissing him. Was about to move nearer when he stepped off the train. She came to the doorway and stood there, looking down on him from her vantage point.

"Look, thanks for everything," she said, not knowing what else to say.

He had to say something meaningful: it was now or never. For some strange reason he already felt as if things had been slipping away, sand between fingers, and he didn't understand why. He hadn't changed. "I really enjoyed last night, Sam." It felt weak, but still took some effort to say.

"Thanks."

The train thrummed in its sunken channel.

"Are you likely to be coming back down to Manchester soon?"

"Up, you mean."

"Yeah, up to Manchester."

"Probably."

It was a tricky situation. Neither of them were committing. Small talk when he wanted big talk.

"Well, here, take this." He handed her the piece of paper. "It's my phone number. I'd really like it if you gave me a bell next time you're here. So we could go out or something."

She was surprised as she held the paper. Then remembered that it was the kind of sentiment someone polite might indulge in. And she had to give him that, he had always been polite to her face. They smiled at each other awkwardly. Then a whistle blew and the doors beeped.

"Look, I'd better go to my seat. The train will be pulling out in a minute."

"Yeah. Sure." He took a step back.

She sat at her table with a magazine she'd kept out for the journey. It had some rare interview with a modern artist as the main feature, and the colours he used had caught her eye, greens that looked like dawn trees. "Reily Breen's Ambiguities" it said. She had enough of those in her life already, what harm were a few more?

The engine revved to a higher pitch and it looked like the platform and Mark were moving away from *her*, that illusion so common to train travellers. They waved as the train picked up speed, pulled out of Piccadilly. And then the station was gone and the city blurred by.

She looked at Mark's slip of paper. Crumpled it up to drop on the floor but couldn't bring herself to let go.

The clunk of metal on metal, cutting wheels on solid rails, cutting off a past and future at the same time.

A trolley rattled nearby.

"Refreshments?"

"Coffee, please." She removed her purse. Put Mark's number inside. "Large," she added.

"Anything else?"

"Better have some crisps."

She paid £1.65 begrudgingly. Took the lid off the cup, sipped, burnt her lip.

"Fucking trains."

She needed a cig badly. Wished she'd gone for a smoking carriage.

"Fucking Manchester. Good riddance."

Then she sat back in her seat but didn't pick up the mag. She gripped the arm rests until her knuckles went white. Beyond the window the sun seemed to bleach *everything* white, transformed the world to bones.

"Fucking Mark. Fuck off. I hate you."

She looked out over the tops of houses, and the brightness became fierce as she started to cry.

the drugs don't work

➢ **Label:** Huc

There's usually a comedown after a high. And so we come to this haunting and heartfelt track, beautifully played and sung, yet with the most horrible imagery of foreboding ever heard in a popular song: "Like a cat in a bag, waiting to drow stripped-back guitar, pained singing and slow orchestr downbeat experience.

s. Drugs here are a doomed attempt to escape, instead just leading to an even darker place, new walls of confinement. They don't ease pain. The only thing that would help is knowing someone else is thinking of you, that you'll see them again. Without that there's nothing else in life, a losing streak with no end but death.

The Verve had a reputation for destructive behaviour: drink and drugs of was once hospitalised for drink-induced dehydration in the US), and band in-fighting. It's a pattern for many bands in this book. Maybe we can only reach the highs after conflict. Or have to be flawed to be great.

Or maybe that's totally wrong, and the song isn't even about recreational drugs, but concerns medication. In interviews Ashcroft said he'd suffered from depression. And some interpretations tie the song to the loss of his father when Ashcroft was a boy.

Mark sat on the front steps of the work building, the sun so bright he was glad he'd brought his shades. Slipped them on, looked up and down the road to see if anyone was glancing his way. No one was. Hunched back over his pad. It was break time and a mug of tea cooled next to him. Rene had told him off earlier for "looking morose" so it was better to be alone. He'd not bothered with the staffroom much recently.

Well, since Sam left. Always back to that.

He drew arrows on his pad.

It had been a week since she went away. He still hadn't heard from her. But he understood it could take a while to settle in to a new place. Maybe she was waiting until she had a definite date for visiting Manchester.

Sam was really something. Or could be. He didn't want to blow it. When she rang he was going to tell her how he felt. It would be hard to say what he wanted to say, to be honest. Hard to break stupid habits. But you can change a habit, once you recognise it. Didn't alcoholics say that? You had to admit you were an alcy. Well, Mark could admit that he wasn't like his dad and brother. He didn't need to "play it cool", keep things to himself. After all, he didn't believe the other stuff they preached. Something good had fallen into his lap, and he was going to look after it, not let it wither and die of neglect.

He drew circles round the names on the paper, connecting Manchester bands by the first names of drummers. When he got stuck he allowed himself to use variations of the surnames for half points. He'd reached the fifth connection when his phone buzzed. And again. Not a text, then. He pulled it from his pocket, excited. A number he didn't recognise. *Sam.*

"Mark here," he said tensely.

"Hello, Mark Here."

The excitement dissipated. It was a male voice.

"Who's that?"

"Mikey."

"Mikey who?"

"This isn't a fucking knock knock joke. Mikey from the garage."

And suddenly it made sense. His mood fell further, slumping down his shoulders. He'd hoped they'd forgotten, or changed their minds.

"You there?" Mikey asked.

"Yes."

"Things are ready. Come along tonight and collect. Just bring your car to the garage, we'll call it a service."

"I don't have a car."

"Jesus. Just bring yourself then. Bicycle or whatever." Mark heard a rattle, then a muffled voice as Mikey shouted "Not got a car!" into the background, followed by laughter.

"I've already arranged something for after work," Mark said.

"Unarrange it then."

"I can't."

"Okay. Tomorrow."

"I'm not in town then."

"That's fine," Mikey said calmly. "I'll bring it to you in the evening."

Mark sighed. "I'd better give you my address."

"No need. We know where you live."

Oh.

"I'll be there to drop off 8pm. Saturday. Be in." Click.

Mark checked the phone while it was heavy in his hand. No missed calls. Put it away. Tipped the remaining tea out on the steps. Tore off the sheet of paper he'd been scribbling on, scrunched it up. There was no joy in it now. His mind was too agitated to make connections.

Piddleseed. *Saturday.*

Mark had lied about having something arranged for tonight. But now he needed it.

Ben's flat was above Quick Pix, a photo-developing and camera shop. Dave stood outside as Mark approached. Ben had been off work that afternoon and they'd promised to call for him and go for a drink when they finished.

"Alright," said Mark.

"Alright," replied Dave.

"How was your last set of deliveries?"

"The usual."

"Have you knocked for Ben?"

"I've sent him a message. Equivalent to throwing stones at his window I guess." Mark noticed Dave had a mobile phone in his hand. "He wasn't ready but should be down soon," Dave added, subdued.

"You okay?"

"Yeah."

Dave fiddled with the phone and read a message on the screen, then said, "Lazy bastard – he'd gone back to bed. He's only just got up." He put the phone in his pocket.

"I didn't know you had a mobile."

"I didn't. Birthday present off Suzannah."

"Happy birthday."

"It's not my birthday until next week. It'll be handy: I can use the phone even if Suzannah's on the Internet. And it's free after six and at weekends, just ten quid a month, so I might as well use it."

"I bet it's nice having someone to talk to."

"Yeah."

"I'm quite happy staying in."

A nod.

"Read a book, watch telly. Music. I'm fine on my own."

"I can take it or leave it."

"You sure you're –"

Ben came out, a big smile on his face. Pretended to fence with an imaginary sword. "The Musketeers ride again!"

Dave turned and started walking.

Mark slowed as they neared Whitworth Street West.

"Whatcha lookin' at?" Ben asked. "Seen a girl?"

"Oh not again," Dave added, grabbing Mark's arm and dragging him. "The Haçienda's *shut*."

"Madonna did her first UK performance there," Mark stated, adamant. "Hardly anyone knows that. Sang Holiday. 1984. On telly. Made her famous over here."

"And?"

"Just one example of how important it was to *all* music."

"So why's it closed then, if it was so great?"

Mark couldn't answer that. "Happy Mondays did a song with the same name," he muttered.

It didn't matter. FAC51 would re-open one day. He knew it in his gut.

The Flea and Firkin was a converted theatre with a dramatic exterior of green and cream brick that dominated the junction. The lads sat in the raised area by the window. From here you could watch Oxford Road roll by. For Mark the outside was less interesting than the inside though: the buildings out there were modern. All the view had going for it was the sun. Whereas in here there was history. Above them was a decorated balcony; Mark could imagine rich people of the past watching shows there, laughing, gripping hands with loved ones at times of emotion. It was like a museum. History is there if you look and think. Helps you get a sense of scale. The sun crept in through red stained-glass windows with spider web diamonds up above, which transmuted the sunlight into the glow of a fire, and the burning warmth of drama. This was how it should be. Use the old buildings, appreciate them, keep the older stuff alive so it wasn't swamped by the new. The shandy tasted better because of it.

Dave grimaced like he'd taken a punch and continued his story. "So she drove to the ASDA Petrol Station. It said Drive Thru at the exit. T-H-R-U. Fuckin' idiots. Why not spell it properly? They're sayin' we're thick cunts, that's why. Think we're all Mancunian scum, brainless lotus-eaters."

Ben and Mark made faces at each other that asked "What's his problem?" while Dave grumbled into his pint.

"You're grouchy," said Mark.

Dave didn't reply. He'd been uncharacteristically snappy all day.

Mark was wondering how he could raise the subject of the shit he was in. It would be good to share it with friends. Maybe they'd have advice, ideas. They were better thinkers than he was, on just about any subject apart from Manchester music.

The smell of the chips that were being eaten at the next table made Mark's stomach rumble. The butty at dinner time seemed so long ago. He yawned.

"Boring you, amma?" Dave asked.

"No. Just tired. I've not been sleeping properly."

"How come?"

"Things on my mind." This could be his chance.

"Don't worry about work," Dave said, before Mark could expand on it. "The reshuffle won't amount to much. We'll keep our jobs but there won't be promotions any time soon."

"Music nerd's had warnings though," Ben added. "Got strikes from Rene."

"Yeah, watch out for that," Dave said. "Keep your snotty nose clean for a while."

Ben was eyeing up an office group at the bar while he finished his current drink, swirl of yellow liquid disappearing down his throat.

"There's other stuff too," Mark began. "I was going to ask you two for advice –"

"Check out the ladies over there," Ben interrupted, whispering conspiratorially. "Especially the redhead. I wouldn't kick her out of bed for farting."

"Stop being a dick, Ben!" snapped Dave. "Can't you be serious for once?"

Ben looked surprised, then hurt; then plonked his glass down. "I've had it up to here," he said, cutting at his neck with a flat hand. He left, ignoring Mark's attempt to detain him.

Was *everything* coming apart?

Dave wouldn't return Mark's stare.

"That was harsh, Dave. Snapping at him for messing around. That's what we always do. Shoot the poop."

"Shoot the *shit*. Say the word. *Shit*. It's not so…" He sighed. "Sorry."

"You know how much he looks up to you."

"Right. I was out of order, happy? Great, now I feel guilty on top of everything else."

"Your dad?"

"Yeah. It's sort of leaching into everything else. He's on shitloads of pills. Mum has to keep lists of what he takes and when. He might have to go on a respirator too, his breathing's pretty bad. Doesn't help that my fucking nephew's just lost his job. He had a chance to kick the drugs and work it out, but he blows every fucking chance. I think he deals in it too. You wouldn't believe the stress it's adding to the family. Dad can do without it. I fucking hate druggies."

"Me too," said Mark, softly. "Have you tried talking to him?"

"Course! Sorry, I shouldn't be snappy. I tried, but he thinks he knows it all. I don't even give a shit about him any more, but it's the way it affects everyone else. People I *do* care about. As if there wasn't enough on everyone's plate."

"Has he tried giving up?"

"So he sez. Half-hearted though. If he really wanted to, he'd have done it."

"It's supposed to be hard."

"For fuck's sake, it's straightforward. I can't be doing with people denying responsibility for what they do. You want to stop being thick? Read a book. Want to give up smoking? Stop smoking. Want to lose weight? Exercise more. Eat less. It's not rocket science. We all know what we should do. If we wanted to do it we would. And if not, stop fucking whining."

"You'd never make it in politics."

Dave flicked at his pint glass, making it wobble. "And Tree Trunk Legs refused me compassionate leave today. She said there's no 'spare capacity'. She's obviously been at the management tapes again. Suzannah's been fucking great though. A brick."

"At least you have someone."

"Yeah. And I'm sorry, me going on."

"S'okay. What friends are for."

"Talking of which, what was it you wanted to ask me? Advice?"

Oh. The guilty feeling told Mark it was hardly the time to talk about delivering drugs.

"I … err … just wondered if there were any good books *I* should read. Broaden me mind."

"Christ, that's it? After all that build up?"

"Yeah. But actually, a better thing: what about Ben?"

"He'll be halfway home by now and won't be in any mood to listen to me. I'll text him later. Apologise. Fuck, I'll go out with him at the weekend. Some crap club. That'll make it up to him."

"Why are you looking at me like ... oh, you want me to come too. I'm really not into that at the moment. Clubs and big nights. Stop it with those bulldog puppy eyes. I really can't on Saturday, even if it'll cheer you up."

"I want the company but it doesn't mean you'll cheer me up. You're a more miserable bastard than I am, Mark."

"Well, I can tell you're perking up again as soon as you start insulting me."

"Arsehole. Do you want another drink?" asked Dave, gesturing with his empty glass.

"No. I'm trying to stick to one. New me."

"'When I read about the evils of drinking, I gave up reading'," quoted Dave. "Henny Youngman," he added to Mark's unspoken question. "Before your time. Soft lad."

"It's actually harder not to drink."

"I suppose it is."

They stood. Mark picked up his shades, slipped them on.

"Rock star, eh?" Dave asked.

"I wish I was." Mark looked down.

"None of us are perfect. But add us together and what do you get?"

"Three Musketeers," Mark answered weakly.

"Yep. Wait – is that you, you dirty dog?" Dave was grinning. Then Mark smelt it.

"Cheese and rice, Dave, good job we're leaving." Mark wafted his hand in front of his face. "That's deadly. Your ricker needs a health warning."

"You're right, it could kill someone," replied Dave. "The coroner's report would say 'ricker mortis'."

Dave was cracking up over his own joke, attracting stares from the chip eaters, but Mark was glad he'd perked up. In the words of Electronic, Dave was his brick wall. The last thing you want to see in it is cracks. Mark would just deal with his problems alone. No change there.

Saturday night. Mark glanced at his phone again. 7.56pm. His stomach flip-flopped. Couldn't put calming music on: couldn't risk not hearing a knock. He sat on the edge of the sofa, staring at the door and tapping his foot arhythmically.

Footsteps on the landing outside. They stopped. Even though he knew it was coming he still jerked nervously when a fist pounded on the door. Yes. They did know where he lived. He took a deep breath to still his yammering heart.

"Hi," Mark said as he opened the door.

"You gonna let me in, or you do your business on the doorstep?"

Mikey was wearing an oily red and white motorbike jacket and carrying a helmet. His hair partly covered the scar on his forehead. Mark held the door open and he entered, moved the stool, sat on it with his back to a wall.

"On your own?"

"Yes."

"Mr Connor told me to ask if you've visited your dad yet?"

"No."

"Then do it. Don't take the stuff with you, you'll be too nervous. One visit without, see how smooth it all is. Take him some other present. Then when you go in with the package you can play it cool."

"You got it there?"

Mikey reached into a pocket at his hip. Slapped a bundle down. It looked like a legless, fat, shaved mouse.

"Pick it up."

Mark shook his head.

"Don't be a pussy. You've got to pick it up sometime."

Mark reached out and lifted it. Denser than he expected. Rubbery greasy surface. Then he realised why. The drugs were wrapped in layers of condoms. Fine string had been tied around, then more condoms enfolded that, giving multiple skins with a long string tail.

"That's got to go…" Mark began.

"Yeah. Here's my tip. Get lube from the chemist. Water-based, so it doesn't affect the rubber. And use a fuckload of it. You could loosen up first, grease up a carrot or something. Make sure you've had a shit too."

Suddenly the lyrics from Holiday, when Shaun Ryder sang about looking up someone's arse, took on a new meaning.

"Oh, and if you wanna be nice about it then douche first," Mikey added.

Mark didn't even know what douche was. An insult? He grimaced at the size of the package in his hand and put it back down.

"Just be thankful it's only the one. I've heard of some situations where a mule has 50 bags of H in their stomach. They have to swallow them. That's riskier." He stood. Slapped a heavy hand on Mark's shoulder. It felt like his dad's, though Mikey wasn't much older than Mark. Always that weight when you had to "man up". "You'll be fine. Keep it well hidden. Tell no one. Do a dry run. Keep your cool and follow instructions. You're not the first or last, so don't make a big deal out of it."

And he was gone. Minutes later a motorbike engine started up, then roared off.

Time passed.

Mark stared at the fat thing.

The light was shifting, gold becoming shadow.

Laughing outside. Saturday revellers. He wasn't going out tonight. It was just him, slug mouse, and fear. Oh, guilt was here too, when he thought of Dave.

Mark would visit his dad. Get the test visit out of the way first as soon as possible. He hated the thought of the package being in his flat, polluting it.

All these negatives, darkness brought by that white powder. He needed a positive to counteract them. Picked up his phone, clicked through numbers in its memory, pressed dial. It rang so many times he was about to hang up when a voice came on.

"Hello?"

"Hi Monksie. It's Mark. Hopton. That helped out a few weeks ago."

"Yorright Mark! Marky the Manc Muso-maniac!"

"That's the one. How're you?"

"Busy busy. Took on an extra venue, bit o' part-time cash, always handy. You?"

"Getting by, I guess."

"Don't sound too good, man."

"It'll pass." Mark stared at slug mouse. "Anyway, I'm happy to help out again as soon as you need me."

"Yeah, sorry for not being in touch."

"No problem."

A pause. "Thing is, my nephew got back early and he was desperate for a job, so I had to take him on. Family and all that. So I don't need any other help for a bit."

"Oh."

"You did good though, got potential."

"Yeah. I see. I thought…"

"Sorry mate. I assumed I'd need you more but never promised it'd be permanent. Still, good for your CV, eh?"

"Good for my CV." That thing professionals had. Not people like Mark. "It's okay, Monksie. I appreciate what you did."

"Great. I like you, my man, don't want any bad blood. And I've got your number. Any opportunities come up and you're first on my list."

"First on the list."

"'Sright. Don't give up. Got to go, was good catching up with you."

"Good catching up."

"Bye, music man."

"Bye, Monksie."

Click.

Time passed and Mark stared at the phone. Then the package. No Monksie. Just mousie.

Later. Mark should have gone to bed but his mind was racing back and forth down dead-end tracks. "No way out," it repeated as a bassline, and it got louder, more insistent. He was sat in his living room chair, picking at the peeling wallpaper with close-bitten nails. Sleep would be impossible. He managed to get a fingerhold and a strip of torn flowers came off in his hand. He let it fall. If only problems could fall away so easy. Peel and drop them, leave them as floral warnings to stop others following.

He needed music to calm the savage beats. Urban Hymns was by the hi-fi so he put that tape in. The chords of Bitter Sweet Symphony rang out and he was in familiar territory. He closed his eyes and let sounds pass through his head, soothing and clearing as they went.

He was almost drifting off in the chair when a muffled bang jolted him upright; at first he wondered if he was imagining it but it happened again, a hand thumping against the front door.

Drug delivery?

He glanced at the table, saw the evidence that it had already happened and wasn't just a bad dream.

Mandy?

Nonsense. She didn't seem to notice him. Must be someone complaining about the music. It was a bit loud for this time of night. Mark assumed it was after 12, but had no clock to prove it and couldn't remember where he'd put his phone.

He lowered the volume, tucked the white package behind the TV, put the front door's chain on – a requirement of living in Stretford – and combined apology words in his head as he opened the door.

"Alright? Tune!" said his swaggering bowl-headed neighbour from above.

"What?"

"Tune! This is Lucky Man." He tapped his fingers on the wall like drumsticks, echoing the tambourine backing as if the music infected him too. "Fucking love it. The album. Classic. Part of me soul, man. Me history. Twists all me melons. Once I got dumped by this girl who was a drummer, I listened to it non-stop until I got her out of my system. Heard that playing just now, realised I had a brother."

"Are you for real?"

"Course! Open the door, I love this bit."

Before he'd thought about the wisdom of the action Mark had taken the chain off, let him strut his way in.

"Bazzy. Bazzy Brown-Rider," the guy said, holding out his hand. "Well, Bazzy Noel Brown-Rider when I fill in forms, but who wants to sound like a Christmas carol, right? Jesus." Mark shook hands with a firm grip, identified himself, heard Bazzy's gold bracelets jangle. Bazzy was wearing a tie-dye top, shorts that revealed hairy legs, and sockless trainers.

"Seen you around," said Mark, leading the way into the living room.

"Course you have. I'm here and there, always ducking and diving, eh? Down, down, down, but I bring them up. The alpha mover and shaker, I say, always will be."

"Cool. A shaker."

"Ha ha. I get it. Kula Shaker. Not my kind of music. Well, Hey Dude's got some energy, but it's all too southern, like Albarn's Bleurgh, not real people like us. Don't get me wrong, their Rice Krispie hippy singer has his heart in the right place. Didn't you have a black eye a while ago?"

"Yeah. Got punched."

"Hope you weren't fighting?"

"No, it was all one way."

"Good. Can't stand fighting, does my 'ed in. Peace and love." Bazzy held two fingers over his heart. "Plus, I'm soft as shite."

"I hear you."

"Course you do. Got the same tastes I bet. I heard you playing some Oasis last night, here's one I bet you don't know: the connection between the two bands." Bazzy looked smug.

"There's loads of connections with The Verve, which one you thinkin' of?"

Bazzy looked less smug.

"I mean, on this album Liam sang backing vocals for one track," Mark continued. "I think he did the clapping on another. They were all mates and did gigs together before Oasis hit it big. And Richard Ashcroft did backing on one of Oasis' songs from Be Here Now. Same year Urban Hymns came out. Is that what you meant?"

"I guess so." But Bazzy looked like he'd been robbed as he said that.

Mark threw him a bone to make up for it. "I heard you playing Fools Gold the other night: you know a connection between The Stone Roses and The Verve?"

"Oh, yeah, that's easy." Bazzy was smiling again, revealing a gold tooth. "John Leckie. He produced the first albums for both bands. Did some work with The Fall too. All the veins meet in The Verve, eh?"

"Not just them. All the bands. It's like secrets if you know where to look."

Bazzy smiled and thumped a foot down on the table. Pointed to his calf. Mark peered more closely at the tattooed squiggle there. It said FAC51: the catalogue name for The Haçienda. Bazzy returned his foot to the floor. "You and me are the same. Kept meaning to say hi."

"Yeah, and I've heard you." Mark pointed at his ceiling. "So I didn't wake you then?"

"Nah, I never sleep! Too busy. What about you?"

"Just thinking about stuff."

"Worrying?"

Mark nodded.

"Bummed. Woman trouble?"

"Not really. It's… Well, maybe a bit. Amongst other things."

"I thought it might be. The moping look you got. I don't know the ins and outs but my general advice is to be nice. Ring her. Don't hold grudges: always be bigger than that. It's about trust."

"Um, thanks. I'll think about it."

Bazzy held his thumb up. "Whatever the problems, don't worry though, man; *everything* sorts itself out."

"I hope so. Do you want a cuppa?"

"Not right now. Got a mate waiting upstairs, trying to teach him chords."

"Guitar?"

"What else? Just decided it was about time I said hi. Timing's my thing. Oh, and if you're down again, just play the music. I'll come." Bazzy glanced at the hi-fi, spun the dial up, making Richard Ashcroft's voice blast out in deafening pain, then back down. "Anything above 13 and I'll hear it."

Mark woke in the chair next morning to low light and traffic sounds. The hi-fi speakers buzzed in emptiness, occasionally clicking in protest that the tape had ended many hours ago. He understood its feelings. Flipped the tape over and pressed play. Never too late to turn over a new side.

Blinded By the Sun

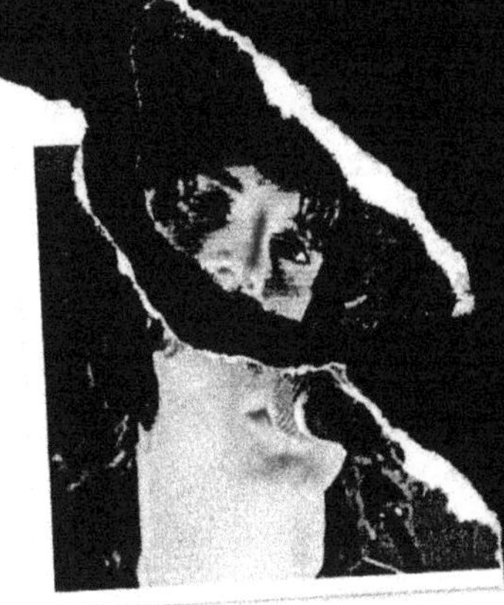

Our sun is the source of life. But if you're not careful you can be burned or blinded. In its presence you can't see clearly, like when you're caught up in emotional times and can't find balance. This song is about the end of a relationship. Some have claimed that Squire was just retaliating against Ian Brown for the many accusations in Unfinished Monkey Business, but that's as preposterous as the rumours that The Seahorses is an anagram of The Rose Ashes or He Hates Roses. Squire isn't credited with writing this song (Chris Helme gets the honour). So let's move on from daft theories. Recriminations only hold you back, rather than setting you free. The only truth is that the closer two people are, the more bitter the split can be.

At the end of Blinded By The Sun's video the space capsule breaks up, spewing the band members into space, drifting away from each other. It turned

to every Mancunian boy
the northern lyrics
will be
echoes of "Don't get clever with me, lad!"

Wednesday 28th June.

Such a bad date. Today, three years ago, The Haçienda closed. And it still hadn't reopened. Mark could do without being in work today, of all days.

He'd not visited his dad yet. Kept putting it off. But Friday afternoon. Definitely. He'd book it off as leave.

Or maybe go at the weekend.

He hawked up a big greeny, spat it against the back of the urinal, then weed on it. Washed it down the drain, sliding in the yellow stream. It felt good. He'd made the world a tidier place. More sane. Control that chaos. It would be great to make a clean start with his life too.

He'd finally asked Emily for Sam's phone number. It took three false starts where he'd got partway to her desk then detoured, pretending he was doing something else while his pulse raced and his ears felt hot. When he finally succeeded – while Emily was on her own – she had laid her pencil down, repositioned it neatly with one pink-painted fingernail … then said no. "If she wants to talk, she'll ring you."

Mark didn't want to argue with her. Had seen what happened when people did that. Plus ringing Sam when she had his number might have seemed pushy, scared her off. It'd happened before.

Better to wait. It would all work out. The future couldn't just be a sucking urinal.

Mark managed to distract himself by distributing payslips, like memos containing good news. In his head he could pretend he was one of them dukes, giving money away to the poor or something. He absorbed flickers of light as he passed each window, a slow and warming strobe. The sun was a beautiful thing.

The task ended when he looked at Sam's empty seat. No slip to leave there. The sun could blind you too.

It's only been 11 days. Time yet.

Back at his desk near the stairwell. It was the losers' corner of the floor. There was a rap of knuckles on wood and Mark was surprised to see Denny grinning at him. He was bristly-chinned as if trying to grow a beard, and a beanie controlled his unkempt hair. He looked like a homeless person.

"Wotcher."

"What are you doing here?" Mark asked anxiously, looking round to make sure no one was nearby. "How'd you get in?"

"Door was open, I just slipped in when the old guy downstairs went toilet. It's not against the law to visit your brother, is it?" Denny dropped into the chair in front of the second desk, wiggled the mouse on that PC absently.

"You'll get me into trouble."

"Dad said you ain't seen 'im yet."

"Not yet. I've been busy."

"Shoulda seen him by now."

"I know. I will. Friday."

"But then you got to go again and –"

"I know!" Then quieter: "I know, right? Weekend. Or Monday, latest. It's sorted."

"Good." He rotated the seat left and right, legs apart. "Hey, when you've done it we can do summat together."

"That'd be good. It's been a long time." He couldn't imagine Denny sitting through a film – too hyperactive – but maybe a drink. Or see a band. Or just hang around in town. Mark didn't care what. He'd never cared as a kid. Just a chance to hang around his brother without Denny being in a bad mood. Down the canals. On the meadows, where Denny and the older lads rode motor bikes. In the Arndale, looking at stuff they couldn't afford and women Denny would never pull. The place didn't matter. The action didn't matter. It was the people. That was what made the difference. Mark needed to feel some good could come from this mess.

"Well, I promised you. It'll be a treat. I know a slag in Sale who'll do anything with anyone. I could fix her up with you. She gave me a blowie in the park."

"Urgh, no. Not that kind of thing."

"Too posh for that are you? Got standards, eh?" Denny rolled his eyes up to the ceiling. "Why'd I get lumbered with this one, not the other way round?" he muttered to someone who wasn't there. Then he looked at Mark again. "That woulda just been me being *nice*. Other stuff is better. There's a two-person deal I've come up with, me as muscle. Real sweet, so I've kept it to myself. Doing that with you would be solid, family-strong. I'd cut you in 40-60."

"That's not what I meant! When I wanted us to do stuff."

"What then?"

"I don't know … shopping, or a game on my Playstation, or go see a band, or –"

"Yeah, as if! Look, deals is what *I* meant, an' I'm older, so that's what counts."

Mark stared at his brother. *Brother.* What did the word mean, anyway? Mark knew they weren't the same. It was clear now: Denny would never change. They'd never be what the other wanted. You can't argue with *never.*

"Fine. We'll talk about it later," Mark said.

"Yeah, great. After you're done we'll get together, hash stuff out. You won't regret it, bro."

"No. I won't regret it."

Denny looked past Mark. "Uh oh, heifer alert. I'll be off." He slunk around the corner, first making a 'phone me' gesture with his thumb by his ear.

During the afternoon break Mark was using one of the monkey PCs, reading through conversations on band discussion boards, when Roger Watson sat down at the computer next to him. His hair glistened in the skylight sun. It looked like it was melting.

"How are you?" Roger asked, in a way that suggested he didn't care about the answer.

"Fine."

"Ah, your payslip." Roger picked it up before Mark could stop him; weighed it in his hand. "Mine's heavier."

"Funny."

"Can I look?" He started to unfold the paper. Mark snatched it back. He didn't want Roger knowing how little he earned.

"Why are you here? Is your PC broken or something?"

"Sort of. I got Sam's, Emily got mine, and the old one was taken away. But I insisted they upgrade them and install Windows 2000. One of my first actions as boss. They were ancient, for crying out loud.

Uncoolio." He logged in. "Oh. Like these. Hot patootie, these are even *older*. What's that, NT 3.5?"

Mark shrugged. They were the only computers he'd ever used. He had no idea what the letters and numbers meant. He just cared how much of his break time was taken up with logging in and opening programs.

"You're in the dark ages over here."

"They work."

"Yes, but like your team: slooooooow."

"You just here to insult us?"

"Why, will you tell Dave on me? Only kidding."

As it loaded he leaned over, scanned Mark's screen, smirked. "Oh, the other reason I'm here is because I let the new girl use my desk."

"New girl? Who?"

"Gita."

"Gita that does advertisingy-stuff?"

"She did: now she's with us. Under me."

"I thought she was only part-time with you?"

No answer.

"And Ben said it was only temporary?"

"Same thing," Roger said petulantly. "So I'm showing her the ropes."

"Nice of you."

"I thought so. Did you know about that, my promotion?"

"I'd heard your team was smaller."

"It's a good break for me. Team leader. And I'm only just 30! Got to go on a training course. It's about time. I'll run things properly. Going to redo the signage and flowline, make it more efficient, make my mark, leave my scent."

"Your idea, that? The signage?"

"Yes, why?"

Mark snorted in disgust. Not worth arguing about though. It would only prolong the time in Roger's company.

"Anyway, is it the usual load of bumf?" By "bumf" they meant circulars, company messages, spam, anything you couldn't be bothered to read, as opposed to "real" emails, which were always social and from friends.

"I don't know. I haven't checked my email."

"No friends."

"No interest." Mark went back to his own screen as Roger finally got to a Windows desktop and opened Microsoft Mail, began reading. After a minute Roger laughed to himself. It was an irritating sound.

"What's so funny?"

"Nothing really. Sam's just got a way with words."

Mark's stomach lurched. "Sam? Sam what left here?"

"Yes. I sent her a CD. She was taking the mickey out of my choice of music."

"A CD?"

"Yeah, you sound like a parrot! For her to listen to before she visits this weekend. Should be a pretty good night."

"Oh." Mark didn't feel too good. He realised he was tapping his fingers against the desk, unconscious drumming, ordered them to be still.

"She says hi to you actually, and hopes you're doing well." Roger chuckled, looking at the screen again.

Mark suppressed his annoyance. "Can I see?"

"No, there's private stuff too."

Out of the corner of his eye he saw Roger flick through other emails then open Netscape Navigator ('Nutscrape' as Dave called it – he'd installed it when Internet Explorer stopped working and was rechristened in their team as 'Internet Exploder'). Roger seemed to be reading the financial news. Mark read and re-read the same paragraph on his own screen three times, still not taking in whether Urban Hymns was alternative rock or Britpop.

Then Gita stuck her head round the corner. Smiled at Mark. She had really silky black hair. The colour reminded him of Sam's. She said, "Roger, phone for you, someone from Web Stationery Supplies, can you speak to them? I'm not sure what they're referring to. Sounds impatient. American accent."

"Oh shit, that'll be Berman. Okay, I'll come now."

He minimised the windows and dashed off without logging out first. He wasn't far away. Roger could just about see Mark if he looked in this direction. At the moment he was picking up the phone.

Mark licked his lips. One moment, balanced on a point. He leaned over and clicked on the MS Mail icon on the taskbar. Spotted Sam's email. He didn't bother to open it, just clicked "Forward" and started typing his address, realising he didn't know it well because he didn't give it out, and he didn't give it out because no one asked. His hands shook slightly.

M-H-e-backspace-r-y-d-e-r-h-backspace-H-a-p-M-o-n- … *idiot, why hadn't he chosen something shorter and simpler?* … @-y-a-h-p-p-backspace-backspace-o-o-.-c-o-.-u-k

His heart was beating quickly as he hit "Send", minimised the window, and leaned back to face his own PC. Roger returned about twenty seconds later.

"Always in demand," he said. "I'd better get used to it, I suppose. Go getter. Trend setter. Not like you lot, unimaginative stick-in-the-muds. Only joking. See you." He logged out. Mark pretended not to notice him, pretended to be calm, and acted as if he was interested in the website on his screen. Then he caught a glimpse of Rene, realised break had ended a minute ago, and logged out too.

For the rest of the day he watched the clock, counted minutes, fantasised about the email. Then he stayed behind tidying bookshelves until the office was quiet and he could log on, feeling dizzy.

One new mail. From Roger.

He opened it. Couldn't help reading the *who* and *when* and *where* first, despite his eagerness. Emails were like books and albums, all stamped, provenance visible, and it was only polite to read the sleeve first. A few more seconds before he'd know the truth. Then he inhaled deeply, and read words which came to life in her voice.

------- Forwarded Message Follows -------
Date: Wed, 28 June 11:16:19 -0000 (GMT)
From: SAMANTHA REES <she-frog27@hotmail.com>
Subject: Re: Balti Balti Bang Bang
To: Roger Watson <R.Watson@packgreen.co.uk>
Reply-to:SHE-FROG27@HOTMAIL.COM
MIME-Version:1.0
X-Priority:3
Priority:normal

Hi Roger,

I had looked forward to receiving your email. I was wrong, and the atatchment was borderline illegal. Please just send words next time. Your song taste gave me great amusment, shame about the (roxy) music. Related to it: a place near me called Briton Ferry. The t is crossed off one sign. Brion Ferry - ta da! Do you get the link and see what I did there? One week in. I love it. I keep telling myself how lucky I am being here instead of there. This place has real people. Though a lad who delivers sandwiches is unbelievably timid, I have never met anyone who start so many sentances (sp?) with "sorry" but it is sweet in a way, hopefully he'll get more confident. He looks a bit like Pee Wee Hermann, even with the half-masts. Reminds me of you. The best thing about selling is that you're allowed to talk - we're MEANT to! Amazing. Not like Pickled Gherkin at all. My uncle is taking us all out for a meal tonight, HUGE family thing. I get to be princess. Uncle Joe is one of my favourite people in the whole world. But he pretended to be annoyed when we watched the rugby on Saturday. We were hoping England would get smashed by South Africa a second week running. He got expensive champagne to celebrate, said with me there it was bound to be a victory. But this time England won. Yeah yeah, you be happy. BTW have you developed any photos from my leaving do? I'd really love copies. I remember when you looked like that sculpture the angel of the north (or something), when you had your arms with a pint in each hand. As to the other issue, since you ask AGAIN, no, nothing happened with Mark, nor would it ever. Just high spirits on my last night. He isn't one of us so this is best I guess. Say hi anyway, but if he asks I'm dead busy. I'll be down by Friday eve, staying with Em. Not sure where the witch will drag me Friday but on Sat night she wants to take me to The Temple. See if you can work out what it used to be and why it reminds me of you. It'll be a cut short visit, I'm coming back on a late train that night, family thing again on Sunday. Oh well I had better go. I am supposed to be doign something, I don't want to get the sack already. Only kidding, it's break time. BTW someone with your name is buried up the road from where I live so I will send him your regards when I visit him.

Sam

Mark read it twice. The office felt hotter and stuffier than usual. Stifling. Only this time he couldn't blame it on the faulty air-conditioning equipment.

His jaw was clenched. After his resolution not to go with someone just for sex he felt tricked. Used. He was so stupid. He sniffed, looked up, wouldn't cry. He scowled his fiercest instead.

He'd wanted to see the universe reflected in her eyes. And it was just lies. Empty words.

"She's a bitch," he heard in Denny's sneering voice.

"A festering cunt," he could imagine his dad saying.

"No! No she's not!" he shouted at the empty office.

He shook, ached, trying to push away the bad feelings. A deep shuddering breath, another, fists clenched in control.

He remembered holding her hand that night. Then hers had slipped from his at some point, lost along the way. If he lost much more he'd have nothing left, not even be a person.

Love. Fool's Gold.

He grabbed a bag from his locker and slammed its door twice, then kicked it as hard as he could. Control. Don't lose control. There was always an escape. And only one person left he could trust. He'd play music on 13 when he got home. Stop it all crumbling. Retreat into a world of music with his new friend.

There was always an escape. Always something you could do. This was no biggie.

Two seconds later he had his back against the locker and was crying, as empty as the office.

Life is Sweet

... music, making the unfortunate ... to the band's will (just as the Chems do with us on the dancefloor). An institutionalised Tim Burgess is also trapped in their claustrophobic nightmare and the confusion of cables controlling things illustrates the bureaucratic truth of places of confinement: so complex they are untameable, errors inevitable, programming can break.

The lyrics are typically obtuse, fractured like a broken mind, so that we only understand fragments of the whole – something about leaving a home because there's nothing to love there any more (coincidentally, the Chemical Brothers' previous release was Leave Home); being far south and wanting love again. More mood than coherent story. Perhaps because of the influence of recreational chemicals (to enhance the dance), or medical chemicals. Take them away and we just have the brothers.

Not blood brothers though. And not Mancunians by blood ... Tom Rowlands were

Sam reset one of the display phones, checked the others were okay, then returned to the counter to process that morning's new contract forms. What her uncle had said was true – managing orders wasn't much different whether it was boxes of phones or piles of books. It was perfect and she threw herself into it.

It wasn't just the job that was working out, either. The location was spot on for a start. Swansea was only a short journey from Neath. The shop was near The Kingsway, perfectly placed for getting food from Govindas at lunch time. And after work, before catching the bus (on the days when she wasn't getting a lift back with Uncle Joe) she could wander down to Oystermouth Road, take her shoes off and walk along the beach for a bit, feeling hot, dry, loose sand between her toes at first, then wet, cool, gritty sand under the soles of her feet at the water's edge. She'd missed the sea.

The tidy house in Neath was ideal too, not far from Victoria Park and the canal. Mamgu and Tadcu had loved the house almost as much as they loved each other. Ever since they met they'd been inseparable right until Tadcu passed on. Such a love. It permeated the walls, it filtered light from the windows, it existed in each gentle creak. And Mamgu had really wanted Sam to have the house. Sometimes she could imagine Mamgu was still there. Not scary, like a bad ghost, just … comforting. Protective. It felt like a house that didn't want anyone to be alone.

Ah, Neath. Birthplace of Welsh Rugby Union. Long rows of old stone terraced houses with teeny front yards. Not far from her house she could stand at the junction of Ropewalk and Greenway Road, and in all four compass directions the long roads and houses would act like three sides of a frame that held hill and sky. In every direction, that reminder of where we come from, painted in living picture.

She'd also re-found some old friends. Her family were giving her space, not calling on her too much – she could imagine the self-control *that* required – but they were there. And having her own kitchen again was luxury. She might even start cooking again. It all fitted, like a key in a lock, and she felt proud of herself. Confident again, like she'd escaped a fog, that impenetrable moisture of painful memories. Leaving Manchester was the best thing she could have done.

Only one thing nagged at her mind.

Sleeping with him didn't get him out of her system as Emily suggested. But time would. She had everything she needed.

Her uncle popped in while she was showing a customer different phone models. Joe pretended to browse, watching her. It was a sale.

"You've got a knack for it, you have," he told her when they were alone.

"It's not so hard."

"Where's Stacey?"

"She's sick today. It's not a problem, we're on top of things so I thought I'd do the front."

He nodded. "See, you're good at this. I did actually try someone else before you agreed."

"You didn't tell me that."

"No point, he was like a fart in a jam pot. Hey, someone yesterday asked me for directions to Ysbyty Hospital."

"You're making this up. What did you really want to talk about?"

He grinned. Always happy. It was infectious. "I'm thinking of changing the name. The business is growing, I want something more classy than 'Jones' Phones'."

"I like it."

"But what about something more trendy? For the kids? Growing market. I could spell phones with an F, 'fones', get it? Or use a letter U for 'you', or the number 4 or something." He was doodling ideas on the pad at the desk.

"No. That's not trendy. It just looks naff."

"Still, see if you can think of a name. Anyway, I got something else to ask. Things are going well, you're doing well … how'd you like to take over managing both shops?"

"I've not long started!"

"Doesn't matter to me. I knows you can do it. It's a bit more work but it's only more of the same. More pay too. And since the other's in Neath, you'll won't need to travel some days."

"What about Pred?"

"That's the thing. I want to branch out. Going to open up a computer shop or two. Jones' Barebones PCs. Pred would manage them instead. You'd be making my life easier."

"You'd need a better name than that."

"I had other ideas too. PC Pentre?"

Head shake. "Too small-sounding."

"So Mega, It Hurts? It's a play on mega hertz."

"No."

"Silicon Chips? Joe's Pro PCs?" Counting on fingers. "2 486 Motorway?"

"486 is old. We had Pentiums at Packham Green. Get Pred to think of something. He's sensible."

"I could also open up a music shop. It's something I've fancied for ages."

"Walk before you run."

"Fair do's. But if I open a PC one, you'll do it? Take on both phone shops?"

"Shouldn't I give you my CV or have an interview?"

"Okay." He sat on the stool. "Miss Rees. You're a presentable woman, so pass the first part. Now onto the brains stuff. What would you do differently if you ran both shops?"

"I'd do all the accounts in one; have a single staff list used to cover shifts in both; stock should be ordered less often, and you could be a bit more bloody organised about it. You could –"

He banged his palm on the counter. "See, I knew it'd be good. Yeah, do all that."

"Okay."

"Gwych. Gizza hug. You got the job."

She hugged him, laughing. It wasn't charity. She really could organise this shit better than him.

"Want to pop out for a *mwg drwg*?" He rubbed his thumb and forefinger together.

"No thanks. I'm going straight for a while."

"Like fuck!"

"True. No booze. Nothing."

"Wow. Rees gone good. Fags?"

She bit her lip. "Getting there."

He laughed.

"One step at a time," she added.

"It sounds boring."

"It feels good."

"Well, that's all that matters."

"Plus, I'm a businesswoman now. Can't afford to make mistakes." The smile faded as a memory crossed her mind. "*Any* kind of mistakes."

"You look great by the way," Joe said. "I meant to tell ya. A real pro." He scratched his nose. "I mean professional, not prostitute."

"Really."

A man was looking through the shop window as they talked, then came in. Browsed the phones. Glanced at Sam.

"Checkout *wnco mwnco*," Joe whispered, nodding towards the customer. "I'm guessing he'll want advice on phones."

"Not such an amazing prediction. It is a phone shop." She kept her voice low too.

"Yes, but he won't buy because he really just wants to chat to you. I say he'll postpone a decision, make it last. Then he'll come back later today, or tomorrow, buy then. I can tell all that from the way he looks at you."

She laughed and Joe slipped out as she went to offer help.

The punter talked for a while, seemed a bit vague; then said he'd think about it and come back. Asked when the shop was open. Left, with a coy glance back.

With Joe's instincts and her sensibleness this could work.

There was no Internet in her house but she could use it in the shop. As she got ready to close up for the day she checked her email. One, with the subject line "PG Tips". The latest of many from Emily giving her the (limited) Packham Green gossip, and saying how excited she was about Sam's weekend visit.

Sam was excited too, even though it would be a short one: she had to come back for Sunday, Angharad's tenth birthday party. She wanted her Auntie Sam there, made her promise because she'd been away so long. It wasn't a huge problem. She'd still get to go out on Friday, and get a last drink and chat on Saturday before catching a late train.

Thankfully there wasn't another email off Roger. She'd ignored some of them as she had the joke emails he sent round Packham Green; she would have ignored the rest but didn't like his sly hints about Sam and Mark, as if he really knew something. She'd done her best to kill suspicion and quash the topic once and for all. It had taken three drafts to get the tone just right. Typing those words hurt.

After she'd sent that email she felt a bit mean on Mark, but it didn't contain any real lies. They were over before they began. She'd written the thing off in her head; the rest would be faded by time.

just when you're thinkin' things over

This song, recorded in Wales

difficult time, the sun going down, needing something to cling to – but there's nothing there. A song to someone sun-connected who doesn't follow the line, someone in the only place that can be a home. Burn everything down and go there.

In the video Tim Burgess tried a new look as a wannabe Manchester gangster, suit and slicked-back hair, a baby-faced Nick Cave. But Tim wa

out of his d

He read the warning signs today. They were everywhere around the prison: Do Not Approach; Caution Razor Wire; No Parking; It's An Offence To Help Inmates Escape. The last one was: Proceed With Caution.

"Too pooping right," he muttered to himself.

Reception. ID check. Quick frisk. Mobile phone taken. Escort to visiting hall.

The room was fuller this time. Fridays usually were. Maybe if people planned to go out drinking that night they'd feel guilty if they didn't visit those inside first. Prisoners talking to girlfriends or wives, reprimands and subdued laughter echoing. More people for prison officers to watch.

Drinks machine, two teas. Dunk, whirr, sloosh, gurgle. Took them to his table. Tapped his toe as he waited. Déjà vu as he stared at the cups, feeling ill. He hadn't been able to put it off any more.

He left the drinks and walked to the toilets, trying not to go so quickly as to look suspicious. His face was hot. He checked that the cubicles were empty then used a urinal. Bogeys were stuck to the wall at shoulder height, dry crusted clots left by scuzzball roving fingers.

Still alone. He licked his lips. Went into one of the cubicles, locked the door, sat on the seat. Put his head in his hands. This was all getting too real.

He jerked upright when he heard the door open and someone came in. Another visitor? He couldn't just sit here in suspicious silence.

Mark flushed, left the cubicle, washed his hands, then wiped his face with cold water. It was a prison officer. Didn't smile. That look: was it suspicion?

They know.

They can't know.

How do they know?

Back out, forcing himself not to run. Back to the table just as the inner doors opened and his dad was escorted in.

Dad was still solid. So much was insubstantial nowadays, touch it and it evaporates. Inbuilt obsolescence, things meant to break, to be replaced. Fancy words and appearances tell you one thing but mean another. Everyone spun the truth to fit their own ends. The

Government, advertisers, shops. Slogans and pictures promised happiness and a good life if you bought their trainers, car, gadget, yoghurt, joined the army. Although it was weird to think it, in some ways his dad was at least *honest*, what-you-see-is-what-you-get; and he was solidly real. Hard. Like a brick wall. Similar to Dave in that regard. Except Dave was the kind of wall you could lean on. Dad was the kind a car smashed into, killing everyone.

"Leaving it a little late, aren't we?" were the first things he said as he picked up his tea.

"Sorry."

"Always put things off. Just makes it worse though, eh? I assume this is the dry run?"

Mark nodded.

"When will you visit me proper?"

"I could come tomorrow. Pretend you asked me for cigs today. That's why I didn't bring any with me."

"Ah. Thinking now. Did they search you?"

Mark shook his head.

"Didn't think so. You're seen as the good lad. Denny, he got a full body search twice."

"So how've you been?"

"Okay. The stuff they serve in here's dogfood, but I'm used to that. I was in segregation again, two days for 'unacceptable behaviour'. A punishment? Peace and quiet, I call it."

"What did you do this time?"

"Nothing much. Threatened another con with a spoon. Hardly worth bothering with. Probably only got done 'cos he was coloured. If it'd been the other way round they'd have turned a blind eye, for sure. What's up with you? Someone shat in your porridge? Oh, I know. Don't be nervous. See, I can reach under the table easy." A compact finger jabbed Mark's knee. "You'll just pass it to me. I take it from there."

"It's not that. I wanted to ask you something."

"Sounds heavy. Go on."

"About when I was born."

"I thought you was going to ask me if I robbed the Post Office! 'Innocent, your honour!' Hey, don't look so serious, that's just a joke."

"Will you tell me then?"

"Nah, I hate talking about the past. You know that."

"If you don't tell me, the deal's off."

"What did you just say?" his dad asked, frowning and leaning forward.

"You heard me, Dad. I want to know more about where I came from. You never said much. And I need to know." Mark held his dad's gaze. Refused to back down this once. What would a few more punches be at this stage? Nothing to be afraid of any more. He was more scared of the emptiness inside.

But his dad leaned back and laughed. "Fuck the judge! Mark grew a pair! That's a first." He slapped the table with a palm. "Well, that almost deserves something. Okay, I'll give you what you want. A reward. Just this once."

You're just worried I won't bring the drugs. Mark settled back.

"I was there when you were born."

"I thought you were in prison?"

"No, that was when Denny popped out and I was in for my first stint. That was a short one. You were between bouts; then I went back in, four years for robbery. The corrupt bastards. Judges – how can any man in a wig command respect? That's why they force you to stand when they come in to court. Punish you if you don't, even if they're perverted little pricks who like prozzies to stick oranges up their arses. It's like an abuse of power, innit? *Fucking judges.* I never voted for them. Then I got extra time in punishment block for belting a screw. Wish it had been the judge. But yeah, I was there for you. You weren't born in a hospital, did you know that?"

"No."

"Middle of winter, icy as fuck. I was with your mum and we'd been driving all day so we stopped at a bar. Too many drinks and too much dancing. We got like that. She was tired and I was too pissed to drive straight so we booked a room in a crummy hotel next door. Then her waters broke just after we'd checked in. Fuck, your mother was sweating buckets, and there was me, trying to sober up and holding on to her hand. Not the best start in the world, eh? I cut the cords myself. That's the man's job. Snip. I set you free of your mum."

"Cords?"

"Aye. Wasn't just you. There was a twin. Woulda been my third lad."

"You never said!"

"Best forgotten, innit? The nipper never made it. I took all three of you hospital, but he moved on. Too sickly. Musta been too much for your mum. Only enough energy for one."

"I'd have had a brother my age…" Mark sighed. "I'd have –"

"What's it matter? He went, you stayed. It happens. Happy now?"

"No."

"See, that's what happens. Eyes bigger'n your belly. You think you want something, ignore me when I say it's bad. Well maybe this'll teach you. Trust me. If I don't tell you something, it's because you're best not knowin'."

"I wanted to know! That would've changed a lot!" Mark couldn't help raising his voice.

"How?"

"I wouldn't have felt so lonely!"

"But it was dead! Not summat you can keep in a box!"

"I don't mean that… Did Denny know?"

"Course!"

"What else, then? What about my mum?"

"What about her?"

"I don't remember her."

"Course you don't."

"Tell me something."

"What? Won't make you happy." He cracked his knuckles. "Okay. She was a bit mad. Saw things sometimes. I blame it on the drink. Seen a few things myself, in my time."

"Tell me something *good* about her."

"Would if I could. Got rid of her after that. Good riddance. I used to wish … ah, never mind."

"What?"

"Well, I used to wish she'd never got herself pregnant. But that changed."

Mark stared.

"Useful."

"That all we are, though? Just good if we're useful?"

"What do you want?"

"Did you ever… *love* us? Really?"

"Don't go fag on me."

"I'm serious."

"And so the fuck am I."

"It's not gay to care about your family."

"It is when we're all blokes."

"Other families don't think that."

"How would you know?" he snapped, crushing his empty plastic cup and letting it fall onto the table to uncrinkle itself, like a struggling wounded mouse that would never walk again.

"Others are kind." The officers were definitely watching Mark's table.

They know.

"You don't know other families. Don't know what it's like. Kind? No room for that. I don't do charity. No one ever gave *me* any help. *Never.* I dragged myself up and carved my own life with my own hands. I was always belted. Ran away. Had to get away or he'd have killed me. So don't tell me what's what." His gaze was accusing. You could almost imagine a trace of twisted vulnerability there. Sometimes it's best to imagine things. The world's bad enough, if you can't make it prettier then at least you can *imagine* it is.

"Sorry, Dad."

"Nah, me too. We're all on edge. Just drop that topic. It's easy to wonder about if there was another way. Of life. When you're on your own. But I can't see it myself. We just do our best. You will, too. I want you to make me proud."

"I try."

"Anything else on your mind. Girls?"

The surprise must have shown on Mark's face.

"I know the look."

"There was a girl."

"Did you fuck it?"

"I'm not even gonna answer that. I don't like the way you're talking."

His dad snarled, but it was a grin. "Ha. Stared me in the eye for once. Good lad."

"Just that I don't want to think bad of her. It didn't work out. End of."

"Women, eh? Don't let 'em control you, son. Don't ever tell 'em the truth, keeps 'em guessing. Don't take any shit. Slap 'em round if they let you down, a black eye marks 'em so people know they're a slag. Always best to get rid of them before they drag you down, lying bitches." His top lip curled as he pushed out air in an imitation of a piece of paper being torn, "ffffittt".

"You said Mum *got* pregnant."

"Yeah."

"Not that you got her pregnant."

"So?"

Mark kept his eyes on his dad's face. Anything. Any detail.

Blankness. "Don't go there, son."

"I just want to know who my family are. Really."

A grimace. "With her, who knew? But who cares. I think of you as mine. Maybe I had doubts, but that's sorted out now."

"And you said you got rid of her." *Was it a Froydian Slip?*

"When?"

"Before. But in the past you said you both split up."

His dad stared at him for a few seconds. "What does a word matter? Same thing."

Mark prodded the hole in his top, making it larger. "What really happened to Mum? How'd she die? I want you to tell me the truth."

A pause. A flicker in the eyes. A shadow of some expression, which could have been fear, but Mark couldn't tell, he'd never seen that expression on his dad's face. Then sudden energy from his dad but it was a second too late. "We argued. She left for some other fella, didn't she? Fucked off. I heard about it later." Pause, cheeks twitched into a resemblance of a smile, like one seen in a glossy magazine photo and not understood. "You were well shut of her. That's it."

His dad had never mentioned her going off with someone else.

Mark got up slowly. Looked at Dad's lined face. No smile lines. No memories of a time when he didn't have an undercurrent of fear. He looked like a stranger.

"Are you top dog, Dad?"

"Yeah. Fucking always and forever. Why?"

"Is anyone making you do this? Smuggle stuff?"

"Are they fuck! No one makes me do anything. Why?"

"Nothing." Mark stared at one of the prison officers who'd been watching him until the officer looked away. When Mark finally spoke it was barely a whisper. "Goodbye, Dad."

Em was waiting on the platform when Sam got off the train. Hugs, squeals, smiles, laughter, a big kiss on the cheek: she certainly felt welcome back.

On the train journey she'd realised that she didn't miss Manchester at all. She missed Emily, and they spoke on the phone or emailed or texted every day, but the absence of the place itself was like a weight lifted. She hadn't realised how heavy it was. All those bricks and walls and buildings were bound to be a backbreaking total.

Instead of going back to Em's flat to drop things off ("Only one night, one bag, let's not waste time", Em had said) they got a taxi to Rusholme for a curry. Em's treat. She even joined Sam in the veggie options.

"You must be missing me."

"You don't know the half of it, babes. Though I wish you'd give up on the lemonade and join me in some Cobras. You've become one of those good girls I have nightmares about."

"I'm still the same inside."

"Hope so." Em leaned forward, eyes eager. "Have *you* missed *me*?"

"Course. It's the people, not the place. And that's the way it should be."

You couldn't beat the curry mile on a Friday night. Lively Bhangra music raising the volume of conversations, moist curries in sunshine yellows and oranges, steaming and carrying the scent of spices. They soon had a selection of balti dishes on their table to share, each sprinkled with chopped coriander leaves, vegetables swimming in oily, creamy sauce. Even Emily shut up for a while, her mouth too full to talk as they used a pile of aloo paratha to mop up the remains of the stainless steel dishes.

"Okay," Em said, unprompted. "That was possibly better than a man."

"High praise coming from you."

"Nah. Just have a low opinion of men."

Mark dumped the full carrier bag on the kitchen table. It clinked and rattled with all the bottles and cans. A selection of the finest from the grocery shop, now rebranded as "Bargain Booze". That said it all. Not just about his life, but about the area, the city, the culture, the future. Fields replaced with roads. Trees replaced with houses. Vegetables replaced with Special Brew.

He found a glass and poured his first drink, a large whisky. Downed it in one, felt the cleansing burn, grimaced, coughed. Did it again.

He was still shaking inside so cracked open a can of beer. It frothed up through the keyhole, ran down the can and over his fingers. He didn't care. Gulped it down. He was lost. But keyholes usually led somewhere. He could find a way in the cans, perhaps.

The flat was full of brooding silence. Always was when he didn't put music on to chase it away, make him feel like he wasn't alone. And this was it. No one could help him. He could hardly ring Dave. "Hey, mate. Can you keep me company? I know you hate drugs and I have a stash in my flat and my family are all connected to drugs but we can still be friends, yeah? Or I'll just keep quiet about it and feel dishonest all the time you're here?" It didn't work like that. He couldn't make things right. Everything was too broken.

After the can he burped, *fizz will out*, rooted through the bag. Took out a bottle of the alcopop Metz.

"Some people ask why I wear a red mask," he muttered, like in the advert. Took a big glug of it straight from the bottle. "It's because I feel guilty." He took another swig. "And because everything's poo." He finished the drink and poured another whisky.

In the living room, another can of lager. The third? He didn't know, didn't care. The more fizzy booze he poured in, the calmer his system became. Bodies were screwed up things. The shakes he felt but couldn't see were now fading. He'd been picking at the wallpaper again. Shredded detritus on the floor around him, like wall dandruff. The place was a mess. But he could live with *that*.

In front of him was the package. He stared at it. More white flakes, powder this time, like snow.

What drug was in there? Had they even told him? He knew the names of some. Speed. Coke. Heroin. Could it be crack? All alien words with no context. He'd never done any of them. Never seen anyone else use them, either.

Sam used him.

He shouldn't think he was special. Because he wasn't. He knew that, and everyone confirmed it.

Still in silence. The whisky bottle was by his chair. He groped for it, knocked it over the first time, spilled on the carpet. It didn't matter. Clean it up tomorrow. Too tired right now. And it was all just a joke.

He tried to pour some into his lager through the little keyhole. Some went in. Some went down the side.

A joke. The punchline was that there'd be another mess to clean the next day, another boring job to do, another insult to swallow, another form to sign, another thing to buy which would break just out of warranty, another hole in your clothes, another rejection, another night alone.

Thanks world! The cosmic joke is so funny! Please can I have the other 2000 that are lined up for me?

It wore him out. Maybe he should listen to Radiohead. Nah, only kidding. But music might help. He pressed play on the hi-fi. Oasis. Gas Panic. But when it got to the bit where they sang "My family don't seem so familiar, and my enemies all know my name" it was too close to home. He swapped the tape for a Charlatans one, side B. Something more upbeat began, cheery piano … ah, Just When You're Thinkin' Things Over. As an afterthought he turned the volume up to 14. Unlocked the front door. Hid the package behind the TV. Slumped back into his chair and closed his eyes to listen.

Yeah, furniture scraping overhead.

Not long after – a knock at his door, in time with the Tim Burgess singing "I'm coming home". Reminded Mark of the James song, Come Home. It sounded like a nice goal, wish fulfilment. It must be great to go home once you've been away. It must be great to go away.

"It's open!" he shouted.

In came Bazzy, wearing a striped tracksuit and Adidas trainers, carrier bag in his hand. "Alright our kid?"

"Sort of. You been for a run?" Mark asked.

"Fashion, not sport." He sat in the chair opposite Mark. The plastic creaked.

Mark held up a can. "Want one?"

"Thanks, but I brought my own." His bag was plonked on the cable spool table. "Got a glass?"

Mark made his way into the kitchen. Slowly. The floor seemed to heave. Found a glass that was probably clean, wiped the rim on the towel just in case.

Bazzy had rolled his sleeves up and was rustling things out of his bag. Mark put the glass in front of him and slumped back into his own chair. Bazzy had gin. A bottle of tonic. A tub of lemon slices.

"You came prepared," Mark told him, breaking into a new can of his own.

"Inspiration break, good to get topped up. What's the matter?"

"What makes you think anything's up?"

"One: you called me down. Usually seem to do that when you're not really with it. Knackered, pissed, borderline depressed. Makes me feel really welcome, y'know? Just joshing. And number two: you got a face like you've seen your arse." Bazzy stirred his drink with a finger tip then leaned back, put his feet up on the plywood table.

"Nothing gets past you."

"Sharp wits, man. Vital."

"I wish I had them. Everything I try goes wrong. I have all these ideas, but they just fall apart. Or I misjudge people. Was never good at that."

"You gotta mix with people if you want to understand them."

"Either way, I'm not sharp."

"You put yourself down."

"People tell me. They're right."

"Oh yeah? Other people are always right?" Bazzy made a "Pfft!" noise with his lips, leaned forward and brushed his shaggy hair out of his eyes. Mark could see a tattoo on his forearm which said "Mother" within a heart shape.

"You got these two voices, right? We all do. One's cool. Call it Miss Positivity. She sits on your shoulder, tells you stuff like 'You can do it! Try that shit! Do something exciting and new!' Then there's this other voice, the vile fucker on your other shoulder, call the cunt Mr Negativity, the one that says, 'You can't do it; don't try and change things, you'll only make them worse.' Problem is, if you listen to that bastard you'll never change your life; even when you feel these brief bursts of inspiration and hope you'll quickly squash 'em, fade back into bitterness and self-loathing and anger. Whereas if you listen to Miss Positivity with her sweet bubblegum breath then it can change things, make your life go in directions you never would've thought possible. And the one you listen to most gets stronger, and it gets easier to ignore the other. So make sure you listen to the right one."

Mark nodded.

"Just want to be clear that you got me – I mean, try and be positive. You got that?"

"Of course! The *Go For It* voice. I'm not thick!"

"Just checking." Bazzy had a grin on his face as he finished off his G&T. "And I'm glad you got defensive. See, you over-rode my insinuation, believed you were better. I said you were sharp."

"Thanks."

"So what's Dad done this time?"

"Who said anything about my dad?" Mark asked suspiciously.

"You were complaining about him last time I was round."

"I don't remember."

"You don't remember being squirted out of your mum's tubes, don't mean it didn't happen."

"It's just ... he's asked me to do something. And I don't want to."

"Ah. Loyalty versus whatever bothers you, eh?"

"Yeah."

"Family. The tie we can't cut easily. You know I can't give you any answers?"

"I know. But it's good to talk to someone."

"Yeah. Helps tighten things up. Only time you don't want a loose fit. You can probably guess what I'd say without me being privy to all the details."

"No."

"What you do, man, you do what's right. That's it."

"Not always easy."

"Nothing worth it is. You gotta find courage where you can. Thinks about Happy Mondays. Bez got on stage during one of their performances and danced, ended up part of the band."

Mark nodded. He knew the story.

"And if you need more: Bez's first name is Mark too."

"I wish you were my dad."

"Nah. I groove around like a baddy."

Mark stared at him. "How old are you, anyway?"

But Bazzy just grinned and shoved his things back into the carrier bag. "Gotta go."

"Already?"

"Can't stay long. Supposed to be writing a review of a new album for NME."

"Wow."

"It's not as great a gig as you'd imagine. Album's shit. Catch you later. Hope you perk up."

And Bazzy was gone.

It was getting dark.

Mark's floppy fringe shaded his eyes. He could hide behind it. He hated it when people moved it out of the way, saying "Let's have a look at you then." His dad was next to him finishing a pint and talking about getting them both chips on the way home. The jukebox tune was the one with sad drums and a sad man who was singing in a deep voice. The one that made Mark want to cry.

"Hey, Jacko. Guess who's walking past?" said a man with a beard and fat arms who sat by the window looking out on to the main road.

"Keep us in suspense, why don't you?"

"It's only the fuckin' Irish. With some tart."

Suddenly his dad's face wasn't smiley. He swallowed the rest of his pint and thunked his glass down.

"Hey now, Jacko," said the barman, "I don't want any trouble in here, we've had the rozzers out twice this week already."

"Won't be any trouble in here," said the boy's dad, getting up quickly. His face was craggier than ever, and there was the mean shine in his eyes. "You stay there, Mark. Don't bloody move."

His dad rushed out the door of the pub. Mark wanted to get up, stop it all, he knew what would happen, felt panic rising, but he was frozen. It was inevitable. The man with the beard started cheering then got up and rushed out too. The barman cursed angrily, shook his head, then went back to talking to the old man on the stool. Commotion outside. A woman cried "Leave him alone!" then started screaming. Someone else was shouting "Put the boot in". There were thumping sounds and yells and something banged against the pub glass. You couldn't see through because it had a misty pattern on it, "frosted glass" his dad called it, but there was a red smear there now, where a bleeding face had rubbed against it. The singer on the jukebox still sounded sad, maybe he was sad that his beautiful music was being ruined. The screaming and yelling went on and Mark couldn't drink any more of the lemonade because he felt sick, like he always did when his dad went from being nice to being angry on someone.

"Don't walk away," the singer pleaded, but Mark wished everyone would. He wished the singer was his dad.

The pub door opened, his dad was there panting and had red on his hand which was clenched into a fist, and now he could hear a woman crying; "Have none of you the decency to call an ambulance for him?" she sounded hysterical, nearly a scream.

"Get the fuck out here quick, Mark, you useless little bastard, we're going!" Dad yelled, and Mark knew there would be no chips as he slid off the bench and ran to the door –

And he woke, wiped his mouth. *It's okay.* He was still slumped in the chair. *It's all okay.* Dark now, streetlights orange, the flat alien, ghostly, not a home, just a place and he was passing through.

Always the dreams. The bad stuff. Always it circled round him. No escape.

He didn't want to be like his family.

His drink was on its side. He'd started on the vodka, that water of life, and remembered his stomach protesting at the glug glug gulps. When he turned his head the world took an eye-blink to catch up, loose and whirling round him like a fairground ride, spinning like a loving crack from a hard hand, the white plastic cogs in his tape, rolling but never getting anywhere except forward in time.

It can't all just be random, life. It wouldn't be fair. There has to be a reason. A cause. Things are connected. He was influenced by the music, his life must mirror it somehow. He could see a pattern if he looked closely enough. He would understand.

He took another mouthful of vodka and looked at the pale glow of the package on the table. The condom-wrapped maggot at the core of this bad apple. It seemed so innocent.

Do what's right.

Yeah, like the line in Wonderwall. "By now you should've somehow realised what you gotta do," Mark muttered.

He stared until he'd finished the bottle.

Love Spreads

timeless and perfect. There's pace. A journey. Believe, and see the light.

Love Spreads is about Jesus as a black woman. About female strength, female power to save, about love and forgiveness. Their previous single had been I Am The Resurrection, also about the depiction of Jesus. Second Coming indeed. The album's opening track is Breaking Into Heaven. A statement of intent? Or because we all dream of meeting the dead again, those we've lost, as referenced in How Do You Sleep? Is it all just about having a second chance?

The album was recorded after a year in and out of studios in Wales. John Squire designed the cover – cherubs from a bridge in Newport, South Wales. Cherubs are angels, and the beings are mentioned in a few Stone Roses songs (for example the happ...

The original home footage UK video (with Ian Brown's best monkey-boy jumping) is far better than the unconvincing US version.

Sam had shared Emily's double bed. She was past sleeping on sofas. Sam wore a pair of light pyjamas with a cartoon frog print; Em had slept in a silky top and bed shorts. They'd agreed to keep to their own sides. When she woke one of Em's legs was sprawled over hers, and despite looking like a slim glamour model Em was snoring like a man. Sam stifled a giggle.

Let the poor mite rest. Never disturb sleeping cats or dogs.

She felt refreshed and awake. It was a contrast to when she lived in Manchester and always seemed to wake groggy, hung over and disappointed. She'd turned the corner. It *could* be done.

Em had got dressed but Sam was still in her jim jams, sat on the sofa eating muesli and watching the news. Em's promise of a big cooked breakfast had fallen through when they looked in the fridge and discovered the only part of it she had the ingredients for was fried tomatoes. Sam borrowed a pair of fluffy slippers off Em, ridiculous pink monster feet, as compensation. They were cosy. It was like being on holiday.

The doorbell rang and Em answered it. Surprise, a male voice, talking. The door closed and two sets of footsteps came up the hall.

"Look who turned up." Em was followed into the room by Roger.

"Morning, Sam!"

"Hi."

"You lazy lumps still lounging? I get up with the sunrise. Choppity chop. I was in the area and thought I'd pop by. I've got to say I was disappointed not to be told where you were both going last night."

"We were thinking about texting you later," Sam mumbled.

"Here, I've brought you something."

He rummaged in a carrier bag. Sam hoped it was photos from her leaving do, but he withdrew a plastic CD case instead and held it out to her. "I made it myself. Got a new twelve speed CD-R drive. Goes like greased doodah."

"Thanks." She felt disappointment as she took it, scanned quickly down the list of tracks he'd written on the white inlay card. Old chart music. Nothing that indicated real *passion* for the sounds.

Em headed to the kitchen. "I'll make us all coffee."

"Don't burn the water," Sam teased.

Middle finger as a reply, the universally accepted sign for "I love you too."

Roger sat on the sofa next to her. Took Sunny Delight from his bag. "How are you today?" he asked between gulps.

"Fine. Thanks."

"It's lovely. The day."

"Yes."

"You funky dory?"

"I'm just trying to eat this." Sam waved her bowl.

"Yes." A second or two passed. He leaned over. "What's that nice smell? Perfume?"

She moved away a bit. "Doubt it. I just got up."

"Yes," he repeated. Then he launched into a description of a new TV programme which was going to start in a couple of weeks. Something called Big Brother. "It's 'reality TV'," he said. "You'll see everything."

"I don't get it. Just watching people? No script or plot? What's the point of that? You'd have to be pretty sad to be interested in what complete strangers do."

"No, it's … oh, never mind." He put the bottle down. Then fidgeted. "Not looked at the CD?"

"Not had chance. Just let me finish this."

Where the fuck was Em?

She resisted the urge to shrug as he told her he'd put Duran Duran on it. And George Michael. "It's a special mix for you."

Wham! She looked at him suddenly, wondering from his tone if there really was a subtext to him, and his eyes flicked up to hers. They had been looking lower down, tit height. She knew. And he *knew* she knew. Sam put the bowl down and fastened the top button on her PJs, hoping he'd take the hint and leave but he didn't. He really was beyond shame.

"I'm your friend, you know. I care about you, Sam," he said, and tried to take her hand. She snatched it away from him as if he held a snake out. A trouser snake.

"Not that type of friend."

He stared at her. "It's Mark, isn't it? You did sleep with him," he blurted out.

"That would be no fucking business of yours!"

"It would be if you lied to me. Why would you keep stuff from me? I've known you longer."

Sam stood. "I'd like you to leave."

Em came in, her face puzzled as she surveyed the scene. "What's going on?"

Roger ignored her. "You're welcome to him then," he told Sam. "Though you might not be so keen if you knew what I knew."

"Which *is*?"

"Wouldn't *you* like to know?"

"If you've got something to say, come out and say it," she told him impatiently, arms folded.

"Alrighty. Just that I overheard Mark boasting about some conquest to the other goons he works with. Sounded like he'd pulled a total slapper. Well, I think that's what it was."

"Mark?" asked Em with obvious puzzlement.

Roger twitched his shoulders, a noncommittal shrug. "Well, only overheard, can't guarantee, but it sounded like it. Being all cocky."

Sam clenched her fists. "Get out," she told him, stepping forward, pleased to see him retreat a step.

"Fine." He snatched up his CD. "But I'm taking this. You don't deserve it."

"I really don't," Sam agreed. "And I don't think we should keep in touch either. Finito binito, as you would say." Roger stared back at her for a couple of seconds then dropped his gaze in resignation.

"Take that too." She nodded towards his bottle of orange.

He picked it up. Held it against his chest.

"I hope you turn yellow," Sam whispered.

When he left, letting the door slam behind him, it resembled a retreat.

Sam took some deep breaths, then flumped onto the sofa.

"What's going on? I am totally confused," Em said.

"I'm surprised at your restraint. How'd you stay out of it?"

"I dunno. Even though I didn't understand what was going on I still wanted to tell him to slip into something more comfortable, like a coma. I'm automatically on your side. But I could see you had it covered. What did he do?"

"He was being creepy."

"That's Roger alright." Em handed her a cup of coffee, put the other two on the low table.

"He was coming on to me."

"Good taste, but surprised he has the balls. I can see why that would make you queasy though. It goes beyond funny. I'm going to batter him on Monday."

"How'd he know where you live, anyway?"

"He came round once after work."

"You didn't –"

"No! He said he needed help with his CV. I was useless anyway. I kept pissing my sides at the bollocks he'd put in it so he left in a huff."

Sam stared into the comforting brown liquid. "Not that I care, but that stuff about Mark?" She struggled to keep her voice from rising in pitch. Mark was many things, but surely not like that? Yet what Roger said seemed too blatant and specific to be a lie. Sam was surprised that even just the thought of Mark talking like that hurt.

Emily knelt on the floor in front of her. "Mark's a stupid prick. For not going after you, I mean. But I don't think any of that stuff is true. He hasn't been cocky. The opposite, if anything. Totally sullen and quiet most of the time. Miserable-looking. Serves him right. I don't think he's told anyone a thing though. Ben would have mentioned it to me. You want to talk about it?"

"No. I want to drop the subject."

Emily nodded. Sam was impressed. Normally Em wouldn't drop anything just because she was told to; she only ever dropped things when she had chewed and worried them until she was bored.

Em changed the topic. "Well, now that you've exorcised Roger from your life it'll be just the two of us tonight. Like old times, but with less booze, snogging and coke. I'm pleased that you seem to be alienating yourself from everyone in Manchester. Makes me more special."

"You're my only affection connection in this whole city."

"Ditto."

"What about you and Ben?"

Em shrugged. "Early days." Then she smiled. "He makes me laugh."

"That's always a start."

"Yeah. I need a giggle when work gets me down. Unwind. Have a break." She sipped her drink, then peeped over the top of the cup. "I hear Wales is tempting this time of year."

"You may not get a sun tan but you can develop a lovely glowing case of rust."

For some reason Em found that hilarious. She sat on the arm of the sofa next to Sam, and brushed her hair while they talked rubbish. And it was good. It's actions, not words, that matter.

Every northern soul dancer *ever* was stomping in his brain at high tempo, clenched fists raised. Nothing else could explain the pain.

He couldn't see anything. Had to use finger and thumb to separate his gummed-up eyes, then whimpered at the brain-stabbing brightness, blinded by the sunlight entering the squinty pinpricks. Hands on head to stop his skull turning inside out. "Oh sweet mother of Oasis," he moaned.

The room tilted and it got his stomach spinning too. He crawled to the toilet. Started retching. He hated being sick. His eyes were cloudy; even the toilet water looked milky white just before he vomited.

He flushed, then managed to stand shakily, using the sink for support. Splashed cold water on his face. Brushed his teeth and tongue, every movement punctuated by a self-pitying groan.

As he shuffled to the towel hook on the back of the door his foot kicked something. He bent down to make it easier for his eyes to focus, but caused a swirling storm of sharp protest in his brain.

Ripped condoms.

Uh? He didn't remember a caveman orgy taking place.

The condoms were powdery.

Nearby was a piece of string…

To the toilet bowl. Although he'd flushed, a fine trace of white remained on the water's surface. A speck on the bowl. A smudge on the carpet.

He was screwed.

Help. Get help.

He made his way into the living room, leaning on the wall every few steps; found his phone in a sticky patch of beer. Forced himself to slow down as he entered a message and sent it.

`Denny. in DEEP doodoo. stuff down the toylet. what shud I do?`

No painkillers in the flat. It would have to be hair of the dog. He found a carton of budget orange juice in the fridge. "From concentrate." Good, he needed to concentrate. He poured out half a glass, added a generous slug of whisky, held his nose and downed it. That should kickstart body and brain respectively.

Oh poopy blasts.

He poured another.

No reply yet on the phone. He felt a bit better though. Awake. Pain in his head easing. The stale hangover dizziness was being replaced with fresh dizziness. Liquids tackling the dehydration. Needed something to settle his stomach so toasted some white bread on the grill, ate it dry. That felt better too.

But the more alive he felt, the more the reality of the situation hit him.

Perhaps he should take up swearing. That might be appropriate right now.

There wouldn't be an easy way out of this. Maybe he could offer money? Pay for the stuff? Then they'd just be a bit annoyed? Would they still break his arms then? But how much had that package been worth? Probably a lot. And he'd spent the last of his overdraft on the bottles and cans last night. Did gangsters let you pay in instalments? He didn't know how the criminal mind worked. But then he cheered up: yes, he did know! He just had to ask himself what his dad or Denny would do if they got ripped off! He thought for a minute.

Oh grease fox turds.

Oh super ships of poopy fuck fuck.

He was screwed.

Last of the small whisky bottle gone. Well on his way to numbness again. This was best. Whatever happened, he wouldn't feel it so much.

Last night he didn't have a clue where he was from or where he was going. But now he could assume the journey would be short and painful. This could be the end. It made sense. Today was the start of July. The month Closer was released. The same month Ian Curtis was born. Yet Ian had died at 23. He was already dead when his album came out. Mark was almost the same age as Ian when he'd died.

Except he hadn't just died. He'd hung himself in the kitchen. It made no sense. He was on the verge of huge success. People loved him. He had talent. A real northern genius. Everything going for him. Whereas Mark … he was a nobody. People wouldn't give a fig if he checked out. Dave had once told him about King Midas. Mark was like that king, but a Manchester version where everything he touched turned to poop.

He was still in control for now. He just had to take decisive action.

Mark yanked the kitchen window up in its stiff track. Breeze. High up. He stuck his head out, looked down at the toy bins, cars and trees below. Fourth floor up. Would that be high enough? Or would he just break his legs, be even worse off?

He went to his bedroom. Two ties in his wardrobe. Would they be strong enough? Maybe if he knotted them to some socks. Then he found a belt. That had worked for Michael Hutchence. Copying that would be the nearest Mark got to musical talent.

He had just lain the items out and wiped his eyes, thought that after another drink or two he'd be ready, when he heard a voice in the hall.

"Alright Marky? Where are ya?"

He froze, heart leaping into his mouth with a combination of fear and guilt as if he'd been caught doing the five finger shuffle.

Denny? Or Mikey?

He held his breath, covered belt and ties quickly with the duvet, looked for a hiding place. Under the bed or in the wardrobe maybe, though they'd be the first places someone would look.

"I had a dream, I've seen the light; the flat below's been fuckin' quiet, where is that brother?" a voice sang.

"Bazzy?"

"Who else?" He came into the bedroom. Smart shirt with a mandarin collar. Round shades on. Mark could have laughed with relief.

"What you doin' here? I didn't summon you."

"Whatever. Just popped down to see if you're okay."

"How'd you get in?"

"Door was unlocked. Might wanna watch out for that. You alright? You look like you've gone five rounds with a bucket of sliced onions."

That got a snort. Mark sat on the corner of his bed, glad to give his shaky legs a rest.

"Bit tired. Bit hung over. I decided to act. Do the right thing."

"Nice one."

"You're always so cool."

"What, way I look?"

Mark laughed. "No, not that. But at the moment you look like someone in disguise. Lennon or Liam Gallagher or something."

"Not in disguise: just to hide hangovers. Lookin' at you, I recommend you wear a pair. Your eyes will be fucked later."

"Ta. Anyway, I meant the way you think. Calm."

"Anyone can do it. What's the deal?" Bazzy leaned against the door jamb, pulled his shades down his nose a bit to gaze over the top. There was something familiar about his pose. Then Mark realised it resembled something Tony Wilson used to do. Just a coincidence.

"I didn't tell you everything last night. Too ashamed, I guess. But my dad, you know he's in prison?"

A nod, making the shaggy fringe wobble.

"Well, him and my brother and some others want me to take drugs to him. Smuggle them in."

"Ah."

"Anyway, I did the right thing. Flushed the drugs down the toilet last night."

"What?" Bazzy stood upright.

"Got rid of 'em."

"You *what*?" And Bazzy was gone. Footsteps thumping into the bathroom. Then: "Noooooooo!"

Mark rushed after him to find Bazzy on his knees.

"Nooooo! Aaaaaaaaaargh!" His primal wolf-like howls made Mark's ears ache.

"What's up?"

"You flushed them away?" He picked up one of the ripped powdery condoms. "Fucking stoning hell!"

"You said to do the right thing!"

"I meant your dad! Your *dad*! I meant it like 'Be a good dude' not 'Waste drugs'! I'd have had this, a month's worth of inspiration. Or sell 'em. Or give them back. Or just refuse. But not *down the shitter*!"

They both looked at the toilet bowl.

"Y'know the Happy Mondays song, Harmony?" Bazzy asked. Mark gave him a raised eyebrow. "Sorry. Of course. Anyway, do you wanna be cut up into bits and cooked, like in the song? Shit." Bazzy rubbed his eyes. "Fuck it." Took a deep breath. "It's done." He pushed himself up slowly. "Maybe you're right. Fuck. Sorry. Just a shock for me. I like to party a bit. Even been known to get a bit crack crazy once in a while. Maybe I indulge a bit more to make up for people like you. Balance the world out, let people live vicariously. Never mind. Irrelevant to this situation. I'm talking shit." Another sigh. "Right. Move on. Focussing on the drugs don't work. Question is, what we gonna do next?"

"I can't see past this."

"Me neither, right now. I need time to think. But keep lookin'. Don't give up. Just this: don't let anyone stamp out your fire, or change what you want to be. Don't forget, you're a man. Be who you're bein'; do what you're doin'; seems like you'll end up good to me."

"Misquoting Happy Mondays lyrics doesn't help me much," Mark replied.

"Sorry. It's often all I have to offer."

"And I might not have a lot of say in the fire stampin'."

"Don't worry. There's usually a way. I'll go. Get some advice."

"Who off?"

"People I know. For now: sit tight. But be ready to move. Don't do anything stupid. Oh, and smarten up. Feel more alive."

"Will do."

Bazzy pointed to his mandarin collar. "When shit goes wrong – at least make sure you've got good cloves on."

Mark saw his guest to the door. Bazzy pointed to the lock. Mark nodded. Flipped the catch as he shut the door on the outside world.

He tidied up a bit. Then rebrushed his teeth. Cold water splashes next, to bring him round. Lots of them. It was so nice he stripped off and got into the shower, turned it to blasting cold, letting it revive him with high-powered ice that left his skin tingling when he stepped out dripping onto the lino. What had Bazzy said? Look good. After towelling dry Mark found clean underwear, black jeans. Then saw the long-sleeved blue top. He'd only worn it once, on the night of Sam's leaving do. A pang. But it was his best.

He was pulling it over his head when the pounding on his front door began.

Bang bang.

"Open the door!"

More banging.

"Mark, open this FUCKING DOOR!"

Mark watched it rattle in the frame, glad that all post went in the private boxes downstairs so there was no letterbox for Denny to look through. If he just stayed quiet enough…

"Open up or I'll kick this fucker down!" Denny counted out loud, then at ten he began booting the door. Should Mark ring the police? There was an ominous cracking noise. Mark rushed forward and put the chain on. Denny must have heard the jingle of it.

"I know you're in there," he said.

"Yeah," Mark replied. No use arguing when the angel of death comes knocking and banging at your door.

"Open up."

"No."

"Why not?"

"You're mad."

"Too fucking right! I get a message like that, what the fuck you expect, you little cunt! So open up!" A fist bang.

"Not when you're like this."

Silence for a second. "I'm calm."

Yes, but how long before he blew, worse than before? Mark remembered having his arm set in hospital when he was fifteen. He'd been playing with Denny's new record player, somehow damaged the needle. Denny hadn't been able to stop himself until Mark's arm made the same noise as this door frame. He might not live through the day but he didn't want it to hurt more than it had to.

"I'll talk, but I'm not letting you in." Mark had to raise his voice so Denny could hear.

"Fucker!" More kicking. Mark wondered how well the door would hold up if Denny was determined to get in. Which would give in first: the door or Denny's foot? He didn't want to find out. Shame there was no furniture in the short hall that could go against the door to reinforce it. Mark leaned against it himself, hoping body weight would be enough.

"Stop it, Denny! I'm listening!"

"Was your text a joke?" he yelled, sounding out of breath.

"No."

"What happened?"

"I was drunk and depressed. Must have flushed it away. I don't remember."

A whack. Fist on wall, maybe. Then a curse.

"They'll throw you down the stairs out here. Drag you back up and do it again. And keep doing it. I *know* this type of people. I can't protect you from them." A pause. "If you're hiding the drugs, pretending, maybe thinking you can sell them on your own – don't. Give it to me, we'll work it out."

"I'm not hiding anything. It's true."

"FUUUUUuuuuuuuuUUUUUCK!" as if he was revolving while yelling. Another bang.

"Calm down, Denny!" Mark was starting to get pissed off with all this.

"No! Look, maybe there's a way out. Maybe you can pay them and just take a good kicking."

Images of Denny's time in intensive care and permanent limp rose in Mark's mind. "No. I'm skint. And I don't want to give money to bad drug people."

"You're a lost fucking cause. Open up now or I'll go down and get a brick from the skip, smash your window, and kick the shit out of you meself, you lanky streak of piss." More kicking.

"Hey, stop that!" A voice further down the corridor.

"Fuck off and mind yer own business you slag!"

"I've called the police! They're on the way!"

Denny's footsteps thudding away; door slam; sound of him kicking someone else's door for a change, and yelling every swear word Mark knew, plus a few more. After that seemed to tire him out he came back.

"Right, I'm going then," he shouted to Mark. "You are *so* fucked. The Connors will sort you out. You're no brother of mine. Not even family any more. You're *nowt.* That's it, forever. Hope it hurts when they get you, you waste of fucking space!"

Even after it seemed like he'd gone, Mark waited, heart pounding, body sweating. Denny might still be outside. Mark put his ear to the door and listened, half expecting another kick. Denny was sly like that. And Mark thought he could hear a stealthy noise beyond.

He almost collapsed when there was a gentle knock.

"Mark? Are you alright? It's Mandy. He's gone."

"Really?"

"Yes. I looked over the balcony. He was limping towards Barton Road."

He took the chain off and opened it, squinting into the bright light and fresh air outside. She was silhouetted by sun, and her face seemed pale under the dark curly hair.

"Hi, Mandy. Thanks."

"Who was that?"

He grimaced. "My brother. He's a bit of a psycho."

"I could tell. Are you okay?"

"Yes." It was the first time he'd spoken to her since he'd gatecrashed the disastrous Lass O' Gowrie work social. Had seen her once or twice and they'd ignored each other. But she did seem concerned now. That was something. "You?"

"I'm fine. By the way, I wasn't lying."

"About what?" His mind raced back to their last meeting.

“About the police.” He must have looked confused, because she added, “I really did call them. They’re on their way.”

“Good. And I’m grateful.” Oh poo.

“I’m…” She had a weird look on her face.

What? What *was* she? The clock was ticking. But she just looked back up the walkway to her own door, which was ajar.

“Thanks, Mandy.”

She smiled, fleeting. “Do you need me to wait with you?”

“No, it’s fine. I want to tidy up.”

“Okay.” She turned to go.

“Goodbye,” he said quietly. She didn’t seem to hear. He closed the front door, rested against it to stop the swaying.

Thought about the ties and belt under his duvet. But his taste for death had miraculously faded. Maybe because he’d faced the reality of violence. Or the opposite: a reminder of what normal people acted like.

He couldn’t stay. The police would ask questions he couldn’t deal with right now. They’d know he was lying: they were trained for that, weren’t they? And getting Denny in trouble would just backfire, make things worse (if that was possible). Plus, they might search his flat. Even if he tidied up they could find drug traces, had dogs and gadgets and stuff.

It all made the decision easy. If he stayed it was a toss-up between a battering by his brother, prison via the police, or crippling and possible death via gangsters. If he was really lucky and they came in the right order, he might hit all three jackpots.

A siren in the distance.

He grabbed his wallet, keys and phone. Slipped on his leather jacket. Found some aviator shades in the pocket so slipped them on too. Then left the flat, pounded down the stairs two at a time, and kept running, taking the opposite direction from Barton Road. He sprinted from the dead-end trap, because wimps like him, baby they were born to run.

Plan: lose himself in Saturday crowds and gain the safety of anonymity for a while. More time to think. When he stepped off the bus, connecting with the hardness of Piccadilly, he still didn’t have a thought, but he had developed a dire need for the toilet. The nearby Wetherspoons became destination one. He could relieve himself, buy a pint, and regroup amongst endless tables, disorientating mirrors and the permanent smell of chips. His table was covered with tottering placards offering a confusing array of food options and various clubs that seemed to meet there on different days. He swept all that distraction to the side, drank a third of the cold pint in one long draught, then leaned back.

What was he going to do?

He needed inspiration but it was blocked by distracting TVs showing sports. A nearby fruit machine "with an £80 jackpot" burbled and bleeped proudly. And the conversations were more than a murmur, the amalgamated bass grumps and mumblings formed a groundswell punctuated by shouts rattling round the open space, amplified kids' canteen noise with highpoints of bottles being dropped into containers with a tinkling crash. Tables of white-haired men in their 60s dressed in white shirts and ties complained about their meals. Groups in their 50s – the young crowd, who wore tracksuit bottoms and trainers but looked like they've never run in their lives, short-sleeved shirts displaying tattooed forearms – were joking and debating loudly, yelling and hooting and gesticulating like drunken chimps. This was a place for the lonely to feel that they weren't alone, to blend in at the edges until the realisation arrived: that being there is sadder than just admitting the truth. This was how it felt when you gave up.

He downed the rest of his drink. Didn't have a destination in mind. Just walked. Crossed Piccadilly, head down. Tried counting items of litter to pass the time, but couldn't concentrate enough, got jostled by the crowds, and lost his place. Every time he got knocked he looked up, half expecting it to be Denny, or Mikey, or Mr Connor, or some other unwelcome face. But it was always just a normal grumpy Mancunian, not a gangster one.

Thinning crowds led down streets of pizzas and fast food. His stomach gurgled to get his attention so he entered a kebab shop. The big meat slab rotated under its red lights, looking like a skinned elephant's leg as it sweated grease. He'd never realised how disgusting it looked in daylight.

"Chips in a pitta please."

"You want sa-LAD with that?"

"Okay. A little bit."

He traded his money for the comfortingly warm paper package. Smothered its contents in vinegar and lemon juice. Walked down the road, picking out bits of lettuce, chips, slices of tomato. Nibbling rather than wolfing it.

He nearly tripped up when his feet tangled in a discarded fish and chip meal, sodden papers clinging to his ankles possessively, slippy squashed potato and batter stuck in the grips of his trainers. He swore, tried to wipe them clean on the edge of the kerb. Why couldn't people use the bins? It was a mess round here, now that he looked properly. Dried remains of stomach acid and bits of food evident on the pavement. Other patches of dried red sticky stuff. He didn't want to think about whether it was ketchup or dried blood.

He left the main road and headed down the long back streets behind bars and restaurants. Probably a better idea if he was trying to avoid attention. Staff in chef's hats and dirty white aprons sat on steps, smoking and looking both miserable and suspicious. It was the other side, without the distracting bright lights and signs and offers and promises. Piles of binbags stacked up in the dark. Like the end of a huge digestive system. The bus was the delivery mechanism to the throat, and he'd just tramped through the guts. Now he was human waste, ready to be dumped.

It was no good. Despite his proper belly hunger, he couldn't eat. The food remainders went in the bin.

It was as if these areas were forgotten, you weren't meant to see them. Left to decay. The pavement and road were eroding: patches on top of patches, as the pattern of crumble and repair continued. Same with double yellow lines on side streets, worn, faded, then repainted. He stared at it, this process he'd never fully comprehended before. It was like seeing below the surface. Literally. The truth of it. Just like the fabric of the city, the principle also applied to the crawlers on top. People came and went, got replaced, the city moved on, emotionless. We don't mean anything. Transient and replaceable.

Too depressing. He switched to Manchester Music Associations, but his mind was dry. He wondered if there were any ways to enliven the game. Could he go off resemblances between people? That would be a new variant. Take Johnny Marr and Noel Gallagher. Similar looks, guitar, talent, attitude, sense of humour. Mark used to wonder if Noel evolved out of his idol, making Marr some kind of proto-Oasis. But Mark didn't think so any more. They both just came from the same source. Manchester. You come from a place, you get forged by it, stamped as much as any book or CD with the place and time of creation.

Oh, he'd drifted from the game. His mind was not sharp today. Maybe he'd been here too long. He'd heard that even vitamin C was toxic if you ate too many tablets. That's it. Maybe he'd just had too much toxic air, it had started to poison him. The only explanation –

At which point he was almost hit by a fancy new Mini that turned the corner without slowing. Horn blasted and he jumped to the side, felt the air as it shot past; he gave the driver the finger as his heart slowed again. There was no pavement on this road and he'd somehow wandered into the middle of it, but still, the driver should have checked before turning. Cars and trams, always machinery ready to crush you, replace you. As if the city wanted him dead. Why? It made no sense. He used to love it. It was all he knew.

As his heart slowed he wondered whether he shouldn't have got out of the way after all. Being knocked down could have been the answer to his problems.

No, don't give up. Not yet. And don't take the antics of city car plonkers too seriously. They were always in a hurry. Too much hurry to look around and see what there was. He wouldn't be like that any more. Make the most of today. He looked around.

Oh. This area wasn't the best to start.

In fact, he wasn't really sure *where* he was.

There was a half-demolished red brick warehouse facing him. It had words formed out of sandy-coloured stone but they were now unreadable mysteries as part of the façade had collapsed. Next to it was the greyness of another car park being born. They seemed to be springing up everywhere; the city was being buried under them. *History* was being buried under them as they were dropped from the sky like giant concrete turds, crushing everything below to dust. It bothered him that they didn't at least add trees, bushes, even flowers. He guessed there was no money in that. And no surprise that if you build a concrete jungle, you get apes.

His phone buzzed. Missed calls. Denny, plus two unknown numbers. And a text.

`Hope all is okay. Ring us. Mikey.`

Such calm language couldn't be good. He put the phone away and walked on.

Yeah, this whole area was changing. Always the clouds of dust and sounds of drills as ancient and solid buildings that weathered the ages were knocked down to be replaced with the kind of modern rubbish he'd seen on nearby main streets, buildings that would need pulling down in 20 years. Why not just repair the old stuff with its … what was the word? Nobility? Sturdiness? He didn't know. But if it was music he'd talk about the classics, the reliables, the songs and sounds that grow out of a place and a history, flavoured with it, adding back in and building up and getting stronger without losing itself.

It made no sense to him. As if he was an outsider stuck on the inside. True in a way. Car parks were bound to seem like alien places when you'd never owned a car. Never even been on a plane or train, transports to exotic places. Like out of the city –

Wales

Ha, who was he kidding. Trains? He was just a plodder in trainers, dirty from walking the streets looking for something that was fast-fading from everyone's memory. He would try to keep it alive in his. Otherwise … well, the old would be lost, no record of it. People were too obsessed with *now*. A match here too. Not just buildings, but music. You've got to educate people before it's all gone, show them what there is worth keeping, worth visiting, what makes a thing *unique*. He wished there was some way to record how it all was. Wished he could do that. In pictures. Or words.

Maybe the answer was staring him in the face. Why did the city want to kill him? Perhaps he was obsessed with the past and that made him part of it, to be covered over, replaced. People like him had no purpose here any more. Things moved on. He couldn't.

Nearby he saw a cobbled alleyway. That looked old. Less depressing. He headed that way. Then grinned. He was facing a battering at the least; had already nearly been knocked over; was definitely hung over; and was depressed about the city in a way he'd never encountered before. On the other hand, he was really enjoying wandering down roads he hadn't seen before, being a tourist in his own home. It was a fringe benefit to opening his eyes wider. You really did see so much more. Bad and good. As if humans couldn't do or be anything which wasn't a mix of the two.

He wondered how old the cobbles were. Jumped from one to another. Water ran from a broken pipe at the back of a building, made its way between the stones as a little set of criss-crossing rivers and he was a giant able to hop from hill to hill. For a few minutes he lost himself again. Like being a kid, playing on his own, with no one – family or otherwise – taking the mickey out of him.

Out of that shady alley to a main road again. Pavement speckled with spit and gum. Inverted detritus constellations.

Remember, eyes wider, up as well as down, see everything and make it all new.

He looked up at the sky, clear blue that seemed endless, like the sea (the one thing Manchester lacked, according to Ian Brown). The sun blazed from it, the source, heating this world. Puffs of warm breeze messed with his hair. Even his hay fever was easing off. Perfect.

He was thinking of getting another pint of beer when he saw the bird. A pigeon on the pavement outside McDonald's, huddled against a bin. There was a small dribble of dark blood behind it. He thought it was dead until he noticed its beak opening and closing. Gasping silently. Maybe it had been hit by a car. He looked through the window. People eating food in there stared back out at him. Gazes seemed blank, corpses in their mouths. They didn't see *him*. Didn't see anything.

He picked the bird up carefully and walked on with it. It wasn't heavy. He'd expected the weight of a chicken. It was warm. There was dried bird poo on top of its feathers. As his hands enfolded it he stroked it with his right thumb and whispered "It'll be all right" every few steps, or "Hush". It still gasped, as though calling, and its orange eyes stared straight ahead.

Denny would laugh at him. "Stupid bird." Mark didn't care. He wasn't thinking of himself. And that made him proud. It was an animal. But so was he. Hadn't Sam said that once?

"Shush. No one gonna catapult you over a wall. It'll be okay. No one gonna put drugs inside you. Or me. We're clean. Gonna die clean."

He knew where he was now. Shena Simon Park, next to the college. He walked past overflowing bins and people eating dinner on benches and students lay on the grass wherever there weren't dog turds, careful not to trip, until he reached a patch of scrawny bushes. He squatted and put the pigeon under their cover. The bird's left leg was bent back, its claws surprisingly big. There was dried blood under a toe. He stroked the bird's feathers and whispered to it; it shuddered twice more and then its head sank down and its lower eyelids rose up, half covering its eyes. He moved it further back into the shade, out of sight.

"It all ends too soon. I'm sorry," he whispered. At least it didn't die in the gutter with the McDonald's packaging and cars driving past. Mark noticed a bit of blood on his top. He sank to the grass. Had he made a difference? Life was like a book. You couldn't tell until you got to the end.

He was not far from Packham Green here. He couldn't escape even on a Saturday. As if he wasn't meant to. Work, that bastion of boredom. Palace of put-downs.

Sam's email.

Roger's smugness.

Pooey Roger.

Mark got up, careful of where he put his feet on the grass, a surge of anger in his veins.

Gets to be on the "cool" team? Gets the promotion? Has the best friends? Mark wasn't jealous, just annoyed.

Sam and Roger up a tree. K-I-S-S-I-N-G.

Okay. Maybe *some* jealousy. And the opposite at the same time. Now his eyes were open he didn't have any trouble seeing both sides, good and bad, new and old. Mark might be angry at Sam but he was also angry that Roger snarked her. What did he say? He'd "run the team properly"? The bumhole. And hadn't he called Mark "unimaginative"?

Oh, he had an imagination all right. Pretty much all he did have going for him.

There was a newsagent's nearby, where Mark bought NME during dinner breaks. The bell above the door jangled as he entered. Load up. Marker pen. Big padded envelope. Marathon bar (he refused to acknowledge the 'S' name on the wrapper, it was always a Marathon to him). Paid with the bulk of his change. He'd need to get some more money out. If luck smiled there was another tenner in his account before he was truly at the overdraft limit. He'd find out soon.

He headed back to the park, eating the chocolate. A pizza box poked out of the overflowing bin. He tore the lid off, ripped it in two. Sat on a bench. Used the marker pen and wrote on the envelope in caps to make it look more professional, as he did with all official forms.

ROGER GELDER, PACKHAM GREEN

CONFIDENTIAL

AND IMPORTANT

Nibbled the end of the pen. Added:

AND PRIVATE

Unimaginative, eh?

Then near the bushes. Didn't care who was watching. Squatted. Put the padded envelope between his legs, held it open with knee pressure. Using the two bits of cardboard as shovels he manoeuvred a large and moist dog turd onto one. As the harder skin flopped and broke it released an awful stomach-wrenching smell from the wetter insides. Mark grinned, impressed by its potency and glad he'd eaten first. Careful not to drop it on his leg, keeping his nose wrinkled, trying not to breathe, he let it slip wetly but neatly into the jiffy bag. Held back a retch. Tore off the sticky strip's covering and sealed the envelope tightly. Skid-marked pizza cardboard into the bin. Surprisingly heavy envelope in his hand.

He needed a name for this operation. Something formed from one of his favourite band's initials, for good luck.

Just Desserts?

Hound Muck?

Turd Vengeance?

Ah, no. The Stone Roses provided the answer. His plan was so bad – meaning good – that is deserved a little swear.

Off to Packham Green and through the letterbox. It fell with a heavy thud. He hoped he'd still be around to see Roger's face on Monday. He'd go blue.

The phone buzzed and Mark twitched guiltily. Looked up at the windows. No one there watching, texting, or filling a bucket with water.

`We know you are not at your home. I would strongly suggest you phone me. Your friend, Mr Connor.`

Ah. Not so good.

Mark heard it in Mr Connor's deep voice. It brought to mind his weight, his inevitability. Mark rubbed a forearm across his face. Ignoring this would be an action as much as replying would. Maybe a worse one. He typed.

`Sorry. I am out.`

Mark knew that there'd be a reply quickly, but it still made him vibrate sympathetically when it came.

`Tell me where you are.`

He could imagine the big fingers pressing keys. The serious gaze somewhere not too far away staring at another phone screen, waiting for Mark's response. Demanding it.

`I will. Later. Sorry about this. Mark`

He hoped that would be enough but the phone started ringing. Impossibly, it sounded more urgent than usual. Commanding. Mr Connor was trying to make a more direct connection with him, like his great shadow was cast over Mark at that very second.

Mark pressed cancel, despite the cold sweat as he realised it was an insult to Mr Connor.

It didn't ring again and he suddenly felt very alone. The happiness about Operation Shitpack Revengeance had pure faded. In the grand scheme of things it had been a childish bit of petty revenge when he should have been worrying about bigger things. Impulsive, too, his urges getting in the way of better judgement like they always did.

And, with a sinking feeling: *incriminating*. Operation SR was *in his own handwriting*. And there was no stamp or full address. It would convince no one. Look like an insider jobbie. There would be an investigation. It would start with the person who delivered the post.

He should have asked the newsagent to write on the envelope for him. He took the marker pen from his pocket, dropped it into the nearest bin like it was hot.

Oh, shitpack.

He was screwed. In every possible way.

Only one thing left to do. He dialled numbers on his phone. Cleared his throat. Noticed the battery was getting low since he'd failed to charge it last night.

"Hello?" the deep voice asked.

"It's Mark. I may be in a bit of trouble. Where are you, Dave?"

"Arndale, shopping with Suzannah. What do you mean, 'trouble'? How bad is it?"

"Remember what things were like when I found out Noel Gallagher had moved to London for good?"

"I'll meet you," he said quickly. Faint but audible bickering words with Suzannah ending in apologies from Dave, then he was back on the line. "Where are you?"

"Near work."

"Meet me in The Shakespeare. I can be there in twenty. Shall I get Ben too? His flat's not far from there."

"Okay. It would be good to see friendly faces."

"Just hang on. No problem's too big for The Musketeers."

Click.

There was a first time for everything.

Before heading to the meet, Mark checked his wallet and discovered a few measly coins. At the cash machine he said a prayer then requested a tenner. It came out. He read the slip in surprise and realised he'd made a mistake, he was not totally skint. Of course! Start of the month, he'd just been paid, and there was some left before he reached max overdraught again, even after the rent had gone out. It was like a bonus for being rubbish at finances. Although this was the money to see him through the month he was unlikely to need it later if he was going to either spend the time in a hospital or morgue. He drew out as much as he could and it went into his wallet, apart from the tenner he slipped into a different pocket. Denny's trick, to keep money in diverse places.

He headed over to The Shakespeare. Past Piccadilly Gardens again. It was as if he couldn't escape from the city centre, a giant concrete magnet. Work. Leisure. Being on the run. His whole life pulled back to the same people and places. So-called Piccadilly Gardens, anyway. Since when was concrete a flower? There was no green at all any more. He remembered a few years ago when it was flower beds, grass, bushes, and a fountain; a real garden before the council paved it all over. He'd heard rumours they were gonna put some grass on top, but it would never be the same, would still just be bits of soil on top of concrete. They'd buried the past like murderous gangsters (Mancsters?), nowt to go back to, no evidence. He remembered something Morrissey had sung on The Smiths' first album. "Manchester, so much to answer for."

As he walked along he got another text. Denny this time. All nice, like.

`get in touch, all sorted now. let me now where U R. its safe.`

Calm words held more menace than Denny's swearing.

The Metro rails were grooves in the ground, full of cigarette dimps like metal-edged ashtrays. He followed the tram tracks. Parallel grooves in the road that seem to come together in the distance. But you know they never meet. Like him and Denny. There was no point wishing for things that couldn't be. Move on.

He soon reached The Shakespeare, just off the main drag to the Arndale. Black and white wood and flower baskets outside. Little painted people above the door. Midgets from old stories. He went in and crossed the studded wooden floor. They were waiting for him in the room to the right. Three pints on a table sticky with drink rings, so he could join them straight off.

"Hi mates," he said as he took a seat and accepted the pint Ben slid towards him.

The pub was proper *olde school.* Curtained leaded windows, diamonds of glass, matching black-framed lights. Dark wood panels. This side room had a big fireplace and decorated mantelpiece. Heavy beams and diamonds against white. They sure liked their diamond shapes in the olden days. Tudor, Dave had taught him on a previous visit.

"Thanks for meeting me. Means a lot. And the drink. And sorry for ruining your shopping, Dave."

"No problem, glad of the excuse to get away. If it was buying sexy underwear for Suzannah I'd be pissed off, but she was buying shoes ... supposedly. Shop after shop, just trying them on. The first pair looked okay. I told her that."

"You too, Ben. You were probably getting ready for a Saturday night date or something?"

He looked embarrassed. "Well, not this time… I got a PlayStation 2 imported from Japan, it arrived this morning. Cost me a fortune, but I couldn't be arsed waiting until November. Set it up on the big telly in my bedroom. Been on it all day."

"I see Mark isn't the only saddo in our triumvirate," Dave said. "Always gotta have technology first, eh?"

"You know me. But I'm meeting Emily tomorrow night." He stretched his arms out, shook his wrist, and yawned. "I should be bored of Ridge Racer V by then."

Glasses raised, cheers said, beer swigged.

"Okay, business. What's up, Hop?" Dave asked.

"Ah. I was in a funny mood before."

"And?"

"I put a dog turd in a jiffy bag and wrote Roger's name on it. Then posted it through the work letterbox."

"No!" Ben said, eyebrows raised.

"Don't believe you!" Dave added.

"Wouldn't lie about this. I called it Operation Shitpack Revengeance."

They both burst out laughing, lager sprayed out like an alcoholic water sprinkler.

"Holy fuckola!"said Ben, slapping the table.

Mark noticed annoyed glances from the blokes on the next table. Scallies in baseball caps and dirty Kappa jackets.

"I think I must be losing it. I did the shitpack thing and was only partly drunk. It's a bit funny," – which set them laughing again – "but I'll probably lose my job. It's obvious who wrote it."

"No," Dave said, controlling himself. "Easy. Whichever one of us does the post Monday puts it in the bin. No one'll know. Though it seems a shame: I'd love to see Gel Head's face if he opened that."

Holy crap-pack. He was right. "Why didn't I think of that?"

Ben slapped Dave on the back. "That's why Dave is the brains in our outfit. We're just the lookers."

"So, problems solved, eh? Not that bad," said Dave. "Or was it something else? It sounded worse on the phone."

Mark thought about the other issue but still couldn't tell the full tangled truth. Certainly not the drugs angle, anyway. It would hurt Dave, lose his respect. Just thinking about how far it had gone made Mark ashamed. No, best to keep their good opinion. Especially if they were the last people to remember him.

"Just a problem with Denny. He's after me."

"What for?"

"A misunderstanding. He thinks I've let him down."

"I could help," Dave said, cracking his knuckles. "I'd be glad to have words with him."

Oh, Dave. There was no easy answer. Mark didn't want to pull them in, risk them being hurt. They could get on with their safe, happy, normal lives. Dave would marry Suzannah. Ben would … whatever.

"No, it'll be fine. I'm glad you offered though. Just to know I have friends."

"You shouldn't doubt it," said Ben.

"Even if we're the only ones you know," Dave added, "You're a good bloke. You can do stuff. I trust you to do the right thing, and you can't say that about many people nowadays."

"Ditto," said Ben.

"Thanks. It means a lot 'cos you both said it." Wasn't diamond the hardest material, most reliable? If so Dave was a diamond bloke. He even went to the bar to get them all another pint.

The conversation of the bunch of scallies on the next table filled the temporary silence. They seemed to be talking about guns; half-heard phrases in their Salford accents about someone being "done in" and "twatted" made Ben frown, uncomfortable. Mark wasn't sure if what he was overhearing was real or just for show.

When Dave got back he asked if that was the extent of it, all his worries.

"Yes. It doesn't seem so bad now I have a handle on it." And was getting tanked up with booze again. "It's like I'm cut free, man. Floating."

"Stop drinking then."

"No. I mean from my family. Done with 'em."

"It's about time. You've got us."

"Yes. Like brothers."

"Ha ha," said Ben. "First white guy who's my brother."

"We're all the same inside," said Mark.

They finished their drinks. Dave had to get back to Suzannah. A good time to call it a day. Mark suspected the aura of nastiness from the next table was a factor too. They weren't as used to it as Mark was.

Once they were outside Dave seemed reluctant to leave and suddenly gave Mark a clumsy hug. Ben followed suit, both clasping him at the same time, Hopton Sandwich. This was a new one. They faced each other, grinning sheepishly.

"Musketeers," said Ben, feigning a sword thrust.

"Yeah. All three. Now go," Mark replied. "I'll be fine. And look after Suzannah. And Emily. You're both lucky, being in love."

"You're acting like this is goodbye," said Dave. "We'll see you on Monday. Don't worry."

"Right."

"We're your friends," added Ben.

"Yeah. You are." With a cold weight in his gut, Mark felt certain he'd never see them again. But in another way it felt good. By keeping the worst to himself he was protecting them. He'd never had anything to protect before today. Let go of something when you're about to fall so you don't break it. He'd had to lie to them. They weren't gangsters, any more than he was.

The scallies in the pub, on the other hand…

Once Dave and Ben were out of sight Mark went back inside.

Be positive. Focus on the good feeling about the scallies. The Happy Mondays were from Salford. Joy Division and New Order were. As was Tim Burgess, Mark E. Smith, Tony Wilson … and Mark.

So they were sort of like family. Focus on that, rather than the scary talk.

He walked up to the four of them.

"Hi," he said, interrupting their sweary banter.

The frowning faces didn't look welcoming. They were all younger than him.

"Fuck off," said one with a gold chain outside his jumper. His baseball cap was offset.

"I wanted to talk about business."

"Oh yeah?" asked one with adolescent pimples and wiry facial hair.

"I overheard you talking." Mark stood there, feeling self-conscious under their aggressive stares. "I wondered if you know anyone who offers protection."

They looked at each other, as if puzzled.

"What do you mean?" asked gold chain. "What kind of protection?"

"Someone's after me. I don't want that person hurt but I want to make sure they don't get to me. So I want someone to keep an eye out for me, I suppose, or – I dunno – watch my flat or something. I can pay."

They looked at each other again. Some subtle communication went on.

"Okay, sure, we can help," said the one with spots. "But we can't talk here, let's go out. The owner don't like us doing protection business inside."

Mark nodded. They finished their drinks. One in a hoodie wiped his mouth on a sleeve. Mark led the way. Once they were outside they glanced around, and one of them tilted his head. The sound of the main thoroughfare faded as he followed them to the back of the pub, into a quiet courtyard of wheelie bins and traffic cones, next to a spiky fence enclosing an electricity substation that sat knee-deep in litter. "Danger of Death. Keep out," the sign warned.

Enough privacy for a deal, definitely.

"Tell us again," said the one with the gold chain. He was smirking. Mark repeated his request for help, explaining that his brother or some other guys might turn up, and he wanted them to be scared off. As he spoke he realised he hadn't thought it out fully, but he felt he was doing okay. "Do you know anyone who could do that?"

"We can do it," he was told. "It's in our line of work."

"Cool."

"Gi' us fifty quid and we'll watch your place for a few days. It's pretty straightforward."

Mark counted out the notes, handed them over reluctantly but also with rekindled hope.

"Now we need your address," said the spotty one, and the others nodded. "So we know where to watch."

Mark told them where he lived. One of them seemed to know the area. Typed something into his phone.

"Are we all done?"

"Not yet," said the gold chain scallie. "We need a key to your flat."

"No you don't."

"Sure we do. So we can maybe spring a surprise on your bruvva."

"No, that's not what I need. I just want you to watch the outside of it."

"Hey, we know what we're fucking doing."

"I've only got the one key."

"Yeah, well you can get another cut in the Arndale can't you?"

"I don't like this. Forget it, give me the money back and I'll sort something else out."

"We don't do refunds."

"You're messin' us about, wasting our time now," said the spotty one. "You can give us a bit extra for that, right lads? Pass us your wallet."

Mark said no, turned to leave, but they were barring his way.

"Don't piss us off," said the one in a hoodie. He took a pen knife out of his pocket. Opened it slowly. Mark couldn't take his eye off it. "Now pass us your fuckin' wallet, you chump."

Great. Cornered. He couldn't get past all four of them. He looked up – so many windows, all faceless. No one to help. Where were people with buckets of water when you needed them? If he shouted he couldn't imagine anyone would come. Well, not until he was lay on the floor, bleeding. Even if someone came, who'd tackle a gang with a knife?

You were always a stupid cunt.

Those words passed through his head in his dad's voice. And he agreed. He'd walked right into this one. He didn't want to fight, get stabbed down this alley. Now the reality of the blade was being waved in his face it didn't seem like an option at all. One of the other lads had his hand in a pocket and kept looking round shiftily. Probably another knife carrier.

Mark sighed. Handed everything over. He wished he hadn't given his real address. The one in the gold chain took the cards and money from Mark's wallet then dropped it through the slits in a grid. It sploshed into the water below. The knife was trained on him all the time.

"Oh, and your fucking phone."

"Leave me with something?"

The knife flashed forward, just missing his face, and he flinched back. They were jumpy, as if this was taking too long. What the hell. If he could get out of this without any perforations then it was worth it. He handed over the phone.

"Cheers man. We'll be seeing you." They left, laughing and jostling each other.

Well done, Mark. You've just screwed up even more. The Salford scummers have a house key and know where you live. It was another group that could hospitalise him if they caught him coming home.

More likely was that by the time he got home there'd be nothing left.

He plodded up the alleyway to the main pedestrian route down to the Arndale. Africans on little stalls were selling bubble guns and handbags.

It's common knowledge that Salford has no centre. Well, it has no heart, neither.

There was a plus side. At least they had the phone. Let them deal with texts from gangsters. Even better, let them all turn up at his flat at once. Everyone who was after him could kick the stuffing out of each other. Maybe they'd be satisfied then.

He was running out of options and time but he still had a tenner in his pocket.

A drink. To think. He could spare two quid for that.

He crossed Piccadilly yet again. Was getting sick of it now. It must be getting on for tea time, the crowds were busier, he had to use his city sense to flow with the right groups, dodge casually between people, all without catching anyone's eye. Faces passed, staring ahead, that feeling of urgency spreading like a pheromone gas cloud. It sucked you in, telling you what to do. *Copy the others.* Normally he did. Not today though. He resisted the urge. Stopped, letting people flow around *him* for once. Aware that people saw him as a blockage, that he was *breaking the rules*, but he hardly cared any more. He was changing. Maybe it was too late, but the process was good to experience anyway.

A woman pulling a suitcase on wheels. She was Stefania. Came from Poland to visit her family.

A group of teenagers laughing at something on a phone. They had met up for an afternoon of bonding in the Arndale and were on their way back to Sale.

A man in a suit, but wearing trainers. He was called Jed McPast. Scottish, and he liked to go fast.

Once you stopped you saw people properly. Could imagine the stories of their lives, distractions from your own. They were all going somewhere.

Then out of the corner of his eye he saw someone who looked like his dad. He felt like he'd been caught nicking toys from the post office, and on reflex he turned his head with hunched shoulders ready to receive a boxed ear. But it was just a craggy tramp with a carrier bag and a grey coat. Like a spectre, he faded away into the crowd again.

Yeah, a drink would be good, right about now. And a seedy bar always made a good chill out room for the soul.

He crossed the rest of Piccadilly and reached the Brittania Hotel. There was a bar underneath it, a cheesy disco-type place called Kicks, which he sometimes visited if he was waiting for the bus. It was half sunk into the basement below ground level but you could see when the 256 passed if you sat by a window and pretended you were a meerkat.

He was using his newfound powers and looking up, instead of down. Take it all in on this last day in the city. It was an impressive building. A huge old cotton warehouse with a pillared entrance. Looking way up above street level you could see carvings on top of each arch – crowned women, sheep, the fronts of boats, naked angels with baskets on their heads, entwined plants. Something to do with the city's trading past, stamped into the stone itself. Geometric shapes were carved into the building too: circles, triangles. And diamonds. Again. Noble but fading, like the last light.

He went down the steps.

Mark sat on a wobbly stool at the bar. The barman was muscly. Tanned, like he'd been abroad, somewhere hot and exotic. He had a short-sleeved shirt on and tattoos up his forearms. He was chatting up a woman who wore lots of make-up and fluorescent plastic jewellery: she felt his biceps and giggled. Otherwise the place was empty.

Music played, cheesy retro. Mark receded into himself as he drank. Listening to the *interior* music. Down inside him, below the thumping surface tune was something bass, deeper, darker. A subterranean mosh pit. But he was the only one dancing. It was just like his cold, empty flat where he put music on to chase away the ghosts.

This was no good. He was tired of being lonely. If everyone had stories, everyone was interesting. And if you talked to people, you were *never* alone.

"Can I have another pint please?"

"Sure," the barman said. "Same?"

"Yes. And can I get you one?"

"Me?"

"That's okay isn't it? One for you. Another for your girlfriend." Mark smiled at her. He would still have two quid left. Enough for a bus fare somewhere.

"Her? She's not my girlfriend!"

"What do you mean by that?" she asked, looking like she'd been slapped. Her voice had a screechy quality to it when it wasn't being whispered.

"Only fun, right?" he said.

"Only fun?" The woman approached him. "Fuck you, Russell!" She threw the rest of her drink into his face. A few drops splashed onto Mark's sleeve when he didn't move out of the way in time. She strode out.

Russell looked shocked. Comical, as the liquid dripped off his face like sweat from a super-workout, wetting his shirt at the front. He muttered something that sounded like, "Not again."

Mark couldn't help it. Started laughing. Pointed at the drips.

Russell didn't seem to get the joke. "Don't laugh," he said aggressively, planting his fists on the bar in front of Mark.

"But it's funny!"

"Oh yeah?" Russell Muscleman grabbed Mark's shirt front and pulled him half over the bar until their foreheads touched. Mark got a good look at the tattoos. They were nice work. Tribal pattern swirls, a big red bird, and a panther.

"You fucking take that back," Russell growled.

Mark knew what his dad or Denny would do in this situation, based on past lectures. A quick headbutt to the guy's nose. He wouldn't expect that. Crunch it in, then smash the pint glass over his head, and run out before he recovered. He felt the tenseness of the situation, adrenaline running, everything slowed to that knife edge of violence that got some people so excited… And it collapsed. This was just a guy. Things don't have to be that way. He could make his own, more peaceful standards.

"I'm sorry," he said. "Ignore me, I'm acting like a todger."

He could hear the imagined insults from Denny and his dad, calling him a pussy, but he could now shut them out without having to play music loud. All the macho crap, fighting and being cool, and hiding emotions – testicles! Do bad stuff, it makes more bad stuff. But do good stuff … well, love spreads, doesn't it? Being able to think like that proved something. He really didn't have any Hopton DNA in him. His family was gone. That left a gap, and nothing to fill it with, but maybe it wasn't such a loss really. Because it meant he was free. No connections any more, to anything. He might not last long, but it felt good right now. Mark smiled at Russell.

"Eh?" The grip hadn't loosened.

"I'm not laughing *at* you. Just at life. So unpredictable. I'm learning to see the funny side."

"What funny side?"

"People told me this would be a year of change. There were parties to celebrate it, weren't there? I didn't understand why it was different. I do now. It's the only one with so many nothings in it. Three of them, following a huge number two. That's my life, innit?"

Russell loosened his grip a bit. Mark picked up his pint glass, then in a swift movement poured the dregs onto his own head.

Russell looked at him, wide eyed, then let him go. Mark slipped back into his seat.

They both started laughing.

"'A huge number two.' I like that."

"You wouldn't if you had to live in it like I do."

Russell handed him a creamy yellow Boddington's bar towel, got another for himself, wiped down his face. Mark rubbed his hair, wondering how stinky it would be, and whether he'd end up with some kind of short, kinky afro.

"You still want another drink?" Russell asked.

"Yep. And your own."

"Don't mind if I do."

Mark looked out through the windows of the bar while Russell poured. You could only see people's legs as they walked past. Endless legs.

"Cheers," Russell said, plonking a pint in front of Mark and raising his own.

Two couples entered and Russell served them, joking and trying to persuade them to have cocktails. They took their drinks to one of the side tables.

It was weird. Today Mark kept drinking, but couldn't get drunk. Maybe it was another power he was developing.

"I like this song," Russell said when he rejoined Mark. It was Roxy Music, "Love is the Drug". Russell sang a few words, gave a little dance.

"Catchy."

"Clever too. The love/drug thing."

"Maybe. I've never had enough to get addicted."

"They'll be gettin' the violins out soon. Man up!"
"I'm not complaining."
"And it's all just about sex really anyway, isn't it?"
"Not all of it."
Roxy Music
"It is." He extended the 'is'.
"No. There's other stuff."
"But that's what it boils down to. Nobbing." Russell grabbed the end of the bar and did a few pelvic thrusts, grimacing comically. "That's what I'm talking about." One of the women looked over and smirked. Russell didn't seem to notice.
"No! Love is ..."
Bryan Ferry
Mark shook his head, bemused.
"What?" asked Russell.
"Wanting someone to be part of your life."
"That's it?"
"That's it. And it's love even if you don't realise it at first."
"Soppy shit."
"Look at it this way. Sex is easy to get. So it's not soppy to go after something rarer. That's the catch with life. Anything that's worth something is hard to get hold of. It doesn't matter if it's diamonds, or a rare promo single, or feelings. The same."
"It's hard to hold on to…" There was a wistful look in Russell's eyes, as if he was remembering something. He wiped his face, maybe a bit of drink he'd missed. Then shook his head. "So you're some kind of philosopher?"
"No. Just not bad for an idiot."
"You had a fallout with a girl?"
"No. It didn't get that far."
"You sound bitter though."
"I'm not. Bitter sweet, maybe. A symphony where someone yanks the needle off before it gets proper started." He sipped his drink. Decided it wasn't as nice as shandy. "It's a shame things didn't work out, but I'm not angry. Life moves on. Anger is a dead end. Fool's gold. I don't want to be that kind of person."
"What was she like?"

Mark closed his eyes and thought for a few seconds. "A summer storm. An amazing sunrise. The only special thing I could see."

"She musta been weird. But I miss my exes sometimes. You look back, don't you, and think: shit, she was something! Shoulda made more effort with that one! Too late though. Always too late you get a knock on the head. And people always fall in love with someone they shouldn't."

"Now it's your turn to cry *me* a river."

Briton Ferry

They both laughed again. Mark liked this bloke. If he had more than a few pound coins he'd hire him as a bodyguard.

On second thoughts, that plan didn't work out too well last time.

It got him thinking though. Mark had felt like his life all went downhill a few weeks ago, but he realised now that it had been going downhill for a lot longer. He couldn't blame Sam for that.

She did hurt him though. She never contacted him, just laughed about him. *Used* him, in a way. And he'd never had the chance to have his say. Nothing nasty, but just to say how he felt.

It suddenly struck him – he'd made a connection with pretty much everyone he knew in the last 24 hours. Made peace or screwed up with each of them. All but Sam. *You've got to make your peace and move on.* Like you do at a funeral. There was a weird certainty in him, that this was his last day here. He couldn't see anything apart from blackness for tomorrow.

"What time is it?" he asked Russell, who pointed to a clock on the wall.

Nearly tea time. He'd pretty much memorised her email. It had said she was going to be in The Temple of Convenience tonight, then get a train back. Maybe things had changed, but he had nothing better to do. If she was catching a train to Wales he imagined she couldn't stay in the pub too late. It was worth a shot. He could at least get his word in. The final chance.

Don't hold grudges: always be bigger than that.

He downed the last of his pint. "Got to go," he said. "Take it easy, mate."

"You're a good bloke," Russell told him. "I think everything will go okay for you."

"Thanks. I need all the good wishes I can get."

Mark headed towards the door, but had forgotten about a step near the bar. He tripped and nearly fell, managing to grab hold of a table just in time. Looked at Russell, who shook his head slowly.

But he was still on his feet. Not bad for a lanky git. He took a deep breath and ascended back up to the road.

He knew where The Temple of Convenience was, of course, but didn't take the direct route. It only added a couple minutes more to come out lower down on Oxford Road. Say goodbye to something else. He zigzagged briskly down roads, slightly wobbly on his legs. Saw some bollards, tilted from collisions. He knew how they felt. Groups of people were wandering around, singing and laughing and shouting. It was the transition time before it switched from shopping city to evening city.

"Hey there, our kid."

Mark spun in surprise to see Bazzy in a green parka that was obviously fashion rather than practical in the heat of the summer, hands in pockets.

"Sweet potatoes! Don't do that. Whenever you appear from nowhere I think it's Denny at first."

"Are you twisting my melons? He's a thug. I'm a happy twenty-five hour party person that exists for music and love."

"It's the voice. Similar, just less angry."

"Like you wish he was. I get it."

"And it's twenty-four hours in a day."

"I play harder than everyone else."

They crossed the road in a moment without traffic, their footsteps in sync.

"I told you to stay put," Bazzy said, squinting at him.

"But to be ready to move. I followed your advice. *All* of it." Mark pointed to his shades, filtering out the rays of the lowering sun.

"Good. You did fine. What's our plan?"

"Say bye to everyone and tie up loose ends."

Bazzy nodded, apparently satisfied. They'd reached Whitworth Street West and stopped. Mark could spare a few seconds for a last glance up that road.

You've got to go back to causes, foundations. Then you understand a thing properly.

"You can't see The Haçienda from here," Bazzy said.

"I can see it in my mind. See round the bend. It's still boarded up and waiting for me at the end of the road."

"You know, though, right? The truth?"

"Yeah." Mark gazed in the direction, saw the empty building in his mind's eye, brick for brick. "It's never coming back, is it?"

Bazzy shook his head.

Mark continued. "I've been holding on for nowt. It's all gone. The good stuff. I'm here just out of habit. If roads lead everywhere, then really they lead nowhere."

Bazzy rested a hand on Mark's shoulder. It was a light pressure. Felt good. "You're not *nowhere*. End of a journey, maybe. But you're *now here*." Then the hand slipped off and Mark turned to him.

"Weren't you meant to get me some help?"

"Not *help* as such. Been talkin'. Friends knew about you. Told me the future."

"And?"

"And told me not to interfere."

"You really know the future?"

A nod.

"I always assumed you were magic or something."

"Well, I am that."

"Is mine painful?"

Sad smile. "Can't tell you, our kid. It's the Cassandra curse all over. Know but can't communicate it. Bloody curses! You'd think we'd have got rid of them in this day and age, eh? Reality sucks."

Mark looked up at the nearly clear sky. Sighed. "But you're not real."

"I know that. Not even convincing. A caricature. Kathy Burke's impersonation in the flesh."

"You're not in the flesh."

"Details. Whatever."

"I wish you *were* real."

"Not me. I'm happier like this. The world's too fucked up. Just wanted to say goodbye."

"So, any advice you *can* give?"
"Time for you to live fully in the real world."
"Great. Anything else?"
"Go wild. Give in to your imagination."
"I haven't got one."
"Oh yeah? How come you're talking to me here while I'm doing a fucking gig in Spain, you prat?"
"I suppose. Still not great advice."
"All I've got. Oh no, one more: no more drinkin', eh?"
"Okay."
"Good lad."
"You not going to see me again?"
"Nah. Comes a time you gotta choose between reality and fantasy."
"Fantasy."
"Wrong answer. Look, Mark, you don't need me any more, you can stand on your own feet. Well, when you're sober, anyway."
"But you've been with me for years. I remember now. You looked different but you're the one I used to see when I was a kid and things were bad. And that time at school. And a few years ago. You keep changing but it's *you*. Always there at the worst times."
"Yeah. But you're stronger now. Got real friends." Pause. "Sorta."
"Well, thanks. I guess. For being around as long as you were."
Bazzy scuffed the tip of his trainer against the pavement, a child-like gesture. "Just … I can't help you any more. Not where you're goin'. So … you know. Be brave about it. Whatever happens. Look, I gotta go, our kid."
"You've always gotta go. Too soon."
"Sorry. Meeting Bernie Hookmarrsy, jam session. The world's gonna vibrate like a fuckin' jelly to our bass grooves."
Mark gave Bazzy a quick hug. The fur of the hood tickled his nose.
"Take care, bro," Bazzy said, separating himself.
"Wish you were."
Bazzy smiled, enigmatic. "I love ya." Then he turned and walked off in the direction of The Haçienda, that confident saunter of his, shoulders back like he owned the world, could do anything, a free spirit that defied gravity. Mark would try to emulate that. Live up to it.

"Bye," he muttered; then added, "brother," as an afterthought while people passed him, occasionally blocked his view. It didn't matter. He'd had his last dance. Bye to all ghostly dreams that would never be real enough to make a difference.

He walked on quickly, dwarfed by seven and eight storey buildings. They were sturdy. They'd existed donkey's years. Mark's time was short. After Sam he would go to the arches, see if anyone was still there. He suspected it wouldn't be empty, but even if it was he could use a payphone, ring Denny, get him to come and to contact the others. Mark could face whatever came next. He felt that he was strong enough now. But he wanted to sort out all his business first. Just in case. Which is why he stared at the canopy above the Temple of Convenience.

The unknown. He'd never been in. Always eyed it with suspicion, those gated steps leading down under the street. He liked to look into a bar through the window first, see what it was like, how ugly or friendly the crowd was, whether there was a jukebox, whether or not a wall was dominated with big TVs showing stupid football.

Maybe she wouldn't be there? That might be easier. He'd been angry when she let him down. How many times recently had he fantasised about seeing her again, then telling her to sod off?

Mark hesitated.

This was stupid.

He took one step away. Stopped.

Calm down, Mark. Treat it like the music it is. Just play it by ear.

Music. Filtering up the stairs with the voices. Oasis. Manchester music. A good sign. He could do this. He could Acquiesce too. He took a deep breath, then headed down, down, down.

Sam looked at her watch. "I've got to go."

"Aw, stay a bit longer," Em pleaded, opening her eyes wide like a puppy. "You said there was another one in an hour?"

"But if I catch the 6.30 it's direct. I hate making changes."

Sam picked up her bag and noticed someone through a gap in the crowd. They were looking around uncertainly, hands thrust into pockets, arms straight. On instinct she went to raise her hand and call Mark's name, caught herself, and just sat dumbstruck until she realised

Em was speaking to her. All she could focus on was the lurch of anger in her stomach on seeing him. He looked good. Slim, casually dressed, quiet, shades on, hair mussed like he was just out of bed, a look she'd seen once before. Déjà vu. Yes, even the top was the same as that night.

Okay, not just anger or repulsion. It was a bittersweet concoction of hatred and attraction she thought had dissipated.

They stared at each other for a few moments, as if neither knew what to do. He only noticed that she was sat with Emily when the latter spotted him and rolled her eyes.

"Hi," he said.

Neither of them responded.

"I've never been in here," he told them.

"What do you want?" Em asked.

"Just a word. With Sam." Then he quickly added, "Please."

"I've got to catch a train," Sam told him.

"Can I walk you?"

"I don't think that's a good idea."

He nodded. Looked around. "I just crossed all of town to catch you."

"How'd you know she was here?"

It had been Emily's question but he replied to Sam. "You told Roger."

"What, and he told you?"

"I sort of overheard. I didn't know if you'd be here or not, but thought it was worth a shot."

"Why?"

"I just want to talk. It's important to me. I won't bother you again."

"You're being creepy," Emily told him. "Best run along and join your boys."

"No," Sam said. "He can walk me."

"But *I* was going to!" Emily whined.

Sam put a hand on Emily's. "I'll be seeing you soon." Emily looked like she wanted to put up a fight, but then nodded reluctantly. Hugged Sam. Gave Mark a glare of shivs.

"Don't be a dick," she whispered to him as she left, nudging him slightly on the way past.

He sat in Emily's seat.

"How are you?" he asked.

"Good. You?"

"Good enough."

He looked at his hands. Playing it by ear was fine in principle. Except he then remembered he had no musical talent. Only obsession with those who did.

"I really do have to go," she prompted, standing,

He nodded, gestured for her to lead, followed her up the steps giving him seconds to think. Seconds that were wasted once he noticed her legs, in a dark skirt, ascending ahead of him; he looked away quickly but – images of her legs bare, being able to touch them, he wanted to touch, not the thoughts he should be thinking… The music faded, swapped for traffic; mysterious darkness with sharp daylight; the fantasy with the reality. There was nothing that could big up his words. No magical backdrop. No excess of alcohol. Just whatever he came up with. Just words: air and clumsy sounds that filled the space between actions.

A further sinking feeling as he realised that in a few minutes it would all be over and he'd be walking to the arches, probably feeling bitter. No, got to get it across. Got to say *stuff.* Tell her how bad she is.

She didn't wait. He had to do stride to catch up.

"How are things going? In Wales?"

"Good."

"Job better than here then?"

"It's a different world. Uncle Joe's the best. He's the one that owns the phone shop."

"Wow. Nice family."

"They all are."

"Where are you staying?"

"I've got a house. It was my gran's."

"Is she dead?"

"What do you think?" she asked, irritated.

"Well, she could have just bought a bigger one."

Sam rolled her eyes.

"Were you close?"
"All my family are. What are you getting at?"
"I'm just being polite."
"Why?" She stopped. They were opposite the Odeon. Red lettering told him he was facing The Perfect Storm unless he performed a Chicken Run. Boys And Girls on screen 3.
"Just finding out! I didn't know any of this, did I? Since I got no *email* off you. It means I know sweet fig all. I just wanted to get an idea of what life's like. *Your life*. Didn't know it was a crime."
"It's not a crime."
"Just a crime to know me."
"What?"
"Well, I'm not cool. Not like your friends. Just something embarrassing. 'High spirits'."
He saw confusion on her face.
"I read an email you sent to Roger. Pretty figging dismissive."
She blushed with realisation. Ah, now he had her.
"He showed you my emails?"
"No, I read it when he wasn't looking. Yeah yeah, such a sneaky sod. But when you say you'll be in touch then don't I'm bound to be curious. I wanted to know why you were treating me like something on the pavement."
"Me treat *you* like shit! That's fucking rich!"
People had to pass on each side of them as they stood in the middle of the path almost shouting at each other.
"What did I do? Pick up a fork with the wrong hand? Forget to say 'please milady' every time I kissed you? I practically treated you like a princess."
"You bastard." She turned, started walking briskly away. He wasn
going to follow her. She was nuts. Let her go.
"Do you turn on everyone?" he yelled after her. "Or just the [illegible]es who trust you?"
She spun round, stormed back to him.
She's going to slap me.
"You fucking two-faced liar!" She looked furious. "I he[illegible]ou!"
"Heard me what?"

“Overheard you slag me off in work. If you're going to accuse me of shit then I'm pretty sure this excuses me.”

Now it was his turn to be confused.

“4 am test?” she added.

4 am? He didn't … what she meant … test …. then guilt as it started to make sense. Things clicked.

Sweet potatoes. Holy pumpkins.

Holy shit.

His face was burning.

“I was trying to put them off. So they didn't rib me about you again. I never meant it!”

“Not good enough.”

“Sam, I'm really sorry. I don't tell them *anything*. But they'd been working out – I didn't…”

“Working out what?”

“I knew someone like you wouldn't be interested in someone like me.”

“And?”

“I couldn't stand it if they started that rumour, me fancying you. I know what it's like. What would have happened. Emily making jokes with the others. Roger looking smug, coming over and laughing at me being common or thick. And you'd hear about it, and would be too embarrassed to talk to me again, because everyone would be laughing behind their hands, so you'd have cut me off, and that would be it. No more chats. No more time with you. Weigh all that up! There seemed no harm in lying to *them*; I couldn't face all that. You *know* that's what it's like. I wanted to keep at least something.”

“So you hurt me to keep face and make things easy on yourself?”

“No, I meant keeping you as a friend. And I'm sorry, because if I'd
known you *were* there I wouldn't have said it. Don't know *what* I would
h[…] said, but I couldn't have said you weren't fit. I lied to others,
ye[…] but never to you. *Never.*”

[…] you didn't mean it.”

“No[…] I fig!” She didn't seem to know what he meant so he added,

“I[…]

[…]me to Roger then,” she said, at normal volume. “Oh,
stupid[…]

"And I'm sorry. Can we forget it ever happened? Just let the past end up even, or something? I really don't wanna say goodbye with bad feeling."

"Me neither. Let's not mention it again. Or think about it."

"I wish I could. I feel bad. Worse than anything today made me feel. But I'll try."

She looked at her watch. "I'd best get moving. Are you still going to walk me there?"

"Unless you tell me not to."

"Come on. Have to go faster." She started walking. Back to normality, back to the flow of people, back to time pressures for both of them.

"Want me to take your bag?"

"No, weighs hardly anything. Thanks."

It was quite a pace. They reached Saint Peter's Square. Beyond the Metro stop, Manchester town hall bracketed the massive, round city library.

"I should've gone the other way. Whitworth Street," she said with a tightening of the face.

"Yeah. Lots quicker.

"Shit! Am I going to make the 6.30?"

"If you keep up this pace you'll get to Wales by then."

She grinned. That was something.

They continued in the direction of Piccadilly Gardens – *again!* – down this road which Mark rarely walked because it seemed to be all banks and art galleries. He didn't have enough money for the first or brains for the second.

"You said you were having a bad day?" she asked as they waited to cross a road.

"You could say that. It's been a bit weird."

"Like what?"

"I sent Roger a shitpack."

The lights changed.

"A *what*?"

"I was annoyed at him. I'd had a drink or three. I ended up putting a dog turd in a Jiffy bag addressed to him. Popped it through the works letterbox."

"No!"

"Yes. I don't know why I just told you that when I know you're friends." He scratched his head. "I always screw up."

"That's brilliant! Tell me again!"

He was surprised at her laughter but repeated the story. Added the bit about the pizza box, but the details of turd transfer to the envelope made her look ill.

"He's not really my friend any more. He's a creep," she told him.

"Ah. I almost feel sorry for him now."

"Don't. That's great though. I love it. A good day, not a bad one!"

"Well, that's just part of it. I got mugged earlier too."

She stopped. "Mugged?"

"Yeah. Guys from Salford. Took my money. Pretty much my pay for the month. My phone too. Oh, and my flat keys. And they know where I live. Probably robbing it now. All I've got left is what you see. Not all bad though, since they didn't stab me in the end."

"That's awful!"

"I thought so too."

"Seriously, this is really horrible. Have you told the police?"

"No point. To be honest, it's not the biggest thing on my mind. But it is something, I suppose. Serious mess. I mean, I've got nothing. I can't go back to my flat. No money, no phone. Probably no job after the dog dirt incident."

"You seem so calm about it. That northern laid-back understatement thing. That's it: you're a proper northern soul."

"Thanks."

"Well, on the bright side, I can do you a good deal on a phone."

"What'll I pay with? Dog poo?"

They both started laughing. But Sam stopped first, and told him, "It sounds like there's more."

He was about to shrug, then over-rode his instinct. "Don't worry. It's just life. I'll deal with it."

"I kind of *am* worried." She looked at her watch. "It's getting tight for time."

"Yes. We'll need to jog a bit."

"I don't mean that. I meant I'll just catch the next train. It's not a problem. Just have to change at Newport, get home a bit later. I want to know more. We could sit somewhere."

"Do you want another drink? There's a bar round the corner."

"I was on lemonade."

"How come?"

"Just changing my life. Cut down on cigarettes and alcohol."

"Wow. That's sweet. I'm impressed. I've been doing that too. I was doing well up until last night."

"What happened?"

"I hit the bottom."

"I've been there. It gets better."

"I'd like to believe you."

"We need to talk, but – coffee!"

They were near the Piccadilly coffee shop he'd visited with her once before. Approached it again. He had enough for two coffees, insisted it was his treat; had to insist again, more firmly, before her protests subsided.

"Two Americans," he said proudly to the man behind the counter. "In pottery cups."

They sat at a different table but it was still a magnet to memories of that Saturday. Time was reset, just for a while. A morning swapped for evening but he didn't mind. It was a second chance, and a touch of the magic was back. Normal things like taking a beating seemed unimportant right now.

She cradled her cup, looked at him, leaving it up to him to speak. No pressure.

"Well, the thing you need to know, is what my family are like. They're probably a bit different from yours. I haven't got a mum."

"Why not?" she asked quietly, concern on her face.

You've got to go back to causes, foundations. Then you understand something properly.

"She was gone when I was young. Maybe left. Maybe … well, I have suspicions. About lots of stuff to do with my family. But I really don't feel up to talking about that right now. So it was just me and my … dad, and my brother, Denny. But Dad was in prison a lot. He's a bit rough. Denny takes after him; he left school at 14 after throwing a desk at a teacher. Then he used to steal cars and thieve. When I was a kid I thought that was normal. I only just made it through school and college myself. It was an achievement if I managed to go in every day in the week, if I could do any homework. So I listened to music a lot. It drowned out Denny shouting, arguing with girlfriends or people he knocked about with. It was hard. But then I moved in with a friend at college, and eventually got my own place. I had some loser jobs, ended up at Packham Green. I was just thankful Dad was mostly in prison and Denny disappeared for months on end, it made it easier to stick to what I wanted to do."

"Shit. And there's me, not knowing how lucky I am, sometimes. Spoilt, me." She put a hand on his forearm for a second, just rested it there as if unsure what else to do. "You've got to have good family ... it's too much to go it alone. They're your past and your future."

He winced as she mentioned the future. "Yeah, you're lucky. Lovely family from the sound of it. I don't want to be too harsh on mine, I mean, they just got by. I don't know what the difference is. Maybe imagination. But I hated the stuff they did. It took me a while to realise but I wasn't brought up, I was dragged up."

"It brings a tear to my eye. True." She sighed, leaned back. He could see pity in her, and didn't know if that was good or not. "Shit. And I thought you were just normal!"

"Well, I kind of am. Don't judge me 'cos of them."

"No. Of course. You're not responsible for them. It just … tips things upside down. I thought you were some kind of indie stud."

He nearly splurted his coffee on her. Had to use the serviette to dab brown stains off the aluminium surface.

"I don't even know what…"

"Y'know. Like your story about that girl you slept with, that was important to you."

"You didn't get it? She was important because that was so *rare.* Cheese and rice, I can't believe anyone thought that about me. I should be chuffed, right, me being pretty ugly. But, y'know, Ian Brown and that."

"You're not."

"I know. Not got any of his talent. But maybe a bit of his style."

"No. I mean, you're not *ugly.*"

He shook his head, looked down.

"No, really. You just don't make as much of yourself as you could."

"People like you find it easy."

"What do you mean?"

"You got looks, you've got family. I don't mean it bad. Just that it must be hard to imagine being someone like me. On the outside, that's where I think of myself. Check this out. When I was a teenager I had a penfriend. She was in Warrington. We wrote every week. I spent ages trying to write neatly, make the letters look as good as hers. Spell things proper. And one time she was going to visit. I was so excited. I was fourteen, she was fifteen. I'd never had a friend like her before. I was going to meet her at the train station, then Denny acted all nice. He had a car, wanted to use it all the time, show off. Said he'd take me. That seemed cool, right? Like having a private car and a driver, like in a film? So he drove me to collect her. I felt so good, even forgot to be nervous. I knew so much about her from the letters, lots of secrets, but had never met her in person."

He took a big breath before continuing. The big night out had started already for some people. A group of lads passed, drinking from bottles and cans. They finished up then just left them on the pavement and walked on, laughing. He wouldn't do that any more. It was like a different type of person from what he wanted to be.

"So I met her on the platform. She gave me a hug. Girls didn't normally do that. No one did. We walked back to the car and I went to get in the front, same as I had on the way there. But Denny said no. 'She's your guest, shit-for-brains, she gets in the front.' I kept hold of the door handle, surprised, thought it was a joke. But it wasn't. So I let her in the front and I got in the back. I didn't know what had just happened, but I felt like a kid. She seemed a bit embarrassed too. Then we drove back and Denny chatted to her almost non-stop, asking questions, and it made me feel excluded in the back, I couldn't chip in, couldn't think of anything to say. As if she was Denny's friend. The more stressed I got, the more I started sinking into myself. She said something to me one time, trying to bring me into the conversation, avoid the weirdness maybe, but then Denny hogged things again. I started to get depressed. I looked stupid, like I could only write letters but not talk to her. Denny appeared all get-going, perky, interested. It was no different back home, Denny being nice, got us drinks, booze. I was just on the outside then. I said I was going to bed, hoped she'd come up, go in Dad's empty room, but Denny told her not to be boring. He was older, looked cool maybe. She didn't follow me up. I just lay in bed and started crying.

"She left the next day. On her own. I didn't even see her. Denny wouldn't answer questions. She ignored my letter. I didn't speak to Denny for ages but he kept being nice to me. I had no one else. So there. That was my family. Anything I had, Denny wanted. Got it, too. But I was never a stud. Rebecca was the only time I'd felt like that."

He paused, looked at Sam. She was focussed on him so intently. Eyes he'd been able to look into once before. Sinking feeling. But he'd gone this far.

"Until the night with you. You're the second girl I've slept with where I felt something good. That meant something. Like a connection. That's why I told you about her. She wasn't one of many, I wasn't boasting. Just being honest. Telling you stuff that was important to me. Stuff I wouldn't tell anyone else."

"I … I really don't know how to follow that."

"You don't need to."

"I did think about ringing you. Even though I was angry."

"Maybe it's for the best. This, today – this worked out. *Just.* But might not have done. Same over the phone, that's always worse. I'm not as chatty then. I'll tell you what, this is all new to me anyway. Dad always said to keep things to yourself, that's what men do. Feelings. The truth. 'Keep the bastards guessing.' But fuck him." A wave of anger filled Mark. "Fuck him!" he shouted, banging his fist on the table.

Sam flinched when he did that, when he'd raised his hand, and it suddenly hurt him inside, the idea of *anyone* raising a hand to her.

"No, not being angry, not to a woman! Not to anyone! Sorry if I scared ya, but I'm not like them, I'm non-violent. And I'd *never* hurt you."

"I know," she said, and took his hand. "I never thought you would."

"Good. Sweet potatoes, if anyone laid a finger on you… No, I hate thinking like that. I thought about you every day since we went Afflecks, you know."

"Really?"

"Yeah. More than that since you left. That's why I'm not bothered about the job. I hate it. Especially now."

"We both fucked up."

"Yeah. But it's okay." He sighed. "It's okay." He was just glad they'd sorted this out. He hadn't wanted anything nasty to happen, not with her thinking bad things about him. Now: whatever. She had liked him. At least a bit. He could be happy with that. And she'd made him a better person. Get her on the train, make sure she was okay, then just deal with whatever came next.

She was silent, thinking. It looked deep. He was jealous. His mind was like the drilling taking place nearby. He interrupted her. "Hey, if we go now then we can take it slower. I'll get you up to the train station. Plenty of time then."

"Okay."

She walked next to him but didn't speak for a while. They were crossing Piccadilly Gardens. Didn't seem so bad this time.

"We've got to talk about all this more," she said. "More than we can do now."

He didn't say anything.

"Phone…" Then she trailed off, looked embarrassed. "How will I contact you?"

"You can't, really. It's…"

"What, you just want to leave it?"

"It's complicated."

"Don't fob me off now."

"I'm not. Just don't know what state I'll be in for a while."

"Why?"

"I don't want to go into it, right? Not now. I'm happy enough, you are, leave it at that. I just want you to get home."

"For fuck's sake. There's being laid-back, and there's being infuriating."

He looked up at the sky for strength. The blues were darkening now. If he kept silent, didn't tell her the truth, then this would become an argument again. And if he lied then he'd be going back on his resolutions with her.

He took a deep breath. Pulled some of that sky in.

"I'm in a bit of trouble."

"What kind?"

"There are some pretty bad men. They wanted me to – argh, I hate telling you this, you might be happier not knowing?"

She stopped walking. They were partway up the approach to the station. The pavement here was textured with spillages: food, liquid, and human. He forced himself to look up from that. She didn't say any words, but that fierce look again. Yeah, that was an answer.

"Okay. My dad. Wanted me to smuggle some drugs into prison. Supposed to be easy. Him and Denny wouldn't let it drop. I got punched. In the end I said yes, but just to shut them up. Thought I'd be able to persuade them against it later, or maybe even hide from them. But I screwed up. I met some people involved. Pretty bad people. And before I knew it I've got this stuff, supposed to take it in."

"What did you do?"

"I tipped it all down the toilet last night. I don't want to be involved with drugs!" Mark's eyes started to water. He wiped his face with his palm. "I hate that stuff!"

"And you weren't even going to tell me?"

"Because it's horrible. I feel ashamed. Like it's dirtied me."

"I'm amazed. That you did that. Mark, you're stronger than you think."

"I don't feel like it. Not right now."

He looked around. Sniffed. Under control. All under control. The shadows were getting longer, the first edges of darkness round the bases of buildings if you knew where to look. The world was running out of sunlight.

"What are you going to do?"

"They know about it. I can't hide from them. So I'll just man up. Go and see them. Take beatings, get it over with." He didn't want to tell her that it might be worse than that.

"But you've done nothing wrong!"

"That's not their view. But really, forget that. It's my problem. I don't want to say bye with that on your mind. I'm just glad there's no hard feelings." He was getting better at all this. He never initiated hugs. But he felt one coming on. "I guess that's it." He opened his arms and leaned towards her, ready for the last few seconds of nice stuff.

She shoved him back.

"How dare you!" she said, jaw clenched.

"It was only a hug!"

"No, how dare you just assume I can go, just sing 'Hob Y Deri Dando' and be on my way? What kind of bitch do you take me for?"

"I don't mean it like that! I know you're not a bitch! I've never met anyone like you. I want you to be happy. To have a good, long life." His voice cracked. But he forced himself on, just a bit more. "I think the world of you. That's why I'm saying goodbye! I've got nothing left. Not even family. You're the only good thing I didn't lose. Please, just go now. Not in a minute. *Now.*"

She stared. He took a step or two back. Wanted to shoo her off, knew it would be a mistake, make her do the opposite. Another step, waiting for her to turn, storm off angry, but okay. And he wouldn't cry, would just go on. There were advantages to being numb.

But she didn't go. She pointed a forefinger at him. "You'd better be telling the truth," she said, with a hard edge that scared him as much as his dad's growl or Denny's frown. "Everything you've said today. It changes things. So you had better mean that completely. Because something that's absolutely true about me, which you need to know, is this: I do not do half measures."

He wasn't sure if he could speak. What was coming over him? It was like he'd had an electric shock. He just nodded.

"There's craziness. In the air," she told him. "But what's so bad about that? Half of life is nonsense. Absurd. It still has value. And you might not think it, but I've felt loss too. Horrible pain. I try not to think about it. But sometimes it tells you what you really want for the future. Mark, we can do *anything.*"

Her, maybe. He could believe that. Not him.

"We both fucked up. But some things can be fixed."

She put her arms around him – *to be held, is to be healed* – a phrase from nowhere, whispered into his mind – and he did start crying, even though he wasn't fully sure why. Man, she was so fucking strong. Solid stone. He felt that, being close to her. A rock, built like an angel five foot tall, a wonderwall.

"This is madness," she told him. He couldn't see her face, pressed against his. "Impetuous. But it feels right. Get on the train with me. Just leave everything, leave Manchester, right now. I'll get the tickets. You can stay with me. Just do it, Mark. And we'll see what happens."

She moved her face back into his line of sight. She was crying a bit too. But smiling at the same time. Man, that strength again. It flowed from her to him. She was right. They could do *anything.* He was changing. Becoming better. Becoming more.

"It's too much."

"No. You saved my life once. The tram, remember? It's my right to repay the favour."

He didn't want to see life as a bad hand in a random world. That's too unfair. No, he had to feel it was all connected. All of it. Music, choices, life, people.

One moment, balanced on a point. Just one step and you've made a decision, already made it happen.

What was eroded could be repaired instead of replaced. It just took time and care.

And hands could be connected too. He took hold of hers shyly. A foreign gesture from a lost past. She didn't pull out of his grip. She just squeezed.

Could he be strong enough to throw everything he knew away, and start again? Rip up his own title page? For her?

Go For It.

He nodded, and she laughed and gave him a kiss on the lips, then they ran towards the station entrance together, and he laughed too.

For her? And maybe a little bit for himself too.

And he'd be worthy of this. Oh man. There were many things that he would like to say to her, and he didn't know how. But he'd find a way. He'd find the words. He knew he could.

Strange ways were past. Wales … here we come.

Acknowledgements

Many thanks to all the people who helped, supported, or inspired me during the *long* process of writing this novel. My personal thanks go to Jennie Cooke (inspiration), Tylie M (support), and Marky H (help); also to those real people who agreed to be in this book, namely Martin the Mod, and Colin from Vinyl Revival. Technical thanks to those who helped me with editing, particularly Francesca Rhydderch, Janet Thomas (Firefly Press), and Gwen Davies (New Welsh Review) – though any errors and flaws in the book are mine alone! Also thanks to Steve Turner, for correcting my misconceptions about what a sound engineer does; and Literature Wales, for a bursary which showed belief in my writing – that boosts confidence more than any cheque. (Cheques are nice, though.)

Huge thanks to musical creators. Please support the musicians and bands mentioned in this book, buy their work, listen to it, appreciate it.

The chapter introductions include extracts from *2000 Tunes: A History of Manchester Music* by M. H. Rees (Harper Collins, 2011), and are used with permission. M. H. Rees also manages Southern Soul, a fantastic record shop in Swansea.

About The Author

Karl Drinkwater is originally from Manchester but has lived in Wales for over fifteen years, ever since he went there to do a degree: it was easier to stay than to catch a train back to Cottonopolis. His writing is most often focussed on themes such as the intersection of rural and urban; England and Wales; past and present; human and non-human; family-as-support versus family-as-cage; and that soppy old thing called love. That may make him a hippy. When he is not writing or editing he loves exercise, computer games, board games, the natural environment, animals, social justice and zombies. He was born M. Hopton but changed his name in 2002.

If you enjoyed this novel then you may also like its partner, Cold Fusion 2000, about a physics- and literature-obsessed Mancunian nerd. Finally, if you have a moment Karl would love it if you left a rating or review online, since they really help him reach new readers. It might even stop him writing biographical details in the third person. Thank you for reading.

karldrinkwater.blogspot.com
facebook.com/karlzdrinkwater
twitter.com/libkarl

Other Books

Cold Fusion 2000

"She stared at him but her intelligent blue-grey eyes were a barrier, not a window. Eventually she leaned her head forwards, eyes closed tight, sighed, and touched her forehead to his. A tingle, echo of the past, the two of them frozen like an art gallery drawing."

Alex Kavanagh is a pedantic, physics-obsessed geek. He's a teacher who hates teaching; a lover who's just been dumped (again); a writer whose articles all get rejected; an adult who still lives at home and gets bullied at the bus stop by teenagers; and he's just had the worst day of his life. So far, so bad. Things can only get better, right?

While drowning his sorrows he sees an ex from six years ago, Lucy Spiers. The point when Lucy dumped him was the point when his life started to go nuclear. He can't help himself: he tells her exactly what he thinks of her. So it comes as a surprise when they go on a date. He didn't expect a spark to be reignited. Couldn't foresee the power of magnetism. He hadn't realised that *he still loved her.*

Holy protons, he hopes she's changed.

She's changed all right. For a start, she's actually Lucy's twin sister, Jane...

Cold Fusion is a story wrapped around an enigma. It's a novel about making peace with the past and moving on.

Discussion Questions

If you're reading this as part of a book group then here are some potential questions to consider.

- What are the themes and concerns of the novel?
- What is the significance of the novel's name?
- How do the chapter names relate to the events of those chapters?
- How many elements of Mark's behaviour, character and interests label him as geek? What are they?
- What does Mark learn?
- What do you think of the claim that the text in the reviews at the start of each chapter are not about the album or song, but actually about this novel?
- What does Sam learn?
- What happened next?
- Is there any relevance to the sex of most characters in Sam's story, and those in Mark's?
- Who actually wrote 2000 Tunes?

- If you could meet any character from the novel and ask them a question, who would you choose, and what would you ask? Why?

You will find information relating to some of these questions in the 2000 Tunes FAQ: tinyurl.com/2ktfaq

Manchester Music Overview
Part 1 (of 2) 1976 – 1986

1976
New bands: The Fall; Warsaw (Joy Division); Buzzcocks.

1978
Joy Division's first TV appearance.
Tony Wilson and Alan Erasmus create Factory Records. Joy Division are their first signing.

1980
Joy Division record second album. Ian Curtis kills himself; "Closer" released posthumously.
New bands: Happy Mondays; New Order.

1982
The Haçienda (FAC 51) opens.
New bands: James; The Smiths.

1984
Stone Roses do their first gig. The Smiths release "Heaven Knows I'm Miserable Now".

1986
Festival of the Tenth Summer, organised by Factory Records; live music includes Buzzcocks, The Smiths, New Order, The Fall.

urce: 2000 Tunes, MH/KD

Manchester Music Overview Part 2 (of 2) 1988 – 1998

1988
New bands: The Charlatans; Electronic.
808 State remix New Order's "Blue Monday"; becomes a favourite at The Haçienda.

1990
Height of Madchester.
Notable releases: Happy Mondays "Kinky Afro" and "Step On"; Inspiral Carpets "This Is How It Feels"; Paris Angels "Perfume"; The Charlatans "The Only One I Know"; Stone Roses "One Love".
New band: The Verve.

1992
Factory Records go bankrupt.

1994
Album releases: Oasis debut "Definitely Maybe"; Stone Roses "Second Coming"; The Charlatans "Up to Our Hips"; Inspiral Carpets "Devil Hopping" (featuring Mark E. Smith).
Debut albums being recorded by Black Grape and Chemical Brothers.

1996
Stone Roses break up; The Seahorses get together.
Oasis at Knebworth.
Noel Gallagher sings on "Setting Sun" by Chemical Brothers.
Albums being recorded: The Verve "Urban Hymns"; The Charlatans "Tellin' Stories"; Monaco (Peter Hook) "Music For Pleasure".

1998
Ian Brown's debut solo album "Unfinished Monkey Business". Ian arrested (sent to Strangeways in 1999).
Electronic start recording "Twisted Tenderness".
New band: Doves.

Source: 2000 Tunes, MH/KD

Lightning Source UK Ltd.
Milton Keynes UK
UKHW02f1822030918
328269UK00013B/536/P